I'LL ALWAYS BE WITH YOU

I'LL ALWAYS BE WITH YOU

NEW YORK TIMES BESTSELLING AUTHOR

MONICA MURPHY

Entangled Publishing, LLC
644 Shrewsbury Commons Ave., STE 181
Shrewsbury, PA 17361
rights@entangledpublishing.com

Amara is an imprint of Entangled Publishing, LLC.

Visit our website at www.entangledpublishing.com.

Edited by Rebecca Barney
Cover design by Emily Wittig
Cover images by loveless_liza.mail.ru/Gettyimages
Interior design by Toni Kerr

ISBN 978-1-64937-598-8

Manufactured in the United States of America

First Edition June 2023

10 9 8 7 6 5 4 3

AMARA
an imprint of Entangled Publishing LLC

O, thou art fairer than the evening air,
clad in the beauty of a thousand stars.
Christopher Marlowe

PART 1

CHAPTER ONE

WEST

SUMMER

Mid-July in Paris is when I first saw her in the flesh—it was hot as balls, thanks to the heatwave that swept over most of Europe. Everyone was sweating on the crowded dance floor at this random nightclub, with the exception of one.

Carolina Lancaster.

I knew who she was. Of course, I did. Her last name is on practically every building at the private school I attend back home, though she doesn't even go there. Then there's the fact that her family moves within the same social circles as mine, not that she's ever around. She's lived outside of the U.S. for years.

It was almost as if she didn't exist. She's more a myth or an apparition: much discussed, yet never seen.

She's a principal dancer at the London Dance Company, or some such shit. A prima ballerina at an extraordinarily young age—or so the media says. What she's doing in Paris, I don't know. But she's sexy as fuck out there twirling on the dance floor, moving to the music. Clad in a pair of skimpy black shorts that show off her long, long legs and the tiniest tank top I've ever seen.

White. Cropped. See-through. Hard nipples poking against

the thin fabric. She dances effortlessly. Without thought and total abandon. Her slender arms wave above her head, her lips curved into a dreamy smile, eyes unfocused as if she's in a trance. She's not very tall, but her legs are endless. She's fascinating. Everyone is watching her.

She doesn't even notice.

Staring at her for so long, I find myself licking my lips like I'm fucking starving. For her. It's like I can't take my eyes off of her. My skin feels electrified just watching her, so without thinking, I take a step forward. Then another. Until I'm out on the dance floor, surrounded by writhing bodies, not moving a muscle, yet sweating profusely while she completely ignores me as I stand just to the side of her.

She sees me, though. I can tell by the way her gaze flicks in my direction, quick as lightning, a flash of interest before she turns her back to me. Pretending I'm not there.

No one pretends I don't exist. Most people—especially girls—can't ignore me. I sound like an asshole, but I'm just stating facts. Everyone knows my family. My last name.

Even me.

The song ends, the DJ announcing the next song in French, and I take my opportunity.

"Hey."

She whirls around at the sound of my voice, and I blink at her, mesmerized by her stunning face. The perfect symmetry of her features. Blue eyes, elegant nose, rose pink lips formed into a pout. Her expression flips to bored in an instant, and she says something in French as her gaze roams over me from head to toe.

I tilt my head, frowning. "What was that?"

She laughs, and I can't help but smile, even though I'm positive she's laughing *at* me.

She repeats the phrase, her blue eyes going wide.

"Fous le camp de moi."

Get away from me.

Playing the cool Parisian to the dumb American, who just so happens to speak French, and I'm totally down for this game.

"You're playing me."

"*Non.*" She shakes her head, her eyes wide—innocent, though I call bullshit on that. Not a single blonde hair falls out of place. It's slicked back into the tightest ponytail I've ever seen, and I don't think there's a lick of makeup on her face.

She's fucking gorgeous.

I stare at her. Hard. She stares back. Just as hard.

"I know you can speak English," I finally say to her.

The music finally starts once more, a slow and jazzy beat, and the majority of the dance floor clears. The remaining couples cling to each other, shuffling around us as they dance, yet neither of us move.

Until finally, she takes a step closer, her cool scent wrapping around me, making me fucking dizzy. This girl is giving off some sort of vibe that has me in a goddamn trance.

"Who are you?" Her voice is thick with a fake French accent.

"That doesn't matter." It's my turn to shift closer, dipping my head so my mouth is at her ear. I inhale sharply, taking in her delectable scent, and it hits me like a drug sliding into my veins. "I know exactly who you are." I hesitate. "Carolina."

She lurches away from me, disgust written all over her face. "Paparazzi, eh? Well, go on."

"Wha—"

Carolina throws her arms out wide, her tank riding up until it rests just beneath her almost non-existent breasts. "Take your photos. Sell them to the rags. Then everyone can gossip about me dancing at a Paris nightclub with my tits out."

I like that she said *tits* in that haughty little voice of hers. She sounds like a princess.

A spoiled, little princess who gets whatever she wants, whenever she wants it.

"I'm not a pap."

She frowns, her slender arms falling back to her sides. "Then who are you?"

"I went to your school." Now she appears even more confused. "Lancaster Prep."

"Oh fuck." She rolls her eyes.

Right before she turns and walks away.

Without hesitation, I chase after her, making my way through the crowd, calling out her name, but she ignores me. She's fast as hell, slipping through the clusters of people filling the nightclub, and at one point, I lose sight of her buttery blonde head.

She appears again seconds later, directly in front of the entrance, pushing her way out of the club.

I speed up, hurrying after her, busting through the door to find her standing on the sidewalk facing the street. A man stands next to her, thin and freakishly tall, and he whips a lighter out of his pocket. That's when I realize she's holding a cigarette and she places it in between her bee-stung lips, leaning toward the guy when he flicks the lighter, the tip of her cig glowing red before she blows out a breath laced with smoke.

Smoking isn't sexy. Not one bit. It's a fucking killer, and it stinks.

But watching Carolina Lancaster puff away on a cigarette makes my dick hard.

She catches sight of me, a look of pure disdain on her face, and she withdraws the cigarette from her lips, murmuring out of the side of her mouth to her skinny friend.

He laughs. Most likely at me.

"You followed me." Her gaze is on me, her tone an accusation.

I approach them slowly, wanting to get near her again, so I can catch another whiff of her scent. Soft and wet like the ocean. Salty and...violent.

Again, like the ocean.

"You ran away before I could explain," I tell her, slipping my hands in my pockets, going for nonchalant. Like she has no effect on me.

"Explain what? I don't care what you have to say."

Damn, this bitch is mean.

I kind of like it.

"You didn't even ask my name." I pause only for a moment, ready to tell her who I am, but she interrupts me.

"Like I said. I. Don't. Care." She sucks on the cig, blowing the smoke directly at me. I grimace and she smiles, pleased with herself.

"I want to know," her friend pipes up. I turn my attention to him, which is fucking difficult, because all I want to do is stare at Carolina all damn night. "What is it?"

"West."

"West. That's a direction, not a name," Carolina mutters, flicking ash on the sidewalk.

"What kind of name is that?" The guy frowns.

I open my mouth, ready to explain, when Carolina interrupts me yet again.

"Probably a family name that goes back generations. Might be short for something. Most likely an old surname that belonged to his mother or his grandmama." She arches a brow.

"Nailed it." I incline my head toward her.

Her friend laughs. She doesn't even crack a smile.

"Well, it's nice to meet you, West. I'm Gideon." He steps forward, offering his hand, and I shake it, smiling at him.

At least he's friendly, though he's not the one I'm interested in.

"I'm bored," she whines, turning to Gideon. "Let's go somewhere else."

"More like you're rude," I tell her, a faint smile still planted on my face.

She glances over her shoulder, her eyes narrowing as she contemplates me, the cigarette still hanging from her lips. She removes it before she says, "Well, look at you, calling me out for my shit."

I shrug. "Someone has to."

"I like him," Gideon says with a nod.

"Thanks."

"I don't," Carolina says, turning to face me fully. It's jarring, how beautiful she is. I try my best not to react as her gaze races over me, taking in every single detail. My skin tingles like she just touched me all over. "The last thing I want to do is spend the evening with an American."

"You're an American," I point out.

"I haven't lived there in almost six years." Her smile is serene, just before she takes another puff on her cigarette. "If I want to fuck a nice, rich American boy, I can go home and find a long list of them."

I'm slightly taken aback by her saying the word *fuck* so easily. She's so dainty and elegant, not what I would consider the usual type to drop f-bombs so casually. "I never said anything about fucking you."

"You want to, though." She sniffs. "I can tell."

Damn it, she's not wrong.

"Let's find another club." She turns to her friend, the suggestion obviously just for him. "I want out of here."

"Okay." Gideon looks beyond her, his gaze locking with mine, a mischievous smile on his face. "West, you should come with us."

"No—" Carolina starts.

"I'd love to." It's my turn to interrupt her, and she doesn't like it.

At all.

She viciously takes another drag off the cigarette, exhaling the smoke with a sexy purse of her lips. I watch her unabashedly, drinking in everything about her that I can visibly see as she continues to ignore me, chattering away with Gideon in fluent French.

The melodic sound of her voice puts me in a trance as she complains about me accompanying them on their night out, and my gaze drifts to her tits. The tiny nipples that are still hard, rubbing against the fabric of her tank. She doesn't have much, but it's enough for me to wrap my hand around one and draw that pretty little nipple into my mouth—

"Stupid American."

I glance up at the sound of her voice, ignoring the insult.

"Come on. Let's get out of here," Gideon says to her, waving his hand, his gaze on mine once more. "Are you going with us?"

Pausing, I think about my friends still inside. Last I saw them, Brent was still at the bar hitting on the bartender. TJ and the others were dancing/grinding on girls.

They won't care where I went. They might not even notice I'm gone.

Fuck it. I'll text them later.

Gideon flags down a cab—why not take an Uber?—and next thing I know, I'm crammed in the back seat of a tiny car, with Carolina in the middle of us. She's pressed so close to me, it's as if I can feel every single inch of her.

Electricity sparks the moment our skin makes contact and she studies me, the cigarette long gone, a mint in her mouth. Between her lips.

On her tongue.

"You wear the uniform of every American teenage boy who comes to Europe for the summer," she accuses me. "Trying to fit in when you do nothing but stand out."

I glance down at my khaki shorts and white button-up shirt. It's untucked, with the sleeves rolled up, and I recall how every single one of my friends is wearing a similar outfit. Some of them are even wearing a hat on backwards.

"Brooks Brothers shirt. Ralph Lauren shorts," she continues, her gaze landing on my lap. My crotch.

"Loafers on your feet." Her voice is tinged with amusement when her gaze meets mine once more. "I can't tell any of you apart."

"You sound like a snobby European."

She shrugs one bare, smooth shoulder, and it rubs against my arm. Sparks fly due to the friction. "I am one."

"You're American."

"As you seem to love to remind me. But like I said, I don't live there anymore. I don't like it." She leans her head toward mine and I inhale as discreetly as I can, taking another hit of her intoxicating scent. "And I normally don't like boys such as you."

"Then why am I sitting with you in a cab?"

Carolina jerks her thumb in Gideon's direction. "It's his fault."

I lean forward, so I can make eye contact with him. "Hey, man. I owe you one."

"I'll collect too," he says with a laugh, going silent when she glances over her shoulder, sending him a look. "What's your problem tonight?" he asks her.

She says nothing, turning so she's facing forward once again, and I unabashedly stare at her profile. Her mouth is formed in a perpetual pout and she works her jaw, her lips parted, her gaze sliding to mine to find I'm already watching her.

The taxi speeds down the road, taking us to another nightclub, and we continue to stare at each other. Gideon is tapping away on his phone, the screen illuminating his sharply-angled face with a silver glow, the only other light coming from outside.

"You're rude," she barely whispers, her voice hardly making any sound.

"You're fucking beautiful," I whisper back, shocking myself. I don't tell girls they're beautiful, especially ones who so obviously know it. I don't need to feed their egos. I prefer they feed mine.

Shitty but true.

Her eyes widen the slightest bit, but that's her only outward reaction. The mask drops into place just as fast, her gaze narrowing, her teeth sinking into her lower lip, like she's thinking about feasting on me. "You're a flirt."

"So are you."

She laughs. "If you think me being mean to you is flirting... then you have problems."

"Yeah." I lean in closer, invading her space. "I do."

My gaze fixes on her mouth, the way she plays with the mint. Swirling it around, teasing it with her pink tongue. I stifle the groan that wants to escape, readjusting myself. Wishing I could get away from her, yet also dying to haul her into my arms.

"Would you care for a mint?" she asks after I stare at her—we stare at each other—for about a million beats too long.

"Yeah." My voice is gravelly, like I just woke up, and I swear I saw something flash in her eyes.

"West." She shakes her head, her lips curling up in the faintest smile. "Such a silly name."

"You should hear my actual name." It's really not that strange. I'm just playing it up.

"I don't want to know," she whispers. Her hand rests on my chest, gently pushing me away before I can tell her what it is.

Frowning, I contemplate her, confused. She's giving me serious whiplash, and fuck, it's torture.

"Come here." She reaches for me, her long, elegant arm sliding up my chest as she tucks her hand around the nape of my neck, pulling me close, her lips brushing mine when she says, "take my mint."

Her hand is a gentle tug, a hint of encouragement, and I dip my head, my mouth hovering above hers. We share the same air, the same fucking breath. I suck in her minty exhale, my forehead pressing against hers. My skin prickles with awareness when I hear the catch in her throat and I lift my chin.

Angling myself just right.

Until my mouth is resting on hers.

Her warm, soft lips part beneath mine, somehow pushing the mint toward me and I lightly suck on her tongue, the mint sliding into my mouth. Every single hair on my body stands on end when I relax my lips, loosening my hold on her tongue. She laps at my top lip like a cat, right in the dead center. The flicker of her wet tongue, the sharp sting of her teeth upon my lower lip making me hiss.

Slowly I pull away, the mint resting on my tongue, my entire mouth tingling, but not because of the winter-fresh flavor flooding my mouth.

No, she's responsible for that feeling. Swear to God I'm shaking, and I note the tremble in her body too. She's watching me with wide blue eyes, her chest rising and falling rapidly.

I offer her a smile, showing that the mint is clenched between my teeth, and she laughs.

"Fine," she says, as haughty as a queen. "You can dance with me."

"What, like it's an honor?"

"One of the highest." Gideon leans over, getting in on our conversation. "She usually dances alone at the clubs."

"It's true." She nods her confirmation.

The air is electric in the cab, and by the time we're slipping out of it, I don't hesitate to reach for her hand, tangling my fingers with hers. She doesn't pull out of my grip, the both of us falling into step behind Gideon. He doesn't say a word until we're in front of the doorman, and Gideon points at Carolina, letting him know her last name.

Apparently, if it's Lancaster, that can open a lot of doors. I don't bother mentioning my last name. It opens a lot of doors too, especially in France.

But she doesn't know that.

Within minutes, we're inside the giant club, Gideon getting us drinks at the bar while Carolina leads me onto the dance floor. This place is somehow even more crowded than the club we left. The air is hotter. Heavier. The music louder, the bass thumping in my body, rattling my bones. When she turns to face me, she begins to dance to the beat, her hips swaying, her arms above her head, while I stand there like an idiot and just watch her as if I'm hypnotized.

"You don't dance?" she shouts at me.

I shake my head, unable to speak. Too captivated with the way she moves her body. The clothes she's wearing don't cover much, and my imagination kicks into overdrive, envisioning her naked.

Spread out for me on my bed like an offering.

Her smile is wicked. Like she knows what she's doing to me. What I'm thinking. "That's a shame. What if you have rhythm?"

"I don't."

She places her hands on my chest, dragging them down. Slowly. Her fingers skim across my stomach, making the muscles tighten and clench beneath her touch. "I bet you do where it counts."

My dick stands at attention at her words, at the suggestion in them.

"You're very fit," she observes, her gaze full of amusement.

"I'm an athlete."

She rolls her eyes. "Of course, you are. Lacrosse?"

I make a dismissive noise. "Track."

Her brows lift. "You throw things? Jump over things?"

"I run." I give in to my need and rest my hand on the spot where her waist dips in, pulling her closer. "I'm fast."

Her hands are still on my stomach, pressing. Burning. "Is that a good trait to have, or a bad one?"

"Depends on how you look at it."

Someone bumps into Carolina from behind, sending her nearly falling into me, and I grab hold of her firmly, my hands on her hips, yanking her closer.

"I don't like fast boys." She rises up on tiptoe when the music gets louder, her mouth right at my ear so I can hear her. "I usually like to take things nice and slow."

I run my right hand over her ass and she takes a step away from me, shaking her head. My hands fall away from her. "Too fast, American."

I stare at her, watching as she digs into the tiny pocket of her even tinier shorts and whips out a crumpled cigarette. "Do you have a light?"

"No."

Without a word, she abandons me once again on the dance floor.

A frustrated growl leaves me as I chase after her, keeping track of her bright blonde head so I don't lose her. Until we're both at the crowded bar, where she's standing next to a dark-haired guy dressed all in black with a thin mustache, a devilish smile on his face as he offers her a light. She leans in close, the flame igniting the tip of her cigarette, and with a laugh she pulls away, shaking her head when he says something to her.

Jealousy consumes me and I march over to where she stands, grabbing the crook of her arm and jerking her around to face me.

"What did he say to you?"

Her smile is small, a gleam in her eyes as she yells, "He wants to take me away somewhere and fuck me."

White hot fury floods my veins. "What did you tell him?"

"I said I came with someone." She pats my chest, like I'm a pet. "Calm down. I won't fuck him."

The fury is still there but not as strong. "Good to know."

"I don't like it when people touch me. Men." She contemplates me for a moment, her blue eyes narrowed, her upper lip curled in an almost-snarl. "They say I'm cold."

"Who?"

"The boys who want to touch me."

"You let me touch you." When she doesn't say anything, I continue, "In the cab. When you gave me the mint."

Her lips curl in a faint smile. "That was different."

"How?"

She shrugs. "I don't know. There's something about you that's approachable. Like a cuddly teddy bear."

I can't help it, I laugh. "No one would *ever* describe me in that way."

"Brooding, scary American boy? I'm sure you ruled the school, am I right? I know the type. You're probably just like my brother." She shakes her head, as if her older brother is a complete disappointment.

Her brother is a fucking legend. Whit Lancaster is an insufferable asshole, who ran Lancaster Prep with an iron fist back in the day when he attended the school. The heir to the oldest Lancaster's empire, Whit is wealthy beyond measure and gives zero fucks about anyone else but his wife and child.

I *aspire* to be as ruthless as Whit, and lucky me, no Lancasters have attended Lancaster Prep since I was a sophomore, when Crew Lancaster graduated. They're always the ones who are automatically in charge. The ones everyone follows with undying loyalty. And now I'm prepared to have that kind of allegiance my senior year.

"I hear your brother is a complete prick."

She laughs and the sound nearly sends me to my knees. "He is. He's terrible." She hesitates. "I get the feeling that you're terrible too."

I shift closer to her, bending my head so my mouth is close to her ear yet again. "Wouldn't you like to know."

Carolina doesn't even hesitate.

"I would very much like to know." She grounds out her fresh cigarette in the ashtray on the bar before taking a step closer. Her hand sneaks beneath my shirt so fast, I suck in a breath when her cool fingers land on my stomach. "Want to be my secret?"

Before I can answer, she's curling her fingers around the waistband of my khakis, tugging me forward. I go willingly, her hand falling away as she turns and heads toward the farthest side of the club. I follow her, my heart racing, my skin still tingling from where she touched me. Her knuckles brushed my abdomen when she curled her fist around my waistband, leaving me with a throbbing hard-on.

Her words didn't help either.

Want to be my secret?

Fuck yeah, I do.

But I'm no one's secret. More like they're always my secret. Not this girl. This girl has me chasing her. Willingly.

She doesn't stop moving until we're in a darkened hallway, the music nothing but a dull throb. A blast of arctic air conditioning brushes my sweat-covered skin, offering instant relief, and when she turns to face me, my gaze automatically drops to her chest.

"You know how to kiss, American boy?"

"I know how to do a lot of things," I tell her. There have been plenty of girls, but nothing too serious. I've had sex. I can make a girl come easily with my fingers.

With Carolina Lancaster, I can imagine us getting pretty damn creative.

"Then show me what you can do." She plasters herself against the wall, her arms slightly spread, palms flat, legs braced.

Slowly, I approach her, remembering what she said. How she doesn't want to go too fast. How she doesn't like to be touched.

The longer I take, the quicker her chest rises and falls. Tempting me. I want to touch her so fucking bad. But will she just shove me away?

Taking my chances, I lightly place my hand on her hip, the sharp edge of bone startling. She's thin. And from the looks of it, nothing but muscle.

I'd guess she works out more than I do.

An impatient noise leaves her, making me smile, and when my gaze meets hers, I find her glaring at me, her expression murderous. Like she wants to hold a knife to my throat and watch me slowly bleed out.

Leaning in, I pause only when my mouth hovers directly above hers, my tongue darting out for the quickest lick. She leans forward with parted lips, as if seeking more from me, and

I smile as I tilt my head, retreating.

"You're mean," she whispers.

"So are you," I remind her, using every ounce of self-restraint I've got to keep still. I squeeze her hip, my touch gentle. "If I move too fast, will you run?"

She nods, lifting her chin, her lids lowering, gaze focused on my mouth. "Yes."

"What if I move slow?" I slide my hand upward along her side. Over the dip of her waist, along her ribs. "Will you run then?"

"I always run," she admits, sounding breathless.

I focus my gaze on her chest, watching it rise and fall rapidly. My fingers tease the hem of her cropped tank, slipping just my fingertips beneath the thin fabric and brushing the underside of her tits. She sucks in a sharp breath and I lift my gaze to hers. "Too fast?"

Carolina shakes her head. "What are you doing?"

"I want to see you." I slip my fingers farther up, over the gentle curve of her breast, my thumb teasing her hard nipple. "Feel you."

She glances around, as if she's afraid we'll get caught. "Someone could spot us back here."

"Let them." With only two fingers, I tug the fabric up, exposing her to my hungry gaze. Her nipples are tiny and pink, and my mouth waters. "Fuck, you're gorgeous."

"Stop." She brushes my hand away, and I step back, the fabric falling back into place, covering her. She's visibly trembling. "You're naughty."

I can't help but chuckle. "I think you like it."

"Are you always so forward?"

"No," I say truthfully, letting the word sink in before I say, "Let's get out of here."

Her frown is so deep, a little crease forms between her eyebrows. "What do you mean, let's get out of here?"

"I mean, I want to leave this place." I crowd her once again, resting my hands on her waist, my fingers burning into her cool, smooth skin. "Take me somewhere that's special to you, fake Parisian girl."

Carolina tilts her head back, her gaze assessing. "You're very bold, you know."

"I could say the same about you." I streak my thumb beneath the cropped hem of her tank yet again, like a dare.

I'm pushing her limits, but she still doesn't run, and I take that as a good sign.

Her eyes darken to the color of the Italian coastal waters— the Sardinia is the deepest, darkest blue I've ever seen, and it's the same exact shade as Carolina Lancaster's eyes, swear to God. "You're also a tease."

"Again, so are you."

The music stops, shifting into a slower tune, and she pushes away from the wall, slipping away from me, glancing over her shoulder as she keeps walking.

"Come on," she calls, and without hesitation, I fall into step behind her.

Pretty sure I'd follow her anywhere.

CHAPTER TWO

CAROLINA

This boy. The tall, lean American with the golden good looks and dark hair that falls over his forehead in the most tantalizing curl. He's attractive, and he knows it, and I usually don't find myself drawn to that sort, but he somehow wormed his way into my evening, despite my reluctance and out and out rudeness toward him.

My behavior didn't deter him, though. It's almost as if he was amused by me, and I suppose I could blame Gideon for allowing West to join us.

Deep down, I wanted this boy to come with us. To see if his touch was as electric as the way his eyes roamed over me. I feel sparks on my skin every time he looks at me, and I...

Don't like it.

The night started out like any other, Gideon and I eager to go out and party, Parisian-style. We broke away from the group earlier, the girls and boys we traveled to the city with. We're here to perform with the *Ballet de l'Opéra national de Paris* in a special program. Only a select few were chosen, and I was one of the lucky ones, along with my partner, Gideon.

My lovely, gorgeous Gideon, who has more disdain for people than anyone else I know, including myself. For whatever reason, he seemed to like West.

I don't. Not really. He makes me uncomfortable. Every time his eyes land on me, I feel…weird. Like my body isn't my own. When he puts his hands on me, my bones dissolve. And when he touched my breasts, I swear I could feel his mouth already on my skin, hot and wet. Making my entire body shake with anticipation.

I want him to do it again.

We leave Gideon behind at the nightclub, not that I think he minds. I spot him at the bar where we left him, giving him a signal that I'll see him later, and he nodded his acknowledgement, with a knowing smile on his face. My friend is most likely thinking, *finally.*

Finally, I'm going to let a boy touch me. Kiss me. I have already let this boy do exactly that, which is so unlike me. I don't like to be touched. Held. And I've never let a boy kiss me.

Ever.

Until this one. West.

His name is ridiculous. I can tell by the way he looks, how he's dressed, that he's wealthy. He gives off that old money vibe, especially with his designer choices. Our families have most likely crossed paths, which is the last thing I want to think about, so I push the thought out of my head.

I've been on a little summer adventure ever since we arrived in Paris a few weeks ago to practice endlessly for our upcoming performance, and Gideon says I'm burning the candle at both ends.

I love Gideon and his quaint, constant usage of cliches. It's adorable.

"Where are we going?" West asks, after we've left the club and we can actually hear each other speak without yelling.

"You'll see." I take his hand, marveling at how big it is. How it completely envelops mine. His skin is warm and smooth, with the faintest hint of roughness on his fingertips and palm. He's tall, much taller than I am. When I look straight at him, I stare at his broad chest. And when I lift my gaze slightly, I can study the strong column of his throat. The way his Adam's apple bobs when he swallows. The faint shadow on his jawline, indicating he needs to shave. I'm tempted to touch his face, see if it's as prickly as I think it might be. "This way."

I lead him down the sidewalk, the streets still crowded with cars despite the late hour, my heartbeat ringing in my ears. He keeps pace beside me, his hand still in mine. The evening breeze washes over my skin, bringing with it the earthy scent of the Seine. I stop at the corner, waiting for the light to change, my eyes closing for the briefest moment, savoring the experience.

This is exactly what I envisioned happening before we left for Paris. I wanted to escape, even for just one night, and possibly even find a boy to escape with so I could forget all of the pressures that come with being...me.

It's almost as if I made my wish come true—with the help of Gideon, of course.

"Hey. Do we have to keep running?"

When I open my eyes, I find him watching me, his dark brows drawn together. I'm amused by his question, considering. "I thought you were a runner."

He smiles, dipping his head for a moment, almost as if he's bashful, which is a complete lie. His arrogance bleeds through his every gesture, but I don't mind. I'm used to this sort of behavior from the men in my family. "I also like to walk. Savor the night, you know?"

My heart turns over itself at his confession. He gets it, and that is such a rare and wonderful thing.

"Oh, I know." The light changes, and I tug on his hand. "Come on. Let's go."

I walk briskly across the street, West keeping pace beside me, swinging our clutched hands between us. People eye us curiously as they walk past, their lips curled in tiny smiles, as if they're in on our secret.

"Are you going to tell me where we're going?"

"Not yet," I say, trying to sound mysterious. "How long have you been in Paris?"

"Only a few days. How about you?"

"The last two weeks." Two weeks of nonstop practice. Of endless work. My feet are aching in the cheap little sandals I bought at a small shop on the Rue Cambon a few days ago, and my legs are tired, but none of my aches and pains will stop me.

Not tonight.

When we draw closer to our destination and I first catch sight of it, my heart swells. The grand staircase in front of the building that is usually filled with people during the day, a street peddler performing songs while standing in front of those steps, his guitar case open for payment. The same man is there every day when we arrive for practice, always singing American rock songs, and he makes all of the younger girls giggle when he tips his hat in their direction, smiling at them. He tried to smile at me, but I only glared, hating how old he was.

He has no business flirting with young girls.

The intricately designed black iron streetlamps that run along the front entrance illuminate the archways, the golden statues that sit atop the building, like blazing candles on a towering cake. I come to a stop and stare up at the building, squeezing West's hand.

"This is where I'm performing," I tell him, my voice so low, it's almost carried away by the rush of traffic speeding by us.

He turns his startled gaze to mine. "When?"

"This weekend. It's a special performance, just for three nights."

The disappointment on his face is clear. "I'm leaving for Spain tomorrow."

"A trip all over Europe then?"

He nods.

"To celebrate...your graduation?" I'm digging for information since he gives so little, but then again, so do I.

Maybe it's better this way, each of us keeping our secrets. This is only one night out of our lives. We'll never run into each other again.

"Sure." He lifts our linked hands to his mouth and brushes the softest kiss across my knuckles, something hot fluttering in my belly.

Lower.

"Let's see if we can find a way inside," I suggest, needing a distraction from the heat in his gaze and the way it makes me feel. All light and shivery and nothing like myself at all. "Come with me."

"Pretty sure we won't be able to—"

I turn on him, stopping in front of one of the grand-arched entryways, clutching both of his hands in mine. "Never doubt me."

His solemn gaze meets mine, and he nods once. "Let's go."

He didn't even hesitate at my request, and I appreciate that. It's in my blood, in my family. Stubbornness. Determination. We get what we want, and no one can stop us. My older brother does whatever he wants. My father is the same. My poor sister is completely controlled by my mother, and I pity her. I really do.

Me? I'm controlled by myself. And dance.

My choice, I think to myself as I pull on every door handle, frustrated that they're all locked. At the center door, I spot an older gentleman standing beside it in a security uniform. I recognize him and make my approach, West right behind me.

"Jean-Jacque!" I exclaim, throwing my arms up as if I'm going to hug him in greeting.

He tilts his head. "Bon soir, mademoiselle."

I speak to him in rapid-fire French, explaining that I left the most important personal items I own inside, in the dressing room behind the stage. It's a plausible excuse. A small stash of items is at my dressing table right now, waiting for me to appear tomorrow and use them. My makeup bag. Extra tape for my shoes.

A few contraband bottles of water, something they frown upon, even though it's necessary for us to stay hydrated.

The Palais Garnier is such an important monument, even water for the dancers is looked at as potentially damaging to the interior.

Jean-Jacque keeps shaking his head, muttering, "non," under his breath, but I don't let it deter me. I talk and talk. Gesture and lament. I even throw out the biggest lie of all, calling West my boyfriend, and explain how desperate I am to get those very, ahem, private items that are inside, so we can spend our last night together...

Intimately.

"I should not," Jean-Jacque says in gruff English, his gaze narrowing on West. "Let the gentleman go to the pharmacy and take care of you."

"Oh, that won't do, not at all, Jean-Jacque." I clutch my hands together, making my eyes as big as I can. If I could will tears to form, I would do so, just to get inside, but I rarely cry. "Please. Please let us in. I promise we'll be out in ten minutes."

A group of teenagers, not too far in age from West and me, start causing a fuss on the steps, all of them shouting at the top of their lungs, singing a popular rap song. Jean-Jacque watches them, irritation in his gaze before he turns toward the door and quickly unlocks it.

"Hurry," he says, cracking open the door for us. "Be careful. There are no lights on inside. Use your phones as flashlights. And get what you need as quickly as possible, do you understand?"

I come this close to hugging him, but I remember at the last second that I don't like touching strangers so I grin at him instead. "Thank you. Thank you so much, Jean-Jacque. I owe you."

We slip inside the entrance of the Palais Garnier and the sound of the grand door closing echoes throughout the massive space. We're shrouded in darkness, and an unfamiliar sensation rises inside me, bubbling in my throat as if I just drank a soda.

I realize I'm giddy. My body is practically vibrating with excitement and it's all because of this night. With this boy who I don't really know.

Who I don't really want to know.

We stand still for a moment, allowing our eyes to adjust. I can feel his gaze lingering on me. He remains so quiet I eventually turn to him.

"What?"

"I can't believe you got us in here. This is one of the most revered buildings in Paris." He sounds awed, and I start to walk, proud that I was able to convince Jean-Jacque to let us inside.

"It was nothing. I'm set to perform here, after all," I toss out at him, my skin warming when he shifts even closer to me, his hand brushing my hip.

I side-step him, ignoring the chills that ripple down my spine as I carefully approach the massive marble staircase. "Shall we go upstairs?"

"Did you really leave your birth control pills here?"

My mouth pops open and I slowly turn to face him. "You understood what I told Jean-Jacque?"

I never deviated from French. And I spoke rapidly, never wanting to give the kind security guard a chance to think about what I was asking to do.

West nods. "I'm fluent."

"How are you..." I shake my head, not wanting to know the details. Prep school French, most likely. "Never mind. I believe you. You don't have to explain how you know the language."

He chuckles, the warm sound wrapping all around me. "If you say so."

"And no, I didn't actually leave my birth control here." They're back in my hotel room. It just seemed like the most scandalous thing to tell Jean-Jacque, and he wouldn't want to talk about it for too long, considering he looks at me and probably just sees a young girl, not a sexually-active woman.

Which I'm not. My first kiss is from the very boy I'm standing with in the middle of the Palais Garnier on a Wednesday night. This entire moment is surreal.

"Let's go up to the balcony." I turn away from West and dash up the stairs, laughing when I hear him chase after me. Once we reach the top, I realize he's not even out of breath, which is impressive. The staircase is massive.

"Where's the balcony?" he asks.

"This way." I take his hand and lead him over to the closed doors, trying the handle to find it's locked. "I can't open it."

West crowds me from behind, his chest pressed against my back as he reaches out and turns the lock above the handle, chuckling. The door opens with ease and we both step outside onto one of the balconies that overlooks the city square.

"Oh, it's beautiful at night." I stop at the balustrade and grip the edge, glancing over it to see that a few people are sitting on the steps that lead into the opera house. The wind is stronger up here, battering against my face, causing a few strands of slicked back hair to break free and I smooth them back, sucking in a sharp breath when West stops directly behind me, just as he did only a moment ago.

He stretches out his arms, resting his palms on the ledge, caging me in. My heart rises to my throat, panic rushing through my veins, and I close my eyes, telling myself not to freak out or push him away.

I've never had someone surround me so completely, and normally, I would feel trapped. Pressing my lips together, I close my eyes for a beat, taking a deep breath, focusing on my core. My heartbeat. The way West stands behind me, around me, not quite touching me. When I open my eyes, a sense of calm comes over me and I turn my head to the side, wishing I could see his face.

"What are you doing?" I ask quietly.

"Enjoying the view." His deep voice, sounding so close to my ear, sends a shiver cascading down my spine.

"The palace is prettier than all of this," I point out, referring to the buildings surrounding us.

"I wasn't talking about the city view." He shifts even closer, the firm wall of his chest pressing against my back, his mouth literally at my ear now. So close, I swear I can feel his lips move against my flesh. "I was talking about you."

Everything inside me loosens, with the exception of my heart. I swear it's going to pound directly out of my chest and leap off the second-floor balcony, running away from me before I can catch it. "I'm sure you say that to all the girls."

"Can't think of one who I've ever said that to." His arms squeeze in even closer on me and I remain rigid out of habit. The cold little dancer with no feelings.

People have called me that before—plenty of times. I had one instructor who said I didn't know how to emote when performing, and when I asked him what he meant, he informed me in front of everyone that I lacked passion. Everyone in the class giggled until I sent them all a cold, hard stare that made them shut up.

Perhaps he's right. I've tried so hard to show that I do, indeed, have passion within me. Passion for dance. For life. And while I always nail the dance moves and the facial expressions, the music sweeping over me, lifting me up, bringing out every emotion that lives within me, it's sometimes still not enough.

I've never known passion with another human being. Sometimes I wonder if I'm incapable of it. Incapable of feeling.

Incapable of loving anyone.

"This is only for one night, right?" I ask the question so softly, I'm afraid he didn't hear me at first. As if my words were carried away by the wind.

He pauses. It's like I can hear him contemplating my question and I wait with bated breath until he says, "I most likely will never see you again after tonight."

I tilt my head down, my ponytail sliding to the side of my neck, the ends dangling against my cheek, and I suck in a sharp breath when I feel his lips rest on my nape. Warm and damp, imprinting on my skin.

My soul.

"You smell so fucking good," he whispers, his mouth brushing my skin. I'm trembling, my fingers gripping the balustrade so tightly, they ache.

Time stops as I wait for him to do something. Say something. Instincts stir deep inside me and I remain quiet, waiting.

Waiting.

When he licks my neck with the tip of his tongue, a soft sound escapes me. He does it again, and I whimper, dipping my head forward, wanting more. Needing more.

Confusion swirls, mixing with a range of emotions and sensations that I don't recognize. His hands settle over mine, keeping me in place, and I ask with a choked sound, "What are you doing to me?"

"Tasting you." His teeth scrape the back of my neck, my entire body melting. Softening. I lean into him, absorbing his heat. His strength. I'm strong, my body formed into nothing but muscle and bone and skin. There's not a single ounce of fat on my frame and I worry for a split second that he won't find me or my body appealing.

I'm too athletic, too skinny, too sharp. Too mean and too cold and too quiet.

He says nothing for a long, pulse-pounding moment, though his breathing deepens. Becomes heavier. I wait, trembling, words stuck in my throat, unable to escape. I'm a wreck of nerves, confused and overwhelmed, and when he finally speaks, I'm relieved to hear it's a command.

"Tilt your head back."

I do as he says, relief flooding me when the back of my head rests on his shoulder. This, I can handle. Being told what to do. Manipulated and molded and formed into what someone wants from me.

His hands settle on my waist, his fingers stretching across the flat expanse of my stomach, and I can't breathe. When he slides them up, oh so slowly, over my rib cage, goose bumps follow, dotting my skin. And when his large hands slip beneath my tank top to cover my bare breasts completely, I moan. A sound so foreign to my ears, I immediately flush with embarrassment.

A deep hum of approval leaves him, his mouth still at my ear as he begins to knead my skin, his thumbs brushing back and forth over my distended nipples. So lightly, I could almost think he's not touching me at all. I arch my back, wanting more, my tank top riding up, exposing me even more, those big hands still covering my flesh.

His hands shift, so only his fingers remain, plucking at my nipples. Twisting them. Hard.

Harder.

I hiss out a breath at the sharp pain and he pauses.

"Want me to stop?"

I shake my head furiously, the words tumbling from my lips as if I have no control over them.

"I like the pain."

His hips nudge my ass at my admission, and I can feel him. Thick and hard, resting between my ass cheeks. Shock courses through me and I push out, rubbing my ass against his erection.

He pinches my nipples extra hard and I cry out. Fuck, that hurt.

But between my legs, I'm throbbing. Wet. If he were to touch me there, he'd find me ready for him. Eager. It's embarrassing, how quickly that happened, and I'm tempted to pull away from him.

But I'd miss it too much. Miss *him* too much. I want West to keep touching me like this.

I want to see how far he'll take it.

He nuzzles the side of my neck. My cheek. His breath is hot, as it fans across my skin, and I turn my face toward his, our accelerated breaths mingling. His lips brush mine, his tongue darting out for a lick, and I turn toward him fully, his hands slipping away from my chest to settle on my hips as we kiss and kiss. Hungrily. Devouring each other. My hands sink into his hair and his hands slide over my butt, jerking me toward him, our lower bodies molded together.

Without warning, he lifts me, setting me on top of the balcony ledge, and I squeal, tearing my mouth from his to stare down at the ground below us. I grip his neck so tightly, it has to hurt him, and he goes completely still, realizing what he just did.

"Don't drop me."

"I won't." He swallows hard. "Fuck, Carolina. I'm sorry. I didn't mean to scare you."

He starts to pull me down and I wrap my legs against the balustrade, not budging. His brows draw together in question, and I slowly shake my head before I settle my mouth on his once more.

"Hold on to me tight," I murmur against his lips, angling my head to deepen our kiss.

He grips me close, his arms tightening around my waist as I lock my legs around his hips. His tongue thrusts inside my mouth over and over, and I grind against his dick, his erection hitting a certain spot beneath my shorts that has me seeing stars, it feels so good.

An orgasm, I think as my mind floats while I rub my body against his. This is what they all talk about. The girls at my dance school, who've discovered their bodies can do a multitude of things, not just dance. It can feel pleasure, sometimes even from the pain.

"You keep that up, I'm going to come in my shorts," he murmurs against my lips.

I laugh, my head falling back, the sound drifting into the air, floating over the city. West kisses my neck, one hand braced against my lower back, his hips working. I whimper and he knows what he's doing to me. I can feel it in the way he's watching me. How he's holding himself.

He wants to see me come too.

"Would that be a bad thing?" I ask like the naïve fool I am. I know how a man has an orgasm, but I've certainly never witnessed it. Not even in porn or photos on the web. I never look that sort of thing up.

It never interested me before. Sex didn't matter. I've never experienced any sort of wanting for anyone.

"It would be a messy thing," he says with a chuckle, his body going still. "And I don't want to risk dropping you."

I glance over my shoulder at the long fall below. I would go splat on those stairs and it wouldn't be pretty. I can see the headlines now.

Dancer heiress falls to her death in Paris!

Carolina Lancaster dead at seventeen after coming too hard on the second story of the Palais Garnier!

A humiliating way to die, for sure.

"It's dangerous," I agree, my expression and voice solemn. "But I—like it."

He frowns. "You do?"

Nodding, I reach out to touch the exposed patch of skin on his chest, wishing I could unbutton his shirt and press my nose into the spot where his heart beats. I want to smell him. Lick him. Eat him up. "I was…close."

He remains quiet, scarily so, and when I finally dare to look up at him, I can see the heat flaring in his eyes. "You want to come?"

Feeling bold, and completely unlike myself, I nod. "Please."

West smiles and leans in, his mouth hovering above mine. "Well, since you asked so nicely…"

His lips find mine, warm and assured, slow and hungry.

So hungry.

I'm just as famished, clinging to him, grinding my lower body against his, our mouths fused. The kiss, frantic. He slips a hand between us, his fingers toying with the leg of my shorts and then they're beneath the fabric, sliding over my front, rubbing my damp panties.

He groans when his fingers press and I lift my hips, seeking more friction. He strokes, his fingers hard on my sensitive flesh, giving me just the right amount of pressure that has chills spreading all over my skin.

Our lips are connected, but we're not really kissing. It's more like we're panting into each other's mouths, his fingers shoving my panties aside to touch bare, hot flesh. I'm so wet, I can hear his fingers slick through my folds. Up and down, circling, pressing, rubbing.

"Oh God," I call out, my voice ringing loud.

He covers my mouth with his, kissing me deeply at the same time he slides a finger inside me, his thumb pressing against my clit. That's all it takes. The next thing I know, I'm coming, shudders completely taking over my body, my heart pounding, my entire body pulsating with the orgasm as it completely sweeps me away. Leaving me an exhausted, overwhelmed mess by the time the last, tiniest shivers linger.

Pressing my face into his neck, I exhale, still trembling, my arms tight around his shoulders, shifting up to his neck. He removes his hand from my underwear, delivering a sweet kiss to the top of my head, and I lie against him for a long, quiet moment, the sound of the city traffic beneath us. The occasional voice from a passerby on the sidewalk reaching my ears. A siren wails in the distance—the song of Paris, there are always sirens wailing—and when I finally lift my head, I find West already watching me.

"You okay?"

I nod.

"Can you speak?"

I shake my head.

"I think I know what might cure that."

Raising my eyebrows, I send him a questioning look.

"Let's go get a crepe."

CHAPTER THREE

WEST

We're sitting at a small metal table in front of an equally small café, not far from the opera house, each of us eating a crepe filled with Nutella and strawberries. Carolina tried to deny she wanted one, and even suggested sharing one, but I told her no way. I wanted my own, and after she just came so hard, I knew she'd polish one off too.

"This is the most touristy thing I think I've ever done," she mutters as she takes a dainty bite of her crepe. "Buying crepes off the street."

"Pretty fucking good, am I right?" I might be as snobbish as she is, but I'm famished. And I didn't even come like she did.

Reaching between my legs, I readjust the front of my shorts, grateful my erection finally died down, though I still have a solid case of blue balls going on. They ache with the need to find release, but no way am I going to get serviced tonight by the richest girl in all of France.

That's okay though. Even though I was petrified I'd drop her, I'm pretty sure half the reason she got off is because she was hanging over the edge of the balcony. This girl likes danger.

She also seems to get off on pain.

Interesting.

"It's delicious," she finally admits, taking a bigger bite and getting a dollop of Nutella on her lip. She doesn't lick it off so I do the noble thing.

"You've got something." I point at her mouth. "On your lip."

"Oh." She touches the corner of her lips and I shake my head, leaning in close. "Where is it?"

"Here." I brush my thumb against her lower lip and show her the remnants of hazelnut spread there, and she darts out her tongue, licking it clean.

Fuck. This girl is going to kill me, I swear to God.

We've kept up a steady stream of conversation since we sat at this table. She tells me about her upcoming performance. I tell her about my trip and where we plan on going next. I'm with my friends, but I failed to mention our parents are with us too. I also lied to her.

I haven't graduated high school. Not yet. I'm starting my senior year in August, just like she is.

Too bad she's not going to Lancaster Prep. We could probably have fun together. Or she'd reject me outright and we'd be in a power struggle the entire school year, trying to prove who's the true leader of the senior class.

She could win just because of her name, which isn't a real win at all if you ask me. At least I've *earned* my position.

"You're salty," she says after she's licked my thumb.

"Only because you are," I point out, considering it's the same thumb that was just pressed against her swollen clit only a few minutes ago.

Carolina flushes about a hundred shades of pink, her eyes downcast as if she's embarrassed. "I forgot that you..."

"Made you come with that hand?" I take a big bite out of my crepe, enjoying her discomfort like a sadistic motherfucker.

"Yes," she whispers, her knees knocking against mine beneath the tiny table while she glances around. "You don't have to say it so loud."

"No one is listening to us," I reassure her. "You can spill all of your secrets to me."

Her expression shifts into closed off, just like that. "I don't have any secrets."

"I've noticed when someone denies that they have secrets, it usually means they have some big ones." Her gaze is full of guilt, I swear. "How about I share a secret with you first and then you can share one with me?"

"Okay." She stretches the word out, sounding unsure.

My brain scrambles as I try to come up with something when it hits me.

"I don't want to take over my family's business," I admit, fighting the shame that always comes when I think about it. "I'm an only child and my father fully expects me to run it someday, but that's the last thing I want to do."

"What do you want to do?" Carolina asks.

"I don't know." I shrug. "Anything but that."

I don't mention what the business is. No need to draw attention to who I am. I like being somewhat anonymous tonight.

"Your turn," I encourage when she still hasn't said anything.

"I'm not normal. I never have been. I don't fit in with anyone," she admits. "I've always felt awkward and…unwanted around other people. Even my family. I don't really have any friends. Not any real ones at least."

"Why?"

"I've always pushed everyone away from me. I don't want anyone to get too close. It makes me uncomfortable. People make me feel uncomfortable. Their emotions are just too much. They're messy and ugly and I don't understand them."

"You let me get close," I point out. "And you definitely felt some strong emotions about me throughout the night." When she frowns, I give her a list. "You hated me. Pretty sure I disgusted you. And then I started to intrigue you. Until I finally—"

She interrupts me. "You're an exception."

"Why is that?" I feel the same way. She's an exception to everyone else. I don't quite understand why I'm drawn to her, but it's there. The attraction. The chemistry.

Looks like she feels it too and is just as confused.

"I'm not sure why." She drops her gaze, like it's too much, looking at me. "Maybe because I know I'll never see you again, so I can be whoever I want when I'm with you."

"And who are you when you're with me?"

Her head lifts, those brilliant blue eyes locking with mine. "I'm not so rigid. Not so—contained. Being with you makes me feel...free. Safe."

The last word is a whisper, as if it were hard for her to confess, and I wonder how chaotic her life has been that no one has ever made her feel safe.

Until me.

"And I never feel that way with anyone," she continues. "Except for you."

We're quiet for a moment, as if we need the words and their meaning to sink in and really take hold.

"I like that," I admit, my voice low. "I'm glad I can make you feel something."

She squirms in her seat, obviously uncomfortable. "It's really late, huh."

I check my phone to see it's already close to midnight. "When do you need to get back?"

"I don't know." She shrugs, but I can tell by the way her eyes skitter to the side that she has some sort of curfew. "Soon."

"You have an early practice tomorrow?"

"I do. Always." She nods, finishing off her crepe with one last big bite, horror dawning in her eyes after she swallows. "I can't believe I ate all of that. So much sugar and carbs."

"I don't think it'll matter much." My gaze wanders over her lithe body. She's so thin and lean, her muscles as hard as mine. She's strong, the way she gripped me out on the balcony, not giving an inch.

"I'll probably throw it all up later anyway." Her gaze flies to mine, panic in her eyes. "I don't have an eating disorder, but I do keep my diet clean, so when I eat garbage, it tends to make me...sick."

I stare at her, wanting to believe she doesn't have an eating disorder. I have no idea what goes on at a dance academy or whatever the fuck it's called, but I can't imagine it's an easygoing atmosphere. I assume it's cutthroat and tough as hell, the days filled with constant dance classes and practices, everyone striving to be the same thing.

On top. Number one.

I can relate. I get off on that. My father has always pushed me to be the best. Considering I'm his oldest son, he has expectations that I'm determined to meet.

Always.

"It can't be easy," I finally say.

"Lots of rigorous training, especially lately. We didn't have a lot of time to learn the dance we're performing this weekend," she admits. "It's a lot in a short amount of time."

"Too bad I can't see it."

"I'm glad you can't watch it." Her laughter is genuine when she sees my shocked expression. "Sometimes I don't like performing for people I know."

"But you don't know me. Remember?"

We stare at each other for a beat and then she's leaping to her feet, pushing her chair close to the table, the metal scraping on the sidewalk. "I'll be right back."

I watch her go to the man taking the crepe orders, and she turns on the charm. Speaking in that rapid-fire French that I can't deny is pretty fucking sexy, batting her eyelashes at the guy who's probably in his late forties or even fifties, judging from the silver strands strewn through his otherwise dark hair. She smooths her hair away from her face, those stray pieces that fell out earlier, thrusting her chest out, showing off those tiny nipples I wish I would've sucked.

My thoughts aren't helping my blue-balls situation whatsoever.

Moments later and she's gliding back toward the table, a lit cigarette clutched between her fingers. She settles into the chair across from mine, a pleased look on her face.

"Bummed a smoke and a light off that guy?" I raise my brows, waiting for her to deny it. I heard enough snippets of her conversation with him to know that's exactly what she did.

She nods, sucking on the end of the cigarette before she blows the smoke to the side, and I appreciate her consideration compared to earlier, when she blew it straight into my face.

"Something else too." She produces a pen seemingly out of thin air, setting it on the table. It starts to roll, headed straight to the edge, and I grab it before it can fall onto the sidewalk. "I need your phone number."

I frown at her, thinking about what she said earlier, about it only being one night. How we'll never run into each other again, and we don't know each other. "You think that's such a good idea?"

Those big blue eyes seem to eat me up the longer she watches me. She finally shakes her head, her cheeks turning pink. "You're right."

"Keeps it simple, you know?" I raise my brows. "We don't need any complications between us."

I get the sense her life is complicated enough.

She nods, sinking her teeth into her lower lip. "I suppose. Though I wouldn't mind leaving something behind so you'll remember me."

"Trust me, Carolina." Reaching out, I tap the end of the pen against her hand. "I will never forget you. Or this night."

Her face flushes a deeper red and she ducks her head, a tiny smile playing on the corners of her mouth. "I have an idea."

"What is it?"

"Give me your hand."

I do as she commands and she turns it so it's palm up, snatching the pen from me before she begins to draw on the inside of my wrist. The pen tickles my skin, making me twitch and she sends me a stern look.

"Don't move."

I keep as still as possible, watching as she scribbles on my skin. The ink is black, and at first, I can't tell what she's drawing, but eventually, it transforms into a ballet skirt.

"I have to get this just right," she murmurs. "The skirt is made of layers and layers of tulle that stick straight out."

Wait a second... "Are you drawing a ballet dancer on my arm?"

"I'm drawing my costume that I'm wearing for the performance on your arm. Or at least I'm trying. This is the bodice." She taps my skin with the pen, then adds tiny dots all over the bodice, like they're sparkles. When she's done, she leans away, contemplating her work.

"Not too bad." She tilts her head to the side, crinkling her nose. "It's much prettier in person."

My gaze lingers on the drawing. It's small, right in the dead center of the inside of my wrist, and I turn my arm this way and that, admiring the drawing. "I like it."

"I'm not really an artist."

Actually, she is.

"I can imagine you in this outfit."

She lifts her eyes to mine, and swear to God, they're glowing. "Really?"

"I can imagine you wearing lots of things," I admit. "Or nothing at all."

Her eyes close and she angles her head toward the sky, taking a deep breath, her eyes popping open. "You must know I don't normally act like that."

"I don't either."

Her head drops, her gaze steady. "So you don't normally finger girls in the Palais Garnier?"

I slowly shake my head. "Never."

A laugh escapes her and she covers it up with her fingers, staring at me as if I'm the best thing she's ever seen. I can't help but sit up straighter, my expression turning serious.

"I'm never going to forget you."

"I won't forget you either," I tell her, meaning every damn word I say.

Later, after we've finished our crepes and the traffic starts to lighten, we head back to the small hotel she's staying at with the rest of her dance company.

"I'm sure your friend is worried about you," I say, my hands in my pockets, so I don't reach out and grab her.

I can feel the invisible wall she's erected between us. It was there the moment we started walking. She's withdrawing now that the evening is coming to a close, reverting back to the quiet, snotty girl she was when I first approached her.

"Gideon? Probably. I don't have my phone with me so…" She shrugs.

That's fucking crazy. What person our age doesn't take their phone with them? And what if I was some sort of creeper who tried to hurt her? Rape her?

Fuck, did she think I pushed myself on her at the opera house? It all happened so fast, and I didn't think of asking for her consent because…

Yeah. Because I'm a dick who just does what he wants, damn the consequences, though I was getting the same vibe from her too.

"Where's your phone?"

"In my hotel room."

"That's really dangerous, you know. Going out in a city you're not from without your phone while hanging out with a guy you don't know."

"Okay, Dad." She sends me a look. "You didn't do anything I didn't want."

I clamp my lips shut.

Never in my life have I met a girl like this. One who's so reckless and rude and charming and sexy. She's unlike any person I've ever known and I already feel so close to her.

Yet I don't know much about her either. Why is she so reckless? Why doesn't she ever go back to the States and spend time with her family? She's fiercely independent and physically strong, yet seemed responsive to my demands.

Oh, and the pain part. She definitely got off on it.

She's a mystery wrapped in a riddle, and I don't fucking get her.

But I want to.

Maybe I'm making it too complex. She admitted she never feels like she fits in, so that's most likely why she acted so reckless and wild tonight. Maybe that's why she stays away from her family too. She'd rather be at peace alone than put herself into a horrible situation with people she doesn't like or understand.

What's that like, living your life feeling as if you don't belong?

I can't imagine.

We walk in silence until she eventually turns on me, stepping directly in my path and stopping me in my tracks. "I can make the rest of the walk to the hotel on my own."

"You sure?"

"It's just right there." She points to a tall building a couple of blocks away.

"I'll watch you until you walk into the building." Nothing is going to happen to her on my watch.

She nods, rising up on her tiptoes and brushing my mouth with hers in a far too brief kiss. "Thank you for a memorable night."

Before she can pull away, I place my hands on her hips, gently pulling her to me, kissing her again. A little deeper this time, sweeping my tongue in her mouth before I slowly pull away. Her hands somehow find the front of my shirt, her fingers clutching the fabric. "Don't forget me."

Her eyes slowly open, the look on her face dreamy. "There's no way that I could."

I kiss her cheek, breathing in her cool ocean scent one last time. "I won't forget you either."

Carolina pulls away from me, regret etched all over her face as she slowly shakes her head. "I don't like goodbyes. Just—you should walk away, okay? And I'll walk away too."

I stare at her, wanting to say more, tempted to ask for her number so we can keep in touch, despite my telling her earlier we shouldn't. If I wanted, I could reach out to her. I know exactly who she is, can find her on any social media site, slide into her DMs and say, "hey, remember me?"

But I won't. Maybe it's better this way. Leaving her on an empty sidewalk in the middle of Paris with no false promises made.

"Okay," I finally say to her, my hands falling away from her hips.

Hers let go of my shirt.

Her eyes are shiny, as if she might cry, and before I can let that get to me, she turns away and starts walking, her steps brisk as she moves further and further away from me. I keep watch just as I promised, my gaze fixed on her blonde head, the swing of her ponytail, her posture ramrod straight. Those long, long legs eating up the sidewalk.

I quickly glance down at the ballet costume she drew on my left arm, brushing my thumb across it. When I return my attention to her, she's even further. Like a tiny blonde speck in the distance.

Look at me, I think. Just one last time, Carolina. Do it.

As if she could hear my mental command, her steps slow and she turns her head, those big blue eyes finding me despite the distance between us. Triumph surges through me and I stare at her, just as she stares at me. She turns around fully to face me, the two of us just standing there. Close, yet so far away.

She raises her hand, wiggles her fingers in a semblance of a wave and then she turns away.

And bolts.

CHAPTER FOUR

CAROLINA

MID-AUGUST

Freedom is dangerous.

I should know. I had enormous, untethered freedom for the last…five years of my life. Oh, at first, I didn't dare push at the rather loose restraints that were given to me. I was young, scared, and I never, ever wanted to disappoint.

The Dance School for Young Girls in London had a strict staff, an unrelenting schedule, and demanded complete discipline from its students. Dance was put above all else. It was more important than regular school lives, our families, our social life. I thrived under the daily regimen. Waking early. Staying up late. Classes where we had to actually learn about nonsensical things such as math and English and history—God, who needed *any* of that?

All I wanted to do was dance.

And dance I did. I danced and danced and danced. I injured myself countless times and danced through the pain. I tortured my body and my mind and my spirit, and God, I absolutely loved it.

After I turned fourteen, I became friendly with the rebellious girls at the school. The ones who smoked cigarettes and drank out of tiny silver flasks they hid under their thin mattresses in their rooms. Sometimes I would sneak a cigarette or a sip from one of their flasks, but never indulged too much.

I was too scared I'd get caught. Too afraid of the consequences.

The mere thought of returning home terrified me beyond reason. No way could that happen.

There were no luxurious comforts at the school, not the kind that I was used to at home, and I liked that too. It was all part of being a dancer. No one cared that I was a Lancaster. My last name, my family, my wealth—none of it mattered.

Everything at the Dance School was a reminder that I was nothing. A nobody. Just another number in a long line of young women who were all striving for the same thing.

To be *the* prima ballerina. The one everyone adored and feared and respected.

I moved on to the London Dance Academy when I was fifteen, and though I was in over my head at first, I worked hard. Harder than I ever had before in my life and by the end of the school year, I was one of Madame Lesandre's favorite students. I preened beneath her attention and praise. I lived for it, my competition eyeing me with disdain. They befriended me and I decided to let it happen. Keep your friends close and your enemies closer, right? My father told me that a long time ago, when I was crying over someone rejecting me as a friend in dance class, though I don't remember who.

"They're just jealous, darling," he'd said. "Look at you! You're perfection."

I knew I wasn't perfection, but I humored him anyway. My father didn't see any of my faults, though I knew they were there, buried deep within my heart. They were dark and ugly and I did my best to keep them hidden.

I have no emotions, and I'm okay with it. I try to, but I don't really care about anyone. Oh, I care about dance and my success and my future. I suppose I care about my family. My brother and sister matter to me, though I can't trust Sylvie, and Whit is so bossy, always telling me what to do that I get sick of him fast. My mother doesn't care about me whatsoever, and the feeling is mutual.

My father adores me to the point that it's stifling. He smothers me every chance he gets, so I do my best to stay away from him.

From all of them. From everyone.

Where I made my mistake? Testing my boundaries this summer. My freedom. We were in Paris to perform and I did things I never thought I would do. Danced at nightclubs. Drank and drank and drank. Smoked so many cigarettes, I made myself sick one night, puking my guts out in one of those tiny public toilettes that are narrow and sit low to the ground. Oh, I was disgusting that night.

I even fell in love a little—or as much in love as I could possibly feel for a boy. A gorgeous, sexy boy who kissed me as if his entire world depended on it.

That was my favorite part.

Those lovely friends, the ones who were my competition? They ratted me out to Madame, who immediately informed my parents of my abhorrent behavior. After the performance though. Oh, she wouldn't let anything interfere with that.

I was perfect that weekend. Still high on the emotions that boy made me feel, I firmly believed I could conquer the world. I could actually be the dancer I dreamed of being my entire life. All I needed was Madame's approval.

And now here I sit with my parents in my father's study at our family home in Newport. In the States—God, I never thought *this* would happen. I should be in London right now, practicing. Always practicing. My feet should be aching and my head full of the music that we dance to. The tinkling piano, the sound of Madame's cane pounding on the floor, her husky, heavily-accented voice demanding, "Higher! HIGHER!"

Instead, I'm sitting next to my mother in the most uncomfortable chair ever constructed, which has probably been in this house for hundreds of years, my father scowling at me, his disappointment palpable.

"You still haven't explained yourself," my father finally says, his voice thick with irritation.

I barely cast a glance in his direction, not wanting to witness his utter displeasure in me for even a second. I'm not used to that. Normally in his eyes, I can do no wrong.

"What is there to explain?" I shrug, keeping my head bent.

I see the way my mother's foot taps against the Aubusson rug, her beige and black Chanel ballet flats battering away at the swirling cream-colored rose like she's trying to crush its petals. "Oh, there's plenty to explain. Like why you ran amok all over Paris like a little whore for two weeks," she retorts.

"Sylvia." Father's voice is sharp. "Don't say that about your own child."

"Why not? It's true. The girl believes she's fully capable of running her own life and doing what she wants, when it's obvious she doesn't have a clue what she's doing. After all of your hard work for the last five years, you're willing to throw it away so you can party in Paris?" The disgust in her voice is thick. *Party in Paris.*

She can't stand the fact that I actually had fun. That I had the absolute time of my life on my own, without being under her complete control unlike my sister. Sylvie can't take a crap without our mother knowing about it. While I'm off doing whatever I want, not that I ever tested the limits until this summer.

And now I'm paying the price.

I can feel my mother's gaze burning a hole through my hair, my skin, as if she's trying to see inside my mind and figure out why I'd done what I did.

"Why is everyone so upset with me? It's not like I'm a drug addict or pregnant." I lift my head, my pleading gaze landing on my father before I turn it into a glare and aim it at my mother. "So I had a little fun in Paris. So what?"

"You're only seventeen," Mother stresses.

"I'm eighteen." I only just celebrated my birthday a week ago, or did she forget? I had reservations at my favorite restaurant in London, and all of my so-called friends were in attendance. It was a party to celebrate me sliding into adulthood, though I didn't have much fun.

Typical.

"You were seventeen when you were cavorting all over Paris with Gideon." My gaze finds Father's again, unnerved by his use of Gideon's name. How much more does he know? "Are you involved with that boy?"

I almost laugh. Should I tell him Gideon is gay? "Of course not."

The look Father gives me says it all.

He doesn't believe me.

"Your father and I have been talking. You need to remember where you come from, who you are. This sort of behavior isn't what a Lancaster *does*, darling." Mother hesitates for only a moment before she plunges on. "You'll be spending your senior year here."

I blink at her, my brain trying to compute what she just said. "In New York?"

There are excellent ballet companies here. Some of the best in the world. It won't matter where I came from or what I've accomplished. It'll be like starting over. I'll have to fight my way to the top of the class, but I can do it.

After all, I've done it before.

Mother shakes her head, her smile growing. "Here. Well, nearby. At Lancaster Prep."

"*No.*" The word automatically falls from my lips, and my stomach sinks into the vicinity of my toes, if that's possible.

"It's what's best," Father adds.

I whirl on him, my mind spinning, my stomach twisting into tight, painful knots that make it hard to breathe. "What about dance?"

"You're on pause," Mother says. "For only a year. Graduate high school and then you can do whatever you want."

"B-but I just turned eighteen." I leap to my feet, my head swiveling back and forth between them, their faces reminding me of blank masks. "I'm coming into my trust fund. I'm an adult. You can't tell me what to do."

"As long as you're enrolled in school, we have complete control of your trust fund," Mother says, her voice irritatingly calm. "You're still considered under our care, Carolina. Just because you're eighteen doesn't mean you're a functioning adult."

"I've been on my own since I was thirteen! In another country, taking care of myself. For Five. Years." I curl my hands into fists, wishing I could pummel both of them. At least Father's expression is full of regret.

"And now you need to be home near us. You can certainly give us one last year as our child before you take off and become a sensation in the dance world." Mother's voice drips with sarcasm.

Staring at her, I take a deep breath, trying to calm my chaotic heart. "You've never believed in me."

"That's not—"

"Don't bother denying it. It's true. You only care about yourself. And my sister." I turn on Father, who's standing as well, his fingers gripping the edge of his desk. "I never expected this from you."

His face seems to break, as if my words are a devastating blow to his heart. "Carolina, you have to understand. We're only doing this to protect you."

"Protect me!" I start laughing, and I can't stop. There are tears streaking down my face, a sob caught in my throat, but I force it down, the laughter still bubbling on my lips. I think I'm in full-blown hysteria. I probably should be committed. "You're doing nothing but hurting me. As usual. I should've known you'd disappoint me."

"So dramatic," Mother murmurs, looking pleased with herself.

God, how I hate this woman.

I loom over her chair and she shrinks back, as if I scare her. Good. I hope I do. I'm sure she hates that I am now taller than her. Thinner. She may have money and experience and she married—only to divorce—the Lancaster name, but I was *born* a Lancaster.

I have more class in my pinky finger than she could ever have in her entire being, and she knows it.

"I expected this from you." My voice is eerily calm. "You don't surprise me at all."

I flee my father's office before they can say anything else, the tears streaming once more, and I wince every time my heels hit the marble floor.

They ache—more so because I haven't danced in days. I run through the house until I'm on the other side, the wing that faces the gardens, and I lock myself away in the ballroom, turning the deadbolt into the elaborate, gold-leaf door with a resounding click.

Breathing heavily, I go to the mirrored wall and stare at myself. My flushed cheeks and red-rimmed eyes. I belong in London. I belong with my dance company and I belong with Madame Lesandre. I need to dance for at least six to eight hours a day and work on my studies for two. That's what's important to me. It's my life.

I can't go to Lancaster Prep for my senior year. I just…

I can't.

Slowly, methodically, I remove my clothing, my gaze never straying from my reflection. Until I'm standing in a pair of thin white boy shorts and my black sports bra that's more for looks than support. Since I don't need it.

I have tiny boobs. Narrow, bony shoulders. And I'm so pale.

I can see the veins in my skin, blue and pink. The blood pumping through them the only thing keeping me alive.

Oh, that and my black heart.

I get into first position, lifting my chin. I shift into second. Third. Fourth. Ending with fifth, holding it before I nod once.

I do it again and again, as natural as walking. Muscle memory is a wondrous thing, I realize as I begin to shuffle my feet, my body moving across the parquet floor. Until I'm leaping and twirling, my skin coated in sweat, my brain blessedly empty of any thought.

They can't force me to do this, I think as I keep my gaze fixed, spinning and spinning, my foot kicking out every single time in perfect sync. I turn and turn until I collapse on the hard floor with a soft cry, and I roll over so I can press my forehead into the parquet, hating my life.

Hating myself even more.

CHAPTER FIVE

CAROLINA

I enter the administration office at Lancaster Prep not so bright and early on Monday. The first day of school. The first day of my senior year.

Headmaster Matthews' secretary lifts her head, her gaze narrowing when she spots me. "You're late."

I come to a stop at the counter, widening my eyes on purpose. "Oh, I am? Sorry."

She can tell I'm not sorry at all, because I'm not.

The woman ignores my fake apology. "The headmaster has been waiting for you."

"Where's his office?" I make like I'm going to approach one of the two closed doors in the area, and she stops me with a firm clearing of her throat.

"I'll go fetch him." She bustles away, her wide hips swinging, and I lean against the old wood counter, tapping my fingers absently as I gaze around the room.

There are awards and photos all over the dark walls. Photos of people I recognize, many of them relatives. The Lancaster family has owned this private school for hundreds of years. The original Augustus Lancaster was a stickler for education and wanted to provide only the best that money can buy. The school is so exclusive, so incredibly difficult to get into, that it's a badge of honor if you graduate from Lancaster Prep.

And here I am being forced to attend. I would gladly give up my seat to any one of the thousands who are dying to go to this hellhole.

The door swings open and the secretary's gaze lands on mine. "He'll see you now."

I push away from the counter and walk past her with barely a glance in her direction, striding into the tiny, messy office and coming to an abrupt stop.

Headmaster Matthews is standing behind his desk, a pleasant smile on his face. He's an attractive man for someone who must be in his late forties. Dark brown hair with faint graying at the temples that gives him a dignified air. Light brown eyes that crinkle pleasantly at the corners and a wide, smiling mouth. He's clad in brown corduroy trousers and a striped sweater in various tones of brown and cream, despite the fact that it's warm outside and will most likely be in the eighties today.

He's giving East Coast Academia vibes for sure.

"Carolina Lancaster." He thrusts his hand out toward me. "A pleasure to finally meet you."

"It's nice to see you." I shake his hand, using the proper greeting anyone who comes from money knows to use. You'd think he'd use it too, considering he's been dealing with the children of some of the wealthiest people in the world for who knows how many years.

I settle into the chair across from his desk and he does the same, his expression pleasant and open. Like he's looking forward to being my friend, which we both know is a lie. I'm sure my parents filled him in on my reluctance to go to this school.

"I'm looking forward to getting to know you this school year, though I won't have nearly as much time with you as I had with your siblings," he says as he turns toward his computer, his gaze roving over the screen, his forehead crinkling in seeming concentration.

I smile and nod, resting my hands on my knees. I'm in the school uniform, hating how the wool skirt scratches my thighs, and the loafers on my feet are incredibly stiff, rubbing against the backs of my ankles. I can't do anything to hurt my feet outside of dance—they're damaged enough already—and I'll have to grab some Band-Aids to take care of the problem before the day ends.

"I've looked over your transcripts. You're an excellent student." His gaze zeroes in on me, dead serious as he continues, "Even with your heavy dance schedule, you were able to maintain a solid A-average your entire high school career."

I'm just as serious when I murmur, "I'm not stupid, Headmaster Matthews."

I don't know why I said that. Wait, yes, I do.

His surprise at my accomplishments feels like an insult. Like I can't manage to devote my life to dance and do well in school at the same time.

His smile falters slightly. "I never said you were, Miss Lancaster."

I merely stare at him in return, a small smile playing upon my lips.

He sits up straighter, tugging on the neck of his sweater as he returns his attention to his computer screen. "Vivian will give you your schedule. Unfortunately, you've missed first period, but you can still sneak into second period. It'll be over in a half hour."

Great. I get to "sneak" into a classroom and everyone will notice me, which is the last thing I want as the new girl.

"I trust your accommodations are up to your standards?" He lifts his brows, as if waiting for me to deny his remark.

"They're adequate." Being a Lancaster means you get to stay in the special suites that aren't part of the regular dorm buildings on campus. I have my own room with an attached bathroom away from everyone else.

"They're still working on converting one of the rooms into a dance studio for you," Matthews says. "It should be done hopefully by the end of next week."

I stuff the panic that wants to rise down deep, painting a pleasant smile on my face. I haven't really danced in days and it feels like my body is changing.

I'm changing. Getting softer.

I haven't even done my daily barre exercises, and I miss it. My body misses it. The discipline. The pain.

I crave it.

"Thank you," I say with as much sincerity as I can muster. "I do appreciate how quickly you've helped me with the studio."

"Of course."

"Any chance they can finish it sooner?" I ask hopefully.

He slowly shakes his head, leaning back in his chair. "I'm afraid not. Supplies can be hard to come by lately, and the construction team is currently working on multiple projects. They hope to have it finished soon, but no guarantees."

If I wanted to act like the spoiled brat that I truly am, I would bang my fist on the edge of the desk and demand the studio be finished on time.

But I do none of that. Instead, I rise to my feet, grabbing the book bag I brought with me and sling the strap over my shoulder. The navy jacket I'm wearing that's part of my uniform stretches tight across my back, thick and oppressive, and I feel myself start to break out into a sweat. "I should go to class."

"Of course." He stands as well, rounding his desk and following me out of his office. "Vivian, do you have Miss Lancaster's schedule?"

Vivian bustles over to the printer and snatches a piece of paper up, handing it to me once I've approached the counter. "Thank you," I tell her.

"Have a lovely day," Vivian trills, turning her back on me and returning to her desk. Dismissing me completely.

Straightening my spine, I glance over my shoulder at Headmaster Matthews, who's openly watching me from his office doorway, his arms crossed in front of his chest. "Good luck today, Carolina. Please reach out if you need anything."

I nod, turning away from him and heading for the door, fleeing the administration office as fast as I possibly can.

Why does it feel like they were both setting me up to fail?

I glance at the schedule, stopping in the wide, empty hall, scanning the list of classes. I have no idea where I'm going, despite being given a map of the campus and all the various buildings. I'm late for my advanced physics class and have American Government next, which will be...interesting.

Considering I've spent all of my high school years in England, I've not learned anything about American history or government since the sixth grade. What do I know about American anything?

I decide to skip the rest of physics and wander around the campus, referring to the map on my phone that's from the school website, trying to get my bearings. I find my locker and test the combination lock on it, opening it on the first try. I find the history building and linger outside of it, smiling at a group of girls who go walking past, their gazes curious and their laughter obvious after they pass me.

They couldn't be laughing about me. They don't even know me.

Finally, the bell rings—a literal bell in a tower that's in the main building. The school is so old, and all the classroom doors swing open, the hall immediately filling with a swarm of students clad in identical blue, green and white. Despite wearing the required uniform, they all put their own mark on it. Some of the girls wear their skirts much shorter, the hems dancing upon their thighs. While other girls don't mess with their skirts at all, the heavy, pleated wool ending at their knees.

Without thought, I reach underneath my jacket and readjust the waistband of my skirt, rolling it higher before I yank my white shirt out a little to cover the flip of my skirt's waistband. I remove my jacket next, mentally noting how many girls aren't wearing theirs, and shove it in my book bag.

I'm desperate to fit in. I don't want to stand out. I don't even want anyone to know I'm a Lancaster, but that's impossible to hide. People will recognize me, and my parents wouldn't let me enroll under a different last name, though I tried. I asked. Begged. Pleaded, even.

They wouldn't budge. *Everyone should know who you are*, my father insisted, pride in his voice. Always proud of me, even when I don't want him to be. Sometimes I wish they wouldn't even acknowledge I exist. I preferred to keep an entire ocean between us, living on a different continent rather than deal with them.

God, my relationship with my parents is so complicated.

Irritated by my thoughts, and by the bulk in my bag now thanks to the jacket, I shove the bag behind my arm and enter my American Government class, choosing a seat in the middle of the room, in the middle row. The desks fill up quickly with loud, chattering students, one after the other, all of them seeming to know each other. I glance around, offering a smile to a boy who watches me with obvious interest.

I turn away from him, not wanting to stare. I think of my old friends, and what they might think about this boy. Simone would always talk of boys as objects that she only used for sex. Is he fuckable or not?

That was always her question when considering a boy, and it would embarrass me to no end. I never looked at a boy and wondered if he was fuckable. I wasn't interested. Not like that. When it came to the many boys I met when I was in London, I never actually wanted any of them.

Until him.

Too bad he already graduated from Lancaster. It wouldn't be so bad, running into West whatever his last name is. At least I'd know someone, even if it might end up being awkward between us.

A stolen night in Paris isn't a normal memory to share with someone, I'm sure, but it's mine.

Ours.

And it's probably best that it stays in Paris. Where it belongs.

In the past.

"You're new," the boy finally says, pulling me from my thoughts.

I turn to find him smiling at me, and I smile in return. "I am."

"I'm Brent."

"Carolina." My smile grows.

His fades. "Wait a minute. You're Carolina *Lancaster*?"

"Yes." I let my smile drop, concerned by the panicked look on his face. How did he know? "Have we met before?"

"Not personally, but I've heard *all* about you." He smothers the chuckle that leaks from his mouth with his hand, his fingers denting into his lips.

His words, how he says them, make me uneasy. "What? From who?"

Brent's gaze goes to the back of the room, zeroing in on the open doorway. "You'll see."

The only person I know who went to this wretched school is my own family and...

The boy in Paris.

Could he have told his friends about us? About me? I thought what we shared that night was private. Secret. I even told him that. I told him so many things. Confessions I would've never made to anyone else.

The possibility that he went and spilled all of my secrets to his friends leaves me feeling terrified. More than that, it hurts.

I turn toward the door, my lips slowly parting when I see who enters the room at that exact moment, clad in the Lancaster uniform minus the jacket, handsome as I remember.

Maybe even more so.

My heart drops, splintering into a thousand pieces, and I turn away from the door as quickly as possible, hoping he doesn't notice me. Though I know my hopes are futile.

He's *here*, the little liar.

West.

CHAPTER SIX

WEST

Senior year. First day of school and so far, so good. I'm finally ruling this campus. It's my kingdom, and everyone else here are just members of my court. I've worked toward this moment for the last three years at this school, and now I'm finally on top.

No one is going to ruin it for me. Not a single soul. Everyone knows their place. What's even better? There are no Lancasters in attendance. They take top spot of the student hierarchy automatically, thanks to their last name. A family you can't fight against, no matter how hard you try. They come in without having to do a single thing to prove their worth, and everyone follows what they say and do.

Only because their damn name is on the building.

First two classes of the day are easy. Advanced physics might be tough as we get deeper into the semester, but I'm guessing there are enough smart girls in the class who'd do my homework for me. Who'd help me with the tests and the labs. Girls who would give anything for some one-on-one time with me.

Am I interested in any of them? Not so much, but my dad always tells me you have to do whatever it takes to stay on top.

I'm walking down the hall toward my next class when I hear

a familiar, feminine voice call my name. Turning, I see Mercedes Browne heading toward me, a coy smile on her elfin face, her dark hair swinging like she's auditioning for a shampoo commercial.

"Mercedes." I flash her a smile, waiting as she makes her way to me. "How are you?"

"Aren't you looking extra fine this morning, Mr. Fontaine." She hip checks me and we fall into step with each other. "I hear Europe was good to you this summer."

"We had fun." That's all I'll admit about my European summer. I'm careful with what I say. My friends might know what happened in Paris and who it happened with, but that's it. Unless the assholes opened their mouths and told everyone.

Wouldn't put it past them. They love to stir up shit, even at my expense. I may have told them about my...incident with Carolina Lancaster, but I gave them zero details. I had to keep some of it to myself.

It's the least I could do. Carolina wasn't just some random girl I fucked around with.

Not even close.

"I'm jealous. I was in Australia." Mercedes rolls her eyes. "With my family."

"I love Australia."

"Me too, but never with my family. At least you made your trip with the boys." She shakes her head, a knowing gleam shining in her eyes. "I'm sure you were all up to no good."

"What's your next class?" I ask her, wanting to change the subject.

"American Government," she says on a sigh. "Boring."

"Lucky you, that's where I'm headed too." Mercedes might be too clingy and overly possessive, but she's smart. This girl will keep me on top of the class when I start slacking, which I've done in the past.

"Oh goodie. A class with West." She touches my arm just as we approach the classroom door. "Should be fun."

There she goes with the possessiveness. Already touching me. I pull away from her seeking fingers, stopping in the doorway with Mercedes just behind me. Brent catches my gaze as if he's been waiting for me, and when we make eye contact, he leans his head toward the girl sitting next to him, mouthing something I can't decipher.

She's blonde, her bright hair flowing down her back in faint waves. Her posture is absolute perfection, her spine straight, the angle of her head...

Familiar.

I'm frozen, Mercedes poking at my side, urging me to move it, but I can't bring myself to put one foot forward like a normal fucking human being.

"West, come on. Let me in!" Mercedes practically screams.

At the sound of my name, the blonde turns, her deep blue eyes meeting mine, her lips parting in shock just before she turns away, like she doesn't want me to see her.

Realization dawns, slow as the setting sun, while it sinks deeper and deeper into my brain.

What the fuck is Carolina Lancaster doing here?

I enter the classroom as if I'm in a trance, Mercedes curling her arm through mine and practically dragging me over to the rows of desks. I fall into the one behind Brent, noting how Carolina keeps her back to me.

She won't even look in my direction. Her posture is so rigid, I'm afraid she might snap in two if she moves too fast. Completely ignoring me when all I want to do is look at her face. Stare into her eyes. Ask her without saying a single word: what are you doing here?

Knowing Carolina, she probably wouldn't tell me.

"Hey, who's the blonde?"

I glance to my right to see my other friend Russ slide into the seat next to mine, his gaze locked on the back of Carolina's head. "Why do you want to know?"

My tone is hostile, and I clench my right hand into a tight fist.

"I get the feeling she's hot." Russ raises his voice. "Hey, blondie."

Slowly, Carolina turns, her gaze sliding over me dismissively, like I don't even exist. The anger rises within me and I let it. Fuck, I marinate in it, I'm so pissed. "Are you speaking to me?"

Her voice is soft. Cultured. With the faintest British lilt. Russ grins at her like an idiot.

"Yeah, babe. Totally talking to you. You new here?"

She inclines her head toward him in silent answer.

"What's your name?"

Her expression is blank. Almost robotic. "Carolina."

Russ grins, nudging me with his elbow. I jerk away from him, annoyed.

"Nice to meet you." Russ thrusts his hand out toward her, that stupid grin still on his face. "Russell Chadwick."

"Carolina Lancaster." Her gaze lifts to mine. Briefly.

I look away as they shake hands, a muscle in my jaw working.

"Lancaster?" Mercedes practically squeaks. "As in *the* Carolina Lancaster?"

Mercedes is big on fangirl behavior. She will fawn all over Carolina, simply because of her name.

"What, like you're a celebrity?" Russ glances around, searching for confirmation.

"She's a ballet dancer. She danced for the London Academy, which is, like, the most prestigious dance school in the world," Mercedes explains.

Carolina just sits there, quiet as a little church mouse, nothing like the girl I met in a nightclub this past summer. Though at least one thing remains consistent.

She won't acknowledge me, just like she did when I first met her. She won't even look at me.

Such a snob. After everything that happened between us, this is how she treats me.

"Why are you here and not at your dance school?" Mercedes asks.

Leave it to her to ask the important questions.

Carolina's cheeks turn rosy, and I remember how her skin was flushed all over after we kissed.

I shove the memory out of my brain, pissed it had the nerve to creep in.

Her lips parting, she pauses, as if she's trying to come up with something to say when the bell rings. Our teacher strides in, slamming the door behind him, and he goes straight to the whiteboard, grabbing a marker and tapping it against the words American Government that he must've written there earlier.

"This is the class you're in. Double check your schedule to make sure you're where you're supposed to be. We've already had some confusion this morning. I'm not in the mood for any more."

There's some quiet chatter amongst all of us, but no one leaves the class, so I guess we're all where we belong. Mr. Harvey is a no-nonsense motherfucker with zero sense of humor and a low tolerance for bullshit. I had him for World History my sophomore year and hated every minute of it, but damn if I didn't learn a few things.

This year, I'm not in the mood to learn shit. I need to take all of the advanced classes to get into an Ivy League school, but it's my senior year. I don't want to do anything too strenuous.

I want to enjoy my last year in high school before it's on to Princeton, Yale or Harvard. Those are the only schools my parents approve of me attending next year. My father says I have to take the requisite advanced courses at Lancaster and look like the overachiever he was. As his only son, he fully expects me to work for the family business, just as he does. The winery business that was started in the lush rolling valley of the Loire in France by my great-great-great grandfather, a man with a vision—a man who was drunk most of his days—the brilliant yet infamous Eduard Fontaine, which also happens to be my father's name.

My namesake is my maternal grandfather, Jonathan Weston. It was at my mother's insistence that they call me West, though my name is actually Weston Eduard Fontaine. She comes from solid American stock in Connecticut, and I was close to my grandparents when I was younger.

Not so much anymore.

I have nothing against our family history, or the fact that we make a lot of money producing some of the most coveted and expensive champagne in the world, but I have no desire to work for The House of Fontaine. Since enrolling in Lancaster, my parents moved to the Napa Valley, where we also have vineyards, and they've been there ever since.

While I'm over here busting my ass so I can get into an Ivy League university for the sole purpose of pleasing my parents. Specifically, my father.

The man is impossible to please.

Harvey launches into a lecture—such bullshit, it's the first day of school—and I lose interest almost immediately, my gaze locking on the back of Carolina's head. All of that white blonde hair flowing down her back in streaming bright waves.

I can't believe she's here. It almost doesn't feel real. And our encounter in Paris definitely doesn't feel real. Not anymore.

I haven't been able to put that night out of my mind, no matter how hard I've tried. Dancing with her at the nightclub, sitting close to her in the cab, sneaking into the opera house, her hand clutched in mine as she dragged me up those endless marble stairs. The look she sent me over her shoulder, her eyes dancing. I could see them even in the dark, the naughty expression on her face.

The way she felt in my arms. The taste of her, lingering on my lips and tongue. Her scent, as cool and mysterious as the ocean. I remember thinking at the end of my European vacation that I'd give anything to smell her again. Just once.

Now, here she is, sitting in my classroom, her back to me, pretending I don't even exist. A living, breathing reminder of what happened on the second story balcony at the Palais Garnier on a hot summer night in July, when I held a girl in my arms and made her come with my fingers.

Maybe what happened between us meant nothing to her. If that's the case…

She can go to hell.

CHAPTER SEVEN

CAROLINA

I can't look at him. I can't. I don't even know what I would say. How do I approach this, approach him?

Glancing down at the top of my desk, I stare at it until my vision starts to blur, the teacher's droning voice becoming distant until I can't make out what he's saying. I'm achingly aware of the boy behind me, his gaze burning a hole into my skin, his disdain for me palpable.

Yet, isn't he the one who lied to me? When we first met, he mentioned he already graduated from Lancaster Prep. But here he is, clad in the requisite uniform, surrounded by his friends. Still attending this school, which means he's my age.

It's obvious that he's popular. What would his friends say if I called him out as a liar?

He'd probably deny it and they'd believe him because he's been here far longer than I have. It's my first day. It's his last year. I have no friends, no one who actually *knows* me.

With the exception of him.

The moment the bell rings, I'm shooting out of the desk like a freaking rocket, practically dragging my book bag behind me, I'm in such a rush. I'm walking as fast as possible down the wide hallway, pushing my way through the hordes of students, ignoring everyone as I make my way to my next class. Statistics.

I hate math.

It takes me a while, but I find my classroom and of course, the period drags on and my stomach rumbles. I didn't eat breakfast this morning because I was too nervous, and now, I'm starving. I arrived on campus only last night and didn't have a chance to check out the dining hall. I'm worried about my food options. I want to eat healthy, especially since I won't be regularly dancing, and I hope there's more than junk food on the menu.

Considering how hungry I am currently though I'd take about anything I could get.

When the bell rings, I'm a little slower to gather my things, not feeling the need to flee like I did in American Government. I don't even notice the girl approaching me until she's practically on top of me, her loud voice making me gasp.

"Hey! You're Carolina, right?"

I nod, taking her in. She's beautiful, her features perfectly aligned. Wide smile, button nose, high cheekbones. Long, wavy brown hair, dark brown eyes. The sleeves are rolled up on her white button down, both of her wrists jangling with a stack of bracelets, and she has a ring on almost every finger. At least three necklaces around her neck and two, possibly three, piercings on each ear that I can see.

"I am," I finally say to her, shoving my new statistics textbook into my bag before I close the flap. "I'm also at a disadvantage since I don't know your name."

"It's Mercedes." Her smile is brilliant, showing off bright white, straight teeth. "We also have American Government together."

Oh. I knew she was familiar. I was so stuck on seeing West for the first time, I didn't really notice anyone else besides the first guy I talked to. "Hi, Mercedes."

"Hi!" Her smile grows, if that's possible. "Want to sit with us at lunch?"

I get the feeling this is an important invitation. "Sure."

We walk together to the dining hall, Mercedes chattering away, pointing out classrooms and rattling off the names of students and staff members as we pass by them. She also shares a shortcut I didn't realize existed to get from one building to another. When we finally arrive at the dining hall, I'm able to sneak in a question.

"How's the food here?"

She wrinkles her nose. "It could be better, but it's not horrible. The pizza is good."

Pizza. I can't remember the last time I ate even a bite, let alone an entire slice. "Do they have a salad bar?"

"They do!" She nods enthusiastically. "The ranch dressing is delicious—it's homemade."

Clearly, Mercedes doesn't have to watch what she eats. Lucky her.

We enter the noisy, crowded dining hall, and I follow Mercedes as she leads me over to the expansive salad bar. I contemplate my options, seeing that there's at least a fat-free Italian dressing available. It'll still be full of calories, but I could add just a little bit for taste...

"Yo, Mer!" A tall boy wedges himself between us, slinging his arm around Mercedes' shoulders, though his gaze is on me. "Who's your friend?"

He blatantly checks me out and my cheeks heat up. I look away from him, uncomfortable by his bold stare.

"TJ, stop!" Mercedes' voice is extra high, and she giggles, flirtatiously. "This is Carolina."

He flicks his chin at me, his gaze knowing. As if he's in on some giant secret and I'm oblivious. "Carolina, huh?"

I nod, taking a step back, needing the distance. I don't know him and if he tries to put his arm around my shoulders, I might lose it. "Hi."

"I've heard about you." His gaze rakes over me yet again, his hazel eyes sparkling. "The dancer?"

"The Lancaster," Mercedes adds.

"Right. We haven't had one of those on campus in a while."

One of those. Like I'm an object, and not a real human being.

"Well, lucky you, now you do." I offer him a brittle smile and leave them where they both stand, my entire body quaking. I go to the end of the line at the salad bar, trying to calm my accelerated breathing.

Was I a complete bitch just now? God, I hope not. Usually I wouldn't care, but I don't want to start the school year off with everyone hating me. I'm stuck on this campus for the entirety of senior year. I need to make the best of it.

I grab a chilled white plate and start loading it with the healthiest options on the salad bar, which, thankfully, are plentiful. I'm even able to grab a small cup that I can fill with salad dressing, so I can keep it on the side. I note how everyone in line adds cheese and bacon bits and croutons to their salads, drenching everything in ranch or whatever other creamy salad dressing they love.

Wrinkling my nose, I take my tray with my salad and go to the cashier, scanning my meal card with a faint smile for the woman sitting at the register.

"Nice and healthy salad you got there," she notes, her smiling eyes meeting mine. "Great way to start your first day of school."

"Thank you," I say, feeling awkward, unsure how to respond.

"You're new here?"

I nod, shoving my meal card into the front pocket of my book bag. "Yes."

"Welcome to Lancaster!" the woman practically shouts, causing what feels like half the occupants of the dining hall to look in our direction, their expressions curious.

I run away from the counter, ducking my head, relief filling me when I spot Mercedes, who's waving frantically at me from a nearby table.

How did she get through the line already?

"Carolina! Come sit with us!" she calls.

I go to the table, noting that the guy who checked me out, TJ, is sitting right next to her. There are other guys at the table as well, plus a few girls. Mercedes kicks out the empty chair next to her, indicating it with her hand. "Sit here."

I settle into the chair, setting my tray in front of me, scanning what everyone else is eating. Mercedes has a greasy slice of pepperoni pizza on her plate. TJ has a cheeseburger and a pile of fries that smell like salt-flavored heaven. The other girls have salads, but you can barely see the lettuce thanks to all the dressing that tops them.

"Everyone, this is Carolina Lancaster." Mercedes says my last name with extra emphasis, which makes me wonder if she's being so friendly because it gets her some sort of popularity points, becoming friendly with a Lancaster.

The girls offer up enthusiastic smiles and little waves. The boys give the standard chin nod and a muttered, "what's up," clearly not impressed with who I am, which is perfect.

But TJ watches me carefully, his gaze assessing before it finally drops to his phone and he starts tapping away at the screen, the unmistakable sound of a text being sent filling my ears.

"Who are you texting?" Mercedes nudges her shoulder against TJ's. "And where's West?"

My stomach hollows out and I stare at my plate, my appetite disappearing at the mere mention of his name.

"That's who I was texting. I have no idea where he is." TJ pockets his phone, his gaze sweeping over the dining hall. "I don't see him."

"Maybe he's at the library," one of the girls says, a knowing tone to her voice.

Mercedes starts to laugh, the sound light. "I don't think he moves that fast."

"You'd be surprised," TJ says with a chuckle.

I feel like I'm missing out on the joke, and my face must convey my confusion because Mercedes takes pity on me and explains.

"West is known for taking girls into the library so they can—fool around," Mercedes explains.

"I heard he had sex with one girl right against the stacks in the Ancient History section," one of the girls adds.

"Oh please, Sam." Mercedes rolls her eyes at me. "Samantha exaggerates."

"Nah, that's true. He fucked Helena Madigan in the library. I think it was in the Autobiography section though," TJ says with a grin, just before he shoves his mouth full of french fries.

The girls start giggling with the exception of Mercedes, who's glaring at TJ. "No need to be so crude. There are ladies present."

"You referring to Miss Lancaster here?" He points at me, rude as hell. "Pretty sure she knows about fucking around with West."

It takes everything in me to remain still and have zero outward reaction to his words. Mercedes' head swings between the two of us, her curiosity growing into a living, breathing thing, though I get the sense she's not brave enough to ask what he means by that.

And I know I won't say a word.

"You know West?" Mercedes asks, her voice so low I almost don't hear her.

"No." I swallow hard, my gaze on TJ's, quietly daring him to deny my answer. "I have no idea who you're talking about."

"He was in our class—" Mercedes starts, but TJ cuts her off.

"Really." TJ's voice is flat, and he leans toward me, his arms crossed and resting on the edge of the table. "Weren't you in Paris this summer?"

"That's public knowledge." I lift my chin, hoping I look strong. Like what he's saying isn't bothering me in the least, though I feel like I could puke if he keeps up this line of questioning. "I performed there this summer."

"Uh huh. Well, I happen to—"

"You know nothing."

At the sound of his voice, we all turn to find West standing directly behind TJ's chair, his stony expression completely unreadable. His gaze is locked on me and he doesn't say a word, his upper lip slowly starting to curl with disgust. There are two other boys standing directly behind him, like they belong to some sort of gang and he's their leader, which makes me realize…

I'm completely out of my element. I've gone to school with nothing but girls and a handful of boys for the last five years, and all of us had the same goal. Each of us were desperately clawing our way to the top. That, I understand. Dance and all of the competitiveness it brings is something I've been comfortable with for years.

The politics involved in navigating an American high school— an elite private school attended by the children of some of the richest families in the country, if not the world—is not something I'm prepared to do. Regardless of my last name.

Pretty sure I'm in way over my head.

CHAPTER EIGHT

WEST

'm fucking pissed.

She really thinks she can pretend she's never met me? Never spent the night with me? That I wasn't the one who made her come with my fingers buried in her sweet, tight cunt on the balcony at the Palais Garnier?

Who the fuck does this girl think she is?

There is no thinking. She knows exactly who she is. Carolina Lancaster has power and influence at this school, but only because of her name.

Me? I earned the power and influence I have. Look at what just happened. With only a few choice words, I got TJ to shut the hell up. I don't need him to reveal anything else about me and Carolina. That's private.

The fact that she pretends I don't exist—that she pretends she doesn't even know who I am—that burns my ass, not that I'd ever admit it. Clearly, she doesn't actually know me. Doesn't know who she's playing with. Doesn't understand what she's doing, or how she's committing social suicide with her words and behavior.

This girl. I thought what we shared was something special, and how fucking sappy do I sound, even in my own thoughts? Well, forget it.

Forget her.

Carolina has made a colossal mistake, crossing me. She thinks she can get away with this?

I'll show her.

Eventually she leaves the table, all by herself. The moment she's gone, Mercedes is talking trash, the little bitch, and I wait for a few seconds.

Then I'm pushing away from the table as well, abandoning them without a word. No one follows me, not even my friends, and not a single one of them call out to me either, though I'm sure they're curious.

I'd bet money Mercedes wishes she followed after me.

I exit the dining hall and immediately spot Carolina's blonde hair. She's heading toward the building where her housing is located.

Fucking Lancasters are so special, they don't have to stay in the dorm buildings like the rest of us peons do.

I slow my steps, still following her, but keeping my distance when she comes to a stop, slowly turning so she's facing me. I don't move. There's no point and I don't give a damn if she sees me or not.

I'm not going to hide that I followed her, though I'm just as baffled over it as she looks. I don't know why she bothers me so damn much. Or why I care.

"Why are you following me?" Her sweet, clear voice rings in the air and I glance around, noting we're the only ones out here.

"Why are you hanging out with my friends?"

She lifts her chin, haughty as ever. "They're my friends too."

I want to scoff. I want to tell her she's delusional because not a single soul at that table gives a damn about her.

Fuck it.

"They're not your friends. You don't even know them. Mercedes talked shit about you the moment you left the table."

Carolina blinks, the shock on her face there and gone in an

instant. "You're just saying that."

"Why would I just say that?"

"Because you're trying to hurt me, that's why." She turns her back on me and starts walking.

And like a fucking idiot, I follow after her, striding into the building and trailing behind her in the hall as she stomps her way toward her room. "Why would I bother trying to hurt you?"

"I don't know," she tosses over her shoulder, never slowing her pace. "Maybe because I ignored you and it makes you crazy? Just because we shared one night together, West, doesn't mean that you matter to me. Because you don't."

I'm on her in a second, my fingers curling around her slender arm, forcing her to face me. She tilts her head back, our gazes meeting, hers the color of the deep blue sea. Look a little closer and I can see the turbulence there. The storm is raging within those eyes, and I know why.

It's because of me.

"You don't matter to me either," I murmur. "Go ahead and ignore me all you want. I don't give a damn what you think about me, or how you feel."

Her eyes narrow, that haughty expression on her beautiful face twisting my insides.

Fuck, I hate that I'm attracted to her. I'd enjoy nothing more than pushing her against the wall and kissing that shitty look off her face. Biting at her lips, licking at her tongue, gripping her tits in my hands, knowing all along she would be just as aroused as I am.

She'd get off on me being rough. Treating her like nothing. Scaring her. She likes it that way.

Carolina Lancaster is attracted to me, and she hates it just as much as I hate my attraction to her.

"You're the one who followed me in here." Her voice is soft. Breathless.

My gaze drops to her chest, noting how it rapidly rises and

falls. She's wearing the required white shirt with a navy sweater vest over it, and she must be hot as shit. How can she stand it?

"We need to make a few things clear." I step closer, my body brushing against hers and she parts her lips, a soft exhale leaving her. "Stay away from my friends."

She tilts her head back, her eyes blazing. "Make me."

Irritation floods my veins, along with a healthy dose of arousal. This girl...

Is purposely trying to make me hate her.

And it's working.

"Don't be stupid." I shift even closer, my leg sliding between both of hers, and I lift my knee, brushing it against the inside of her thighs. "I'll make your life a living hell, if that's what you want."

"You already have," she whispers.

"Right back at you, babe." I curl my fingers around her chin, forcing her to meet my gaze. "You know what frustrates me?"

Carolina remains quiet, her entire body trembling, and I see it flicker in her gaze.

Desire.

"I can't stop thinking about that night. The sounds you made. How wet you were. So tight, your pussy gripping my fingers like a vise."

"Shut up." Her cheeks turn pink and she tries to pull out of my grip, but I don't let her, my fingers tightening.

"You hate the fact that I'm the one who made you come, don't you?" I chuckle, though the sound lacks any humor.

"It's all Gideon's fault," she spits out, and now I really do want to laugh. "He should've never let you get into that cab with us."

I let go of her face, pressing my cheek against hers so I can whisper in her ear. "I don't remember you complaining when you slipped that mint into my mouth with your tongue."

She shoves at my chest with all of her might and I stumble back, shocked at her strength, though I shouldn't be. I know she's made of nothing but pure muscle.

"You're a dick."

"Sad you didn't get to sample it?" I grab at my junk for emphasis like the asshole that I am.

Carolina barks out a laugh. "God, you're disgusting."

"You love it, babe."

"I hate you." Her voice trembles, and for a split second, I feel bad. Because that's fear I hear in her voice.

Is she scared someone will find out what we did?

Or is she scared of me?

Cruel, I know, but I hope she is scared of me. Because...

She should be.

CHAPTER NINE

CAROLINA

"How's school, darling?"

I sigh into the phone, not bothering to hide my exasperation from my father. He should know exactly how I'm feeling about being here, because it's awful. And maybe if I suck up to him enough, he'll let me come home. Or even better...

Let me go back to London.

"It's terrible."

He chuckles. "Tell me how you really feel."

"Oh, I will," I say, my voice strong, running right over his laughter. Like I'm a big joke—that hurts, not that I'll ever admit it. "The classes are boring, the teachers are terrible, and my studio still isn't ready."

"I heard from Matthews myself this morning. He mentioned that the two of you—spoke, and that you weren't happy construction is taking so long."

"I'm not happy at all." Matthews and I didn't "speak." It was more like I barged into his office and yelled at him, while he just sat there and took it. "I've been here for almost three weeks, and it's still not done. I was told it would be ready within a week of my arrival."

"Matthews can't control the supply chain, darling. It's not his fault that some items aren't available. Just—be patient."

"That's not my best trait," I mutter.

He starts to chuckle again, which is just beyond infuriating. "It's not a strong trait among any of us Lancasters. We want what we want and we want it now."

"I'm glad someone understands." I flop onto my bed, staring at the ceiling while I clutch my phone tightly in my hand. "I'm just so homesick."

"You should come visit me at my apartment this weekend," he suggests.

"I'm homesick for London," I correct, wincing when I hear the catch in his breath, as if my words might've hurt him.

Which they might have. He has to understand, I have no real reason to be homesick for his apartment. I've spent very little time there. After our parents' divorce, I left for London to escape the tension and the fighting and the struggle between my parents as they tried to lay claim to their children. Mother snagged up Sylvie as hers. Father reluctantly chose Whit, but only by default, since Whit was thoroughly disgusted by our mother's antics during that time.

Funny how my brother stood by our father's side while he was a cheating, thoughtless bastard. Men. I will never understand the way they think.

"You know how your mother and I feel about you being in London." Father's voice shifts into stern mode. "You took your dancing so seriously. It wasn't fun anymore. The fun you sought was more on the dangerous side, and we were concerned with your safety. That's why you're here. Back home, where you belong for one last year. Once you graduate high school, you can do whatever you want. If that means returning to London or maybe heading somewhere else, that's fine. But until then, you are stuck here. With us."

I've heard it before from him, countless times. I'm constantly trying to get him to cave, to give into my demands and let me return to my dance school, but he won't budge.

It's so frustrating, but I'm not giving up. I can't.

My entire body feels tight, like it hasn't received the proper exercise it needs, which it hasn't. I've been running the last week or so. In the late afternoon, when the football team is out on the field practicing. I jog the track, ignoring the catcalls and lewd remarks, withstanding their attention because I need the exercise and I don't necessarily feel safe jogging out on the beach. It's so far.

I suppose I can handle a few teenaged boys yelling at me.

I don't have many friends yet. Mercedes still speaks to me, and even includes me at their table in the dining hall during lunch, but most of the time, I leave the moment West shows up. Or sometimes I don't sit with them at all, much preferring to sit outside and enjoy the still warm weather. The gentle breeze cooling my lurid thoughts.

All of them filled with the many ways I could possibly destroy Weston Fontaine. Of the champagne and wine Fontaines, who originally descend from France. My father knows about West's family because, of course, I asked, as casually as I could.

How pathetic I must've looked to West, being incredibly rude toward him while pretending to be French. I'm fluent, but so is he. I'm positive he understood every single word I said, and most of them in reference to him weren't kind.

God, I was such a bitch that night. I don't regret my behavior toward him any longer though. He's just as mean, just as cold now as I was then. It's almost as if he seduced me on purpose, but for what reason? To brag to everyone at school? His closest friends act like they know something happened between us, which is infuriating. How much did he tell them? What sort of personal details do his friends know about me? And how could he betray me like that? Besides the fact that he lied, telling me he'd already graduated.

I don't understand him. Worse, I cannot stand him. He's a

horrible human being.

A gorgeous, horrible human being.

"I hate this school," I murmur into the phone, my throat suddenly thick with tears. I close my eyes, fighting the overwhelming sense of dread threatening to wash over me and I brace myself for the inevitable, *it's all going to be okay*, remarks from my father.

"Give it a little more time," he says. "You'll eventually make friends."

"They all hate me." Oh, I sound pathetic.

I think about Mercedes and her shallow offer of friendship. It's mostly her asking me questions about my family or her droning on about how rich hers is. They got their money in tech. Her dad is an app developer. That's so *nouveau riche*, I don't know why anyone at this Godforsaken school would give her the time of day. She even admitted to me her mother named her Mercedes because it's her favorite car brand, which is just...tacky.

I can't stop thinking about West warning me that she talks shit about me when I'm not around. I know I should expect that sort of behavior from someone like her, but it still hurts.

I come back to the States and I've turned soft, allowing a known mean girl to get under my skin. In London, I didn't care what anyone said about me. I just wanted to be on top. The only dancer Madame truly believed in.

"Or they want me as part of their circle because of my last name," I continue. "They don't even try to get to know me."

"You should try and get to know them instead," he suggests.

"None of them talk to me like that. It's all so...fake."

He's quiet for a moment and I press my lips together, scared a sob might burst out of me. Why am I sad? Why does having a friend matter to me? I've never felt so alone. Even when I was in London, I had people surrounding me, pretending to be my friend. Some of them might've actually liked me, but it's doubtful.

There's not much to like about me.

I swallow the near-sob down, willing my body to cooperate. Something I've always been able to do when I'm dancing. *If I think it, I become it.*

You won't cry. You're stronger than that. You will not cry.

The ache in my throat slowly eases and when I open my eyes, they're not blurred with tears anymore.

"Try your best to make new friends. Sometimes you can be rather...unapproachable, you know," my father so graciously reminds me.

Right. Unapproachable. That's a kind way of being called cold. Closed-off. Distant.

I don't know why I'm that way. Sometimes I try to act open and warm and willing to make friends, but it's so hard.

It's not me. And I wish someone would just accept me for who I am.

"I'll try," I tell him.

"I made lifelong friends while I attended Lancaster Prep. Men and women I still speak with on occasion." He chuckles. "Most of them are Facebook friends, but that still counts, right?"

There's no point in arguing with him that no, that doesn't count, because he'll deny it.

"I have to go. I'll talk to you later?"

"Call me whenever you want, okay? If you're sad, if you're lonely. I'm here for you, sweetheart. I am."

"Thank you, Dad." He likes it when I call him Dad. Much less formal than Father, which is how Whit and Sylvie always refer to him.

"Anytime. Love you."

I end the call without saying I love him too, which also makes me uncomfortable. Saying those words out loud.

Affection, physical or verbal, makes me squeamish. My parents weren't particularly demonstrative growing up, and once I went away to dance school, I had no one giving me any physical affection. I got so used to it that now, I'm always uncomfortable when someone tries to touch me. I can tolerate it when I'm dancing, but only when absolutely necessary. I'm not one to dance with a partner. I've always preferred to perform solo. When I did dance with a partner, I'd tense up every single time they put their hands on my waist. My back. My arms.

I shiver just thinking about it.

That's why it's so shocking that I let West touch me in Paris. That I let West put his fingers inside my body while he kissed me and gave me an orgasm. Afterward, I told Gideon what happened and he flat out didn't believe me, no matter how hard I tried to convince him. He called me a liar.

Instead of trying to prove myself, I let it go. Like I usually do.

I always let things go. Sweep them under the rug. Pretend they didn't happen.

It's just my thing.

It's nothing personal.

It's lunch time and I've just joined my usual group in the dining hall, sitting next to Mercedes and listening to her drone on and on with the boys. I don't think she even cares which one is paying attention to her. She just wants one of them to listen, and to care. And maybe even ask her out.

So far, none of them have. And it's making her frustrated. I only know this because she tells me. I've learned since my encounter with West a few weeks ago that I shouldn't say anything to this girl, so I don't. She can talk all the shit she wants, but I refuse to give her any ammunition to use against me later.

I really need to find new friends, but everyone else is either afraid to approach me or simply not interested.

"West, we've been flirting for the past two years," she starts out the moment West arrives at the table. On the opposite side of where I'm sitting, I might add.

How we continue to coexist in the same circle, I'm not quite sure.

"Three," he corrects her, his voice stern.

I keep my gaze focused on my salad, which I've eaten every single day for lunch since I've arrived here.

God, I'm sick of salad.

"Oh yes, three years." Mercedes giggles, flipping her hair over her shoulder. "I was just wondering if you were ever going to work up the nerve to finally ask me out."

The entire table goes silent and I lift my head, gauging everyone's reactions. Mercedes appears to be holding her breath. Marcy and Samantha are wide-eyed, their mouths hanging open. The guys are all nudging each other and whispering amongst themselves, TJ even saying loud enough for us to hear, "Girl's got some balls."

West is quiet, his perfect lips quirked up in the faintest smirk. I watch him, my own breath lodged in my throat, my heart beating erratically.

He better say no. He absolutely, one hundred percent should turn her down.

"Well?" Mercedes prompts when West takes too long to answer.

His gaze slides to me, his expression dead serious as he says, "I'd love to ask you out on a date, Mercedes."

I can't look away. It's like I'm watching a train wreck and I can't stop staring at the bloody carnage. Or as if I've walked in on him and Mercedes while they're having a sexual encounter and can only watch in absolute horror as he fucks her slowly, his gaze never straying from mine the entire time.

It's the worst feeling in the entire world.

"Oh yay! Shall we go out to dinner Friday?"

"Make it Saturday and you've got yourself a date." He's still watching me and even Mercedes' gaze flickers to mine, her brows drawing together in confusion. I finally duck my head, staring at the pile of lettuce and vegetables on my plate, wishing I could hurl it at someone.

At West and his perfectly handsome, perfectly awful face.

"Sounds amazing. Oh my God, this will be so much fun!" She claps her hands together, West's focus already on someone else. His friends, who waste no time giving him grief. Then, within minutes, all of them rise to their feet, West pausing at Mercedes' chair so he can reach out and tuck a strand of hair behind her ear, murmuring, "Can't wait till Saturday."

Then they're gone.

Mercedes literally squeals like she just won a billion dollars, bouncing in her seat. "I cannot believe that just happened!"

"I can't believe you just asked him out on a date and he agreed," Marcy says wryly.

Mercedes frowns, her laughter gone just like that. "What, you think it's weird that West would be interested in me?"

"No, it's not that. It just—he didn't even protest. He agreed and now you're going out with him." Marcy shrugs, obviously uncomfortable.

"I was tired of wasting my time with him," Mercedes says, waving her fingers in the air in a nonchalant gesture. "I've been waiting for him to make a move for years. I finally decided to make a move instead."

"Good for you," Samantha says. She's Mercedes' little cheerleader, always there to openly support her friend, no matter what. Even if Mercedes treats her like shit, which she does.

Often.

"Do you think it was a mistake, Carolina?"

I lift my head, my gaze meeting Mercedes' triumphant one. "What was a mistake?"

"Me pushing West to ask me out. Was that a mistake?" Her eyes are wide, her expression one of total innocence.

But I see a glimmer of something conniving in her gaze.

Like she knows I hate that she's going on a date with West this Saturday, which I do.

I hate it with my whole being.

"No. Not at all." I shake my head, my smile polite. "I mean, it's not something I would do." I rest my hand to my chest. "But it looks like it worked for you, so…"

I let my voice drift and I offer up a little shrug.

The scowl on her face is obvious. She doesn't like my answer, but is she going to call me out for it?

"Well, at least I have a boy interested in me, right? Unlike you." Mercedes rises to her feet, grabbing her tray. She didn't even touch her lunch yet. "Come on, Marcy. Sam. I need to go to the bathroom."

She doesn't say my name. Doesn't even look in my direction when they all leave me alone at the table, looking like a loser. I glance around the dining hall, noting the pitying looks on some of the other students' faces. It feels like everyone is watching me. Like they all witnessed the faux pas that just occurred and they feel sorry for me.

Frustrated, I push away from the table, leaving my salad behind as I flee the dining hall. I head for the administration building, bursting through the door, relief flooding me when I notice Vivian, the secretary, isn't at her desk. She must be on her lunch break.

Perfect.

Noting that Headmaster Matthews' door is cracked open, I approach it carefully, peeking inside to see he's sitting at his desk, staring at his phone while he munches on a sandwich. He must sense my presence because he lifts his head, his shocked gaze meeting mine.

"Carolina. I wasn't expecting you."

I feel stupid for just showing up, but I didn't know what else to do. "I can come back later. I don't mean to interrupt your lunch."

"No, come in. I was just scrolling social media." He waves

his hand at me and I enter his office, glancing around the messy space. He really needs someone to come in here and organize it. "Is there something you wanted to talk about?"

"I hate it here," I blurt, wringing my hands together. I might've come in here to put on an act that I'm miserable at this stupid school and I want to leave, but I really do hate it here.

I really am miserable.

"Sit down." He points at one of the chairs in front of his desk and I settle in, stretching my skirt out over my legs, hating how my knee bounces, a familiar signal that I'm nervous. "Why do you hate it here?"

"Everyone is mean. They all have their cliques and it's hard to make friends." I press my lips together, hating how whiny I sound, but I can't help it. "The academics are lacking too," I add, though it sounds lame.

"You think our teaching staff is lacking?" Matthews pulls out a pen and starts writing on his little notepad.

Not really, but I'm feeling mean. "They lack inspiration more than anything else."

His gaze lifts to mine. "We have some of the finest staff in the country, though I'm sure they're not on the level of what you experienced while in England."

I shrug, feeling dumb that I came into his office to have a hissy fit. If he only knew the academic teachers at the dance schools I attended over the years put in the bare minimum in order for us to pass our classes. We didn't receive the best academic education. Our dance instructors, though?

Some of the best in the world.

He rests his arms on top of his desk, clutching his hands in front of him, a serene expression on his face. "I know it's been an adjustment for you, attending Lancaster."

I say nothing, but I can feel the sulky expression on my face. I'm pouting. Upset with myself and my surroundings. Wishing more than anything that my life could return to normal.

The normal I know. The normal I'm comfortable with.

"And I know you're upset your studio isn't up and running yet, but I have good news." His smile is faint. "It will be completed by the end of the week."

Hope makes my heart swell. "Really?"

"Yes. It's taken far longer than projected, and for that, I apologize. I understand how important dance is to you, and that you want to maintain your skills while you're attending school here."

I'd need instructors and rigorous training to maintain my skills, but that's impossible. I swear I can feel my muscles slowly turning into mush with every day that passes at this Godforsaken place.

"I wish I was back in London," I murmur, unable to help myself. "I never wanted to come here."

Headmaster Matthews tilts his head, contemplating me for a moment. "May I make a suggestion, Carolina?"

I brace myself, not sure if I want to hear what he has to say. "Okay."

"You can either make yourself miserable while you're here and wish to be somewhere else, or you can reconcile with yourself and realize that you're here and there's nothing you can do to change it, so you may as well make the best of it."

His vaguely inspirational words, while accurate, are also annoying. "Sometimes pitching a fit gets you what you want in life."

"And sometimes, it makes you look like nothing but a spoiled little brat." His smile never falters and I'm taken aback by the stern edge to his voice. "I've been in near constant contact with your father, Carolina. I report to him what's going on every single day. I don't think throwing a fit—or throwing me under the bus, so to speak—would work in your favor."

I blink at him, startled by his tone. The words he's saying. Of course, he's in daily contact with my father. I'm not surprised.

Daddy did always love to keep tabs on me.

Rising to my feet, I huff out a breath. "Clearly talking to you won't get me anywhere."

"It did get you the good news that your studio is almost finished," he reminds me.

"Only after being delayed for the last three weeks," I retort.

"Two and a half," he corrects.

"Whatever." I'm about to leave his office when he calls my name and I pause, glancing at him from over my shoulder.

"Be careful who you spend your free time with," he says, like a warning.

Or maybe a threat.

When I frown, he continues.

"Mercedes is a user."

"I know."

His eyes widen slightly at my admission. "And West Fontaine is…"

Matthews goes quiet, my irritation growing. "He's what?"

"Not kind."

My frown deepens. "What do you mean?"

"If you spend any amount of time around him, you'll understand."

"If he's so terrible, why don't you do anything to stop him?"

"We never actually catch him breaking school rules." Matthews shrugs. "But I hear the stories. I know what he's about. I would advise that you avoid him at all costs."

"Maybe I could be the one who stops him." My older brother ran this school with an iron fist. He got people kicked out of school for looking at him wrong, never to be seen again. Whit was ruthless.

"If anyone could stop him, it would be a Lancaster." His smile is brittle, his tone almost mocking. "Good luck, Carolina."

CHAPTER TEN

CAROLINA

The next day at school is more of the same, with me avoiding everyone in the dining hall because Mercedes has chosen to ignore me completely. I think she's angry I insulted her for the way she got West to ask her on a date.

I still can't believe he's taking her out Saturday. Just the idea of them together. Of him touching her. Kissing her...

I cannot stand it.

At lunch, I hide out in the library because it seems like the safest place. Hardly anyone is in here and the librarian is an old woman with curling gray hair and a permanent scowl on her face. Like she sucked on a lemon and it was so bitter, her expression got stuck.

I steer clear of her desk and make my way to the back of the building where I find an empty table tucked deep within the stacks. I settle in and open my book bag, about to pull out my sandwich bag of baby carrots when I hear someone clear their throat.

Glancing up, I look around, seeing no one.

Shrugging to myself, I open the bag, pulling out a single baby carrot and putting it in between my teeth. The crunch is so loud, I swear I hear the librarian shush me from the other side of the room, along with a faint giggle.

Someone is back here with me, and it's a female someone.

I swallow down the carrot and take a sip from my water bottle, waiting for the mystery person to show themselves. I swear I can feel their eyes on me, watching. Amused by my confusion.

Exasperated, I finally have to say something.

"It's rude not to show yourself." My gaze scans the rows of bookshelves in front of me, searching for a face peeking between them. "And it's really rude to stare."

A sigh sounds then finally, the mystery person reveals herself.

"Hey." The girl waves at me and I take her in, mentally noting her features. Long red hair, pulled back into a low ponytail, her fresh face dotted with freckles, her expression shy. She's wearing the Lancaster uniform, even the jacket, and there's not a wrinkle in sight. "You're Carolina Lancaster, right?"

Here we go. If she has something awful to tell me, she may as well just come out with it. "Whoever sent you, you can tell them to go fuck themselves."

Her golden-brown eyes go wide, a shocked gasp escaping her. "No one...sent me here."

"Then why are you looking for me?" I arch a brow.

"I've spent every lunch in this library since school started, so if anything, you're infringing on my territory." Her voice trembles on the last couple of words and I almost feel sorry for her.

I contemplate her and she watches me right back, shifting from one foot to the other, clearly uncomfortable. "No one sent you to look for me?"

She slowly shakes her head, her ponytail swinging.

"Not even Weston Fontaine?" I hate the fact that I said his name out loud. Hate it.

"He doesn't even know I exist." She rolls her eyes.

I sit up straighter, relief flooding me. "Be glad. He's the last person you want acknowledgment from."

Her smile is faint and she takes a single step forward. "So, you are Carolina."

"I am." I tilt my head. "Who are you?"

"Sadie Swanson." She tucks a stray hair behind her ear, that tiny smile still curving her lips. "I'm new here. Just transferred like you."

Her circumstance is nothing like mine, though I don't bother correcting her. "You're a senior?"

She shakes her head. "A junior. But I've been doing online courses the last couple of years and I can graduate this year if I want to. My mom wanted me to experience high school like a real American."

Maybe our circumstances are similar after all. "Where have you been?"

"Traveling all over Europe with my family. They're not big on conventional lives but when my father had a heart attack, his cardiologist suggested he slow down for a bit. My parents bought a house in Brooklyn and decided my brother and I needed to go to school like real kids. My brother is twelve. He's having the time of his life away at boarding school, but me?"

"You're not?" A house in Brooklyn. That sounds...depressing.

Sadie shakes her head. "My brother is loud and obnoxious and I'm just...not. I prefer to hide away in the library."

"This is where you've spent every lunch since school started?" We've been here almost a month.

She nods. "I don't mind it in here. If you avoid Miss Taylor, it's not so bad."

"Who's Miss Taylor?"

"The librarian. God, she's mean." She laughs.

I can't help it, I do too.

The hopeful glint in Sadie's eyes is obvious. "Can I sit down?"

"Sure." I wave a hand at the chairs across from me and she eagerly pulls one out, settling into it and scooting closer to the table. She rests her arms on top of the table and watches me with a contemplative glow in her gaze.

"So what's it like?" she asks after a few seconds pass.

"What's what like?"

"Being at a school where your family owns it?"

"You want the truth?" I glance to my left, then my right, like someone might be lingering nearby and could hear me. I lean across the table, my voice going low. "It's fucking awful."

A shocked burst of laughter leaves Sadie and she covers her mouth with her fingertips, stifling the noise while Miss Taylor shushes her from her post at the front of the room. "I totally agree. This school is an absolute nightmare."

Her admission also makes me laugh. "They're all such snobs."

"And mean," Sadie adds.

"Terribly mean," I agree.

"My first day on campus, this one guy ran right into me, almost like he did it on purpose." Sadie shakes her head. "He knocked my books right out of my arms."

"Did he apologize?"

"Of course not. When I yelled at him, he shrugged and said I should've had everything in a backpack."

"Why didn't you have a backpack?"

"I don't know. I was trying to figure out which books I could leave in my locker and which ones I needed to take with me. I'm a disorganized mess. My dad always likes to say I bring chaos everywhere I go." Her expression turns somber, her gaze distant. "I miss him. I hate being so far from my family."

"Have you ever gone to boarding school before?"

She shakes her head. "My mom did and she wanted the same education for me and my brother, so here I am."

I push my plastic bag of baby carrots toward her. "Want one?"

"Sure." She takes a carrot and chews on it thoughtfully, her gaze locked on the bag. "Is that all you're having for lunch?"

"I haven't been exercising like I usually do since I got here, so I have to watch what I eat or I'll get fat," I explain.

Her brows shoot up. "You're not even close to fat. Aren't

you a famous dancer?"

"I don't know about famous." I grab another carrot and munch on it, swallowing it down before I answer. "But yes. I'm a dancer."

"In London." When I nod, she continues, "I saw your performance in Paris over the summer."

My entire body stiffens at the memory of Paris. The connection I have to stupid West. "Oh really."

"It was beautiful. You're a gorgeous dancer. When I was little, I thought about being one. I dreamed of it actually. I wanted to perform in The Nutcracker and wear a giant pink tutu." A sigh leaves her at the memory.

"Thank you." I've danced The Nutcracker many times, in a variety of roles over the years. "You've traveled a lot?"

"Everywhere. My parents, um, they have a…YouTube channel," she admits hesitantly.

It takes me a moment, but then realization clicks in my brain. "Wait a minute. Are you part of the traveling Swansons?"

Sadie nods, her cheeks turning pink. "Yeah. It sucks."

Her family is known for traveling all over the world and filming everything along the way. They lead an unconventional lifestyle, the kids never in school, wandering the world like nomads and making endless discoveries.

"That's so interesting." Her parents—the entire family—are famous. Internet famous. "Don't they have like ten million subscribers on their channel?"

"Closer to fifteen but who's counting?" She laughs, throwing her hands up in the air in a helpless gesture. "I hate it. The entire world has watched me grow up and it's embarrassing."

It felt like the world watched me grow up too, but not in the same way they obviously did to Sadie. "There are probably some embarrassing videos out there, huh?"

Her cheeks turn pink and she hides her eyes for a moment. "The absolute worst videos you've ever seen. It's so humiliating but my parents don't care. They think it's cute." She makes a face. "This is why I hide out in the library. I don't want any of those assholes figuring out who I really am."

I can relate, because I feel the same way. I don't want people knowing who I am, though it's already too late for that.

"Have you made any friends at all?" I ask, keeping my voice gentle, like she's a wild animal I don't want to startle and make run away.

"Not really. Everyone is so stuck up here. Someone said I don't belong here because they'd never heard of me before, and I was blown away by that. Like, what does it matter what my last name is, or what old-moneyed family I come from? Can't they just try and get to know me for who I am? Sheesh." She curls her arms together on the table and rests her head on top of them, hiding her face. "It sucks here."

Her muffled complaint hurts my heart and I actually reach out and touch her, resting my hand on her arm. "It's going to be okay."

Shock courses through me the moment I touch her and I retract my hand, settling it in my lap. How...strange.

I actually feel bad for Sadie. And I don't even know her.

But I can definitely relate to her.

She lifts her head, her expression bleak. "You really think so?"

I nod, offering her a smile.

I have to think so. Otherwise...

What do either of us have to look forward to?

CHAPTER ELEVEN

WEST

Mercedes Brown is boring. Thoughtless. Borderline brain-dead. She prattles on about the most nonsensical things, like what she says matters. As if she believes I'll be interested in what she says, hanging on her every word.

I'm not. I hate listening to her. Her voice is irritating. The way she constantly gestures with her hands and drops constant slang as if she's creating a social media post and trying to seem relatable.

She's intolerable. My biggest regret is agreeing to take her out on a date. We're at an Italian restaurant downtown, not too far from campus, and Mercedes is shoveling fettucine alfredo into her mouth like her life depends on it.

"God, I love carbs." She moans, her eyes practically rolling into the back of her head. Has she watched porn recently? Does she believe this sort of behavior will make me find her attractive? "But they're so bad for me. They make my ass big."

Her ass is big. So are her tits, which are practically sitting on top of the table, thanks to the low-cut neckline of her dress. Normally, I like this sort of thing. I'd pick up the vibe she was trying to send me, and respond positively.

Not with Mercedes. Not tonight. I didn't agree to this date

because I want her. I agreed to this fucking date because I wanted to get under someone else's skin. I wanted to make Carolina Lancaster positively green with envy. I wanted her spitting nails and shooting fire from her eyes when she glared at me.

Instead, she barely reacted, simply lifted that delicate little nose in the air like the true snob she is and never said a damn word to me.

We still haven't spoken.

And it's driving me fucking crazy.

"Stop eating so many carbs then," I say calmly, taking a sip of my water.

Her fork falls to her plate with a clatter, her mouth popping open. "That was rude."

"Not really. I'm just trying to be logical. You said carbs make your ass fat, so stop eating them." I shrug, glancing around the crowded restaurant, envious of the tables where it appears that they're having a good time.

I'm not. This date is awful. I've just completely led Mercedes on and it's going to be hell trying to get rid of her, but what's done is done. I can't change anything about the situation.

She pushes her plate away and bats her fake eyelashes at me, smiling prettily. "What do you want to do after dinner?"

"Go back to campus."

"And do what?"

"Tell you goodnight after I walk you back to your dorm building."

Her smile falters. "What about—"

"What about what?" I interrupt her, wanting to see if she'll just flat out ask for it.

I'm not the first guy from our friend group to take Mercedes out. TJ has fucked her a handful of times, and also complains that she's boring.

More like vapid, but I have a more descriptive vocabulary than he does so boring still fits.

"I don't know." Something nudges at the hem of my black trousers and I realize it's Mercedes' toes brushing against my calf. "I thought we could spend a little alone time together."

"I don't fuck on the first date."

She snatches those toes back. I can even hear her shove her foot back into her shoe. "That's not what I heard."

An irritated sigh escapes me and I don't even care. "I don't think you're my type, Mercedes."

She blinks again and again, like she's got something in her eye. "And you're telling me this now? While we're mid-date?"

"Better than asking for a blow job and abandoning you completely after I convince you to swallow."

We stare at each other from across the tiny round table, and I can feel her anger rise. The server magically appears with the tab and I hand him my credit card without hesitation, grateful I pulled it out of my wallet a few minutes ago in preparation for this.

"Why did you ask me out then?" She sounds hurt, but there's something about her tone that rings false.

"You basically goaded me into it, don't forget." I shrug. I'm doing that a lot tonight. "I've heard some things about you from my friends and I wanted to see if they were true."

Her gaze warms. Does she actually like the idea of us gossiping about her? I've seen her nudes. TJ shared them, and while I can't deny she has a nice curvy body, that's not my thing. Not lately.

I like mean, skinny blondes with shitty attitudes.

"What did TJ say?" Mercedes asks.

Love how she just name drops him. Why pretend she doesn't know who I'm talking about?

"He said you gave good head." That's not a lie. He did mention that a time or two.

"It's true." Her eyelids grow heavy and she leans across the table, her tits blatantly on display. "Want me to show you out in the parking lot?"

I make a face. "No, thank you."

She sits up straighter and crosses her arms, covering her chest. "God, you're no fun."

"You're right." I pick up the steak knife sitting beside my plate, tapping the edge of the blade against the table over and over. "I'm in a mood."

I almost said I was sorry to Mercedes, but I'm not. I am in a mood. It's all Carolina Lancaster's fault. I can still feel her slender thighs clutching around me. Can still catch a faint whiff of her delectable pussy.

Clearly, I have issues. I'm not one to become obsessed, but I'm aware enough of the fact that I have a problem.

"Yeah, you are." Mercedes pastes her smile back on her face, her gaze flashing with hope. "I can help you relieve that."

"Yeah, no you can't." The server reappears and I take the bill from him, opening it up and signing the receipt with a flourish before I shove my credit card back into my wallet. "Ready to go?"

The drive back to Lancaster Prep is filled mostly with Mercedes trying to tempt me with sex, while I do my best to discourage her. I'm not interested. I don't know how else to make that abundantly clear, since she doesn't seem to be getting the message.

"Are you sure you won't come to my room? I don't have a roommate."

Even the comfort and privacy of her single dorm room doesn't entice me. I can see it now. Me sitting on the edge of her narrow bed, my dick out, her lips wrapped tight around it, tits hanging out of the front of her dress, her big eyes locked on mine.

No fucking thank you.

"Maybe you should hit up TJ instead," I tell her before I climb out of the car and slam the door.

She's scrambling out of the car quickly, huffing and puffing as she shuts the door, her eyes blazing with fury as she glares at me. "You're a prick, Fontaine."

"Tell me all about it." I shove my hands in my pockets, watching her fume, enjoying myself despite my lack of interest in her.

"Thanks for the dinner, asshole." She flips me off before she stalks toward campus, heading straight for her dorm building, which is right next to mine.

I watch her go, hands still in my pockets, fingers clutched tight around my key fob. I hit the button, locking my car, and I wonder what the fuck I'm going to do for the rest of the evening.

My gaze catches on a flash of blonde hair. A tall, lithe figure running along the walkway on the opposite side of campus. She's clad in a dark green bra top and matching booty shorts.

Carolina.

Without thinking, I head toward the building she was just running in front of, my gaze tracking her as she disappears through the double doors. The building where she stays. Where all Lancasters stay when they attend this school. No one else should be in that building.

Just her.

Trying one of the double doors with a gentle tug, it opens easily, and I stride inside, careful that the door doesn't slam and announce my entrance. There's a hushed silence as I make my way down the wide corridor, and I pause when I hear music. The tinkling of a piano.

My steps slow, then stop completely, just outside the open door of the room where the piano sounds the loudest. I carefully peek around the edge of the doorway to find that the cavernous room has been turned into some sort of dance studio. The floors are smooth and bare, and one wall is mirrored from the floor to the ceiling. There's a barre attached to the wall and Carolina currently stands beside it, her fingers curved around it as she shifts her body into different positions.

Her hair is in a high ponytail, the ends swinging as she dips and moves, her arm going out, curved elegantly in front of her. The piano music comes from a small speaker sitting on a chair, her phone hooked up to it, and when the song ends, her heels settle flat on the ground, her arms dropping at her sides.

The next song starts, this one dramatic. A full orchestra plays and she makes her way to the center of the room, her back to me, her gaze on the mirror as she gets into position and holds it for a few beats.

And then she begins to dance.

I watch, mesmerized by the way she glides across the floor so effortlessly, her feet barely touching the ground. She flings her body into the air, doing a couple of spins before she lands in a matter of seconds, again and again. She completes every jump perfectly, twirling over and over, lost in the music. I enter the room fully, leaning against the wall, watching her, but she still doesn't notice me.

Her body is a work of art, fluid and purposeful. Her dancing? Some of the best I've ever seen. I'm not an expert, not even close. I don't even particularly enjoy watching ballet, and it's something I've been exposed to here and there throughout my life.

But I could watch Carolina dance for hours.

The tempo rises, the drums heavy, the strings insistent, and I'm breathless, caught up in the story her body is trying to tell. She spins in a circle, her arms coming up, her fingers tangling in the hair of her ponytail and her gaze goes to the mirror, clashing with mine. A jolt runs through me the moment our eyes lock, and I stare at her, unable to look away.

She comes to a complete stop, her breathing heavy, her chest rising and falling. Sweat gleams on her skin, all of those slender muscles defined. She whirls around, so she's facing me, her gaze narrowed.

"What are you doing?" She's completely out of breath, her chest heaving, wild strands of hair sticking to her pink cheeks.

"Watching you."

The music continues to play and she presses her lips together, as if she's trying to control her breathing. Or control herself from saying something more to me. My gaze roams all over her body, noting the long length of her legs. How the shorts mold to her skin. Her slender hips. The gentle flare of her ass.

She is perfection.

"Go away." Her tone is dismissive, like I'm an annoying bug she wants to swat at.

"No."

She turns her back on me and marches over to the chair with the speaker on it, picking up the phone and stopping the music. The silence that follows is deafening, and then I hear her rapid breaths. How the air seems to shudder in her lungs.

"West..." Her voice is a warning, her back still to me. "You should leave."

I push away from the wall and stalk toward her, stopping just behind her. Her entire body is still, as if she's waiting for me, and the temptation to touch her is strong. I clench my hands into fists and dip my head, my mouth level with the delicate shell of her ear as I repeat the very words she said to me not too long ago.

"Make me."

She keeps her head bent, the slender column of her neck beckoning me, and it takes all the strength I can muster not to press my mouth to the spot where her neck meets her shoulder. To feel her pulse flutter beneath my lips, rapid and insistent. Her skin shines with sweat, and fuck, I can smell her. Clean and salty, with a hint of her unique ocean scent.

"How was your date?" Her tone is snide, with an underline of disgust, and I get a sick sort of pleasure from hearing it.

"Love that you remembered," I whisper against her skin, noting the goose bumps that dot her nape.

I back away from her and she straightens her shoulders, turning around to face me once again. My gaze drops to her chest, lingering on her hard nipples that brush against the front of her sports bra, and yet again, I'm tempted. Mercedes put her tits on blatant display during dinner and I could give a shit.

I see Carolina's little nipples poking against fabric and all I can think about is how they might feel on my tongue.

"How could I forget? Mercedes was practically salivating over the chance to suck your dick."

Her anger only fuels my amusement.

A chuckle escapes me. "Jealous much? Wish it was you instead?"

"Absolutely not," she retorts. "Why would I want to go on a date with someone like you?"

I'm not even offended by her remark. "Someone like me? You *have* gone on a date with someone like me."

"That didn't count." There goes the nose in the air.

"Right. It didn't count." I smile at her.

She scowls.

"It didn't count that you grinded on me in a nightclub. That you had me chasing you all over a goddamn opera house in the middle of Paris. That I made you come with my fingers and you almost fell off a balcony. None of that mattered, am I right?"

Her gaze flickers with annoyance, her lush lips formed into a frown. I hate that I just said all of that, like it mattered, like *she* mattered when, apparently, I didn't.

I don't do relationships. I don't allow women to hurt me like this, and I sound like a stupid little baby, even to my own ears. I clamp my lips shut, not wanting to say anymore.

We both remain silent until she finally murmurs, "At least I'm not a liar."

I'm taken aback by her accusation. "You're calling me a liar?"

"Yes. You told me you already graduated from Lancaster Prep. You promised you wouldn't tell anyone about us." She glances down her nose at me, which I don't even know how it's possible since I'm taller than she is. "Lies."

"And you said you didn't go here, so who's the one lying now?"

I forgot I even said that. It didn't matter then. I was never going to see her again.

"I never told you that. My showing up at Lancaster Prep happened at the very last—" She presses her lips together, as if she realized she's revealing information she doesn't want me to know. "You've been mean to me from the moment I started here."

"You were the one who ignored me from the moment I saw you in class." I approach her and she takes a step backward, creating distance I don't want. I keep walking toward her and she keeps stepping back, until she's pressed against the mirrored wall and I've got her blocked so she can't escape. "You started all of this."

"I was in shock over your obvious lies." She glares at me. "Why did you do it?"

"Do what?"

An irritated sound leaves her. "Lie to me!"

"What does it matter? I thought it was for only one night. I could say whatever I wanted and you'd believe me." If she only knew how truthful I'm being in this moment.

"I hate liars. They can't be trusted." She reaches out, her fingertips barely touching me, as if the mere thought might disgust her. "Move."

"No."

"Move!" She shoves me with both hands, surprisingly strong, and I crowd her, slapping my hands against the glass on either side of her head, glaring at her as my breaths come hot and heavy.

She tilts her head back, falling onto the mirror, her lips parted. Her eyes dilated. The air between us becomes electric, making every part of my body tingle, and on pure instinct, I lean in, settling my mouth on her neck.

A low moan sounds in her throat when I lick her there. Kiss her there.

Suck her there.

"I hate you," she murmurs when I lick at her pulse, moving my hands so they settle on her slender hips. "You're an asshole."

"I hate you too." I nip at her neck, scraping it with my teeth. "You're a shitty dancer."

Her hands press into my chest, pushing with all of her might, and I stumble away from her, startled once more by her strength.

"Lying again." Her smile is smug, her confidence ringing clear. "I'm probably the best dancer you'll ever see in your life."

Exuding confidence that reminds me of the night we first met, she glides toward the chair, picking up her phone and turning on the music before she begins to dance. I turn so I can lean against the wall, watching as she twirls across the floor, the small speaker practically vibrating with how loud the music is.

Damn it, I can't take my eyes off of her and she knows it. I see the triumphant smile on her face. Hear it in her joyous laughter as she passes by me. She gets off on proving me wrong, and deciding to take my life in my hands, I approach her slowly, careful not to get in her way, until I'm standing in the middle of the floor and she's dancing around me.

When she draws close enough, I snake my arm out and grab her waist, pulling her into me. A gasp escapes her, her breaths coming quickly once again, her skin shining with the faintest sheen of sweat. I bend my head, licking her shoulder, and the shock in her voice is obvious.

"What are you doing?"

"Tasting you." I push my face into hers, her wide blue eyes filled with unfamiliar emotion. "I want to taste every inch of you."

Her face hardens, and without warning, she slaps my face. Hard.

My hands fall away from her and she takes a step back. Then another, horror written all over her pretty face.

"What the hell was that for?" I touch my cheek, hissing in a breath.

"You're disgusting." She wraps her arms around her middle, her gaze dropping from mine. Like she can't look at me. "You hate me."

I remain quiet.

"I hate you," she continues. "You don't want to—*taste* me."

I'm still silent and she lifts her head, her eyes filled with confusion.

"I don't understand you."

"I can still hate you and want you at the same time," I admit, curious as to her answer.

"When I look at you, I feel nothing." She marches over to that damn chair yet again, turning off the music and clutching her phone in her hand. "You're nothing to me."

The finality in her tone has me fuming. Fuck this girl.

Fuck her.

CHAPTER TWELVE

CAROLINA

I lock myself in my room once I make my escape from West, stripping off my clothes and stepping into the shower, turning the water until it's scalding hot. I need to burn his touch off of my skin, his words out of my mind. He's cruel and awful and he says the worst things.

The most confusing things.

The water slides over me, and I stand under it, closing my eyes. But it doesn't help. I can still see him. Feel his hands on my body. The way he licked my neck. My shoulder. When he said he wanted to taste every part of me. My body automatically reacted when he said those words.

It's reacting now, my pulse throbbing between my legs, heavy and insistent. I reach down, my fingers sliding, sinking into nothing but hot wetness.

Oh. I cup myself, remembering how he touched me. So confident, so firm. I press my fingers against my clit, resting my other hand on the tile wall of the shower to brace myself as I start to stroke.

Within seconds, my orgasm is already building, and I lean into the wall, rubbing furiously, tight little circles on my clit. I remember how I gripped West's hips with my legs, his mouth fused with mine while we were out on that balcony, and how scary that was.

How exhilarating.

I hate him. I really do. But I also...

Want him?

I see his face in my mind, too handsome, too smug. I think of how he had a date with stupid Mercedes, yet somehow sought me out after, and I don't understand what that means.

The orgasm hits me out of nowhere, making me gasp. Making me shake. I moan into the cold tile, nearly stumbling, and when it's over, when I've come back to my senses, I realize my entire body is still shaking.

I fantasized about his stupidly handsome face and fingered myself to an orgasm, and I hate myself for it.

I hate him even more.

The next morning I move through each class as if I'm in a trance, unable to focus during the lectures, answering a question wrong when I'm called upon in American Government. People laugh at me and when I chance a look at West, his expression is stoic.

Immovable.

Like I don't even matter.

When it's lunch, I don't bother going to the dining hall. I find myself in the library, in search of Sadie, and when I come upon her sitting at a table in the very back of the building, I almost sag with relief at seeing her friendly face.

"Are you okay?" Her brows lower, her expression one of concern when she sees me.

I settle into the chair right next to her, not about to go into detail over what happened between West and me. I hardly understand what happened, or why I let him get to me so much.

"It's just a Monday," is what I say to her, which is the lamest excuse ever, but she accepts it.

Sadie nods. "Oh, I totally get that. Mondays are the worst. I had a pop quiz in American History. Who does that sort of thing on Monday morning, and in first period? Sadists, that's who. I did terrible, but I think we all did, so I'm not too worried about it. Hopefully, he'll grade on a curve."

I listen to her babble on, grateful that she's keeping up the conversation and I don't have to say a word. My stomach growls, but I choose to ignore it. I hardly ate anything the entire weekend, too upset over the thought of West with Mercedes.

Too upset by West's attitude and the things he said to me Saturday night.

It feels as if he's in control of my every emotion and I hate it. I can't let this boy do this sort of damage to me, especially because he doesn't give a damn. I need to focus on something else so I will stop thinking about him. I should concentrate more on my studies. Work hard, get good grades and get the hell out of here.

"I have a question for you," I say, interrupting Sadie mid-sentence.

She brightens, like she's thrilled I want to know something about her. "What is it? I'm an open book."

Her first problem, though I don't tell her that. "Is there a boy at this school who interests you?"

Sadie leans back in her chair, her brows drawn together like she has to really consider it. "I don't know."

"You don't know if there's anyone who interests you, or you don't know if you want to tell me?"

"Both." She laughs, and I envy her carefree attitude. "There are cute guys here, I can't lie. But most of them are such snobs, don't you think?"

I am the biggest snob at this school. She just doesn't realize it yet. "Some of them are, yes."

"Most everyone is. Except for you."

I can't keep up the pretense. "I'm horrible, Sadie."

She appears shocked by my words. "No, you're not. You've been so nice to me!"

I slowly shake my head. "You caught me during a vulnerable moment. I hate everyone."

"You hate your parents?"

I nod. Then shrug. "I can tolerate my father. My mother is vile."

Sadie's eyes are so wide I'm afraid they'll pop out of her head. "Do you have siblings?"

"Yes. My brother is an asshole and my sister probably belongs in a mental facility."

Sadie blinks. "Do you have any friends?"

"Not here." Not back in London either. Oh, I called them my friends, but what a lie that was. They were my competition. We were all pretending to like each other when really, we'd have no problem slitting someone's throat to get to the top of the dance company.

"You have me," she says with the utmost sincerity.

My cold heart cracks a little at her words. "And I appreciate that. Though I probably don't deserve your friendship."

"Of course, you do. Everyone deserves friendship. Like I said, you've been nice to me. I don't know why you'd say you're so mean." She smiles and reaches out, patting me on the arm.

I automatically jerk away from her touch, but she doesn't even notice. "Lancasters aren't nice people."

"You're telling me the entirety of your family isn't nice? You're all a bunch of snakes in the grass."

I contemplate what she says, thinking of my family members. My immediate family plus my aunts and uncles and cousins. "Pretty much."

Sadie laughs, like I'm telling her a joke. "I find that hard to believe. Maybe it's not that you're horrible, it's just that you don't know how to make friends with people. Why is that?"

Her face is so open, her question so genuine, that I don't

hold back when I answer.

"I don't trust people."

"You don't trust anyone?"

"Everyone wants something from me, especially when they find out who I am. Who my family is. They want to be around us because we have money. Our name opens doors. Our name gets you into places that other people can't ever obtain. I've been handed everything I've ever wanted my entire life. I don't have to work hard, which means I'm spoiled rotten. I deserve nothing."

My voice is flat, and I'm repeating words that have been said to me to hurt me. My mother has said that. Various people at any dance academy I was at, both staff and students. I've been told the same thing over and over as they try to hold me back and it hurts.

It hurts that no one believes in me. That no one thinks I work hard. It's all I've been doing since I first discovered my love for dance. The only thing I do love is ballet and dance and performing, but they all try to hold me back. They all say I don't deserve it. I don't put in the work.

It's as if I've been gaslighted my whole life, and no one realizes it.

"Are those your own thoughts talking, or do people actually say that sort of stuff to you? Because if it's the latter, I feel the need to go cut a bitch," she says with such vehemence, I start to laugh.

And it's as if I can't stop.

Within seconds, Sadie is joining me, and we're leaning in close, our shoulders brushing. I don't recoil. I actually enjoy the sound of her laughter mixed with mine, and how nice it feels to be honest with someone and not feel the need to throw up a wall all the time.

"Thank you for talking to me," I say once our laughter has died. "I needed that."

"Anytime." Sadie grins. "That's what friends are for."

CHAPTER THIRTEEN

CAROLINA

Just as all good things must come to an end, there came a point where I couldn't avoid Mercedes and her wrath any longer. I knew a confrontation was brewing. I just didn't realize it would happen so soon.

It's in American Government, of course, where everyone who's anyone in the senior class at Lancaster Prep is in this class period. I'm sitting in the back of the room, trying to mind my own business and stay away from my so-called friends who haven't spoken to me since Friday at lunch when I realize someone is standing right next to me, her cloying perfume making my nostrils twitch.

"Sitting in the back with the rest of the losers, huh?" Mercedes asks, venom lacing her voice.

I slowly lift my head, glaring at her from narrowed eyes. "What did you just say to me?"

"You heard me." She grins, casting a knowing glance in Marcy's direction, who looks away quietly and settles into her desk.

Smart move on Marcy's part.

"Are you really calling me a loser?" I look her up and down, wrinkling my nose, trying to keep calm.

Deep inside, the storm is starting to rage.

"Yeah, I am. I don't care what your last name is." Mercedes grins, and I realize in that moment, she's a complete imbecile. "You don't scare me."

"Why would I, you stupid little piece of trash. You're too dumb to realize who you're dealing with." I sniff. "Your mother named you after her favorite car, for God's sake."

There are a few nervous titters from the other people sitting in the classroom, pretending not to notice what's going on.

Mercedes glares at all of them before returning her attention to me. "Who are you calling a piece of trash, huh? No one gives a shit about you, you know. You're the loser Lancaster. The invisible one."

Her words hurt, not that I can ever let her know it.

"And you're just jealous that West asked me out on a date and not you," she continues, hitting way too close to home. "That he wants to be with me and not you. I see the way you look at him."

Alarm races through me. Is it obvious that I look at him? Does she know about our one interlude in Paris?

God, did he tell her?

"Aren't you the one who essentially goaded him into taking you to dinner?" I remind her, noting the flare of anger in her eyes. Her cheeks turn red and her smile fades into a frown. "I'm pretty sure that's how it went down, right?"

I glance around the classroom, noting the way Marcy nods, like she can't help herself. Mercedes catches it too.

"Marcy, fucking support me for once in my life, *God*." With that, Mercedes flounces out of the room, Marcy knocking into her desk as she slides out of the chair and runs after her.

The moment they're gone, everyone starts talking amongst themselves, and I sit there alone and ignored, trying to calm my racing heart.

"You're right, you know."

I glance up to find West's friend Brent turned around in his chair facing me, his expression serious. "I'm right about what?"

"That Mercedes pushed him into asking her out. He doesn't like her. Not like that."

"Then why did he go out with her?" I regret the question the moment I ask it, wishing I'd kept my mouth shut.

"Because he knew it would bother you." Brent grins. "We were all there with him last summer, you know."

Realization dawns and I blink at him, trying to come up with something to say. I remember West saying he was traveling with friends. Meaning Brent was one of his friends? Who else was with him? Who else knows?

"And we know what happened between you two. Don't worry," he adds when he must see the panic written all over my face. "I'm not saying anything. Neither is TJ."

I swallow past the lump in my throat. "West told you?"

He nods, looking around the room before he leans in closer to me. "We didn't think anything of it, you know? Yet another hookup in Paris. Lucky West. We sure as hell didn't expect you to show up on campus and go to school here."

Another hookup in Paris? How many hookups were there? How many girls has West been with? I'd have to be a stupid little fool to think West hasn't been with anyone before. He was far too skilled for that to be possible.

It still hurts though. He might've left a lasting mark on me, but I didn't matter to him. Not really.

An ominous feeling settles over me, the hairs on the back of my neck standing on end and I watch as Brent's expression transforms, his gaze on something else.

Someone else.

"Brent." The familiar voice makes a low buzzing sound start in my ears and I brace myself, not wanting to look at him. "Carolina."

West.

His clipped tone tells me he's unhappy for whatever reason

and my initial thought is Mercedes ran to him and told on me, when she's the bitch who started our fight in the first place.

"Hey," Brent says as he slowly eases away from me, his gaze fixed above my head. "What's up?"

The air sizzles for a beat, leaving me breathless.

"What are you two talking about?"

His tone is clipped. Full of anger and I can feel West's gaze on me, hot and foreboding. I finally dare to look up, doing my best not to recoil from the fury blazing in his eyes. "Nothing," I say at the same exact time Brent does.

We seem guilty, when our conversation was actually pretty innocent.

The silence stretches for so long, I feel like I'm going to snap in two when finally, West speaks.

"Uh huh. Sure." His drawl is heavy with sarcasm and I keep my head bent, not wanting to antagonize him further.

Why I care, I don't know, but I'm not in the mood to fight anymore. Standing up to Mercedes took it all out of me.

He breezes by the two of us, settling into his desk, and Brent scrambles out of the one in front of me, going to sit next to his friend and placate him, I'm sure.

For the rest of class, nothing happens. It's just another Monday and our teacher gives us yet another lecture. Marcy slinks back in just as the bell rings, but Mercedes doesn't show her face at all. It feels like a win, but I know it's temporary.

If she's brave enough to talk to me like that in a classroom full of witnesses, she'll do it again.

The moment the bell rings, I'm out of there, in the hall and headed to my next class when I feel fingers wrap around my elbow. A yelp escapes me and I jerk out of the hold, turning to glare at whomever dared touch me, to find West standing there, unbearably handsome in his uniform, his tie already loose around his neck, like he can't be bothered to fix it.

"What do you want?"

His gaze never wavers from mine. "I want to talk to you."

"If this has anything to do with Mercedes, there's nothing left to say."

He frowns, seemingly confused. "Mercedes?"

I roll my eyes and start walking once more, irritated when he keeps pace with me. "She didn't tell you we got into a fight?"

"A fight? Are you talking about a physical fight?" He sounds surprised.

I come to a stop at the point where two corridors intersect, stepping out of the way so people can pass by us. West does the same, standing directly in front of me, his gaze so intense, I can't look away. "Of course not." I hesitate, regretting that I even mentioned it. "She didn't tell you?"

West shakes his head. "I haven't talked to her since Saturday night."

For a fleeting moment, I feel triumphant, knowing that he hasn't spoken to her since then. But the feeling is brief when I remember they had a date that night.

And after he left her, he found me.

Annoyed, I start walking again, heading in the opposite direction of where my next class is. "Stay away from me," I tell him from over my shoulder.

The boy flat out doesn't listen. Instead, he chases after me, trying to grab me again, and I whirl on him like a wild animal, ready to snap.

"Don't touch me," I hiss between my teeth.

He doesn't move. In fact, he shifts closer, his body heat radiating, the scent of him wrapping all around me, his voice low, downright menacing, before he murmurs, "Stay away from Brent."

That was the last thing I expected him to say.

"What do you mean? Why?" I shake my head, confused by his change of subject.

"Don't fall for his shit. He uses girls."

"He uses girls," I repeat, remembering what Brent told me. "Like you do?"

"What the fuck are you talking about?" he practically snarls.

"All your hookups in Europe?"

West scowls. "What hookups?"

"I don't know. Brent mentioned them." I take a step backward, needing distance from his intensity.

The scowl deepens. "He mentioned my European hookups?"

I'm getting in too deep with this conversation and I don't want to have it anymore. "I'm done with this."

I walk away, my steps quick, my head held high. He follows me yet again; I can sense him, how he's keeping close, not saying a word. I pretend he's not there, and just as I'm about to walk into the classroom, he suddenly is there, right next to me, his hand on my arm, barely touching me.

"You need to stay away from him," West repeats, his voice practically a growl. "Do you hear me? I mean it, Carolina. Keep away from Brent."

I smile, rising on my tiptoes, so my mouth is level with his ear as I whisper…

"Make me."

The idea floats in my brain until lunch, and for once, I don't head for the library and seek out Sadie. I send her a text, letting her know I won't be there today because I don't want her thinking I ditched her or forgot about her.

Sadie: *What are you doing for lunch then?*

Me: *I have a plan. I'll tell you all about it later.*

I enter the dining hall with my head held high, a faint smile curling my lips as I walk past people, nodding a greeting, acting like I'm queen of the fucking court. I spot my victim a few feet away, already in line with an empty tray clutched between his hands, and the situation couldn't be more perfect if I planned it.

Putting a little pep in my step, I approach him, shimmying my hips like I'm going to knock myself into him, my tone flirtatious. "Hey, Brent."

His startled expression isn't surprising. I've barely spoken two words to him since our conversation on the first day of school. Oh, and our rather informative conversation earlier. "Hey, Carolina."

"Mind if I cut in line?" I pull out one of Mercedes' tricks and bat my eyelashes, knowing it probably won't have the same effect since I don't have eyelash extensions.

"Sure." He gestures ahead of him with his tray and I'm grateful he's clutching that thing.

It means he can't touch me.

I slip into line ahead of him, my smile fading when I look at all of the hot lunch options. We have an excellent kitchen at Lancaster Prep, but all of this food is fat on fat and will go straight to my already spreading hips.

It doesn't matter how many hours I dance or exercise in my new studio. It's not the same as the rigorous training I endured while at the London Dance Academy. This is a vacation and my body is already softening.

I hate it.

Brent reaches around me and grabs a plate with a greasy slice of pepperoni pizza on it.

"Is the pizza any good?" I ask weakly, my stomach growling at the scent of garlic and oregano wafting in the air.

"You haven't tried it yet?" He sounds incredulous. "It's the best thing in the dining hall, hands down."

I can't stomach the idea of greasy pepperoni, so I grab a plate with a slice of cheese pizza, setting it on Brent's tray. "Will you carry it for me?"

"Yeah, no problem."

My brain scrambles, trying to come up with something else to say to Brent as we move through the line, drawing closer to the cashier, but I come up empty. I'm not good at this. Flirtatious banter and mindless small talk. I don't go on dates. I never really talk to boys. Gideon was a close friend, but all we ever talked about was dance, our teachers or our classmates. Gideon is a vicious gossip, and I enjoyed trading stories with him, talking badly about everyone we danced with at the Academy.

Now that I'm gone, I'm sure he's gossiping about me and why I left, and that realization cuts like a knife.

When we finally reach the cashier, I go ahead and pay for Brent's meal—his slice of pizza, a Dr. Pepper and a bag of Doritos, disgusting—and mine, smiling at the cashier when I hand over my meal card.

"You want to sit at a different table?" Brent asks me once we leave the cashier. When I give him a questioning look, he rambles on, "I figured you didn't want to sit near Mercedes, and she's already at our usual table, holding court with West."

My gaze immediately goes to that table, where Mercedes is literally sitting on West's lap, trying to feed him a french fry while he dodges her efforts. She's giggling, tossing her hair over her shoulder, her gaze finding mine as if she already knew I was watching.

I look away, nodding at Brent. "I think that's a good idea."

"Let's go."

I let him lead the way to an empty table on the other side of the hall, as far away from our usual table as possible. I take my plate from Brent, studying the pizza slice with disappointment.

"Eat it fast before it gets cold," Brent suggests before he shovels half of his slice of pizza into his mouth.

I take a swallow from my water bottle, picking up the pizza with dainty fingers, trying not to get them too greasy. I nibble from the pointed end, the mixture of dough, sauce and cheese hitting my tongue.

Oh shit. It's good.

Within seconds, I'm devouring it, Brent watching me with amusement after already finishing his slice and now digging into the bag of chips. When I'm finished, I lean back against my chair, wiping at my mouth with a napkin, surprisingly not full of regret.

"That was delicious," I declare, making Brent chuckle.

"You sound surprised."

"I am." I toss my wadded-up napkin on top of my plate, hiding the grease stain left behind. "I can't remember the last time I ate pizza."

"Really? I eat it like five times a week." His gaze finds mine. "I probably need to eat a salad sometime, huh?"

"Definitely." I smile at him, hating myself for using him. He seems nice enough. Harmless enough. Attractive enough, with warm brown eyes and dark hair that curls a little at the end. His uniform is pressed neatly, not a wrinkle in sight, and he has a nice smile.

But he does nothing for me. Not a single thing.

I watch as he eats a few Doritos, shaking my head when he offers me the bag. I can hear Mercedes' voice, loud and obnoxious, and I refuse to look in her direction, give in to her baiting me.

"Brent, can I ask you a question?"

"Go ahead." He munches on another chip, then washes it down with a sip of Dr. Pepper.

"Why did you agree to sit with me over here instead of sitting with your friends like you always do?"

He shoves another couple of chips into his mouth, chewing and swallowing it down before he says, "You looked like you needed a friend."

Normally I would take Brent's comment as an insult, but he isn't too far off the mark.

"Thank you," I murmur, trying to ignore the itchy feeling forming between my shoulder blades. I'm not used to thanking people for much and it feels weird to say. "I appreciate that."

"You're welcome." He grins. "Plus, I hate Mercedes. She's so fucking annoying."

I can't help but laugh, and I make sure it's extra loud. I hope *he* can hear.

West.

I hope he sees me and thinks I'm having fun with Brent. I hope even more that he's pissed off that I didn't listen to him and chose to hang out with Brent anyway, despite his warning.

I don't know who Weston Fontaine thinks he is, but I do know one thing.

He can't tell me what to do.

CHAPTER FOURTEEN

WEST

"You're not even paying attention to me," Mercedes whines, like an annoying fucking gnat in my ear. She touches me—she hasn't stopped touching me since I hauled her onto my lap the moment Carolina walked into the dining hall—her fingers sinking into my hair, and I jerk away from her always grasping hand. "West, what the fuck is wrong with you?"

The entire table goes silent at her question and I glare at all of them until they drop their heads, picking their conversations back up as if she never said anything.

"Leave it," I tell her with a glare.

Mercedes huffs, removing her hand from my hair, thank God, and taps her long, bright pink fingernails against her pursed lips, watching me with thinly-veiled disgust. Giving me Carolina vibes, if I'm being real right now, though it's more like she's the brass version while Carolina is pure eighteen carat gold.

"You're tense," she observes.

"No shit." This girl is a complete dumbass. Can't she see there's a reason for me being tense and angry? And she has nothing to do with it.

"Let's get out of here," she whispers, her gaze turning sultry, those long fingernails now streaking across the top of my thigh.

"We could sneak off somewhere for a little bit."

I'm not tempted by her offer whatsoever. "Mercedes."

She pouts, her hand still on my leg, her nails digging into my skin, even through the fabric of my pants. "What? Come on, I know what you like. We have almost twenty minutes until the bell rings."

She has no idea what I like. We've never messed around and I'd like to keep it that way, despite her persistence.

I settle my hand on top of hers, about to remove it from my thigh when I hear it. The sweetest sound floating in the air, drifting toward our table clear across the cavernous dining hall.

Carolina Lancaster's laughter.

Clutching Mercedes' fingers tightly to stop her from reaching for my dick, I glance over my shoulder, spotting Carolina's bright blonde head immediately. She's leaning her head back, a smile on her face, laughing at whatever Brent said while he watches her looking like a goofy motherfucker, an idiotic grin plastered on his face.

I want to smash his face in. Brent is one of my closest friends and I want to wreak unholy violence on him for even looking at her like that, let alone making her laugh. Sitting with her at lunch because she chose him.

"Ouch, West, you're hurting me." Mercedes tries to pull her fingers from my grip, but I rise to my feet, practically dragging her up with me.

"Let's go," I say gruffly.

"What? Are you actually agreeing to this?" Her pain forgotten, she sounds downright shocked as I pull her through the crowded tables in the dining hall, purposely going in the wrong direction, so I can pass by Brent and Carolina's table. "West, where are you going?"

"A shortcut," I tell her, pulling her closer and letting go of her hand, so I can sling my arm around her shoulders, tucking her into my side. "I know just where we can go for a little—privacy."

She snuggles closer, her body practically vibrating. "Oooh, that sounds perfect."

I slow my steps as we draw closer to their table, my head swiveling, so I can look directly at Carolina. She watches me with amusement, her blue eyes dancing with mischief, like she knows I'm putting on a show for her and she just doesn't give a damn.

Frustration ripples through me and I tug Mercedes even closer to me with my arm, resting my mouth right on hers, my gaze still locked on Carolina's.

The gleam leaves Carolina's eyes like the dimming of a light switch and she jerks her gaze away from mine, saying something to Brent that has him frowning. He glances in my direction, sees Mercedes and me together, my mouth resting on hers, though not actually kissing her, and the bastard slowly shakes his head.

What, like he's disappointed? What does that jackass know? What the hell does he care?

"Come on," I say irritably as I remove my arm from Mercedes' shoulders and take her hand once more.

"Where are we going?" Mercedes asks, her voice shaking with excitement.

This bitch has been horny for me since freshman year. I'm about to make her dreams come true, so she better appreciate this moment, the same one I know I'll regret later. After whatever we're about to do, she'll cling even harder, trying to turn this into something more, and I'll have to avoid her every chance I get. To the point that I'll eventually have to be cruel and say something shitty in order for her to leave me alone for good. Even then she'd probably come back around after a few months—make that a few weeks—of avoiding me.

Mercedes has a pattern and it's obvious to all of us. We know how this girl operates.

We exit the dining hall, the warm, early fall breeze smacking me directly in the face. I come to a stop, glancing first left, then right, when I spot a janitor's supply closet in the near distance.

"Over here," I tell Mercedes as we head toward the door.

"They lock those normally, don't they?" The worry in her voice is surprising, and I send her a look to see that, yep, she's not looking forward to this particular idea.

"They never lock them." I test the door handle and it opens with ease, the scent of antiseptic and bleach wafting out of the tiny space. "And this is definitely private."

She pulls her hand from mine, crossing her arms in front of her ample chest. "No way."

"What?" I glance into the darkened closet, noting the shelves of cleaning supplies. "You scared of the dark?"

"No, I just—I'm not getting on my knees for you in there, West. The floor is solid concrete. I'll bruise."

I want to laugh. "Don't want to bruise those precious knees any more than they already are, am I right?"

Mercedes frowns. "Are you trying to insult me?"

"Never." I pull her in for a quick hug, giving her a gentle pat on the back that's this side of patronizing. "Some other time then."

"Wait a minute. I'm not saying *that*. We should still totally hook up. What about an empty class—"

"Another time," I repeat, baring my teeth at her in an attempt to smile.

"West." She rests her hand on my chest, drawing her fingers in a straight line right down the middle. "Are you mad at me?"

"Not at all. You have a valid point." I pull her into my arms and she kisses my cheek while I pat her on the butt. "Maybe tonight."

"Really?" She sounds so damn hopeful.

Not a chance, is what I want to tell her, but I just nod and smile. "Maybe."

Her phone buzzes with a call and she checks the screen, her gaze never lifting. "I need to take this."

"Go," I encourage, and she's already gone, walking away briskly, the phone held to her ear as she immediately starts talking.

God, she has a big mouth. She whines. She's pushy. And so fucking obvious. She was practically dry humping my leg earlier when Carolina happened to spot us together, and while it felt good that she caught us in that moment, everything was fucking ruined and pointless when I saw who she decided to go sit with during lunch.

Fucking Brent.

I told her to stay away from him and she defied me. Stupid, idiotic girl. Brent is my friend, but he's careless with girls. He's only out for one thing, and if he thinks he has a chance with Carolina Lancaster?

The asshole is going to go for it—and then brag to all of us how he had her naked and crying out his name while he rammed his pencil dick inside her.

Yeah, I can't fucking stand the thought of that.

My phone buzzes with a text and I check to see that it's from my mother. Ignoring it, I pocket my phone before I reach out to close the janitor closet door when I spot movement out of the corner of my eye.

Carolina, exiting the dining hall.

Alone.

She glances around, her head aimed in the opposite direction, and I grab hold of the door, making sure she can see at least a part of me, my head angled just so that I can watch her. She finally looks in my direction, her gaze settling on me, and I send her a knowing smirk before I enter the closet and shut the door behind me.

What the fuck am I doing?

Within seconds, I can hear her footsteps just outside the closet. Can see her loafer-covered feet through the slats near the bottom of the door. She shifts from foot to foot, like she doesn't know what to do, and I lean against the door for a split second, letting out a soft groan.

Let her think I've got Mercedes in here with me and she has

a mouthful of my dick.

A frustrated sound escapes Carolina, which makes it easy to know that her hands are curled into fists. I press my lips together, trying not to laugh, and when the rapid-fire knocking starts, I almost jump out of my skin.

"What are you doing in there?" she demands, her voice shrill. Reminding me of an uptight teacher—no, reminding me of our uptight librarian, Miss Taylor. That woman is always getting pissed at someone for being too loud.

I remain quiet, sinking into the shadows, wondering what Carolina could be thinking. I hope her mind is filled with all sorts of filthy visions, every one of them involving me and Mercedes in some sort of sexual act. The most basic one would be a blow job, because we all know that girl would be on her knees sucking my dick at this very moment if she'd only had a pillow to rest them on.

Jesus. I don't know what to think of Mercedes bailing on me, but if I was really into her? I'd have aching blue balls, that's for sure. She's such a fuckin' tease.

Carolina leans against the door, and I can hear her voice loud and clear. "I know you're in there. I can hear the two of you breathing."

I'm smiling. I can't help it. She's got this so wrong.

"I should go tell on you two for making my life miserable today." The determination in her voice is obvious. "I'm going to Matthews right now to let him know that the two of you are hooking up in a closet. He's going to be so pissed—"

Without warning, I swing the door open, and she nearly falls into me, she's standing so close. I grab hold of her, pulling her deeper into the shadows, pressing her against the shelf and slamming the door with a singular kick of my foot.

"What are you doing? Get off me." Carolina slaps at my chest, my face. Her hands are in constant motion, trying to hurt me.

Trying her best to get away from me.

I grab hold of her wrists and pin them to my chest, holding

her there despite her still constant struggle. "I had to stop you from being a nasty little tattletale, though it doesn't surprise me, you wanting to run off to Matthews."

Her breaths are quick. Shaky. She lifts her head, her hair brushing against the shelf behind her, knocking into something that tips over, the sound making her jump.

I take both of her wrists in one hand and run my fingers over her shoulder. Down her arm. Gently. Barely touching her.

She doesn't like to be touched. I already know that much.

"Where's Mercedes?" she demands.

"I don't know." I whistle like I'm calling a dog. "Mercedes! Where the hell are you?"

"Shut up," Carolina hisses. "Are you telling me she's not in here?"

"Nope."

"Then what the hell were you doing, running into the closet like you just did? Did you do it on purpose to get my attention?"

I say nothing, letting her draw her own conclusions.

An exasperated sigh escapes her and she shoves at my chest, her hands curled into fists. "God, you're obnoxious. I think you enjoy torturing me."

"Right back at you." I practically thrust my face in hers, noting how wide her blue eyes are. "Nice move there, hanging out with Brent at lunch."

Her lips form into a knowing smirk. "He's not so bad."

"He's an asshole."

"He's your friend."

"And he's still an asshole. Don't be fooled by his 'aw shucks' persona. It's bullshit." I lean into her, pressing her against the shelving, letting her feel every inch of me. "You're playing with fire with that one."

"More like I'm playing with fire with you," she retorts.

We're quiet for a moment, the only sound our mingling breaths, and I would give anything to know what she's thinking.

I can't figure this girl out and it drives me fucking crazy.

"Did Mercedes actually turn you down? I can't imagine her missing out on a chance to suck your dick."

I'm shocked little Miss Proper Lancaster would say such a thing. "She got an important phone call."

"Interesting," she murmurs.

"Where's Brent? He let you get away from him for a few minutes?"

"There is nothing going on between me and Brent."

"Just like there's nothing going on between me and Mercedes."

"I don't believe you."

"It's true. I don't like her. She does nothing for me." It's easier to tell the truth when we're in a darkened closet, where I can't really make out Carolina's features.

"Then why did you let her sit on your lap?"

I grin. I can't help it. "Bothered you, huh?"

"Not at all."

"Wish it was you?"

"Of course not."

"Really? If it was you, it would've been a different scenario."

"I would never sit on your lap like that in public."

"What about in private?"

"I wouldn't do it then either."

There is something about her snotty tone that is such a fucking turn-on, which means I should probably get my head examined. I'm hard just listening to that haughty voice of hers.

Fuck it. I'm going to fill her in on a few fantasies of mine.

"If I had you in my lap in the dining hall, you know what I would do?"

Chapter Fifteen

CAROLINA

His question hangs in the air and all I can think is, *please don't answer.*

Please don't answer.

I remain quiet, but it doesn't matter. He keeps speaking, letting go of my wrists and bracing both of his hands on the shelf behind me, caging me in completely. I'm surrounded by him and God help me, I like it.

Despite everything he's said and done and how he taunts and tortures me, I crave more of him. More talking, more touching, all of it. Just knowing he's watching does something to me. Makes me feel alive.

Makes me feel wanted.

"I'd have you sitting just so, your little plaid skirt flared out so I could feel the backs of your bare legs, the soft cotton of your panties resting against my thigh. And guess what?" He tips his head, his mouth at my temple when he murmurs, "They'd be damp. Fucking soaked for me."

My panties are soaked right now just at his words.

"When no one was looking, I'd slip my hand beneath your skirt. Trace the leg of your panties, right at that spot where your pelvis meets your thigh. Then, I'd run my finger up and down, right along the edge, and I'd slip my finger beneath the fabric and finger-fuck you right there in front of everybody. Your skin would start to flush, get all rosy, like it does right before you come, and I'd give you an orgasm. You wouldn't be able to stop it, wouldn't be able to control yourself because I know what you like, Carolina. And I know just how to give it to you."

His voice is a hot rasp against my skin, his words filling my head with thoughts. Too many chaotic, naughty thoughts.

"Of course, who am I kidding? Everyone would be looking at us and everyone would know I'm knuckle-deep inside Carolina Lancaster's tight little pussy, making her come right there in the middle of the dining hall. Mercedes would probably be pissed as hell, but it would be a fun little show to put on, don't you think?" He shifts, backing away from me, and I nearly collapse to the floor, not realizing that the only thing holding me up was his body pinning me to the shelf.

"You're disgusting." There's no anger in my voice and I'm sure he knows I don't mean it.

Because I don't. What he just described rattled me to my very core. My entire body is strung tight and the throb that started between my thighs the moment he pulled me into the closet has only become stronger.

It's all I can focus on.

"You fucking love it." He is relishing every moment of this and I want to hit him.

I also want him to slip his fingers inside my panties and do to me exactly what he just described.

A whimper leaves me and I press my lips together, trying to stifle it, but there's no use.

He heard me.

"I can smell you, you know." He's back, his body next to mine, his mouth brushing my forehead as he speaks. "You're hot for it, aren't you?"

I say nothing, trying to control the trembling that wants to take over my body.

His hand brushes the hem of my skirt and I hold my breath, my chest growing tight when he slips his fingers beneath my skirt. They brush my thigh, sliding up, and a ragged sigh escapes me when he does exactly as he described, tracing the edge of my panties, right at the spot where my thigh meets my pelvis. "It probably wouldn't take much, would it?"

Much what, is what I want to ask, but I keep my mouth shut. I don't trust myself to say anything right now.

"You'd probably go off like a firecracker." His fingers slip beneath the thin fabric of my panties, streaking across my pussy, and I spread my legs slightly, my feet sliding across the concrete.

I can see his grin in the dim light of the closet, and I know he loves that I obey him without words. That I want him like I can't help myself. I lean my head back, resting it against the shelf, my eyes falling closed when he sinks his fingers into my pussy and begins to stroke.

I'm so wet, the sound of his busy fingers fills the confined space, but I don't care. All I can focus on is the way he touches me, his breaths hot and heavy against my forehead, the sloppy sounds of my juices as he slides his fingers inside my body, testing me. Stretching me.

"You're so fucking tight," he mutters, and I gasp, my inner walls convulsing around his fingers, the orgasm slamming into me out of nowhere. I shudder and shake, his body holding me up, his fingers pumping inside me, his thumb brushing against my clit.

The moment stretches on for what feels like forever, my mind going blank, all the air escaping me until I can't breathe. I never touch him. It feels as if he's holding me up with just his fingers buried inside my body, and when the orgasm is finally over and I can focus again, I realize his fingers are still in me, his mouth at my temple, his soft chuckle rippling across my skin.

"That was too easy." He pulls his fingers from my body, my skirt falling, covering me completely and then those same fingers are at my mouth, trying to pry my lips apart. "Open up."

I do as he says and he fills my mouth with his fingers, the salty, musky taste of me hitting my tongue.

"Suck," he demands, and I do as he says, lapping at his fingers, sucking every bit of myself off of them until he finally makes a growling sound of satisfaction, pulling his fingers from my mouth.

I wait for the shame to wash over me, but it doesn't come. My skin feels electrified. My mind is spinning and my toes are tingling and I wonder if this is normal.

"Did I hurt you?" he asks, his voice low.

I shake my head, surprised at his concern. "Not really."

"Not really?"

"I—liked it." I miss the pain from dancing. The rigorous training my body used to go through is gone and there's an empty spot inside me now that longs for it. Pushing myself beyond my limits. I want to be exhausted. I want my muscles to be weak and shaky and I want my mind to be blank.

I've discovered the closest thing to that feeling is engaging in sexual acts with West.

The moment the final bell rings, I escape my class and head for my suite, eager to be alone in my room so I can explore a few things. Bask in my memories of what happened just before lunch ended. When West fucked me with his fingers and made me come in a matter of seconds.

I'm still waiting for the embarrassment and shame to hit me, but it hasn't come yet. So when I run into him hanging around the entrance to my building, I come to a complete stop, staring at him, pleasure and shock mingling in my blood.

That I'm happy to see him doesn't really surprise me. It's more the fact that he's here. Seeking me out.

"What do you want?" I ask, my voice calm.

He shoves his hands in his pockets, watching me. "Just checking on you."

"Are you concerned for my welfare? I appreciate it, but I'm fine. Really." I go to the double doors and pry open one of them, wincing at how heavy it is.

He's there in an instant, directly behind me, opening the door and taking the brunt of the weight. "What are you doing?"

"Going to my room." He follows me into the hall, the door slamming behind us, shrouding us in echoey silence. We're the only two people in this entire building. "Do you want to join me? Are you hoping I'll say yes after Mercedes turned you down?"

I'm goading him on purpose and it works. He's grimacing, his gaze filled with disgust.

"I don't like her like that and you know it."

I come to a stop and so does he, the two of us facing each other. "I do? I don't know. You had her on your lap at lunch."

"And I had my fingers inside you right after. She's not the one I want."

The unspoken words say so much and I tell my hopeful heart to get over it. Whatever West and I are about to embark on is nothing close to normal. I can admit this—we want each other. I'm curious about him, but I'm also not comfortable touching another human like that.

Like what he wants.

And I have no clue how to do it either.

"Are you embarrassed?" he asks when I remain quiet. "About what happened?"

"No," I admit, deciding to give in a little. "I liked it."

His expression remains serious. "You're all I can think about."

I blink at him.

"I had a test in sixth period and I couldn't concentrate for shit. I could still smell you on my fingers and I couldn't stop thinking about the sounds you made. How your cunt tightened around my fingers right as you came." He shakes his head, rubbing his jaw with his hand. "You're bad for me, Carolina."

I don't even take offense. "You're bad for me too."

"Show me your room."

I shake my head. "Wait for me in the dance studio."

He frowns. "What do you mean?"

"You know where it's at. Wait for me." I start walking, heading toward my suite, not looking back when I say, "The door's unlocked."

I can feel his gaze on me as I practically run into my room, and the moment I'm inside, I turn the lock, so he can't barge in.

Not that he would. I think he might enjoy the game as much as I do. The anticipation.

I go to the full-length mirror and stare at myself, taking in my reddened cheeks, my wild eyes. I shed all my clothes until I'm standing there completely naked, my nipples hard and red, that rosy flush he spoke of earlier coating my skin.

He does this to me, I think, as I touch my breast, pinching my nipple, making me wince.

He makes me feel this way, I realize as I slip my fingers between my legs and stroke myself once, pulling them out and staring at them. They glisten, my scent clinging to my skin, and I rub one nipple, then the other, wondering if he'll notice.

Knowing without a doubt he will.

Turning away from the mirror, I throw on a pair of black booty shorts that don't really fit me well and the thinnest, tiniest sports bra I can find. It's black and strappy and barely covers me and it's exactly what I want.

I wore my hair down today and I leave it that way, though I never dance with my hair down. It gets in my face, turning into a sweaty, gross mess. But there will be no dancing this afternoon, not with West.

I don't know what he wants from me exactly, but I know enough. And whatever I can't figure out, I'm sure he'll guide me.

When I arrive at the studio, I find him standing in front of the window that overlooks the campus gardens, his back to me, his hands still in his pockets though he's removed his jacket. The white cotton shirt stretches across his shoulders, his back, and I stand there, silently admiring him, twisting my hands together while I worry that I might be in over my head.

Slowly, he turns his head, glancing over his shoulder to find me standing there, his expression impassive. No emotion shown whatsoever. "I don't normally wait for girls."

I want to roll my eyes. Of course, he would lead with a statement like that. His ego is boundless.

"Not sure if I'll be worth the wait." I move toward him, keeping my steps purposely slow. I decide to be completely honest. "I don't know what I'm doing."

He turns to face me fully, his gaze roving over me, my skin warming everywhere his eyes touch. "I'll show you."

I come to a stop in the middle of the room, my entire body trembling in anticipation.

"Is the door locked?" he asks.

"No." I'm such an idiot.

"Go lock it then."

I turn on my heel and run to the door, turning the lock with a finality that rings through the hollow room. My feet barely touch the ground as I make my way over to him, gliding across the floor like I'm dancing, and when I stop directly in front of him, I fully expect him to reach out and pull me into his arms.

I brace myself, ready for the onslaught of sensation I experience every time someone touches me, both dreading and looking forward to the moment, but he does none of that. Instead, his hands remain in his pockets and his gaze is heavy as it settles on my face.

"You don't like to be touched." He states it as fact.

Being called out for your faults is never easy. I've had it happen to me again and again over the years in dance, and I thought I'd hardened myself enough to withstand it, but West making that simple statement nearly sends me to my knees.

"Why don't you like it?" he pushes when I remain silent.

"I don't like...showing emotion. I never have."

"Why not?"

"I don't know." I shrug. I've been to therapy, alone and with my family. I've been forced to talk about my feelings and issues in front of my parents, right after they expressed their worry for my wellbeing, which coincided with their divorce announcement. I withdrew into a shell, horrified by their arguments, by Whit's cruel and cold behavior, and Sylvie's chronic health issues.

I couldn't take it. None of it. I tried my best to emulate my brother's cold, callousness and I still do, but there's a tiny part of me buried deep that feels too much.

It's so much easier to feel nothing at all, I realized at an early age. Don't react. Don't cry. Don't smile. Don't let anyone touch you. Throw up that wall and don't let anyone penetrate it.

I begged my parents to let me go to London to dance. It was the only thing that gave me pleasure, I told them. The only thing that mattered to me. They were reluctant, my father protesting loudly when my mother gave in to rid herself of me, but in the end, I got what I wanted.

Lancasters get what they want. I lived by that mantra once I was aware of it, until I was forced to go to this stupid prep school that doesn't mean shit to me, even though it's supposed to, thanks to my family owning it. And while I'm still despondent over the fact that I'm missing out on my regular dance classes and I'm afraid I'll end up behind everyone else and never be able to claw my way back to the top, at least I have this.

At least I have West.

CHAPTER SIXTEEN

WEST

I curl my hands into fists, keeping them in my pockets, so I don't do something crazy like reach for her, scare the shit out of her and have her running from me.

I can't risk it. Not now. Not after what happened in the janitor's closet.

Hottest moment of my life. All I ever seem to do is finger-fuck this girl in ridiculous locations, and it only makes me want her more. She's never really touched me. She's never even said anything to indicate that she wants me. Yet, here I am, desperate for her. Desperate to touch her, kiss her, strip her of what little clothing she's wearing and feast on her. I want to fuck her pussy with my tongue and my cock, my gaze never straying from her face as I make her come over and over again. I want to pin her to the ground and force feed my dick into that lush mouth of hers, until she's choking on it, tears streaming from her eyes. I want to humiliate her and fuck her and mark her and make her mine.

It's the strangest fucking thing.

She's strange. I can't deny it. I can't even describe her as classically beautiful. She's so thin and wiry, nothing but muscle and skin and bone. Her hair is a bright blonde, when I've mostly been drawn to brunettes, and she's pale, her skin nearly translucent. I can see the veins in her skin now, the faintest pink and blue, her chest rising and expanding as she breathes heavily, those pillowy lips parting as she stares at me, her tongue sneaking out to lick at the corner.

Jesus.

Mentally, she's probably completely unstable, but guess what? We all are. I'm hanging on by a thread most days, always filled with an inexplicable rage I can't quite pinpoint on why exactly I feel that way.

I just do.

"Do you dance every day?" I ask, needing to change the subject. We shouldn't get into all the reasons Carolina Lancaster avoids physical touch and enjoys pain. That subject is far too complex for this Monday afternoon.

"I try."

"Do you want to dance right now?"

She slowly shakes her head, her hair sliding over her pale shoulders. She wore it down today, which is rare, and it smells so fucking good. I had to restrain myself earlier from burying my face in it when we were in that damn closet.

I glance around, spotting the chair with the small speaker on it and I go to it, setting the speaker on the floor before I settle in. I spread my legs wide and pat my thigh. "Come here."

Carolina glides toward me, and when she gets closer, I can see that she's visibly shaking. Is she scared? Or just excited?

"Sit down." I point at my thigh and she does as I ask, perching her skinny ass on my leg, her posture stiff, her back ramrod straight. She weighs barely anything and I don't touch her. Not yet.

She rests her hands in her lap, her head bent, her gaze downcast and I observe her, letting my gaze roam over her, restraining myself from what I really want to do.

Run my mouth down the length of her elegant neck. Lick at her ear. Bite it. Push the strap of her sports bra off her shoulder, slowly exposing her to me.

My cock swells and I shift my position, Carolina slipping closer, her hand coming out to brace herself against my chest. She lifts her head, her gaze meeting mine and I see fear in her gaze. Fear mixed with curiosity and something else. Something unnamed.

I keep my hands at my sides while she slides her hand up my chest, her fingers toying with the knot in my tie, tugging on it, loosening it from around my neck. I still don't touch her, letting her completely undo the tie. She wraps it around her wrist, tying it around and around, a little smile playing upon her lips.

"I want to keep this."

"It's yours."

Her gaze meets mine. "Do you give up your possessions this easily all the time?"

I slowly shake my head. "Never."

"Are you saying I'm special?"

Giving in, I lean in so my face is in hers, my gaze serious as I murmur, "Yes."

She tips her chin up, our lips brushing. Clinging. Before I can do anything more, she withdraws, her teeth sinking into her lower lip, her hand at my throat once more, her fingers slipping over the buttons of my shirt, undoing one. Then another. She keeps her gaze trained on my neck, swallowing hard as she exposes me, her fingers brushing over my chest. My ribs. My stomach. Until every button is undone and my shirt is completely open.

"I've touched my dancing partners before, but never like this," she admits, her fingers hovering above my stomach.

Every muscle is strung tight, the anticipation of her hands landing on my skin once more, nearly undoing me. "How do you want to touch me?"

Her gaze never straying from my chest, she reaches out, tentative fingers settling on my stomach. The muscles ripple beneath her fingertips, my entire body shaking in relief, and she traces her fingers up, streaking across my ribs. Down the center of my belly.

"You're firm."

"I told you I was an athlete."

"Track." She rolls her eyes, amused.

"That counts."

"I know." Her gaze meets mine. "It shows."

She becomes bolder as she continues to touch me, and still, I don't touch her in return, afraid I might scare her off, desperate to see what she does next. When she curls her fingers around the waistband of my trousers, I bite my lip, stifling my groan when her knuckles brush the flesh just above my boxer briefs.

I feel like I could come in my pants at any second and all she's doing is touching me in a mostly nonsexual manner.

This is fucking torture.

"Are you hating this?" she asks, her shaky fingers fumbling with the button of my trousers.

"Not at all." My voice is strained, my mind growing hazier when she undoes the zipper. White hot anticipation flows through my veins, leaving me weak. Something I never feel when it comes to sex.

"I want to see you." She scrambles off my lap, the disappointment crushing, though it immediately disappears when she settles in front of me on her knees, both hands on the front of my trousers, spreading the fabric wide, tugging at the waistband like she wants them off.

I toe off my shoes and lift my hips, letting her take my pants off, until I'm sitting there with my shirt undone and my dick straining against the front of my charcoal gray boxer briefs, my heart pounding so fucking hard I can't help but wonder if she hears it.

She stares at my erection, her eyes wide, just before she reaches out with her index finger and traces the length. My dick jumps beneath her touch, twitching, and she blinks, her gaze lifting to mine.

"It wants what it wants." I shrug, trying to make light of the moment.

"What does it want?" She gulps. "Me?"

"Yeah," I rasp.

Carolina cups me fully, her fingers coming around my length, her touch gentle. I want to tell her to squeeze it, grip it harder, but I keep my mouth shut.

I'm doing this on Carolina's terms. Letting her come to her own conclusions, go at her own pace. To push her would be a mistake.

I'm not putting anything at risk. Not today.

"You're hard." Her gaze drops to my dick. "And big."

My cock jerks beneath her touch and she's about to snatch her hand back, but I'm quicker than her, settling her hand on top of me with mine covering hers. "Grab it. Don't be shy."

She wraps her fingers around me, over the cotton, and I shake my head, lifting her hand with mine, sliding them both beneath my boxers. Until she's touching my bare flesh.

A shuddery exhale leaves my lungs when her fingers grip me, her gaze stuck on watching her hand beneath the gray cotton. She begins to stroke, her movements jerky at first, until she finds a rhythm.

Jesus, that feels good.

"Take these off," I demand, tugging at my boxer briefs, and she's scrambling, pulling them off, until my bare ass hits the chair and my boxers are crumpled around my ankles.

If anyone were to come in and catch us, there would be hell to pay. Shit, anyone could walk by the giant windows and see us like this. But I don't give a damn.

Can't worry about it. Not with Carolina's fingers wrapped tight around my dick, stroking me, slowly but surely.

"You're soft, yet hard," she marvels, squeezing the top of my cock until a bead of liquid appears in the slit. "Are you already coming?"

I bark out a laugh. "Not quite. Pretty sure you'd be aware of it when it happens."

Her cheeks color with embarrassment and her hold loosens, like she's going to slip away. I slap my hand over hers once again, keeping her right where I want her. "I wasn't laughing at you, Carolina."

She presses her lips together, swallowing hard before she whispers, "Can I lick it?"

Holy shit. Like I'd say no.

I nod, unsure if I can even speak.

Rising up, she leans over my lap, darting her tongue out to lick the tip of my dick, lapping up the liquid that was there. She licks again and again, her tongue soft and delicate, as if she's eating an ice cream cone on a hot summer day and when I'm just about to beg her to stop, she wraps those delectable lips of hers around the head of my cock and draws it into her warm, wet mouth.

"Fuck," I bite out, unable to tear my gaze away from the visual of my cock sliding between Carolina's lips.

She removes me from her mouth with an audible pop, frowning. "Am I doing it wrong?"

"You could never do this wrong," I say vehemently. "Don't fucking stop."

Her siren smile is a revelation, and I wonder if this is the moment she realizes the power she has over me.

I know it's the moment I realize the power she wields.

And I'm too fucking gone over her to worry about it.

She remains on her knees, her hand coming up to grip the base of my cock as she continues to lick and suck. I let her play with me for a while, sliding my fingers into her soft hair, careful not to get the strands tangled in my watch band. Exerting a little pressure to indicate I want her to take me deeper. She bids my silent request, a moan leaving her when she sucks me deeper. Harder. The vibrations of her mouth make my balls draw up tight and that familiar tingling starts at the base of my spine.

It's not going to take much and I'll be coming. I'm fucking sweating just thinking about it, restraining myself, desperate to regain control of the situation.

"Stop," I demand, and she automatically removes me from her mouth, frowning. "Keep your lips open for me."

She parts her lips wide and I lift my hips, sliding my dick in between them before I pull back out. She lowers her head, following after me, her hand resting on my thigh, her other hand circling the base of my cock, and I fuck her mouth, my hand coming up to hold the back of her head.

Keeping her in place.

Her eyes are watering, just like I imagined, as I push inside her so deep, I bump the back of her throat. I fuck her hard, grunting with every thrust, my hips bucking, her fingers digging into my thigh, cutting into my skin. The prickle of pain is strong, immediately wiped out by the sensation of my orgasm sweeping through me, taking over until I'm a shuddering, groaning mess.

She doesn't move away as I feel that first blast of semen hit the back of her throat. She swallows it down, every fucking bit, and when it's finally over and my chest aches, she finally removes me from her mouth and wipes the back of her hand across her lips, leaning back on her haunches.

"That was a lot."

I frown at her, my chest heaving. "What do you mean?"

"All of the—semen." Her cheeks are pink and she rubs at the corner of her mouth with her finger. "More than I expected."

"Yet you swallowed it all."

"I thought I was supposed to." She frowns. "Was I not supposed to?"

Damn. This girl.

She is unlike anyone I've ever known.

CHAPTER SEVENTEEN

CAROLINA

I feel different, I think as I walk around campus, clutching my books to my chest since I forgot my bookbag in my room earlier this morning. I'm more forgetful. Completely preoccupied. My father called me last night and I was so disinterested in our conversation he even said something.

"Are you okay? You seem distant."

"Lots of homework," I told him like the little liar that I am.

I can't admit to my father that I can't stop thinking about the fact thWat I had West Fontaine's dick in my mouth. That's the last thing he wants to hear, but it's the truth.

I can't stop thinking about it.

The look on his face while he watched me. The way he tangled his fingers in my hair, tugging on it until my scalp stung, his hips forceful as he essentially fucked my mouth. I let it happen, the tears streaming down my face, the head of his cock touching the back of my throat and nearly making me gag. It was painful and it was delicious and when I felt that first spurt of cum hit my tongue, I automatically swallowed it down, shocked when it kept coming.

The entire moment was filthy and kind of degrading and I enjoyed every single second of it.

It was a little awkward after the fact and I basically asked him to leave the dance studio once it was over. He slipped his clothes back on, covering up that glorious cock of his, leaving his shirt unbuttoned as he slung his jacket over his shoulder and wandered out of my dance studio, whistling an unfamiliar tune.

The entire moment was surreal.

I want to do it again.

Anticipation throbs in my veins and between my legs as I enter American Government, my gaze searching, looking for West, but he's not in the room yet.

Mercedes is though. Sitting in her usual spot with her minions surrounding her, her gaze ghosting over me as if I don't actually exist.

Fine, I don't want her acknowledgement. Would much rather sink into the shadows and pretend I'm not here.

Brent walks in, his gaze finding mine before he quickly looks away, not acknowledging me at all. I frown, ready to call out to him, but then West wanders in, a knowing smile on his face as he settles into the desk directly behind me.

"What are you doing?" I hiss at him, glancing around. I don't want anyone noticing that he's sitting right next to me, especially Mercedes.

"I told Brent to back off. He won't be bothering you anymore." That's all West says, confidence bleeding into his every word.

With that, he rises to his feet and makes his way to the center of the classroom, sitting in the desk directly in front of Brent.

Directly across from Mercedes.

I'm fuming. Why would he choose to sit next to her? It doesn't matter that it's his usual spot. That it's where he always sits. I'm feeling irrational. Territorial.

After everything that happened yesterday, he actually still chooses to sit by her.

I hate him.

Our teacher announces the quiz he warned us about on

Friday and I feel stupid for forgetting, staring blankly at the test questions once he's passed them out, my mind scrambling to come up with the proper answers. Thankfully, it's only multiple choice and true/false questions, so I answer them the best I can, keeping my focus on the test, trying not to be tempted by what's happening in the classroom behind me.

I feel someone watching me and I quickly look up to find Mercedes staring at me, blatant hatred blazing from her gaze. I don't know what I did to her, or why she's so angry with me, but I immediately look back down at my test. I'm not in the mood for a confrontation with her today, or any day.

It already feels like she won. He's sitting next to her still. Guess it doesn't matter what happens between us. West is still going to choose his other life. His public life.

While I'm more like his sick, little secret.

I take most of the class period to agonize over the quiz, and once the bell rings, I gather my things, awkward with the stack of books I got out of my locker earlier. I leave the classroom and hurry to said locker, so I can dump off the ones I don't need any longer. I'm not paying attention when someone sticks their foot out and I trip, falling to the floor with a grunt, the books scattering everywhere, my knees taking the brunt of my fall.

The entire hallway fills with laughter and there's a breeze brushing over my backside. I close my eyes, reaching behind me to check that yep, my skirt flipped up, exposing my pale pink panties to everyone.

"So clumsy," I hear Mercedes say, just before she cackles with laughter like the witch she is. I hear other girls laugh—her minions I'm sure—and I quickly sit up, brushing my hair out of my face before I lean over to gather my textbooks.

A boy crouches beside me, grabbing my books for me, and I scowl when I realize it's West. I track his movements as he rises to his feet, offering his hand to me.

"Let me help you up." His deep voice reaches inside my chest and squeezes my heart, and I stare at his outstretched hand, wishing I could refuse him.

But like the secretly obsessed girl I am, I rest my hand in his, tingles sweeping over my skin when he curls his fingers around mine and hauls me to my feet. There's a scowl on his face as he hands over my books, his gaze searching the faces of those who surround us, and I realize he's mad.

"Who the fuck tripped her?" he demands.

No one answers. I wouldn't either if I saw the look on West's face.

"Mercedes?" His tone is extra sharp.

She rests her hand against her chest, the picture of innocence. "I would never."

She so would, and we all know it.

"Keep the fuck away from Carolina," he tells her, his gaze sweeping over the crowd. "All of you."

They all shuffle away, a few nervous giggles and chuckles filling the air as they walk past us, and I shove at West the moment they're gone.

"What was that for?" he asks incredulously.

"I can defend myself."

I start walking, and as always, he follows behind me. "You weren't doing such a good job of that a few minutes ago."

His words infuriate me and I toss my head, my hair flying. "I can handle things on my own, West. I don't need you running to my defense."

"They hurt you." I come to a stop when I hear the fury in his voice. And I swear it's mixed with pain too, which is…mind-boggling. "They need to leave you alone."

"Who?"

"Everyone." His lips thin into a straight line as he murmurs, "Mercedes."

"I don't know if she's the one who tripped me."

"If it wasn't her, it was someone she told to trip you." He takes a deep breath, running a hand through his hair and messing it up in the most adorable way. "Just—watch out."

"I will."

"Tell them to back the fuck off." His searing gaze meets mine. "Don't forget who you are."

I frown at him.

"A Lancaster, Carolina. You're a Lancaster."

I bypass the dining hall at lunch, seeking out Sadie in the library, and I find her in our usual hangout spot, nibbling on a sandwich while she draws something on a sketchpad. The moment she spots me, she's flipping the sketchpad closed, her cheeks tinged pink, and I settle into the chair across from her, my tone purposely nonchalant.

"What are you drawing?"

"Nothing." Her cheeks are now bright red. "A boy."

Hmm. "Who?"

"I don't know his name. He's a senior."

"I might know him." I'm getting to know them, but not all of them.

"Oh, and he's gorgeous. Friends with the popular crowd." Sadie rolls her eyes. "He doesn't know I exist."

She knows who West is so I'm guessing she's not talking about him. "Let me see if I recognize him."

"The drawing isn't that great. You probably wouldn't be able to recognize him."

I reach for the sketchpad and she slaps her hand over it, preventing me from snagging it. "Come on, Sadie. Let me see."

Her hold loosens, and I slip the sketchpad from beneath her palm, setting it in front of me before I start flipping through the pages. There are a few landscape sketches. A couple of profile sketches. One of a horse that I pause over, the details so intricate I can't help but admire it.

"That's my old horse. I've worked on that drawing for years."

"You're really good, Sadie." I lift my gaze to hers, offering her a faint smile. "I love it."

She covers her face with her hands. "This is so embarrassing."

I find the last sketch, the one of the boy she was working on when I first came to the table. I recognize him instantly, taking in the fine details that she captured, marveling at how well she drew his handsome face.

"I know him."

"Of course, you do."

I lift my gaze to hers. "His name is Brent."

Sadie's cheeks are red again. "I know."

I frown. "You said you didn't know his name."

"I do. I lied. I didn't anticipate showing you the sketch." She tugs the pad out of my hands and flips it over so she can study her drawing. "If he ever saw this, he'd laugh at me."

"If he ever saw it, he'd most likely be impressed with your skills. You're an artist."

She shrugs. "I suppose. I've always dabbled in art. Drawing. Painting, though I prefer pencil sketches."

"Are you taking an art class here?"

"I'm in Art Four." Sadie rolls her eyes. "Brent is in that class too."

"Brent is into art?" I'm shocked. He doesn't seem the type, though I guess that's limited thinking on my part.

"He's into sculpture. He's really good." She leans back in her chair with a sigh, shaking her head. "And he doesn't give a crap about me."

"Have you tried talking to him?"

"No."

"He's really nice." I think of how kind he was to me yesterday at lunch, though I only used him which makes me the rude one.

West told him to back off for no reason other than he was jealous, and now Brent will probably never talk to me again. "You should try to talk to him in class."

"Easy for you to say. You're a Lancaster. Everyone will talk to you automatically, thanks to your last name. I don't know why you bother hiding out in the library with me. I'm sure they all want you to be their friend."

I tell her about Mercedes and how friendly she was toward me at first—until she completely turned on me. And how she's determined to make my life a living nightmare every chance she gets.

"That's really stupid of her," Sadie says when I finish my story. "Why would she come after a Lancaster? Doesn't she understand your influence? I've only just started at this school, but even I understand that."

"I think she's so secure in her position, she doesn't give a damn what my last name is." Mercedes is sitting on a house of cards. I have a feeling I could make them topple with a few choice comments in front of her group of so-called friends.

"She's a bitch," Sadie says with complete disgust. "I'm sorry she's so awful to you."

"Don't worry. I have a feeling she'll get hers soon enough." I pin Sadie with a look. "I have a suggestion, and I want you to be open to it."

"Oh God," Sadie groans, but I forge on.

"Have lunch with me tomorrow. In the dining hall. I think I can get Brent to sit with us."

The panicked look on Sadie's face is almost comical, but I know the feeling is real, so I'm definitely not laughing. "He won't want to sit with us."

"Yes, he will." I pause. "I ate lunch with him yesterday. Just the two of us."

"What, is he interested in you? I don't want to interfere—"

I cut her off with a shake of my head. "He's not interested

in me." Even if he was, he wouldn't be now, thanks to West's warning. "He's just a friend. He's a nice guy, Sadie."

At least I think he is. According to West, he uses women, but I get the sense West was just saying that to keep me away from him.

I don't know how to feel, but I'd like to at least try to pair the two of them together and see what happens. It can't hurt to try.

"He seems nice enough. I don't know. I don't trust these guys here. They all seem very…calculated. Like every move they make is deliberate."

I think of West. Is everything he's doing with me deliberate? Planned out? Is he setting me up to do something…terrible to me?

My stomach cramps and I rest my hand over it, hating how breathless I feel.

How worried I suddenly am.

CHAPTER EIGHTEEN

CAROLINA

I'm in the studio running through my barre exercises, staring at myself in the mirror when I spot a shadowy figure in the doorway. I know immediately who it is, and I pretend that I'm annoyed though deep down, I'm thrilled he unexpectedly showed up.

West.

"What do you want?" My tone is snide, my attention…not on him. I want him to believe he doesn't matter. I want to believe that too, but I'm starting to worry.

The last thing I should do is allow this boy to mean something to me. Nothing else does. Only dance.

I can't let him worm his way into my thoughts. Or my heart.

"Always so rude." He leans against the doorframe, crossing his arms in front of him. He's wearing a gray crewneck sweatshirt and black joggers, pristine white sneakers on his feet. His hair is freshly combed and his face is smooth. Handsome as ever.

I'd guess he just took a shower, while I'm verging on being a sweaty mess.

Dropping to the balls of my feet, I let go of the barre and turn to face him, trying to gain control over my chaotic thoughts.

How glad I am that he's here. How frustrated I am with him

still. How he confuses me more and more as each day passes.

"What can I say? You bring it out of me." My words are soft, without any heat behind them.

As if he senses my mood shift, he enters the studio fully, glancing over at the tiny speaker sitting on the chair. "No music today?"

"Not yet." I lift my chin, mimicking his position by crossing my arms as well. "What do you want, West?"

"I wanted to check up on you. Make sure you're okay." He drops his arms at his sides, his gaze dropping to my legs. "You fell earlier. Did you bruise?"

I glance down at my legs quickly before returning my gaze to his. "Not that I can see."

"You so sure about that?" He starts walking toward me and I do my best to calm my breathing, which only ratchets up the closer he gets.

"I stare at myself in the mirror all the time. I'm fairly certain there are no bruises," I say wryly, turning my back to him and reaching out for the barre once again. "You can go now."

"Are you dismissing me?" He sounds amused. When I meet his gaze in the mirror, he's even smiling. He slips his hands in his pockets, devastatingly handsome without doing a thing beyond existing, and I dip my head, desperate to break eye contact.

Even more confused by the emotions swirling within me.

"Do you enjoy watching yourself in the mirror?" he asks when I still haven't said anything.

I lift my head, my startled gaze meeting his. He's far closer than he was only moments ago. Close enough to touch me. Close enough that I can feel his body heat seeping into mine.

"It's part of dance, watching ourselves move. Making sure we're perfect. Precise. Or we're watching our instructors, mimicking their movements," I explain.

"Do you like to watch?" His gaze roves over me, lingering on my chest. My boobs are so small, and they look even smaller in the dark green sports bra I'm wearing. The fabric is so thick and stretchy, it flattens my chest.

"It's just...it's what I do." I shrug, sucking in a breath when my shoulder brushes his chest.

"Hmm." He crowds me, not quite touching me, settling his hands on the barre on either side of my body, trapping me where I stand. "I like to watch."

My breaths come even faster. His scent lingers, clean and fresh, and I bring my arms in closer so I don't touch him. "Watch what?"

"You." His gaze holds mine in the mirror. "Everything you do fascinates me."

I'm trembling. From his nearness. From his words. From the look in his eyes. "Why?"

"I don't know. Maybe because every time we see each other, you leave me wanting more."

"More of what?"

"More of you." His hands shift, his arms inching in closer and I hold my breath when they brush against me. He's so warm. And strong. "You tempt me even when you shouldn't."

I can relate to that. He absolutely shouldn't tempt me, yet he does.

All the time.

"I wish you weren't so afraid of me touching you," he admits, his voice hushed.

"I'm not afraid," I immediately insist.

"What is it then?"

"It makes me...uncomfortable. Personal human interaction. Touching. Affection." I close my eyes for a moment and swallow hard, surprised I'd say something like that to him.

But Weston Fontaine has always been able to draw my secrets out of me.

"Your parents must've really done a number on you," he murmurs, his mouth terribly close to my hair.

"You don't even know how much," I say, my smile sad.

"Can I confess something?" His hands inch even closer together on the barre, his arms closing in on me and a shuddery breath leaves me when he seems to wrap me up, his front pressed against my back. "I think about what we did in this room all the time."

The memory comes back to me, when I gave him a blow job. How much he seemed to enjoy it, despite my inexperience. I was so afraid of messing everything up, and he made me feel comfortable. He has this…easy way about him sometimes. He both riles me up and calms me down, and it's so confusing.

My feelings for him are—complex.

"Do you ever think about it, Carolina?" His voice is a whisper, making me shiver.

I nod once, my gaze finding his in the mirror.

"You'd never done it before, yet you let me come down your throat," he continues. "You were fucking perfect."

The shame I thought I might feel at his words doesn't come and I hold his gaze, noting the way my skin starts to turn pink. The knowing look on West's face tells me he notices too.

"Are my words turning you on?" He gently reaches around me, resting his hand on my bare stomach and I let him. I savor the heat of his fingers. How possessive his touch feels. "Are you wet?"

Growing braver by the second, I keep my gaze locked on his when I say, "Check and find out."

A faint smile curves his perfect lips and he slowly slips his fingers beneath the waistband of my booty shorts. They skim along my skin, light yet with purpose and when he slides down further to find that I'm not wearing any panties, the pleasure in his gaze is unmistakable. "Dirty girl."

I say nothing. Just revel in the way he made those two words sound like a compliment.

"Spread your legs," he whispers and I immediately do as he says, hissing in a breath when he parts me, his fingers sliding into my wetness. "Fuck, you're soaked."

My gaze drops to his hand moving beneath my shorts, stretching out the dark green fabric as he starts to stroke. I can't stop staring, feeling and seeing what he's doing to me, my lips parting when he brushes his fingers against my clit over and over again.

"Does dancing turn you on? Or is it me?" His hand pauses, his fingers resting against my pussy and I strain toward them, wishing he would stroke me more.

"It's—you," I choke out, relief flooding me when his fingers begin to move once again.

"Good girl," he murmurs. "Right answer."

He touches and teases, humming against my temple when a whimper escapes me.

"Take off the shorts," he demands.

I reach for the waistband with shaky fingers, shoving at the Lycra fabric, pushing them down past my hips and exposing my lower half completely within seconds. They fall to my knees, binding me in place and he reaches down with his free hand, pushing the fabric further down, helping me get rid of them completely.

Until I'm standing there with him fully clothed behind me while I'm only in my sports bra, his large hand completely covering my pussy, his busy fingers stroking me into oblivion.

"Look at you." He turns his head toward me, his mouth on my cheek, sliding down to my neck, his breath warm against my skin as he kisses me there. Tiny, tender kisses that make me shiver. "Are you close?"

My nod is almost frantic, a moan sounding low in my throat when he presses his fingers hard against my clit. He rubs it in small circles, the pressure just right and leaving me panting.

Wanting.

"Keep your eyes on me," he murmurs against my cheek, his gaze going to the mirror, meeting mine. "Don't look away, Carolina."

I couldn't even if I wanted to. My gaze stays on his as he continues stroking me, his pace growing faster, making it hard to breathe. To focus. I stare at his busy hand, my trembling thighs, my hips that I didn't even realize were moving. My head falls back, leaning against his shoulder, everything centered on that one spot he keeps rubbing. Pressing. Stroking.

The sensations build, growing stronger and stronger and I strain toward them, angling my hips just so, seeking his touch in a particular spot. It's as if he can read my mind, my body, because his fingers are exactly where I want them. His speed increases, going faster and faster and I'm breathless.

Weightless.

I pitch forward when the orgasm hits me, a choked groan falling from my lips as I practically bend in half. He keeps me upright, his fingers holding me there as I rub shamelessly against his palm, the electrified sensation racing through my limbs, my blood, pounding in my very soul.

When I come back to my senses, I'm a shaky mess and West gathers me in his arms, holding me close. His fingers tangle in my hair and I press my face against his chest, trying to calm my breathing. Taking in his delicious scent. He slips his fingers beneath my chin, tipping my face up so he can kiss me and the press of his lips upon mine is gentle. Sweet. His tongue a delicious tease that I respond to with a sweep of my own.

Slowly but surely, he calms me down, though my body still quivers. He whispers soothing words against my ear, reassuring me that I'm going to be okay but I don't know.

When it comes to what West and I share, I have no idea how I'll survive it. But I know one thing.

What a beautiful way to go.

CHAPTER NINETEEN

CAROLINA

"How's school? How are your classes?"

I tap my pencil against the edge of my desk, staring out the window that overlooks the campus grounds. It's late afternoon and a storm is rolling in. The clouds are dark and heavy with rain and all evening practices and campus activities have been canceled for the night in preparation.

You'd think it had never rained at Lancaster Prep before, which is ridiculous. I just spent the last five years in London, where it rains all the time. I don't understand the worry and the hype. Where I used to live, it was just any other day.

"It's all right. My classes are boring," I tell my sister, Sylvie. I'm shocked she called me. Usually, she's so wrapped up in her own bullshit, she rarely thinks about me. "Why are you calling?"

"Can't I call my little sister and check up on her?"

"Can't you just text me and be done with it?" I return.

She sighs, and I can hear the irritation in that one simple sound. "Mother asked me to call you."

"Why can't she call me herself? Oh, I know why. I'll just ignore it and not answer." I toss the pencil across my bedroom, watching it land on the floor and roll underneath my bed.

"She's worried about you."

"Is that what she told you to tell me or did you come up with that yourself?"

My sister aggravates me, but not nearly as much as our mother. It feels like Sylvie doesn't have a mind of her own. Like my sister's life is completely run by our mother, and Sylvie has no problem with it. I couldn't live like that.

That's the reason I left home so young. To get away from my mother—not that she cared.

"I know she's worried about you, Lina. She tells me all the time that you never talk to her."

"I don't want to talk to her. She's psychotic."

"That must be where I get it from," Sylvie says, her voice tinged with amusement.

Her mental health issues—along with her physical health concerns—are well known yet confusing. No one can figure out exactly what's wrong with my sister. Not any of the medical teams or group of specialists our mother has taken Sylvie to see. I personally think it's all in her head, but maybe I'm wrong.

And then again, maybe I'm not.

"Are your classes hard? Is Matthews still there? He was headmaster when I went there," Sylvie says, sounding nostalgic.

"Matthews is still headmaster, and no, the classes aren't hard, save for American Government. I'm practically an English citizen, how am I expected to know and understand how the government here works?" I'm whining, but it's Sylvie, and I know she'll understand.

"I barely graduated, so do better than me, okay?" She makes a tsking noise. "At least you'll be able to go back and dance once you're done."

"Hopefully." My stomach dips. That's my biggest worry. Will I be welcomed back with open arms at the dance company, or will they flat out reject me? Will I need to find somewhere else to dance? I'm sure I could, but I don't want to. I want to go back to London.

I need everything to go back to normal.

"Oh, you will," Sylvie says with the utmost confidence. I wish I felt that confident. "I can see it now. You'll be dancing in London, the star of the show."

We chat for a little longer until I say I have to go, ending the call on her before she can protest. I let my phone drop on my desk and rest my elbows on the edge, burying my face in my hands.

Talking to my family is exhausting. Pretending everything is perfectly fine is par for the course with my sister and especially my mother. I'm allowed to be a bit more vulnerable with my father, but with my brother? I don't know how to act around Whit most of the time.

So, I avoid him at all costs.

Rising from my desk, I walk over to the window and stare outside. West and I haven't really talked much, but we've definitely continued seeing each other. In class, during lunch, we act like we barely know each other, but after school he'll show up at my dance studio and we'll do...things.

All sorts of things.

Lots of kissing. To the point where my jaw hurts and my tongue is tired. I don't flinch anymore when he touches me. Not really. I think I'm growing used to him.

I start expecting him to show up, anticipation curling through my blood, leaving me weak every time he appears. I could get addicted to this boy if I don't watch it.

Maybe I already am.

He's steering clear of Mercedes and I'm doing the same with Brent. Why would I provoke West? It's pointless.

I did try to get Brent to have lunch with me and Sadie the day after she confessed she had a thing for him, but he kept putting me off. And Sadie essentially begged me to leave it alone, so I did.

Reluctantly.

I'm all for pairing up Sadie with Brent, but publicly pairing myself up with West? I don't know if it's logistically possible, and besides, it might be a terrible idea. Being with someone else. Letting someone have that kind of power over me completely.

It's scary.

The longer I stand at the window, the further the sky darkens until the sun all but disappears and all I can see is gloomy skies. Lightning flashes in the distance, a silvery bolt of light across the sky, followed by the low rumble of thunder, and I wrap my arms around myself to ward off the sudden chill.

I spot someone walking along the sidewalk, his wide steps eating up the space, his gait determined. I recognize the color of his hair, the way he moves, and my heart leaps to my throat, threatening to cut off all my oxygen.

West.

And he's heading right for my building.

Turning away from the window, I go to the full-length mirror hanging on my wall, grimacing at the sight that greets me. I look a mess. I'm still in my uniform, sans the jacket and my shoes, still wearing knee-high socks and my skirt, my white button-down wrinkled and untucked, hanging so long it practically covers the hem of my skirt. I wore my hair in a ponytail and there are so many stray strands sticking up all around my face, I look like I've been electrocuted.

Desperate, I run my fingers through my hair, trying to straighten the mess before I give up and tuck the shirt back into my skirt. I glance around, wishing I could change into something else. Something that would make me feel pretty and feminine, and just when my gaze lands on a few dresses that are hanging on the back of my closet door, there's a loud, rapid-fire knock.

Swallowing hard, I move toward the door and lean my head against it. "Who is it?"

"It's me," West says, his voice brimming with confidence, he's that assured I know who's waiting for me on the other side.

Trying to hide my sudden desperation, I do my best to school my expression into something bland before I fling open the door and let him in, not surprised at all when he makes his way inside, his gaze curious as it slides all over my belongings.

"What do you want?" I ask, still keeping the door open.

He sends me a smirk from over his shoulder, walking deeper into my room. "Nice to see you too."

I shut the door, silently reprimanding myself for sounding borderline hostile. "I'm just—surprised. You don't usually come to my room."

"I know. Guess I'm trying to change it up." He hesitates. "I thought about it, and what if someone caught us in there? Together?"

God I'm so stupid. I always get so caught up in what we're doing, I never think about someone finding us. "That would be..."

"Awful," he finishes for me. He must see the alarm I suddenly feel in my expression because he's quick to say, "Not that it's bad we're spending time together. We just don't want to be—exposed yet. Right?"

"Yes." I nod. "Right. So that's why you're here? In my room? Because it's more private?"

"Yeah." He turns to face me fully, his expression so neutral it's almost annoying. "And I guess I also...missed you."

I lean against the door, shocked by his admission. "You did?"

He stops next to my desk, his fingers drifting across the top of it, picking up a pen and holding it in his fingers, clicking it again and again. "Yeah. I did."

My heart feels like it might crack in two, but I tell it to get over itself. "Well, I didn't really miss you."

"You didn't?" He grins, seemingly pleased by my denial.

I lift my chin, giving a singular shake of my head. "We just saw each other earlier in class. And I've been busy. Between my studies and dance..."

"So you haven't thought about me."

"Nope." I'm such a liar.

"Not at all." He drops the pen on my desk and starts to

approach me, his expression dark. Almost feral. As if he's thinking of the many things he wants to do to me, none of them proper or kind.

My legs wobble and I lock my knees.

"Uh uh."

He stops directly in front of me, his hand reaching out to hook into the space on my shirt between the buttons, sliding a single finger inside, brushing against my stomach. "I don't believe you."

"Y-you d-don't?" I close my eyes, hating how I stuttered my words. Hating even more how weak I sound. He's got me exactly where he wants me, and I'm positive he knows it.

"If I've been on your mind even half the amount of time that you've been on mine, then I'd call you…" He tugs me to him by pulling on my shirt, and I have no choice but to stumble my way toward him. "Obsessed."

It's the way he says the word, as if he's tasting it. As if he's imagining tasting me and I dare to lift my head, to find his gaze locked on my face, heavy and full of—dare I say—longing.

"You haven't been to the dance studio yet?"

I frown. "How did you know?"

"You're still in your uniform," he points out.

"So are you," I return.

"We should rectify that." He removes his hold on my shirt, his fingers returning to the line of buttons as he starts to undo them.

I pull away from his grasp, turning my back to him, completely overstimulated. Panic grips at my heart, making it race, and I mentally tell myself to calm down. I had become somewhat used to his touch, but this moment feels different. You can't just come into my room and start undressing me."

He's silent, and I worry I might've upset him. Maybe he's even preparing to leave but then he speaks.

"You're right. I shouldn't assume."

Shock courses through me, but I remain standing in front of my window once more, watching as the first drops of rain hit the ground, dotting the sidewalk over and over again until the concrete is a wet, dark gray. I brace my hand against the window frame, a shuddery breath leaving me when I feel him shift behind me, his breath stirring the hair at the back of my neck.

He doesn't touch me. He doesn't say a word. Just stands there and lets me get used to his presence. Oh so slowly, I find myself leaning back, leaning into him, knowing he'll be there for me, which he is.

My spine connects with his chest and I close my eyes, melting into him. He reaches around me, his arm hovering, as is his hand, and I give my permission with the tiniest nod.

West settles his hand on my stomach, his fingers splayed, touching so much of me I feel owned. Possessed.

"Who did this to you?" he whispers, his voice so faint I almost don't hear him. He just asked this question a few days ago, and it's like he can't let it go. "Who made you hate physical touch so badly?"

I dip my head and open my eyes, watching as he slides his fingers toward the buttons on my shirt, his fingers dropping, teasing at the hem. "I already told you. No one did it to me. I just—I trust no one."

"You seem to trust me." His hand swoops beneath my shirt, hot fingers resting against my stomach, burning into my skin.

"Not quite."

"Enough for me to do this." He toys with the waistband of my skirt and I watch his fingers slide beneath it, fascinated.

"I can't stop wondering what you taste like," he whispers in my ear, his hand sliding farther down, fingertips skimming along the top edge of my panties. "I've licked my fingers after they've been inside you, but it's not enough."

Thank God he's holding me or I'd probably collapse on the floor.

"The visual of you on your knees with my cock stuffed in your mouth lives rent free in my mind," he continues, and I lean my head back, resting it on his shoulder.

That memory lives in my mind too. It's a good one.

Too good.

"All the times in your studio—it just gets better and better," he says.

I don't respond, but I definitely agree.

It does get better every time we're together.

"I shouldn't admit this to you. I'm sure it makes me sound weak." His fingers creep beneath my panties, moving downward until he's firmly cupping me. "But I can't stop thinking about you."

His fingers slip between my lower lips roughly, making me gasp. Making my pussy flood with moisture. He lifts up, like he's trying to carry me with his hand curved around my pelvis and I lift my head, my neck fully exposed, his hand gripping my sex as if he wants to render me into two pieces.

"Always so wet." His mouth moves against my neck, making me shiver. "I wonder how many times I can make you come tonight."

"West." His name is said on a moan, and I close my eyes, thrusting my hips forward as he continues to rub me aggressively, my clit already on fire. "Please…"

"Please what? Please stop? Please make me come? Please do it harder?" His fingers pause, my entire pussy throbbing, protesting when he stops rubbing me. "What do you want, Carolina?"

I don't know how to tell him what I want without saying it in the crudest way possible, so that's exactly what I do.

"I want you to fuck me."

He goes completely still, the only thing moving is his thumb, which lightly brushes my distended clit. Every pass on my flesh lights a spark deep within me, making my breaths come faster and making me feel as if I'm going to collapse into convulsions.

"Not yet," he mutters into my neck, his hand shifting so his palm presses directly into me, grinding on my clit, "I want to put my mouth on you first."

A flash of lightning illuminates the sky, casting light into my room and my heart jumps. West remains unfazed, his mouth drifting up and down my neck as I ride his palm, thrusting my hips forward, trying to get more of that delicious friction.

"I told myself I would stay away from you tonight and give you a break, but I can't." He releases his hold on me completely, so fast I stumble forward and nearly fall onto the bed. "Get undressed."

I do as he says without protest, confusion swirling within me. Why is he able to command me so easily? Why do I give in every single time?

Can't worry about it now, I think as I undo the buttons on my shirt with shaky fingers, whipping it off my body and tossing it onto the floor. Next is my bra, which unhooks in the front and is gone in a matter of seconds. Years in dance, competing, recitals, rehearsals...teaches you how to change quickly.

I'm about to take off my skirt when his firm voice makes me freeze.

"Leave the skirt on." He pauses. "But take off your panties."

I stare at him, surprised by his demand. Surprised even more at the way my panties flood with moisture at the image his request brings to mind.

Never taking my gaze off him, I slip my hands beneath my skirt and reach for the waistband of my panties, slowly tugging them down until they appear just beneath my skirt, wrapped around my knees.

"Let them fall," he says, and I stand up straight, my panties falling down my legs until they land around my ankles. "Kick them off."

I step one foot out of them, then kick the scrap of cotton to the side with the other. Until I'm standing there, basically naked, with only the plaid skirt covering me. My nipples are so hard they ache, and I flinch when another flash of lightning shines into my room. I feel blatantly on display, the sound of the cold, harsh wind outside making me shiver, and I jump when West says, "Sit on the edge of the bed."

Again, I do as he says, appreciating the commands. I have no idea what I'm doing and it's obvious that he does, so I'm grateful for the instruction. It's almost like dance. I'm told how to position myself. Where to go and how to do it. I've been treated this way my entire life.

There's comfort in that, as odd as it sounds.

I sit there with my hands twisted in my lap, my head bent, my hair falling like a curtain on either side of my face. I watch the floor as he takes a few steps forward, until his feet are directly in front of my bare ones, his black dress shoes so shiny, I can almost see my reflection in them.

He's completely dressed, while I'm basically naked, and everything within me draws up tight at the realization. I curl my bare toes inward, suddenly ashamed of my ugly dancer's feet, and when I feel his fingers drift over the top of my head, I almost cry out in relief. His touching me feels like approval and I desperately need it.

"All this pretty blonde hair," he murmurs. "You Lancasters all look the same."

His words almost hurt. I don't want to be lumped in with the rest of them.

"Yet you're blonder. Your eyes." His fingers slip beneath my chin, tilting my face up so I have no choice but to meet his gaze. "Bluer."

I'm trembling. Nervous. Excited. The back of my arms rub against my nipples, making them ache even more, and he strokes his thumb across my chin, looking pleased.

With me.

"Lie back," he practically croons, and as if I'm under his spell, I lie down on the bed, my gaze never shifting from his, my skirt rising with the movement, nearly exposing my most private spot.

West takes a step back, his gaze roaming over me, heat

lighting my skin everywhere his eyes land. What he's doing to me is exquisite torture, and I don't ever want it to end.

Why did I stay away from him again? Why did we maintain our distance from each other? It doesn't make any sense. Not when we could've been doing this for the last few days.

"Lift your skirt," he says, and I curl my fingers around the hem, pulling it up slowly, until I'm fully exposed. "Spread your legs. I want to see it."

I spread them, the air hitting my damp pussy, making me suck in a breath.

He's silent, studying me, and I want to squirm. I want to cry out in frustration and beg him to do something. Anything.

"Touch yourself."

I go still, lifting my head a little in question.

"Go on." He nods, waving his hand. "Touch yourself. I want to watch."

I rest my right hand on my stomach and slide it down. Over the slope of my belly, until my fingers are touching my pubic hair. I don't dare go any farther, suddenly afraid.

I've never really touched myself like this before. Well, I did earlier but that doesn't really count. I've never viewed my body as a sexual vessel. I've always seen it as a machine that could twirl and spin and jump and leap. That's it.

"Do it, Carolina." I close my eyes, fighting the humiliation I feel over my hesitation. "If you don't touch yourself, I won't touch you either."

CHAPTER TWENTY

CAROLINA

I don't know what has come over me—over us. I didn't know it could be like this. I mean, I've heard of things like this. Dominance and submission. Being told what to do and getting off on it.

I just didn't realize I would actually like that sort of thing.

"Carolina." West's voice is sharp, and I automatically slide my hand down, cupping myself. Testing myself. My pussy is hot. And so wet—embarrassingly so. I didn't know it could get this wet, and when I start to stroke, the sounds fill the room.

"Touch your clit," he directs, and I press my finger against it, a sizzling jolt of electricity pulsing through my veins. "Rub it."

I wish he was the one who was touching me. I love that he's telling me what to do, but I want more. I want him to be the one who's stroking me.

I want to know what it feels like, to have his mouth on me.

Increasing my pace, I rub my clit in tight circles, my stomach clenching, my entire body electrified. I brace my feet on the mattress and bend my knees, lifting my hips toward my busy hand as I continue stroking myself. I could come like this, I think, my mind growing hazier and hazier. I could come over and over again, knowing West was watching.

"Stop." He's on me in an instant, his hands on my ankles as he yanks my legs down, spreading them as wide as they can go. I open my eyes just in time to see his face. His eyes wild, his skin flushed. "It's my turn."

Thank God, I think as he bats my hand away from my pussy, his hot gaze drinking me in. He reaches out, his fingers tracing my slit, gathering my juices before he brings his fingers to his mouth and sucks them between his lips.

His gaze never strays from mine as he licks his fingers before returning them to my pussy. His touch is gentle, barely there, and I strain toward him, needing more.

Needing it harder.

He dips his head and kisses my stomach, his lips hot. Soft. A sigh leaves me as he blazes a trail across my skin, his body shifting between my legs, his mouth drawing closer and closer to where I want him.

I rest my hand on top of his head, my fingers curling in his thick hair. I tug on the strands, testing to see how hard I can take it, but he doesn't say a word. Just continues licking and kissing my skin, his mouth sliding over me, his tongue a hot rasp against my sensitive skin.

When he settles his mouth directly on my pussy, I nearly bow off the bed. He rests his hand on my stomach, keeping me in place as he sucks my clit between his lips, his other hand braced on the inside of my thigh, squeezing tight.

It hurts in a delicious way. The contrast of his soft tongue and hot lips and the firm grip of his hands has me spiraling. I'm on sensory overload, and I can already feel the orgasm pressing down. Drawing closer. I pull my legs in, clamping either side of his head with my thighs, and he pushes a finger inside me, then adds another.

Then another.

He stretches me full with three fingers, slowing pumping them in and out while he attacks my clit with his mouth. Shuddery moans leave me and I arch my neck, my mouth falling open when the orgasm slams into me out of nowhere. Like a punch to the stomach.

I'm coming. Heat radiates through my blood, along my skin. I'm trembling, my stomach heaving, my heart racing.

It's too much. It's not enough.

When it's finally over, I lie in the middle of my bed in a boneless heap, only just noticing the sounds of the storm raging outside. Wind batters at the windows, rain splattering against the glass, accompanied by the low rumble of thunder.

I feel like that storm. Chaotic and destructive. What West just did to me...

Is hard for me to wrap my mind around. How my body could react to his touch, his words...his commands. It's as if I have no control over myself.

He's the one who controls me. At least in this way.

The mattress shifts and I open my eyes to watch him climb off the bed and walk over to the window. He stares out at the darkened sky, his brow furrowed as he watches the storm, his fingers tugging at his bottom lip. I'm sure his face smells like me.

I want to kiss him and see, but I'm suddenly shy.

"I should probably go," he says, his voice low, his gaze still on the window.

"It's too stormy outside." I sit up, realizing my skirt is still on so I tug it down, covering my lower half. "Maybe you should wait it out."

"No." He barely glances at me. "I'm leaving."

I blink at his stern tone. What's wrong with him? Is he mad? Upset with me? What did I do? Grind on his face and come all over his mouth? Is that a crime?

Maybe in West's eyes, it is.

"You don't care, do you?" He turns to face me and I take in his messy hair and flushed face. His rumpled shirt that's untucked, hiding what I assume is a raging erection tenting his pants. I remember feeling it against my leg, so I know it's there. "You don't seem like the cuddly-after-sex type."

Not sure why, but I'm offended by his assumption. Even though he's right. I don't like cuddling. As he well knows, I'm not fond of physical touch.

But for some odd reason, I want him to hold me close. Whisper reassuring words in my ear, making me feel wanted instead of used.

That's how I feel right now. Used. Even though I'm the one who got off, I still feel that way, and I don't like it.

"I'm out." He heads for the door, his tone so casual I almost don't believe he made me come with his mouth and fingers just a few minutes ago. Only my still throbbing pussy and aching thighs remind me that's exactly what happened.

I remain quiet, unable to speak thanks to the lump in my throat. Besides, what would I say? Don't go? Please stay?

That's not my style. It's not his either.

"See you tomorrow." He rests his hand on the door handle and glances back at me from over his shoulder, his gaze finding mine. There's no emotion in his eyes. They're almost...flat? "Bye, Carolina."

The door shuts at the same time I whisper, "Bye," but he didn't hear me.

I remain rooted to the bed, bending my legs at the knee and wrapping my arms around them, curling my body into a ball. I'm shivering, the angry storm not helping matters, and I rest my head on top of my knees, closing my eyes.

I don't know what just happened, but I'm rattled.

And I'm pretty sure West is too.

. . .

The next day dawns dark and dreary, the clouds hanging low in the sky, fat with rain. It drizzles all morning and by the time I'm in American Government, I'm a mess of nerves, both eager to see West, yet dreading it too.

He probably won't even look at me.

Brent enters the classroom, his gaze landing on me, and he heads straight for my desk, settling into the one behind mine.

"How do you know Sadie?"

I turn around to face him, trying to contain my excitement. Did she get up the nerve to talk to him? I'm so proud of her. "How do *you* know Sadie?"

"She's in my art class." His cheeks turn the faintest pink, as if he's embarrassed he takes art. Men. Toxic masculinity is strong here at Lancaster Prep. "She mentioned that you two are friends. I have no idea who she is."

"She's new here and she's really sweet." I tilt my head. "How did you two get to talking?"

"We were assigned to work on a project together. We just sort of started talking and it was—easy." He shrugs, purposely trying to seem like it was no big deal. Which gives me a hint that maybe he likes her? I don't know. I'm probably reading too much into this. "She's nice."

"She is. I like her a lot. We hang out at lunch together."

"I've never seen the two of you together at lunch."

"We hang out in the library together." I smile at him. "You should join us sometime."

"I don't know—"

"Don't you two look cozy?"

We both glance up to find Mercedes standing in front of us, Marcy next to her, both of them wearing matching shitty smiles.

"You finally going for it with her, Brent? Like you said you would?" Mercedes' eyebrows lift.

Something tells me Brent never said anything like that to Mercedes. She's just trying to cause trouble. Possibly to get my hopes up, only for me to be let down.

Ah, if she only knew who had his face buried between my legs last night, she'd die of mortification, wouldn't she?

"I, uh…" Brent glances over at me before he ducks his head, as if he might be embarrassed.

"Aw, did I expose you just now? Sorry." Mercedes makes a tsking noise and Marcy laughs, like what her bitchy best friend said is soooo funny.

It's not.

"Why don't you mind your own business and go sit down?"

I'm shocked the words came out of my mouth, but then again, I'm not. This girl keeps pushing me and I'm tired of it.

Mercedes' eyes narrow and there's a sneer on her face. "What did you just say to me?"

"You heard me." I lift my chin. "Stay out of my business. Not that I should bother telling you, but Brent and I are just friends. Right, Brent?"

I send him a look when he lifts his head and he nods in agreement, the relief on his face obvious. "Yeah. We're friends."

"Right." Mercedes frowns. "Friends who fuck maybe? I've heard stories, you know. Brent has a reputation around campus."

"Mercedes—"

"As a matter of fact, no, Brent and I don't fuck. Ever. West, though? You should ask him all about us. Like what we did together last night." I smirk at her, not even caring that I blew our cover. That I exposed our secret. This shitty girl deserves to hear it. To know that West isn't interested in her.

He's interested in me.

Mercedes laughs in my freaking face like the bitch she is. "Please. You wouldn't know what to do with West's dick if he slapped your cheek with it."

"I'm fairly certain he'd rather slap my cheek with his dick rather than yours, but maybe I'm wrong? Maybe we should ask him." I raise my brows, doing my best not to contain my own laughter.

Her good mood fades, her face contorting into an ugly, angry mask. "You wish. I can't wait to tell him about you acting like he's into you. Please. You're just a child. A sheltered, little good girl who's scared someone might dare to touch you."

How does she know I don't like to be touched? God, did West tell her? He would never.

Would he?

Class eventually starts and West is nowhere to be found, which leaves me confused. Where is he? Where did he go? Is he sick? Did he leave campus? Did he ditch school?

By lunchtime I scan the dining hall, but he's not there. Before I get caught by Mercedes and her rude crew, I head to the library, grateful when I spot Sadie's smiling, excited face in the back of the building.

"I talked to Brent," is how she greets me.

I settle into the chair beside her, trying to get caught up in her good mood versus wallowing in my bad one. "I know."

Her smile slips. "How do you know? Oh God, are people talking about us? About me?"

"No, no. He told me. Asked me how I knew you." I give her a reassuring pat on the arm, snatching my hand away from her when I realize I'm voluntarily touching someone else and not minding it either.

"Was he nice about it? Or does he think I'm pathetic?" Sadie's worried expression almost breaks my heart, she seems so distressed.

"He doesn't think you're pathetic. You're completely overreacting. He had nothing but nice things to say about you."

"Okay." She nods and exhales loudly, her lips pursed. "That's good."

"Don't freak out. Just—take it slow and see what happens." I smile at her and she smiles back, but it's tentative at best.

There's no way I can tell her what happened with Mercedes. How she's spreading rumors that Brent and I are a thing—though maybe I should tell her and confirm that it's not true.

She'd know it wasn't true though, right? I'm not interested in Brent like that. He's nice, he's good-looking, but when I talk to him, I feel nothing.

All West has to do is look at me and I'm a trembling mess.

Instead of bringing any of that negativity up, I let Sadie ramble on about her interaction with Brent, slowly but surely losing focus, my thoughts returning to West. Where is he?

Why did he run away?

CHAPTER TWENTY-ONE

WEST

I received the text from my father last night, discovering it just after I made Carolina come with my mouth, while I was standing at the window watching the storm rage outside. His text made me feel as angry as that storm, barely able to contain myself.

We need to talk.

No one wants to receive a text like that, not even me, especially not from my father. Our relationship is fraught with tension. It always has been. He fully expects me to take over the family business, but I have no interest in it, not that he cares. This is the problem with being an only child.

All expectations fall on you.

I got out of Carolina's room as fast as possible, knowing full well I confused the hell out of her, but I couldn't help it. Having my father text out of nowhere is unusual, even for him. I know he loves a good surprise attack, but this is odd.

We spoke on the phone when I returned to my dorm, though he really didn't say anything substantial. He basically requested that I come to New York City and talk to him, so here I am in a suite at one of the swankiest hotels in Midtown, sitting at a boardroom table all by myself and fidgeting in my seat. I let Matthews know I couldn't make it to class today and he was fine with it. Well, his secretary was.

I check my phone, hoping for a message from Carolina, but then I realize she doesn't have my phone number, so I squash that hope completely.

Stupid.

I would've taken things so much farther last night if not for that damn text from dear old dad. I'm dreading what he wants to talk to me about. Something to do with the business, no doubt. I turned eighteen over the summer, and he insisted I sign a bunch of paperwork along with all of the members of the House of Fontaine board. Something to do with a transfer of power in case of my father's absence or death. I don't even fully understand what I signed, but at the time I didn't really care either.

I'm not attached to the vineyards or the wine and champagne making like my father is, and his father before him. It's not in my blood, the need to wander the vineyards and check for the best grapes. Perfecting the right blend to bottle and sell. I enjoy drinking it—we make some of the best in the world and I'd fight anyone who challenged that title—but I don't want to run the business. I don't want it to consume my life like it does for my dad.

But shit. I have no idea what I want to do with my life.

The door swings open and my father appears, regal in a black Brioni suit, his white shirt and red tie appearing extra crisp, as usual.

The man is intimidating, with a shark's smile and foreboding dark eyes. He doesn't fuck with much—meaning not many people can get something over him. He's sharp as hell and quick-witted, and while I know I have some of his traits, he always knows how to get the best of me.

And it sucks.

"Weston." I automatically rise to my feet when he says my name, letting him hug me. I return the gesture, lightly patting him on the back, the two of us not exactly comfortable with expressing affection.

I'm reminded of Carolina and how I'm slowly getting her used to my physical touch, and I realize there's hardly a moment that I can't relate it to Carolina somehow.

"Hi, Dad," I tell him when he withdraws, remaining standing until he settles into a chair at the head of the table. I sit in the chair to the right of him, waiting for him to speak, trying to ignore the nerves that gnaw at my insides.

"You're looking well." He inclines his head toward me and my gaze drops to the black leather portfolio sitting on the table directly in front of him. I don't recall seeing him bring that in, so I'm not sure when it appeared.

"Thank you. So are you." The formalities between us are excruciating. I wonder if he can feel it? If Mom was here, she'd be the buffer between us. Her presence eases the tension between Dad and me. We haven't really even said anything, yet it's always there, brewing between us like that damn storm last night.

"How is school coming along?"

"My grades are good." I shrug, knowing for a fact that he's already checked my grades. He logs into the school portal and looks at them almost daily. He told me that once, and I never forgot.

The line of questioning feels like a formality. A bunch of mindless small talk before we get down to the real business.

"Did you join cross country like you mentioned to me?" His brows lift.

"No." That was a fleeting idea at the end of my junior year, when I was still on a high after winning the state championship, and I never wanted to stop running. "Decided it wasn't my thing. I prefer short distance."

"Probably can't pace yourself for long distance." The insult is small, but its aim is true—straight to my ego.

I decide to ignore the comment and be more direct. "Why are you here?"

They've lived the last few years on the West Coast—specifically the Napa Valley. There's a Fontaine vineyard there that my father has been working on, overseeing the creation of new wines.

"I went to France first and spent some time at the vineyard. The soil is changing. The sun is too hot for too long. We've been making accommodations, but it's not quite working. Yet." He smiles, but I see the worry in his gaze. He's been worried about the weather changes for a while. All of France and even the UK are worried too. Less champagne is being produced, yet it's more in demand than ever.

"How was your visit?"

"Productive. Fruitful." He smiles at his subtle pun. "You should've come with me."

"You didn't ask."

"I knew you'd turn me down," he counters. "Though you're exactly where you need to be. Working on your studies. Enjoying your last year of freedom."

Dread coats my skin and I go completely still at his use of the term, *last year of freedom*.

How fucking ominous of him.

"What do you mean?"

"A—complication has arisen, and I don't know how to work around it." He rubs his chin, his gaze turning thoughtful as he stares off into the distance. "There are going to be changes."

"Changes in what?"

"Your life. Mine." He finally meets my gaze and I notice how hollow his cheeks are. His eyes dark, almost haunted. "I'm not well, son."

My mind has a hard time processing what he's saying. "What do you mean?"

A ragged sigh escapes him and he leans back in his chair, reaching out to pluck at the edge of the leather portfolio in front of him. "I'm sick."

My ears start to ring.

"Cancer."

My head joins in, making it hard to hear.

"Where is it?" When he stares at me blankly, I clear my throat. "The cancer. Of what?"

"Oh. The lungs. The liver. Everywhere. I let it spread." He chuckles, shaking his head, his gaze dropping. "I didn't believe them when they first told me. An entire team of doctors ran tests on me and I didn't want to believe the results. I went to other doctors. Other specialists. Holistic healing. Natural herbs and pastes and treatments. I have done all sorts of things over the last six months."

The last six months? And he didn't tell me?

"I didn't want to worry you. Your mother is stressed and anxious and had to be put on medication. She believes I'm healed, only because that's what I told her." His smile is more like a baring of teeth, his skin stretched tight over the bones in his face, giving him a skeletal appearance. "I'm dying."

The two words are like a slap to the face, and despite the tension and the animosity and the anger this man has made me feel over the last few years, it takes everything inside me not to break down and cry at the finality of his words. His tone.

He's dying.

"What do you need me to do?" My throat is dry. All of the moisture in my body seems to be welling in my eyes, and I close them tightly, mentally telling myself not to cry.

I can't cry.

Not in front of him.

Not in front of anyone.

I need to remain strong.

"Finish school. Hopefully I'll be around until you graduate." His smile grows, and I feel a single tear slide from the corner of my eye, making its way down my cheek. "Aw, don't cry. You know I was hard on you for most of your life. You don't need to shed any tears over me."

"You're my father." I swallow down the sob that wants to escape. "Of course, I'm going to be emotional when you tell me you're—dying."

"It's all part of life, son." His expression is somber. "Something you'll have to get used to. We have things in place in case I pass before you graduate high school, but the moment you do, I need you to step in and take over."

"Take over what?"

"The business. This is my legacy, what I'm leaving you with to carry on our family name. You're young, just a baby, but you can step up. Step into my role. There are people at Fontaine who will help you. Guide you." His gaze turns almost pleading, a look I've never seen him wear before. "You could graduate early and I'll guide you myself."

I'm shaking my head, bracing my hands against the edge of the table. This is the last thing I want to do. The last thing I expected him to say to me.

"I need you." His voice breaks, and he presses his lips together as if he needs to compose himself. "I need you to come back to Napa with me."

"I—"

"Please." He shakes his head, a chuckle leaving him. Almost as if he's laughing at himself. "I'm not one to beg, you know this. But I need you, Weston. I need you to come back with me and help me take care of the business. Let me teach you whatever I can. I know I mentioned that you're getting your last year of freedom, but my own selfish needs are rearing their ugly head right now and I-I need you. Your mother needs you."

Pulling out the mom card is a low blow. She may drive me crazy sometimes, but I love her. She's my mom. And I hate the thought of her being alone, suffering through all of this and never telling me what's going on.

They've both suffered in silence and it's fucking weird, but par for the course. Our family is all about secrets, mostly when they're unnecessary. My parents claim they prefer to keep their business private, but they take it way too far.

Like this, for example.

"Why didn't you tell me that you had cancer?" I ask him, letting all my hostility bleed into my voice.

"Like I said, we didn't want to worry you."

"Right. Great excuse. Instead, you keep it to yourselves and try to deal with it, only to spring all of this on me in a matter of minutes." I throw my hands up in the air, frustrated. "I can't just drop everything and go to California with you. I have a life here. I'm going to school. I need to graduate."

I'm just a fucking kid, is what I want to tell him. His expectations are way too high, but they always have been.

"And you have a life and responsibility waiting for you in Napa as well." He shrugs, very much an 'oh well' gesture. "You're right. I didn't handle this correctly. I never said I was perfect. I truly believed I would recover and be in remission in no time. That's not how it worked out for me, and unfortunately, that means I need your help. I know you're young and what I'm asking from you is a lot, but we need you, West. This business is an empire. You're set for fucking life. You'll barely have to do anything to manage it beyond make decisions with the board and staff, and you'll have consult teams to check in with on your every move. It's simple. It's already a smooth-running machine."

He doesn't mention how no one will respect me, and there are sure to be more than a few employees pissed that I was handed the reins without having to do a damn thing to earn them.

"You should sell it." That's what I've always wanted. Huge luxury conglomerates have been buying up a variety of brands, including alcohol and specifically champagne. I know a few have made offers to my father over the last few years, but he's always turned them down.

Dad shakes his head. "Never."

We'd make a shit ton of money. We're already set for life, but a deal like I just mentioned would take care of Fontaines for generations to come.

"And I don't want you selling it either," he tacks on, his voice firm, his gaze intense. "This business has been in the Fontaine family going back almost two hundred years. And I want it to stay that way."

I remain quiet, hating my thoughts.

Once he's dead, he won't know what I do with the business. And if I have my way...

I'll get rid of it.

For good.

CHAPTER TWENTY-TWO

CAROLINA

West hasn't been on the Lancaster Prep campus for almost a week. And I don't know where he is. He hasn't called me or tried to reach out. Not that he has my phone number to call or text, but it's just weird, how he disappeared without a trace.

People talk about him at school, but no one else seems to know where he is either. Not even his friends. I cornered TJ and Brent right before American Government and they both claimed they haven't heard from him. I find that hard to believe, but as the days go on, they seem just as perplexed as I am.

At least with West gone, Mercedes has moved on from terrorizing me. She's found a new man to dig her claws in—some poor, dumb soul named Cooper, with a handsome face and a cocky grin. He's a year younger than us and completely enraptured with her, so I wish him luck.

He's going to need it.

I spend my lunches with Sadie, trying to pump her up and get her to ask Brent to hang out with her after school, but she won't do it. And neither will he, so the two of them merely circle each other like sharks in the water, reluctant to take the first bite out of each other.

It's ridiculous.

The week drags, and I get to the point where I can't take it any longer. I'm antsy. Anxious. Every room I'm in feels as if the walls are closing in on me and I eventually become so frustrated by not knowing where West is, I call the one person I'm confident can find him.

My older brother.

"You want me to find who?" he asks, after I explain the situation to him over the phone, careful not to reveal too much information.

I'm already regretting my decision. "Weston Fontaine."

"From the champagne Fontaines?"

"You know them?" I really hope he doesn't know West.

"I know of them. Eduard Fontaine is a ruthless businessman—and I admire him for that. And he knows how to make a damn good champagne." I can hear Whit tap away at a keyboard. "Is Weston his kid?"

"His son."

More tapping. "His only child. You should ask Sylvie for his information. She knows how to dig up dirt on people."

"I don't want to deal with Sylvie," I admit, feeling bad. "Besides, she's better at hacking."

"Not so much anymore. She sort of gave that up." He taps at a few more keys and pauses, going quiet, which I assume means he's reading over something. "I think he's in California."

My blood runs cold. "What do you mean?"

"I'm looking at a photo on a random Napa Valley website of Eduard and his wife, and there's a sullen-looking teenaged boy standing with them who's been identified as Weston Fontaine. It's dated two days ago. He's definitely in California." Within seconds my phone buzzes with a notification. "I just sent you the photo."

I pull my phone away from my ear to study the photo, my gaze racing over West's handsome face, lingering. Trying to find some hidden message. My brother is right—his face is sullen. He doesn't look happy to be there.

Why is he with his parents all the way in California? Why didn't he tell anyone where he was going? Why didn't he tell *me?*

Maybe because you don't matter to him.

I push that shitty little voice inside my brain to the darkest depths and focus on what my brother is saying.

"...you into this kid? You're never into anyone. I figured you were asexual."

An irritated noise leaves me. "Just because I'm not some sex-crazed maniac like you doesn't mean I'm not into anyone."

Whit doesn't even protest the sex-crazed maniac comment. "You've got to admit that you've never really focused on any guy—or girl—ever."

"I was too focused on dance," I remind him.

"Being at Lancaster Prep causes the hormones to ramp up, huh?"

"Oh, fuck off," I mutter, making my older brother laugh.

"Look, you're smart to go after a guy with that level of family wealth. He'll never be as rich as us, but he comes from major money," Whit says. "He'd be closer to our level if they sold the company."

"How much is their business worth?"

"Estimated in the billions," Whit answers.

We chat a little more until I finally tell him I have to go and end the call, my mind filled with all sorts of things.

More like all sorts of questions.

I do a little research myself, trying to find the same photo and article Whit found on my own but I'm unable to locate it, which is frustrating. I do find other articles about the family, the business, his father, his mother.

West looks like his dad. I stare hard at the photos over the years, noting that his father looks thinner and paler in more recent photos. As if he's not well.

Is his health poor? I think of my sister. Sylvie's weight fluctuates depending what medications she's on, or how ill she is.

Eduard Fontaine is thin and nearly as pale as me. When you compare the photos to ones from even two years ago, it's a dramatic difference. He was stockier. Tanner. And he smiled much more too. He looked like a man who enjoyed working outside, and now?

Now he doesn't look very well at all.

Giving up on my internet quest, I try to focus on homework, but no matter how hard I try, I can't. Instead, I throw on a leotard, knot my hair on top of my head and go to my dance studio, putting on the comforting sound of piano music that reminds me of ballet class in London before I go to the barre and start on my daily stretches. Again.

I danced earlier, before classes started, because I couldn't sleep. I was too worried, too confused by West's disappearance. So here I am again, stretching my already loose body, trying to lose myself in the mindless task of my exercises.

I don't hear the studio door open, and I don't hear the faint shuffle of footsteps across the floor either. It's only when I glance up and see him in the mirror's reflection, standing just behind me, appearing in the room like a ghost.

A gasp escapes me and I turn to face him, baffled that he's here. Standing in front of me.

"Where did you come from?"

West doesn't move from where he stands in the center of the floor. "I just got back."

The music still plays, the lilting piano cheerful and seemingly false in the otherwise somber mood of the room.

Of him. Judging from the stiff way he holds himself, the stark expression on his handsome face, he doesn't appear happy.

"Where were you?"

A ragged sigh leaves him and he rakes his fingers through his already disheveled hair. He looks tired. His face is drawn and there are bags under his eyes. His cheeks and jaw are lined with stubble and he's clad in a navy blue hoodie and gray sweatpants, but despite the exhaustion I see in his eyes, he still looks good.

I missed him. My entire body is leaning in his direction, and I yearn to run to him. Feel his strong arms wrap around my waist while I circle his neck with my arms, resting my cheek against his chest, so I can hear his thundering heartbeat. The need to actually touch him is so strong, I swear I can feel it vibrating in my bones.

But I do none of that. I remain in place, my breathing erratic, thanks to my stretching and his being here.

"I went to New York to meet with my father. He summoned me," West starts, wandering over to the chair where my speaker sits. He turns it off and sets it on the floor before he settles into the chair. "He wanted to talk."

I'm afraid to ask what about, especially because he has to be lying to me. He wasn't in New York. He was in California.

"How did your talk go?"

"It was…fine." He angles his head to the left, staring out the window. "I went back to California with him."

All the tension leaves my body at his admission. "Your parents live there, right?"

"Yes. They moved there when I started high school. I don't spend a lot of time with them anymore."

"Do you miss them?"

"Not particularly." Another sigh leaves him. "It's difficult, being the only child. The only son. A lot of expectations are put on me."

I think of my brother and all the expectations riding on his shoulders. How my parents don't do that to me at all, just because I'm female? Or because I'm the youngest? I'm not sure. Maybe it's a combination of both. "My brother deals with the same thing."

He cuts his gaze to mine. "Are you close with your brother?"

"Sort of." I shrug, careful not to mention I just spoke with him, and the conversation had everything to do with West. "It feels like as we get older, we get closer. Plus, I was in London for so long. I rarely spoke to either of my siblings."

"How was that? Being so far away from your family in London? I thought it was bad that my parents moved across the United States, but you lived in another country."

"It wasn't awful. I left by choice, really." Panic rises, threatening to close my throat, and I close my eyes for a beat, dredging up the courage to tell the truth of my fucked-up family. "My parents were fighting all of the time. My father was involved in a long-term affair, and my mother was focusing on my sister Sylvie instead of her marriage because, deep down, she knew it was crumbling. My brother had turned into a raging asshole— basically the entire family was falling apart and I wanted out. I wanted away from it. The only thing that was important to me was dance, and I used that as an escape."

"An escape from your family?"

"An escape from my entire life." I swallow hard, surprised by how much I just revealed to him. I don't talk about my family problems with anyone.

"Come here."

I startle at his rough command, the emotion thick in his voice. The look on his face is unfamiliar. Troubled. His gaze is clouded, and when he lifts his eyes to me, I go to him, perching my butt on his leg and breathing a sigh of relief when he slips his arm around my waist, pulling me into him.

It feels...good. Comforting, having his strong arms around me, my body leaning into his. I absorb his warmth and his scent and his strength, my arms going around his neck, just as I envisioned. He holds me closer, until I'm pressed completely into him, and I close my eyes, savoring it.

Savoring him.

"I missed you," he murmurs into the skin of my neck, and I cling to him harder, wishing I could say the words out loud.

I missed him too.

His fingers streak down the side of my cheek, slipping beneath my chin to tip my face up, our gazes meeting. Locking. He stares at my lips, his own parting, and I lean forward, brushing my mouth with his. I stay there, our parted lips close enough to touch, inhaling his exhales and he tips his head up, his mouth closing on mine.

He's kissing me, soft and slow. Our lips connect. Break apart. Meet again. Over and over, his tongue sneaking out for a teasing lick. Mine sliding against his.

I turn to face him fully, straddling him on the chair, pressing my torso against his as the kiss deepens. He cups the back of my head and I drown in him, our tongues tangling, our breaths increasing. I've got my hands buried in his hair, and he's got both hands gripping my ass, pulling me into him, so I can feel how hard he is. How hard I make him.

Power sizzles through my veins at the realization, and I grind against him, lifting my hips so his erection presses right against me. Sparks light up my skin at the connection, making my pussy throb. It would be so easy to come like this.

He ends the kiss, breaking away from me as if he needs to catch his breath, angling his head to the side. I stare at him, taking in his flushed cheeks. His sparkling eyes. His swollen, damp mouth.

"I can't do this," he says, his voice pained.

I frown. "You can't do what?"

"Lead you on." He grabs me by the waist and lifts me off him, rising to his feet and gently setting me to the side as if I don't weigh a thing. "We can't keep doing this. Hooking up at random times. It's unfair to you."

"What are you talking about?" I follow him as he heads for the studio's door, my mind awhirl with what he's trying to say. "You're not leading me on."

He comes to a stop, his expression grim. "I can't be what you want from me."

I gape at him, at a loss for words. "I never expected anything from you."

"I can't even give you what you consider nothing. It's too much for me right now." He rests his hands on his hips and glances down at the floor, his breathing deep. Ragged. "I'm leaving."

"Fine. Go." I wave a hand at him, hating how close to tears I feel. There is no reason to cry over this boy. He doesn't mean that much to me.

He doesn't.

"You misunderstood me." West lifts his head, his expression full of remorse. "I have to leave here—soon."

I'm confused. "And go where?"

"Help my family with the business." I see it in his gaze that's the last thing he wants to do.

"Why? Doesn't your father run it? Doesn't he have a full staff and a board and whatever else that comes with the House of Fontaine? Aren't you going to college first?"

"I don't know where I'm going after I graduate. I don't know what's going to happen." He sounds positively miserable and my heart aches for him.

"Well, you don't have to worry about that yet, right?" I try to smile but it feels so forced, I let it fade immediately. "Let's just enjoy this time together, okay? We have the rest of the school year to do whatever we want. All of our family responsibilities can wait."

"That's my problem—the responsibilities can't wait. And it's all crashing down on me, you know?" His gaze lingers on mine. "You probably don't. You seem to have it pretty easy."

I glare at him, his words infuriating me. "You think I have it easy? You've got to be kidding me."

"You run away from your problems, right? That's what it looks like to me. Hiding away in London for the last five years so you didn't have to face anyone," he says, and I wonder for the quickest second if he's trying to goad me on purpose.

It feels like he is.

But I let it happen anyway.

"I didn't run away from anyone. I chose to go to London because dance means everything to me. Just like I'm choosing to spend time with you right now. I'm not the one who's trying to run away." I pause, letting that sink in. "That would be you."

My words hang heavy in the air and he flinches, as if I physically hurt him. "You're right. I need the distance."

That's all he says before he turns around and heads for the studio door, pulling it shut with a loud slam only seconds later.

It's my turn to flinch. Tears are streaming down my face and I don't even realize it until I taste the salt on my lips. Now I'm even angrier. I don't cry, especially over some dumb, random boy I made the mistake of getting involved with one hot summer night in Paris.

So stupid.

Once I hear the distinct clang of the building door sound in the distance indicating that he's gone, I fall to my knees, burying my face in my hands.

And I weep.

CHAPTER TWENTY-THREE

CAROLINA

Weeks go by and I've fallen into a dependable pattern. I wake up early and stretch. Go to class. Endure the boring lectures and try my best to focus, intent on doing as well as possible on tests and busy work, so I can graduate and get out of this hellhole.

I spend lunch in the library, most of the time with Sadie, though lately she's been spending her lunch hour with someone else.

Brent.

I can't be mad at her for making her dreams come true, but I miss her. And I'm a little jealous. I wish West wouldn't have ditched me so easily.

After school is over, I dance more. I spend hours in the studio, devoted to it, to pushing myself to the limit and ending most sessions in a satisfied, yet exhausted heap. I dance so hard, I'm asleep pretty much the moment my head hits the pillow, and I wake up all over again the next morning to do the same thing.

I'm staying busy and it's keeping me preoccupied. I almost feel like I'm back in London at the dance company, where I ate, breathed and slept dance. It's what I need, what helps me focus, so I don't get distracted by other things.

Like West. Like his group of friends. Mercedes is still there, trying to cling to his side and make something happen between them yet again, I'm sure. I'm fairly certain she did something to scare poor Cooper off, and he now stays far away from her. West does his best to ignore her. I see the way they interact in class. More like how she tries to interact with him while he pretends that she doesn't exist.

He does the same thing to me. Pretends that I'm not there, looking right through me. I hate it. His blank stares and blatant lack of awareness makes me angry, and I nurse that feeling, keeping it close to my chest. It's easier to be pissed than sad over the situation. Sadness is such a useless emotion. All you can do is wallow in it and cry.

Anger? It can fuel you, and it's exactly what I need to remember how West made me feel when he turned me away. When he said he couldn't do this anymore, without any real explanation.

I don't need an explanation, is what I constantly tell myself. His rejection was reason enough.

I'm about to go to my last class of the day when I run into Headmaster Matthews outside the door of my classroom, as if he'd been waiting for me.

"Oh, there you are." Matthews approaches me, reaching out to grab hold of my arm, but I dodge out of his grip just in time. He drops his hand, his brows drawn together in confusion. "Can you come back to my office with me, please?"

"Why?" I ask warily. What could he want from me?

"You have someone here to see you. Don't worry, I'll write up a pass for you to miss this class."

Curious, I walk back with him to the admin building, tucking my uniform jacket closer to me to ward off the bitter chill. Ever since the rain storm that one night, the weather has been gloomy. Heavy with clouds that don't allow the sun in. Dark like my mood.

When we enter the administration building, my heart drops to my toes when I see who's waiting for me, an overly bright smile pasted on her face.

"Darling! I've missed you." Mother throws her arms open as if she's going to scoop me up in a big hug but I dodge away from her at the last second, not about to let her get her hands on me.

I don't trust the woman. Look at my sister. She's almost died multiple times and I believe my mother is somewhat responsible for it.

"What are you doing here?" I ask, sending Matthews a look when he hovers near the open door of his office.

I'm not about to have this conversation in front of him.

Mother senses my reluctance and smiles at the headmaster. "Could you give us some alone time, please?"

"Use my office," he says, indicating the door with a wave of his hand. "I'll wait right out here for you."

I scurry into his office, Mother hot on my heels, and the moment she closes the door I'm turning on her. "What do you want?"

She rests a hand on her chest, appearing shocked at the hostility in my tone. This woman needs to get a clue, I swear. "I wanted to see you. I am your mother after all."

"Not that you ever act like it, since you don't give a damn what I'm doing." I cross my arms in front of my chest, reminding myself of a pouty little child. "What do you want from me, Mother? Tell me the truth."

Her face crumples the slightest bit and she falls into one of the uncomfortable chairs in Matthews' office. "I just want one of my children to love me and want to see me. Is that too much to ask?"

I restrain myself from rolling my eyes and stand in front of Matthews' desk, leaning against it so I'm facing my mother. "What did Sylvie do to you now?"

"Nothing." Her face screws up in a bitter little mask. "And that's the problem. She won't talk to me. She doesn't reach out to me anymore, and we were so close. Her husband died and now I never see her."

I don't bother telling my mother that the moment Sylvie's much older husband died, she took it as her moment to be free, once and for all, from any constraints—including those put upon her by our mother.

"She's in mourning," I remind her, unsure what else I could say to her to bring her the comfort she doesn't deserve. My mother and sister were close only because Mother made Sylvie be her constant companion. It was never a choice. "Give her some space and time to herself. She's trying to figure this out."

When Sylvie married that much older man, I sort of stopped talking to her. Okay, I never talked much to her in the first place. Not over the last few years. There was no point in trying to get close to her. She was erratic and untrustworthy—and I'm afraid she still is.

Mother's smile is faint as she studies me and she rises to her feet. "I was hoping you would go to an early dinner with me."

I frown. "You came all the way out here to complain about Sylvie and then ask me to dinner?"

None of this makes sense.

She nods, glancing around the crowded, messy office, grimacing, though her face doesn't really move. She's had some recent work done, and while I see no problem with cosmetic procedures, it feels like she's looking younger and younger every time I see her.

"I've missed you. We never have one-on-one time, so I was hoping I could spend a few hours with my youngest daughter. You could tell me how school is going, and what you hope to do once you graduate."

I'm not in the mood to play mother/daughter catch-up today, though I don't see how I'm going to get out of this. "It's a Wednesday, Mother. You should've shown up here on a Friday."

"I'll do that next time. That way we can spend the entire weekend together." She clasps her hands in front of her, smiling so widely it looks fake. "Come on. I'll sign you out and we can go shopping. Then go out to dinner. There's that one Italian restaurant your sister always raved about to me. I want to try it."

Pasta is nothing but carbs. But maybe it would be good for me to load up and then dance for at least ninety minutes after our meal. I would definitely have enough fuel to burn off. "Fine," I say with a sigh, glancing down at myself. "Maybe I should change."

"You look fine. Beautiful in the uniform."

"I hate it." The wool skirt is scratchy and the entire getup makes me feel sweaty and hot most of the time.

"It's not necessary, Carolina. Now come on. Let's go."

I guess I have no choice but to go with her.

We wander the quaint downtown area, popping into shops, Mother not finding a single thing she wants to buy, which doesn't surprise me. If it doesn't have a designer label on it or isn't worth thousands upon thousands of dollars, then she's not interested.

By the time we're finished with our so-called shopping, she finally takes us to the Italian restaurant my sister supposedly loves. Despite the still early dining hour, the restaurant is busy, though luckily enough, we're shown to a small table that's near the front of the place, thanks to Mother name-dropping to the host, who I'm pretty sure is a manager and might even be an owner.

I scan the giant menu, holding it up to cover my face as my mother prattles on about family gossip. Whit is going to marry his girlfriend Summer soon. My cousin Grant is having another child with his wife. My other cousin Arch is gearing up to start at Lancaster Prep next school year as a freshman and his father—my uncle George—is furious at him.

"He's a troublemaker. The worst sort. Can't keep his dick in his pants," Mother says, sounding absolutely disgusted.

"He's like…in the eighth grade." I still can't believe my mother said the word dick out loud.

"He should already be a freshman. His mother purposely held him back in preschool for one more year because she fretted over him not being ready. The poor dear." Mother rolls her eyes. "He acted out every chance he got, from a very young age. Your father described him as a holy terror."

I don't remember him much, thanks to the age difference. By the time I would've started talking to him, I was already gone. In London.

"He's very handsome." Mother shows me a photo of my cousin on her phone. He reminds me of Whit. The icy blue eyes, the darkish blond hair. "And an absolute nightmare."

"I think you're getting off on the nightmare part," I tell her, enjoying the offended look that appears on her face.

"*I am not.* You take that back. I can't deny that I get a bit of—enjoyment from talking about how awful this boy is, but I definitely do not get off on it. What kind of person do you think I am?"

"You don't want me to answer that question." I reach for my water glass, ignoring the way she's staring at me. As if I've suddenly sprouted two heads.

The server shows up at our table, saving me from saying something else to offend my mother, and we give her our orders. The moment she's gone, Mother is leaning over the table, her eyes narrowed and her voice a nasty little hiss.

"A salad? Are you serious?"

"I don't want to gain weight." I shrug.

"Darling, I hate to say this but…do you think you have an eating disorder? There is no reason for you to think you need to lose any more weight. You're as skinny as a rail and completely fit. You're taking this eating thing too far."

I'm offended she would so blatantly ask me that question, especially after dealing with my sister's own mental issues over the years. "I don't know, Mother. I feel completely out of control most days and the only thing I can control is what I put in my mouth." I stare at the basket of bread sitting in the center of the table. I push it toward her. "Have some bread."

She pushes the bread basket toward me. "No, thank you."

"Why not? Do you have an eating disorder too?" I widen my eyes, trying to look purposely stupid, and she ignores me, draining her glass of wine and indicating to the server that she wants another.

"Let's change the subject." There's that overly bright smile again. "Tell me about the boy in your life."

My stomach sinks. "What boy? There's no boy."

"You don't have to lie to me. I have eyes and ears all over this campus. I know what's going on with you and…it's Weston Fontaine, isn't it? A fine choice. Far better than what your sister and especially your brother chose for themselves." She shudders for emphasis.

God, I hate her. I hate that she has spies planted at the school. People she most likely pays to give her information about everyone. About me. I can't get away with anything here without her knowing about it, and I wonder who the rat is.

Probably everyone on the staff, meaning there are multiple rats. I bet even Matthews is one. Oh, I bet that Vivian bitch rats us all out on the daily. I always see her lurking around campus, where she has no business being.

"His family is worth a lot of money that goes back generations. I love that." Her eyes are sparkling, she's so excited. "And he's very handsome."

"Don't get your hopes up," I say, dropping my gaze to the table. "We're not together."

"Oh, darling. What happened? Were my sources wrong?" Her

gaze catches on something in the restaurant. Or more likely someone. "Wait a minute—Is that him over there with that large group of kids?"

I whip my head around, glancing over my shoulder to see a bunch of people I know settling in at a large table. Well, I don't *know* most of them, but I recognize their faces. Students from Lancaster Prep, including Brent and Sadie. TJ and a few other boys and girls, including Marcy. And of course, West.

With Mercedes right beside him.

Our gazes meet and she smiles, her eyes glittering with cruelty when she reaches out, running her hand down the length of West's arm, as if she owns him. He doesn't even acknowledge her, he's so busy having a conversation with a boy I don't recognize, and I turn away, trying to school my face into a neutral expression, but it's no use.

Mother saw my misery. And now she'll most likely use it against me.

"Why aren't you with them? I thought you'd made friends and were accepted into the fold," Mother says, digging the knife a little deeper into my already stabbed and bleeding heart.

"I don't know." I shrug, trying my best to make it seem like their appearance doesn't bother me. "I've been keeping to myself lately."

"And why is that? You need to get out and meet people. You're a Lancaster, for God's sake. You should be ruling that school, as your brother did before you."

"Sylvie didn't."

"Sylvie was barely there." Mother waves a hand, dismissing my comment.

"I only just started. None of them really know me. How can I rule over a school when I'm a stranger, who only happens to have the last name Lancaster?"

"It doesn't matter if they know you or not. They will know *of* you merely because of your last name. Isn't that enough? That

should make you powerful in your own right, being a Lancaster."
Her voice drops, attaching an edge to it. "Don't be weak, darling.
Be strong. Remember who you are and what you're capable of.
And don't ever forget that you're a Lancaster. No one can take
that away from you. Not even some pretty rich boy who toys
with your emotions."

I sit there in shock, surprised that she's giving me advice.

Surprised even more that it was decent.

CHAPTER TWENTY-FOUR

WEST

I'm surrounded by people, my supposed friends. A group of us decided to go to one of the local restaurants to celebrate TJ's eighteenth birthday at the last minute. I should be having a good time. I have my real friends with me, and while Mercedes is a complete nuisance, I can ignore her presence easily enough. Yet I'm completely miserable.

The problem?

The girl sitting across the restaurant with a woman, who I'm pretty sure is her mother.

What the fuck is Carolina Lancaster doing here? What are the odds that she'd be here tonight of all nights, when we're here too? I figured tonight would be my one chance to get away from her for at least a few hours. Where I wouldn't have to think about her and worry about her fucking feelings.

Instead, here she is, a constant, physical reminder of what I told myself I can't have only a few feet away. Looking completely miserable as the woman—I'm fairly certain that is Sylvia Lancaster she's sitting with—is giving her a lecture, her mouth never seeming to stop moving.

"Hey." Someone slaps my arm and I glance over at Brent, who's studying me with concern. "I thought you were looking forward to tonight."

"I was. I am." I paste on a smile, but the dubious look my friend gives me tells me I'm fooling no one. "I'll be fine."

"You've been in a shit mood since you disappeared, and that was a month ago." He slaps me in the arm again, harder this time. "Snap out of it, man. You're a real downer lately."

"Yeah. I'll try." I haven't told anyone about my father's condition. He asked that I keep it private and that's exactly what I'm doing, but fuck, it's hard.

I have no one to talk about it with. And the one person who probably would've listened to me, I pushed away.

I'm a complete idiot.

"You have been in a bad mood for a while." This comes from Mercedes, who curls her arm through mine, like she's trying to claim me. I see the way she keeps glancing over at Carolina's table. She's trying to send a message to her and it's the same old bullshit.

It's also completely untrue.

I'm not interested in this girl. She's too obvious, too forward, too much. She's also clueless. As in, she can't figure out that I have zero desire to be with her, let alone talk to her. I shift my arm out of her possessive grip, wishing she'd take the hint.

"I'll get over it," I tell her, my voice clipped, my gaze going in the same direction as hers.

Toward Carolina.

I drink her in, shocked to see she's still in her uniform, her hair in the usual high ponytail, bright blonde and silky soft. She's staring at her mother while the woman talks, her fingers absently stroking up and down the length of her neck and I wonder what she would've done if I'd grabbed her by the neck and held her in place while I fucked her. Would she have liked it?

My instincts say yes.

But I'll never get a chance to do that. I ruined what we had. The only reason I pushed her away is because I didn't want to hurt her. I'm leaving soon. The plan is for me to leave over winter break for California and not return to Lancaster Prep. My father has been given six months tops, and he wants to take whatever remaining time he has and train me. To have me take over one of the biggest champagne producers in the country, if not the world, once he's gone.

It's unbelievable, his expectations.

I'm only eighteen fucking years old. The man is delusional if he thinks I can do it as well as he does. He's got a solid thirty-five years on me, experience-wise.

"I don't understand your fascination with her."

I turn to face Mercedes, at the disgust in her voice, noting the equally vile expression on her face. When she hates someone, she gets ugly about it. "You're just jealous."

Mercedes' face turns about twenty shades of red in approximately ten seconds. "Why would I be jealous of her?"

"Oh, I don't know. Maybe because she's got more class in her fucking pinky finger than you do in your entire body. You constantly tear her down to anyone who will listen to you babble on while Carolina remains quiet and doesn't say a bad word about you to a single soul. All you ever do is talk, Mercedes, and if you were smart, you'd learn how to keep that big mouth of yours shut."

She gapes at me, obviously shocked that I would call her out for her shit. Well, someone had to.

"You're an asshole," she finally manages.

"And you're a bitch. Guess we're even." I rise to my feet, ignoring Mercedes' muttered curse words streaming after me. Also ignoring my friends calling my name, no doubt curious as to where I'm going.

I walk through the restaurant, weaving in and out of the tables, purposely making my way toward Carolina's. She catches me out of the corner of her eye, doing a double take when she sees my intention, those big blue eyes going wider with every step I take closer to her.

Does she believe I'm going to say something shitty and make her look bad? Act like an asshole, like Mercedes just called me?

"Carolina." I nod at her when I stop at her table, her mother's gaze full of approval when it lands on me. "Nice to see you."

She stares at me, unblinking. It takes her mother furiously whispering her name to get her to speak. "Hello, Weston."

I feel about a thousand pounds lighter hearing her say my name. Just being in her presence. I stare at her, shoving my hands in my pockets, a crooked smile curving my lips.

"I'm Sylvia." Her mother draws my attention away from the girl who haunts my every waking thought by thrusting her hand toward me, giving me no choice but to shake it. "Carolina's mother."

"I believe we've met before," I tell her, extracting my hand when I realize she's not going to let go first. "At the Met fundraiser last summer."

"Oh, perhaps we did. I know your parents. Well, in passing. Lovely people. How are they?" Sylvia asks politely.

I flinch, hating that I have to lie. "They're well."

Such a lie. My mother is doped up on antidepressants and my father is dying. They are both the farthest thing from well.

"Are you celebrating something?" Sylvia inclines her head toward the table I just abandoned. "With your friends?"

I glance over my shoulder to find them all laughing and talking amongst themselves, save for Mercedes, who's tracking my every move.

"A friend's birthday. We planned it last minute." I send Carolina a look. "I would've invited you to come with us, but—"

"You don't need to lie to look good in front of my mother," she snaps, that sexy, haughty expression on her face. She won't look at me, her posture rigid, her lips pursed, as if she's contemplating spitting in my face.

I get off on an angry Carolina, for whatever strange reason. When she's mad, she's sexy as fuck.

And the best thing? She doesn't even realize it.

Grinning, I run my hand along my chin, impressed with her bravery. I love how she doesn't hesitate to stand up to me and tell me off. "You're right. Guess I shouldn't bother with the excuses then."

"Carolina, my goodness!" Sylvia sends me an apologetic look. "I'm sorry, Weston. My daughter is impulsive and sometimes speaks out of turn."

"She's not wrong though. I wouldn't have invited her tonight, even if I had run into her." I bow like I'm in front of the Queen of England and slowly back away, turning on the charm. "You ladies enjoy your meal and have a lovely evening."

I turn tail and head for the bathroom, my original destination, my steps hurried like I can't get away from them fast enough.

That's a lie. I would've stayed there longer, but I know Carolina would've completely lost it. I don't regret talking to her and her mother though. Stopping by Carolina's table just to bask in her presence for a little bit, to listen to her sweet yet biting voice—it was worth it. Seeing that flare of anger in her beautiful blue eyes doesn't make me feel bad. Not even a little bit.

I made an impression on her mother at least.

Might not have been a good one, but fuck it.

I'm washing my hands when the door swings open and Carolina enters the restroom, planting herself against the door as soon as it closes, her hair falling out of the ponytail, her expression frazzled.

Someone seems upset.

I turn off the water and stick my hands under the automatic air dryer, shouting over the droning noise. "What are you doing in here? Pretty sure you took a wrong turn."

"I wanted to talk to you." She sniffs, disgust written all over her pretty features. Funny how she can be mad at me and still look beautiful, while Mercedes is angry and looks like a freaking beast. "You should've never stopped at our table."

"Why not?"

"Now my mother thinks I have a chance with you." She crosses her arms in front of her, pouting. "You're an asshole."

"That's the second time someone's called me that tonight." I vigorously rub my hands together under the blast of hot air, enjoying every second of this.

I'd rather argue with Carolina for only a minute versus having a regular conversation with anyone else.

"Who else called you an asshole?'

"You don't want to know."

"Mercedes?"

I smile helplessly and shrug.

"God, I hate that I agree with her," she mutters, her hand reaching out for the door handle. "I should go."

"That's all you wanted to do? Bust into the men's bathroom to tell me that you think I'm an asshole?"

Her hand drops, her scowl deepening. "Don't make this into something it's not."

"I'm not making it into anything." I pause. "You are."

She pushes away from the door and marches toward me, her loafers practically on top of my feet when she stops. "You're the one who said you couldn't do this."

"I lied." Oh fuck. Here I go. "I still want to do this."

Carolina blinks at me, her lips parting, her hands coming out...

And shoving me in the chest, so I go toppling backward, bumping into the slick-tiled wall behind me.

"Fuck you, Weston." She shakes her head once, exiting the bathroom.

CHAPTER TWENTY-FIVE

CAROLINA

I go storming out of the men's bathroom, glaring at the man who was about to open the door, almost laughing when I see the confused look on his face.

I don't laugh though. I'm too furious. Freaking West.

Mercedes is right—he is an asshole. I can't believe he stopped by our table. My mother practically convulsed with joy when he spoke to her, his rich, deep voice stirring something deep inside me that I hate.

Fine, I don't hate it. I hate my reaction to him. The power he has over me. It's annoying.

Confusing.

"Carolina!" West is shouting, and I look over my shoulder to see he's in hot pursuit of me, a determined look on his face.

I run faster, heading for the front of the restaurant, pushing my way through the crowd of people waiting in the lobby before I exit through the double doors, the early fall breeze washing over me, immediately cooling my angry thoughts.

"Why am I always chasing after you?"

Turning, I find West standing directly in front of me, breathing heavily. "Maybe you should take it as a hint."

"What exactly are you trying to tell me?"

"I want you to leave me alone. I tried to ditch you in Paris. Multiple times. I've tried to ditch you at school. And just now. Yet you still chase after me."

"Look." He steps closer, crowding me, yet I stand my ground, feeling defiant. I thrust my chin up, glaring at him, but there's something in his gaze that makes me soften. He seems...hurt.

Raw.

Real.

"I fucked up," he murmurs, reaching for my hand and bringing it up to his chest, so I can feel the thunderous pounding of his heart against my palm. "I told you I couldn't do this because I was going through some—personal shit."

What in the world is he talking about?

"I should've never pushed you away. I could really use—a friend right now."

I'm gaping at him, my mouth hanging open, shocked by his words. "You want me as a friend?"

"I want you any way I can get you, Carolina." His smile is small, though it doesn't quite reach his eyes. If anything, West appears completely tormented.

By me? Or life in general?

"Why did you come here tonight with Mercedes?"

"I didn't come with anyone. We're celebrating TJ's birthday. She tagged along, that's it." He pauses. "Your friend Sadie is with us."

I go completely still. "How do you know Sadie is my friend?"

"She told me. Us." He tilts his head, his fingers clasping tighter around mine. "You're pretty fucking paranoid, you know that?"

"You give me reason to be." I yank my hand out of his touch, tucking it into the sleeve of my uniform jacket. "It's hard for me to trust people. Especially those who toy with my emotions."

"Got it. Like me. You don't want to forgive me. I don't blame you. I treat you like shit and make you come, all in a matter of hours."

Oh, his words completely infuriate me. I ball my hands into fists, wishing I could sock him in his beautiful face so he could feel actual pain. This boy who sails through life without a care in the world. With all the money and prestige and privilege that comes with it. People could say the same about me, but I come from a messed-up family, who all use each other in some sort of sick, twisted game. I tried to escape it and did so for years, but here I am, having a shitty night out with my mother, running into my ex...lover? I don't even know what to call him.

I don't know how to feel about any of this. I just need to—go.

"You always have to bring sex into it," I say, my voice low.

"Sex is a part of what we share, don't you think?" He tries to grab my hand again, his watch snagging on a loose thread coming from the sleeve of my jacket, and I tug on it, watching as the very expensive watch unbuckles and almost slips off his wrist.

"Watch it," he says at the same time I apologize, my gaze snagging on what looks like a tattoo on the inside of his wrist as he rebuckles the watch, the band completely covering it.

Hmm. I never noticed that before.

"Do you have a tattoo?"

"No," he says far too quickly.

Now I'm the one reaching for him. "Yes, you do. I saw it."

"You didn't see shit." He lifts his arm above his head and I circle my hands around his bicep, startled at the feel of it beneath my palms. He's as hard as a rock.

In all sorts of places.

"West." My voice is firm, like I'm a parent talking to a naughty child. "Let me see it."

He shrugs my hand off of him, turning so his back is to me. "No."

"Come on, this is dumb. I want to see it."

"There's nothing to see." He starts walking, heading toward the restaurant's entrance, and he glares at me from over his shoulder. "You're making a big deal out of nothing."

I watch him go, puzzled by his reaction, how quickly he retreated. This boy...

Is so freaking confusing.

I wait a few minutes before I go back inside, heading straight for the table where my mother sits, scrolling through her phone, which is resting in her lap. There are already two salads sitting on the table, hers untouched.

"You should've started without me," I say as I slide back into my seat.

She glances up from her lap with a frown, irritation gleaming in her eyes. "Where have you been? You've left me alone in here for at least ten minutes!"

"I had to use the bathroom."

The concerned look on her face is hard to ignore. "You weren't...vomiting in the bathroom, were you?"

I think the woman wants me to have a major eating disorder, I swear to God. She enjoys seeing her children suffer. "I haven't even eaten anything yet. What could I throw up?"

"Fine, you're right. I'm sorry I even mentioned it." She straightens her shoulders and puts on a smile. "Are you hungry? This salad looks delicious."

She doesn't ask what I was up to; it had to be obvious what my intentions were. I took off after West left our table with a distracted, "I'll be right back," and she's not questioning me, so I should be relieved.

Instead, I'm annoyed. My mother is so wrapped up in her own bullshit, she barely notices mine, which is normally a good thing.

But right now, I feel the need for some motherly comfort, despite knowing deep down, I'm never going to get it.

"Weston seems like a nice young man," she says, when we're a few bites into our salads. "Good manners."

Oh, if she only knew. He's really just a giant perv who enjoys eating pussy, but I don't want to ruin the illusion.

"He's whatever." I shove more lettuce into my mouth, so I

can't say anything else. I can feel her heated glare, but I choose to ignore her.

"You're at Lancaster Prep for what, two months, and you've lost all semblance of manners?" She shakes her head, forking up a dainty serving of salad before she carefully inserts it into her mouth, chewing quickly and swallowing before she says, "Maybe it was a mistake, bringing you here."

The fork falls onto the edge of my plate, the loud clattering noise startling her, but I could give a damn. "My life isn't a game, you know."

She wipes at the corner of her mouth with the cloth napkin, setting it in her lap before she answers me. "I never implied your life was a game."

"Yet you treat it like one. Pulling me out of one of the most prestigious dance companies in the world after I had the performance of a lifetime, because I needed to be reminded of my roots? Or were you just toying with me because Whit doesn't let you in his life, and Sylvie ran off and married someone old enough to be her grandfather?" I think I'm the angriest I've ever been toward her. Toward anyone. Like, my blood is boiling, I'm so pissed.

She brushes her brittle blonde hair away from her unlined forehead, and I'm reminded of my sister. Our mother isn't a real blonde, but her hair matches Sylvie's. Her face matches it too.

"You were misbehaving and someone needed to control you. As your parents, we have that right."

"Making me return to the States ruined *everything*. Not that you care. My future in the dance world. I was destined to become a prima ballerina. If I'd stayed there, I would already be on my way."

"They just filled your head with grandiose ideas, while we paid for your tuition. We funded the theatre's renovation, helped pay for various productions. They used us—and you—to get what they wanted."

My heart starts to race. "You're lying."

"It's true." She shrugs, nonchalantly. Like what she said didn't just shatter my entire image of the dance company.

"I am a dancer." I bang my fist on the table, making the plates, the silverware, the water glasses shake. "They wouldn't let just any old person dance at the *Palais Garnier*. I had to earn my spot. I worked hard. I put in the time. I auditioned—and I was selected."

"You earned your spot with all the family money that funded their failing dance company. They're well taken care of for years to come." Her smile is bitter. I think she's enjoying this moment. "Face it, Carolina. You're just a rich girl playing at being a dancer."

Her words are evil. Mean. So is the look on her face. She wants to hurt me. But why?

What did I ever do to her?

"God, I hate you." I jump to my feet, tossing my napkin in her face. I throw it so fast, I hit my target, and she bats the napkin away, her expression horrified that I'm making such a public scene. "You're such a bitch."

Before she can respond, I'm walking out of the restaurant with my head held high and my footsteps hurried, my entire body trembling with a combination of anger, adrenaline and fear. I have never spoken to my mother like that in my life. I've never spoken to anyone like that.

Somehow, I manage to make it outside, the air having turned even colder since the last time I left the restaurant, and I wrap my arms around myself, shivering. Desperate to calm my racing heart and my shattered self-esteem, I take deep, gulping breaths, closing my eyes as I turn my face toward the sky. The breeze washes over my face, cooling my angry thoughts, and I blink up at the sky, wishing I was anywhere but here.

"Hey. Are you all right?"

I turn to find West leaning against the building, basically in the same spot as I left him, his phone clutched in his hand and a curious look on his face.

I can't believe he's standing in front of me. "What are you still doing here?"

He frowns, pocketing his phone. "Waiting for my Uber. They're taking fucking forever."

I'm this close to crying at finding him. If anyone can comfort me right now, it's him. Despite everything that's happened between us, it's like I know I can count on West. I don't understand why I feel that way.

I just do.

Without hesitation, I rush toward him, my gaze on the restaurant's entrance, afraid my mother is about to bust through those double doors and start yelling at me. "I need to get out of here. Now."

"Let's go," he says without hesitation, slipping his arm around my shoulders as he steers me toward the sidewalk, turning down a side street when we get to the intersection a short time later.

He doesn't ask me why I need to leave, or what's wrong. He just agrees, and I almost collapse with relief at his unspoken devotion.

But I say nothing. I let him lead me down the sidewalk, farther away from the restaurant, walking deeper into an older, rather quaint neighborhood full of beautiful, small homes that are well-kept, with lush green yards filled with flowers and shrubs, shaded by large trees. It's quiet here, and I squish as close to West's side as I possibly can, without impeding his ability to walk.

He squeezes my shoulders reassuringly, and I close my eyes to ward off the tears that want to spill. I keep my head bent, dashing my fingers under one eye, then another, before I dare attempt to speak.

"What about your Uber?"

"I canceled it."

I turn my face to his, frowning. "How are we getting back to campus?"

"We'll figure out a way." We come to another intersection, and he turns right, taking me with him, and I realize we're on the other end of the downtown area. The scent of coffee suddenly fills the air, and I can hear jazz music playing on a speaker outside.

"Let's get something to drink," he suggests as we slow in front of the cutest coffeeshop I think I've ever seen. The exterior is painted white brick with dark gray shutters framing the windows and inside it looks warm and cozy.

Inviting.

I smile at him in relief, on the verge of tears yet again, though I don't quite understand why. "Thank you," I murmur.

His smile is probably the sweetest I've ever seen. "Just trying to prove to you that maybe I'm not such an asshole after all."

CHAPTER TWENTY-SIX

CAROLINA

Once we're inside, we make our order and then find a table that's in the back of the coffee shop, a quiet little corner with a small round table and two chairs. West heads back to the counter to wait for our drinks and I check my phone, frowning when I see I have a bunch of texts from my mother.

Where did you go?

Carolina! Call me back.

Text me NOW.

I'm going to call your father and tell him what you did. What you SAID.

You ungrateful little brat. You're lucky I don't demand you come home with me and homeschool you the rest of your senior year.

I tap at my screen and hit the block button with a trembling finger, knowing that will only piss her off more, but I need to save my sanity if she's going to keep this up.

Then I immediately text my father.

Me: *Mother and I got into an argument.*

He responds immediately.

Father: *I already heard. Where are you?*

Of course, she already told him about it.

Me: *Promise not to tell her?*

Father: *I'll just let her know you're safe. I won't tell her where you are or who you're with.*

I'm sure she assumes I ran off with someone from school. Maybe even West, especially since he never reappeared in the restaurant. I wonder if she noticed?

Me: *I'm safe. I'm at a coffeeshop waiting for an Uber.*

Father: *Are you alone?*

I think about telling him I'm with West, and then decide not to.

Me: *Yes. My ride should be here soon and I'm going back to campus. Please don't make me go home with her. She says she wants to homeschool me.*

Father: *Your mother would rather die than have to teach you guys anything. She's as dumb as a stick.*

He sends a bunch of laughing emojis, which makes me both smile and feel bad.

He really thinks our mother is that dumb? Why did he marry her then? What does that say about him?

Father: *Don't worry. You're staying at Lancaster Prep. I'll make sure of it.*

Me: *Thank you.*

Father: *Love you, sweetheart.*

I don't respond that I love him too. It's not easy for me to use those words, and I never say them in a careless manner. I need to mean it, and I rarely do. There are very few people in this world who I actually love. My father is one of them. I just…

I'm not comfortable saying it.

"Here you go." West appears in front of the table clutching two steaming coffee cups in his hands. He sets one in front of me and I can't help but smile when I see the heart design in the foam of my vanilla latte.

"It's so cute." I glance up at him. "Thank you."

He settles into the chair across from me, his knees knocking into mine. "You're welcome."

I take a sip from my cup, but it's so hot I immediately burn my tongue. "Watch out. it's hot."

"Noted." He leans back in his chair, contemplating me, his gaze assessing. "Are you okay? Feeling a little better?"

I shrug. "Not really." Though he's making it better. Not that I can say that to him out loud. I don't want him getting any ideas.

"What happened?"

I shrug, reluctant to share the details of my horrible conversation with my mother.

I can't even think about what my mother said to me. Did she mean all of that? And is it true? If it is, does that mean I've been lied to my entire life and I'm just a shit dancer? Someone they tolerate merely because my family pays a lot of money to keep me in dance? And in turn pays them a lot of money to make me happy?

That's so fucked up.

"Does it have to do with your mom?" His expression darkens when I remain quiet. "Or did Mercedes say something to you?"

"Mercedes? No. I didn't talk to her." I shake my head. I forgot she was even at the restaurant. "It was my mother. We got into an argument."

"Ah." He nods, like he understands. And maybe he does. "I always argue with my dad when we're together."

"For me, it's my mother. For all of us, really. My brother and sister, too. My dad, even though they're divorced." I wince. "She's...a lot."

We're quiet for a moment and I try to take another sip from my drink, blowing on it first. It's disconcerting, how carefully West is watching me, and I'm tempted to start wiggling in my chair when he finally says something.

"I'm sorry she upset you."

"It's okay," I croak, swallowing past the thick emotion suddenly clogging my throat. I rarely receive sympathy from anyone. I'm only stating facts, because I never let anyone see me like this. "She's just watching out for me."

That's actually not the case, and I don't know why I'm making excuses for her. But I definitely can't tell West what she said to me. It'll make him look at me different, when that's the last thing I want to happen.

"When they do shit like this, our parents claim they're watching out for us, but they're really only making things worse. Or just protecting themselves." His tone is bitter and he takes a big swig from his coffee mug, leaving a film of latte foam on his upper lip when he's done.

I point at his mouth, a giggle escaping me. And I never giggle. "You've got something on your upper lip."

He sticks out his tongue, licking at the corner of his mouth, and something warm and thick unfurls in my stomach—actually, make that lower. "You want to lick it off for me?"

"Ew, no." I shake my head. Lying through my teeth.

"You probably would've a month ago." He grabs a napkin and wipes at his mouth, the foam disappearing with one swipe. "Look, I feel bad."

"About what?" I glance around the café, relieved to find it's not very crowded. It's so nice in here though. Quiet, with the jazz music playing in the background, mixed with the sound of low chatter. It smells good and the coffee is delicious, meaning I'll have to come back here soon. Maybe Sadie would go with me.

Sadie…I didn't even make eye contact with her at the restaurant, though I know she was there. With Brent. This is huge. Major. He brought her along with him to hang out with his friends, and I love that for her. I really do.

I also wish I could have that. With a boy.

With West.

"I pushed you away and it was fucked up on my part. I was going through a lot of shit at the time and I was totally being selfish. I think I hurt myself more than I hurt you." He ducks his head for a moment, staring deeply into his cup of coffee before he lifts his gaze to mine. "Or maybe I did hurt you more. I don't know. I just feel shitty about it and I'm sorry. I'm not good at this sort of thing."

"What thing?"

"Caring about someone else. A girl. Relationships." He shrugs, his gaze fixed on his coffee mug again. "Thinking about other people's feelings."

I can relate, though I'm not sure if I can tell him that. I don't worry about anyone else. I don't like anyone else. Not really. I tolerate my family because I have to. I made so-called friends in dance school because I needed to align myself with the proper group. The only people I can actually say I like currently are Sadie and...

West.

And I'm mad at him, so the vote is still out on that opinion.

"You're all I think about," he admits, his searing gaze returning to mine. "I can't get you out of my head, and it fucks with everything I try to do. Every decision I make. You fucking haunt my thoughts, Carolina. What are you doing? What's going on in your life? I never see you in the dining hall anymore."

"I don't like it there."

"I see you in our one class and that's it, and you sit in the back of the room on purpose. You buzz in at the last second before the bell rings, and before I can even get my book in my backpack when class is over, you're already gone."

I didn't think he noticed.

"I don't want to keep going on like this." He leans forward, resting his arms on the edge of the table, his knees bumping into mine again, making my skin tingle. Any time we make contact with each other, I feel it. Even his eyes on me feel like the stroke of his fingers. "I fucked everything up between us and I want to make it up to you."

I sit up straighter, my posture rigid, a shuddery breath

escaping me. What he's asking for, I don't think I can deliver. "I don't do relationships either, West."

He stares at me, absently shredding the napkin with his fingers. "Okay."

"And I'm leaving. As soon as we graduate, I'm going back to London." I have no idea if that's actually part of my plan, but I'm going to make some calls starting tomorrow. I can't trust my mother or my father to take care of it for me.

I have to handle my future on my own.

"I'm leaving too," he admits. "I have to go to California and help my father."

"You're not going to college?" That's something we've never really discussed before. I have no idea what West's goals and dreams for the future are.

"No. I can't. My dad needs me, so I guess I'll be getting an endless amount of hands-on experience. Family business, you know?" His smile is grim and I can tell.

He doesn't want to go to California to help his father.

"Are you okay with that? Is that what you want to do?"

"Sure." His smile is false as he takes another drink of his coffee. "Sometimes we have to do things we don't think we want, but it'll all work out in the end, right?"

I swallow hard, hating how resolute he sounds. As if he's accepting his fate, even if he doesn't like it. "You don't have to do what other people tell you all the time."

"I do when it comes to my father. I don't have a trust fund set up in my name that'll take care of me for the rest of my life. I am the only heir to this business, which means I get it all, but that's a lot of pressure, and he wants me to work at the House of Fontaine. There are certain...expectations set on me that I have to live up to."

It's an automatic reflex when I willingly reach out and touch his hand, my fingers streaking across his knuckles. He turns his hand over, palm up and I let him grasp my fingers, keeping me there. For once, I don't try to pull out of his grip. Instead, I let my hand relax in his, and when his gaze meets mine, my heart starts to race.

"We don't have a lot of time," he murmurs, and I frown, confused at his choice of words. "Let's make the best of it while we're here. Together."

We have the rest of the school year. Yeah, it'll go fast and next thing we know, we'll be graduating and out of high school forever, but is that what he means?

"What are you trying to say, West?"

He ducks his head for a moment, suddenly bashful, which is the most un-West-like thing I've ever seen him do to date. "Let's try and make this—" he waves a finger in between us "—work."

I'm quiet for a moment, absorbing his words.

"Are you saying you want to be with me? That you want other people to know that we're together?" I need it spelled out plainly before I agree to anything.

"Yeah." He clears his throat, and I wonder if that was hard for him to admit. "I mean, we don't have to come right out, if you don't want to. We can keep this quiet. It's nobody else's business what we do."

"Are you wanting to keep me a secret?" My voice is sharp, and I can't help but take offense at what he's saying. Though, deep down, I also think I get it.

Letting people in...letting them know we're trying to be a thing, could end up being a lot. We'll draw unwanted attention, and I'll probably gain more enemies.

Not that anyone was really on my side to begin with at this school.

"No, not at all." He shakes his head, his expression stressed. "I just—people suck. They're nosy. They'll spread rumors and speculate about our relationship. It'll get around to everyone, you know? Staff, admin. Everyone."

Everyone like my mother, thanks to the plant she has

somewhere on campus. Though I'm pretty positive there are multiple plants collecting information for her.

Knowing her, that's exactly what she's doing.

Just the idea of every single person at Lancaster Prep knowing I'm in a relationship, thinking about what I'm doing with West when we're all alone is...

Scary.

"I'm a very private person," I say primly, trying to pull my hand out of his.

He won't let go. He even goes as far as to interlace our fingers together, our clasped hands resting in the middle of the tiny table. "I know. That's what I like about you."

He smiles at me, another one of those sweet smiles that are so very much not like the West I've gotten to know.

"This is going to be...weird for me."

"It'll be weird for me too. I've never really had a girlfriend before."

"You haven't?" I'm shocked by his confession.

He slowly shakes his head, his thumb skimming back and forth across the top of my hand, soothing me. "How about you?"

"I've never had a girlfriend either," I say with a straight face.

He presses his thumb against the top of my hand hard, making me laugh. "You know what I mean."

"Then no, I've never been in a relationship. I'm not sure I'm built for one." When his troubled gaze meets mine, I feel the need to explain further. "I just want to be honest with you."

A ragged sigh leaves him, but he smiles. "Yeah, same. I don't know if I'm cut out for this either. I guess we'll just figure it out together."

Together.

I like the sound of that.

CHAPTER TWENTY-SEVEN

WEST

'm a selfish prick.

I didn't tell Carolina I'm leaving Lancaster Prep at winter break and not coming back. I don't know how to tell her. I'm also afraid she would've said no to my asking her to be my girlfriend if I'd confessed I wasn't going to be around much longer.

I wouldn't have blamed her either. What's the point in us doing this if I'm leaving in a couple of months?

This is why I'm a selfish prick. I did it for me. I did it because I need her support. I want to keep her around. There's something about her that I'm drawn to, something that I can't quite put my finger on, but it's there nonetheless. Reminding me that she makes me smile, she makes me laugh, when no one else in this entire fucking world does that.

Only her.

It's been a week since that fateful night at the restaurant. Since TJ's birthday dinner and Carolina got into that argument with her mother. When she got into somewhat of an argument with me.

Our coming out publicly as a couple has been slow, and I haven't pushed for anything because I don't think it's necessary. Let people come to their own conclusions when they see us together. It's fairly obvious, what's going on.

We walk together to almost every class, even if I have to sprint across campus to get to my own classroom before the bell rings. We sit together at lunch with Brent and Sadie, using them as sort of a shield. So far, it's working. Even Mercedes has mostly left us alone, though I'd guess she's slowly dying inside.

She wanted her chance with me and she blew it. Hell, she never really had one. I was never that into her.

Not like I'm into Carolina.

She's been keeping me at arm's length since we've started this relationship-type thing though, and I'm trying to be patient, but she's testing me. And I think she realizes it too.

I also think she gets off on it. Creating distance between us. Putting on a little show for me, waving that invisible sign that says, *look but don't touch.*

I can only take so much.

It's near the end of fifth period when I get a call from my mother, my phone ringing right in the middle of class. The teacher frowns mid-lecture, and I immediately turn off the ringer, trying to ignore it. But she calls again. And when I still don't pick up that time, there's yet another call.

"It's my mother," I tell him when he can blatantly see the flashing screen of my phone as it sits on my desk.

He inclines his head toward the door. "Go ahead and take it."

I hurriedly exit the class and call her back once I'm in the hallway. She answers on the first ring.

"It's your father," she blurts before I can even say anything. "He's not doing well. They just admitted him into the hospital."

I grip the phone tightly, staring out the window as I stand in the empty corridor of the school. "What happened?"

"He passed out. I found him in the living room, collapsed on the ground and unresponsive. I called 911." She starts to cry and I grimace, wishing I was anywhere else but here. Listening to her. Knowing this might be the end for my father. "I don't know what to do without him, Weston. What are we going to do?"

She's wailing. And I almost end the call on her mid-cry because this is way too heavy for me to take.

Instead, I inhale deeply and start asking her a series of questions, all of them having to do with my father's condition.

"The doctor's here. Let me call you back." She's gone in an instant and I start pacing the hall, gripping the back of my neck, hating how fucking anxious I feel.

If she needs me to come back now and be with him, I'll do it, but fuck. I only got a week with Carolina? I know the moment I go to Napa, I won't be coming back. Not to Lancaster Prep. Maybe not even to the East Coast—at least for a while.

And what's going to make Carolina want to come and see me? I'll be wrapped up in paperwork and trying to figure out my new place at a fucking business that has been run by a middle-aged man with over thirty years of experience. What the hell do I know about champagne besides that what we create is some of the best out there?

I know nothing. I'm a kid. It doesn't matter how we feel while we're here, my friends and me. Like we're the big men on campus. The seniors who rule the school. It's bullshit.

We're babies. We don't know what the hell we're doing.

Within minutes, my phone rings, and I answer it without checking who it is, relieved to hear my mother's not as frantic voice in my ear.

"Your father is going to be okay. They just diagnosed him with pneumonia. They put him on antibiotics and said he should be feeling better within the next few days."

"Pneumonia? How did he get that?" It's not even cold season yet, especially in California.

"I'm not sure. His immune system isn't in the best shape. He's susceptible to all sorts of things lately." Her voice lowers. "I do wish he would've done chemo, but he was insistent on taking the holistic approach."

I remember that my mother believes my father is in remission, and thank Christ I didn't say anything different. "He's going to be okay then."

"Yes. They're keeping him in the hospital overnight for observation. They'll most likely release him tomorrow." She releases a shuddery breath. "Unless something else happens."

I swallow hard and ask, "Do you need me to come out there? I can book a plane the second I get off this call."

She's quiet for a moment, and I press my forehead against the cool glass window, closing my eyes. Praying she says no.

"I'll be all right," she finally says. "Your father mentioned you'd most likely stay there for Thanksgiving."

He did?

"But you'll come home for Christmas though, right, sweetheart?"

I crack my eyes open, pushing away from the window. "Of course."

"I'm glad, darling. We miss having you around."

Her words infuriate me. They didn't miss me enough to stick around when I started high school here at Lancaster Prep. The moment they got their opportunity to go to Napa, they left. Who cares if their son was across the country attending boarding school?

Business comes first.

With the Fontaines, business always comes first.

You'd think being their only child would give me some sort of prestige—or a reason for them to want to make sure I'm okay, but it never does. Most of the time I feel like an afterthought.

Until they need me for something.

Emotional support for my mom. Taking over the biz for dear old dad.

The bell rings, and within seconds, the hallway is flooded with students eager to head to lunch. I move in the opposite direction of most of them, needing to go back to my classroom to get my stuff where I left it at my desk, when I spot Carolina making her way toward me.

"Where are you going?" Her expression is the friendliest I think I've ever seen her, and it's kind of mind-blowing for a moment. This girl takes her scowls seriously.

"I left my stuff in the classroom." I take her hand and start dragging her along with me. "Come on."

She doesn't say a word but at least she doesn't try to pull her hand out of mine like she used to. She follows me into the classroom, my teacher just about to leave when we meet him in the doorway.

"I left my stuff in here," I tell him.

He nods, flicking off the lights, the room going dark. "Grab it and go. The door will lock behind you on your way out."

He sends us a stern look and then he's gone.

Carolina turns to face me, her brows drawn together. "Are you okay?"

I think about blowing her off and acting like everything is fine, but it's like I can't. "No."

Her frown deepens. "What's wrong?"

"My dad." I blow out a harsh breath, glancing toward the closed door. "He's sick. At the hospital."

"What's wrong?"

He's got cancer. He's dying. But I can't tell her that. I promised my father I'd keep it a secret. "Pneumonia. He's being treated and my mom just called me. He's staying overnight at the hospital, but he's going to be all right."

For now.

I lean against the teacher's desk, my butt resting on the edge and Carolina takes a step forward, touching my cheek lightly with her fingertips, her gaze meeting mine. So much concern swirls in the depths of her blue eyes, and when she cups my cheek, I lean into her palm, closing my eyes for a brief moment.

"You're scaring me," she whispers.

I crack open my eyes, offering her a wan smile. "It's okay. I'm just—worried. About my father. And my mother. I'm all they've got. The only child. Sometimes, it feels like a lot of pressure."

She stares at me, her fingers sliding down my face before they drift back up, pressing against my cheekbone. "Is everything all right? You've been acting different lately and I can't help but wonder if it might be because of…us."

"No, not at all," I say immediately. "It has nothing to do with you."

Her expression turns knowing. "So there is something else going on. What is it? You can tell me."

The truth is on the tip of my tongue, ready to spill all over the place, but I press my lips together to stifle the words. I can't tell her. Once I open my mouth, I won't be able to stop and then what's really going on with my family, my father's health, will be out there, and I won't be able to take it back. It could turn into public knowledge and my father would be furious.

It's not that I don't trust Carolina. I just don't know her well enough. My father reiterated to me how his health affects everything with the House of Fontaine. He's reassured board members and staff that he's in remission, which isn't fucking true.

My father is a liar. And he's made me become one too.

I hate that.

Instead of telling Carolina the truth, I lean in, slipping my arm around her waist at the same time I press my mouth to hers. Distracting her with a kiss, which is a distraction for me too. This feels like the first time we've been alone together in a while, and my need for her has been building. Rising within me and now that I've got her in my arms, I don't want to let her go.

Not yet.

She opens to me easily, her tongue tangling with mine, a soft sigh leaving her. The sound goes straight to my dick, making it ache, and I wrap both of my arms around her, hauling her into me so she can feel it.

Feel me.

"West." She rests her hand against my chest, pulling away from my still seeking lips. "We can't do this in here."

"We're fine. No one knows we're here." I try to kiss her again, but she dodges to the side and I end up planting my lips on her throat.

"West, we probably shouldn't…"

I feel her shiver when I race my mouth down her neck, licking at the spot where her pulse pounds. "It's okay."

I kiss her again before she can say anything else and she sinks into my lips, her tongue meeting mine, her arms winding around my neck. I can hear people walk by the closed door in the hallway, the low hum of their conversation drawing closer before it eventually drifts away. It happens over and over again, to the point that I choose to ignore it, confident that no one will bust in on us.

We won't be discovered, which only emboldens me.

Slowly, I slip my hand beneath her skirt, drifting my fingers along the back of her firm thigh. She shudders at my first touch, a whimper sounding low in her throat as I memorize her warm, soft skin with my fingertips. I trace the curve of her ass before sliding my fingers up, funneling beneath the thin cotton of her panties.

"West." My name is a harsh whisper against my lips when I palm her ass cheek. "We can't—"

"We can." I thrust my tongue in her mouth at the same time I slip my fingers inside her from behind, encountering nothing but wet heat. I pull away from her so I can see her flushed face. "You like it."

She doesn't disagree. She even spreads her legs a little wider, giving me better access as I essentially finger-fuck her in the middle of the empty classroom, while all of our friends are in the dining hall, no doubt wondering where we are.

"Oh." She moans when I push extra deep, her hands moving

to my shoulders, where she grips me tightly. I nip at her plump lower lip, adding another finger in the mix, stretching her wide. "I think—"

"Don't think," I murmur against her lips, increasing my pace. "Just come for me."

There's no more talking. Just the sound of our accelerated breaths, my fingers moving inside her cunt, the shuffle of her feet as she tries to remain standing. I tug her closer, making it easier for me to reach her pussy from behind, and she nudges her hips against mine, as if she's trying to create friction.

My dick threatens to burst out of my trousers, it's so hard. Doesn't help that she's rubbing herself against me, her breaths coming quicker, soft whimpers sounding in the back of her throat. I stretch out her panties with my hand, my fingers as deep inside her as I can get them, and a choked sound comes from her, followed by my name.

She's coming. Pulling her face away from mine, my eyes pop open just in time to catch her staring at me with wonder. Her eyes close, her head falling back, exposing that long, graceful line of her throat, and I bend my head, planting little kisses there while she rides her orgasm out on my hand.

When it's over, I let my hands fall away from her as she steps back, brushing the hair out of her face with shaky fingers. Her cheeks are pink, as is her neck, and I'd bet big money she's flushed like that everywhere.

"That was crazy," she says once she seems to have found her voice again.

I smile at her. "It's like every time I make you come, we're doing something crazy."

"It's all your fault then."

"Nah, I think it's all you." I bring my fingers to my mouth, the undeniable scent of her pussy still clinging to my skin. I breathe in deep, just before I wrap my lips around them and suck every last bit of her into my mouth. "You taste good. Next time, I think I'll bend you over a desk and go down on you from behind."

Somehow her cheeks get even pinker, and I realize something. She's just the distraction I need.

CHAPTER TWENTY-EIGHT

CAROLINA

I feel like we're living on borrowed time, West and me. And I can't even begin to explain why. Maybe it's the way he acts. Almost like he's desperate. He holds on to me like he never wants to let me go. I catch him looking at me like he fully expects me to disappear at any moment. When we're in public together, he rests his hand on me somewhere, anywhere he can reach, as if he's trying to claim me. Remind me that I belong to him.

Or maybe he's reminding himself that I'm right there, by his side.

He doesn't say much. We talk about surface things, like what's going on at school or with our friends. He doesn't speak of his family, not even his father who was hospitalized with pneumonia recently, but seems to have recovered fully.

My family is my least favorite subject to speak of, so it's easy for me not to talk about them. I don't talk about the future either. That part is scary—I have a feeling we won't be together. We never made any promises to each other, and while at the time of that rather odd conversation in the coffeeshop, I was fully intent on going to London the very second I graduated from Lancaster Prep, now...

Now I don't like thinking about my life without Weston

Fontaine in it.

Stupid, I know. I've turned into the very girl I used to make fun of. The one who would be lovesick over a boy who everyone knew they didn't have a future with. I always wondered why girls would waste their time with boys like that. We're too young. People change. Our lives take us in different directions.

I was so smug, so confident that I would never subject myself to a pain like that, and now here I am, neck deep in my feelings over West, knowing that something will eventually happen and we'll be over.

Sometimes late at night, when I'm lying in my bed alone and can't fall asleep, I think about the many ways I could end things with him. I could be brutal and just tell him I don't care about him anymore, but that would hurt. Or I wouldn't be able to choke the words out. I could tell him dance comes first in my life always, and I almost believe he would understand that. He might not have something like dance to give him purpose, but he's got the family business he's going to be responsible for someday. It will have to be important to him too.

Sexually, we've not done much beyond oral sex, and I know he wants more. He wants to fuck me. He's told me that already. Multiple times. But I keep pushing him away, making him wait.

I'm scared. That once I give that last little piece of myself that solely belongs to me, I won't be able to get it back. I'll become someone else. Someone who belongs to a man. A man who I won't actually be with forever. Instead, he'll become that constant reminder, that one guy who took my virginity and now I'm forever linked with him.

Why is there so much importance put on a girl's virginity? A boy can fuck whomever he wants and no one makes a big deal about it, but a girl should save herself. She's pure that way. Untouched. Innocent.

It's kind of gross.

I can't stop thinking about it. To the point that I'm starting to reverse my feelings on the subject and I bring it up to Sadie one lunch period when we're at the library instead of the dining hall with our boyfriends. We like to get away and have conversations on our own, like we did when we first met.

"Have you had sex with Brent yet?" I ask her.

She practically chokes while taking a drink from her water bottle. "A warning would've been nice," she sputters.

"Sorry." I watch as she wipes at her face with the back of her hand before recapping her bottle of water. "So, have you two had sex?"

Her gaze meets mine, her expression blank. "That's a very—private question."

I roll my eyes. "Come on. We're friends. Tell me."

"Yes," she admits, and I must give her a look because panic floods her features. "I know we moved fast, but oh my God, every time we're alone together, we start going at it and I swear he makes me so hor—"

I hold my hand up, stopping her. "That's enough. I don't need all the details."

Sadie laughs. "I gather you two haven't done the deed?"

I shake my head. "I think I'm putting too much pressure on myself, preserving my virginity for whatever dumb reason."

"Those are societal issues that we have nothing to do with," Sadie points out. "You can't let that make you feel guilty. Just go with how he makes you feel."

He makes me feel completely out of control lately, and I don't like that. I've been in control of everything in my life since the age of thirteen—save for the moment my parents made me come here, and now with my relationship with West. "I don't think our relationship is like yours and Brent's."

"What's that supposed to mean?" She sounds vaguely offended.

"I'm not knocking it, I promise. You two are just...moving faster than me and West."

"I see the way he looks at you." Sadie's smile is sly. "I think he's ready to move it as fast as he possibly can with you."

I didn't realize he was that obvious about his feelings toward me. "Maybe. I don't know. Sometimes he seems...troubled. Like something is weighing on him."

"Like what? You think he's having a hard time with all the talk around campus about the two of you?"

"What talk?" This is the first I've ever heard of "talk." I know people are gossiping about us. Of course, they are, we're a couple now. He's never had an actual girlfriend, and I'm a Lancaster. We automatically produce gossip.

"The usual stuff." She shrugs. "Mercedes tries to start a lot of talk about you two. How you stole him from her for one."

I burst out laughing. So loudly, Miss Taylor, the librarian, shushes me from her desk at the front of the building. "Please. She wishes I stole him from her." Seeing Sadie's confusion, I continue, "He was never hers to steal in the first place."

"Oh, right. Well, she loves to spin a good story. She's kind of awful." Sadie makes a face.

"She's totally awful. I hate her." I glance over my shoulder to make sure she's not lurking behind a book shelf, ready to use whatever I say against me. "She needs to go find a new victim to torment."

"Agreed." Sadie offers me a thoughtful smile. "If you think something is bugging West, you need to just ask him about it."

I nod, though I don't say anything. What she says sounds so logical. So simple. I should just ask him what's wrong, but will he tell me the truth? I feel like anytime I ask about his family, he evades the question. Or flat out changes the subject. Maybe it's upsetting, knowing his father isn't doing well, health-wise. Maybe he feels helpless that he's stuck here while his parents live in California.

They're the ones who went there. Who left him, just as he was barely starting his freshman year at Lancaster Prep. He shouldn't feel guilty.

They should.

"What about Halloween?" Sadie asks, changing the subject.

"What about it?"

"Are you two going to wear a couples' costume? That would be fun, don't you think?" Sadie opens her phone and starts scrolling. "I have some ideas, but everything I suggest to Brent he totally shoots down."

We spend the rest of lunch talking about Halloween costumes and it's just the distraction I need to focus on something that's fun versus worrying over West all the time.

And as I walk back to my building after class, I tell myself that he's basically an adult. We may be in high school, but he's eighteen. And when he's ready to discuss with me what's bothering him, he'll come to me. Maybe he's still trying to process things. Maybe his parents are evasive with him and he has no choice but to be evasive with me as well.

I enter the building and head for my suite, unlocking the door and pushing my way inside, stopping short when I see what's waiting for me on my desk.

A giant bouquet of the palest pink roses I've ever seen. Two dozen of them at least, maybe more. The flowers are already open, their delicate petals turned toward the sun and I drop my bag on my bed as I make my way to the desk, plucking the cream-colored envelope that's nestled in the arrangement and tearing it open.

It's from West. I recognize his handwriting, and while I knew before I even saw the note that the flowers were from him, it still gives me a little thrill, seeing his name signed on the card.

The color reminds me of you.

Xo,

West

"You like them?"

I turn to find him standing in my open doorway, his hands braced on either side of the doorframe. He's wearing the uniform trousers but no jacket, his biceps straining against the white fabric of his shirt, the sleeves rolled up, showing off his strong forearms.

My knees go weak and I smile at him like an idiot. "I love them."

He drops his arms and enters my room, stopping when he's standing directly in front of me. "Brent and I went off-campus at lunch and bought our girls gifts."

My heart leaps over itself at the words our girls. "What did Brent get Sadie?"

West grins. "I'll let Sadie tell you." He yanks me into his arms, holding me close. "I meant what I said in the note."

"About the color reminding you of me?" I brace my hands on his chest, my fingers curling into the fabric of his shirt.

"Yeah. You turn that shade of pink when you're embarrassed." He leans in and drops the softest kiss on my lips. "And when you're turned on."

I kiss him back, trying not to be embarrassed.

"The deepest pink on the roses? That's the color of your lips." Another kiss. "Your nipples." This kiss is deeper, with plenty of tongue. "Your pussy."

"West," I whisper, full-on embarrassed now. "Seriously?"

"Seriously." He starts to walk, guiding me backward, until the backs of my legs hit the bed. "I'll show you."

He releases his hold on me, and with a gentle push of his fingers on my shoulder, I fall back onto the bed, my gaze never leaving his. He stands in front of me, his hand going to his belt buckle, absently undoing it.

"What are you doing?" My voice is shaky with excitement, my entire body trembling. I recognize that look in his eyes.

He wants me.

"I've missed you." He pulls the belt from the loops of his

pants, letting it drop onto the floor with a loud clank.

"I've been right here all along," I remind him, my lips parting when he untucks his shirt from his pants, flashing me a glimpse of his flat stomach.

"I've been preoccupied." He must see my confusion. "Family stuff."

Right. The stuff we can't talk about.

"And I think I've been neglectful." He undoes his trousers, sliding down the zipper, exposing his black boxer briefs. "Toward you."

If he means because we haven't messed around lately, I figured that was because of midterms. They've been particularly intense, though for me that's because I rarely had an intense testing schedule when I was in London. Only for dance.

"I didn't feel neglected." That might be a minor lie, but I don't want him to ever feel guilty. I've always been an independent person, who doesn't need to rely on someone else for their entertainment. Most of the time growing up, I preferred to be alone. I did my best to escape from Sylvie, who was too needy, every chance I got. She wanted constant entertainment, mostly to keep away from our mother.

I suppose I can't blame her.

"Good." He lets his pants drop, toeing off his shoes before he kicks them off while also unbuttoning his shirt. "You should get undressed."

Laughing, I shake my head, my hair sliding over my shoulders. "Why don't you undress me instead?"

With a growl, he lunges for me, pouncing on the bed and making me squeal. His mouth is on my neck immediately, his hands working the buttons down the front of my shirt, undoing each one with smooth precision. No shakiness involved, no frazzled nerves on display. Just my sexy, confident boyfriend undressing me while he kisses along my jaw. My chin. Until that soft, warm mouth finds mine.

I sink into his kiss, our tongues tangling lazily, the bedframe squeaking when he shifts his weight more on top of me. I part my thighs, giving him room to settle between them and the moment our torsos connect, hot sparks singe my skin. I can feel his erection rubbing against me perfectly and I lift my hips, desperate for the connection.

"Hey." He grabs my wrists and pins my arms above my head, holding me there. I open my eyes and stare up at him, drinking in his every feature. His beautiful eyes and dark eyebrows. The way his longish hair hangs over his forehead. His firm jaw and square chin, offset by that sweet, sexy mouth of his. His chest is on display, leanly muscled and smooth, warm skin. "No getting off too fast."

I pout, struggling against his hold but that only makes him tighten his grip. "You're no fun."

"And you're always the one who's rushing toward the fun." He dips his head, his mouth moving against mine when he speaks. "Let's draw this out a little bit. There's no need to rush."

My problem, I think when he kisses me again, his tongue sweeping through my mouth, is that all I want to do is rush once he touches me. I'm chasing after that feeling only he can provide. The delicious tingles. The clenching low in my belly, the throb between my legs. He's responsible for my impatience.

He spreads my shirt open wide, his mouth never moving from mine, his hand cupping my breast, kneading it as he drifts his thumb back and forth across the front of my plain cotton bra. I should get lingerie. Something sexy and lacy, instead of boring and functional. I want to tell him my plan when he breaks away from my lips to mutter, "Your sweet little cotton bras drive me fucking crazy."

Sweet?

He rains kisses on my neck and chest, shifting downward, his fingers fiddling with the clasp on the front of my bra. "Same pink as the roses," he murmurs, flicking the tiny bow stitched above the bra's clasp.

Before I can say anything, he has it undone, the cups falling away from my chest, my nipples hard and pointing toward his mouth. I watch, breathless as he tongues one hard, pink point, drawing it into his mouth and sucking it deep before he lets it go. My hard flesh glistens from his lips and tongue, the cool air hitting it, making me shiver, and I cup the back of his head when he does the same to the other one, holding him to me. The more he sucks, the more restless I become, and that familiar, needy throb intensifies down low.

"You're so little," he tells me once he lifts away from me slightly, his fingers drifting over my ribs. My stomach. "But so strong. You're nothing but muscle."

I used to worry he might not find that attractive, but right now? He's worshiping my body with his hands and mouth. It's obvious he likes me.

"You could probably kill me with these muscular thighs of yours." He presses his hands on the inside of my thighs and spreads me wide open, my skirt riding up. "We need to get rid of this."

Within seconds, the skirt is gone. So is my bra and shirt. Until I'm lying there with just my panties on, my shoes now on the floor but my socks still on my feet.

"West." I squirm beneath his visual assessment, both loving and hating how he watches me so carefully. "I wish we could…"

My voice drifts and I press my lips together, wondering if I can say it out loud.

"You wish what?" He sucks my nipple back into his mouth, his teeth nibbling, making me cry out in both pain and pleasure. "Use your words, baby."

Never before has he called me baby and any other time I would be like, ew, no.

Not this time. A surge of moisture floods my panties at the endearment and I thrust my hands in his hair, holding him to me.

"I wish we could fuck."

The words leave me in a breathless rush and he lifts his head, staring at me with those intense brown eyes, my core tightening in anticipation of the promise I see in their depths.

There's a loud clatter that comes from nearby—possibly the hallway? Like someone dropped something to the floor. We both lift up, staring at the door, which is still standing wide open.

Shit. We forgot to close it.

"Stay here," West commands as he rises from the bed and pads over to the open door, carefully peeking his head out to survey the hallway. It swivels left, then right, and he stares for a long, quiet time until he carefully closes the door, turning the lock before he returns to the bed.

I'm shivering by the time he returns, completely freaked out. Did someone just witness us together like this? Did they hear what I said? Was it someone on staff?

It could be anyone.

"No one was out there." He gathers me in his arms and holds me close, murmuring reassuring words against my temple but just like that the mood is ruined. I can't stop thinking about what happened.

Who was out there? Who snuck in?

And are they going to tell anyone what they saw?

CHAPTER TWENTY-NINE

CAROLINA

Halloween is not a holiday I usually celebrate. When we were children, we didn't go trick-or-treating. That was far too beneath my mother's standards, walking around our neighborhood begging for candy "like poor people" I heard her say once.

Considering she also regaled us with stories about her own youthful trick-or-treat endeavors, I always thought that was rather hypocritical of her. She just didn't want to deal with the ritual.

When we were very young, me almost too young to remember, every year, my mother would throw extravagant costume parties the weekend before Halloween for her friends' children and us, of course. I don't remember having much fun. I specifically recall crying one year—I must've been four—because Whit dressed as a vampire and chased me around the house with his fake teeth and "blood" dripping from the corners of his mouth. Sylvie laughing the entire time.

My siblings were the worst.

My subtle dislike for the holiday grew over the years until I flat-out ignored it when it came around. I dressed up in costumes all the time for the stage. Beautiful, glittering costumes were my life. Why would I need to wear an ugly, cheap one for a useless

holiday where fattening candy is given to children in some sort
of morbid ritual that has pagan origins?

No thanks.

This year, I'm faking my joy for the holiday for Sadie. She's
so excited about the party that's being held at one of the old,
burned-out buildings on campus after hours that I think she
might pass out and miss the entire event. I actually got an edible
from Brent to give to her to nibble on so she'll mellow out while
I work on her makeup in my suite.

"I love it back here. Your room is so big," she says as she
wanders around my suite, going to the window so she can stare
outside. "It's so private though. Do you ever get freaked out,
being out here all alone?"

I think of the afternoon a couple of days ago, when I'd
hoped West and I would finally have sex but were interrupted
by something—or someone. "Not really." That was the only time
I felt nervous, and I've tried to put the moment out of my mind.
"The doors are locked every evening and it's pretty secure. I like
the privacy."

She glances over at me, watching as I go through the various
cosmetics that I have in my vanity table drawer. "You do seem
to like your alone time."

"I don't have a problem being alone," I correct, noting the
way her brows draw together. "You don't like being alone?'

"No way." She shifts away from the window and plops on the
edge of my bed closest to the vanity. "With all of my brothers
and sisters growing up, I was never alone. Then I came here and
I was completely ostracized. That was the worst, spending those
lunch hours in the library with no one to talk to. Until you."

I smile. "Until me."

"I'm glad we're friends, Carolina. Sometimes I think I might
irritate you because I don't ever seem to stop talking, yet you still
want to spend time with me." She scoots forward, throwing her
arms around me and squeezing me tight so quickly, I'm frozen

in place for a bit. I didn't expect her to touch me, so I didn't have time to prepare for it. "Thank you for being my friend."

"You're welcome." I reach around her, patting her back awkwardly until I finally just give in and squeeze her back. It's not so bad, hugging people you like. "You have other friends now. And Brent."

"All of those other girls are fake bitches compared to you. At least you keep it real." She pulls away from me. "And yeah, I have Brent. He keeps it real with me too. I think I'm in love with him."

Love. She tosses the word around so carelessly. I can't imagine saying that about West to someone else.

I can't imagine telling him that now.

I love you.

The words would sputter on my tongue and I would make a complete fool of myself. Besides, I can't bring myself to say something I don't know the meaning of.

Do I love West? I'm not sure. I like him a lot. He's kind to me—now. He's interesting, though he's also secretive. I am too, though. Sometimes I feel as if we're just circling each other, waiting for the other to give in first.

Give in to what, I'm still not sure.

"Really? You're in love with him?" I ask when I realize she's waiting for me to respond. "Why do you say that?"

"I get all tingly every time I catch him looking at me, which is often. He makes me laugh. Like all the time. And the sex is so good. Like, I didn't know it could be like that." She bites her lip, just before she starts giggling. "I feel like a grown-up."

"You're only seventeen, right?" I'm in the grade above her. Have lived mostly on my own for years, yet I still don't feel like a grown-up. Not even close.

"I'm actually eighteen. I got held back one year because of my family traveling all the time. Mom's homeschool regimen wasn't as great as she thought it was." More laughter as she bounces up and down on my bed. "Want to get started on the makeup?"

I have whiplash from my conversations with Sadie, but I'd rather do her makeup than talk about feelings and how much we love our boyfriends. "Yes, let's do it."

"Yay! We're running out of time. I want to be out at the old building by nightfall."

The boys are out there already, setting everything up. The party is a tradition, started by my brother of all people, who hosted his own wild Halloween party his senior year back when he was here at Lancaster Prep. Once that started, the students kept the tradition going, and West and his group of friends are the ones in charge of it this year.

I sort of felt like I should have had a hand in some of the planning since I'm a Lancaster and my brother started this, but West reassured me that they had everything under control. Unless bad weather prevented the party from happening, there wasn't much needed at the location anyway. Lights, electricity, plenty of alcohol and music was all that was required.

"What are you dressing up as? You never did tell me," Sadie says as I start working on her foundation, which is so pale it's almost white. They're going as vampires—my brother would surely approve.

"A flapper." I found the cutest dress for the costume, and West ordered a suit costume on Amazon. "We're from the 1920s," I explain when I see her little frown.

"Like *The Great Gatsby*? Oh, I loved that movie!"

"We just read the book for English," I tell her.

"Meh, I won't read it. Hopefully everything they test us on is in the movie. I'll need to rewatch it! I'm a total fan of Leonardo." She starts shimmying and I give her a stern look, which makes her stop. "Just think, I could possibly be his girlfriend one day. He doesn't like them over twenty-five, remember?"

That's just gross. "What, so he gets older yet all of his girlfriends stay the same age?"

"Essentially. When you're Leonardo, I guess you can get away with that."

I dab some concealer under her eyes. "What about your relationship with Brent?"

"What about it?" When I send her a knowing look, she shrugs. "If you're implying Brent and I will end up together forever, I'm going to have to say probably not. We're young. I still have another year in high school after you guys graduate. I'm pretty sure we're not going to last."

I almost admire how breezy she is about the entire situation. "And you're okay with that?"

"We're in high school, Carolina." She grins, and I nearly poke her eye out with the concealer wand when she moves. "I'm not looking for an epic love story when a fun high school romance will suffice."

"Suffice? Nice word choice." I set the concealer on the table and grab a sponge, blending the concealer with little dabs. "And I thought you were in love with him."

"I am. But we both know it's nothing serious. I can love him and not want to marry him." Her eyes widen the slightest bit. "Are you saying you're in love with West and can imagine the two of you together forever?"

"Absolutely not," I practically snap, leaning back to check out my work. Sadie looks ghostly pale, which I think was her intention. "I don't know how I feel about him."

"You're not in love with him?" Sadie sounds shocked. "I see the way he looks at you. How he's always touching you."

I'm tingly at her just saying that. "That's just lust, not love."

"I don't know about that." Sadie sounds skeptical, but I can't let her reaction get my hopes up. "He seems pretty concerned about you all the time. I think you mean a lot to him."

She doesn't know, I think as I start shading her cheekbones to make them appear hollower. I might mean something to him, but is it enough? No. Not really. We're not serious. I shouldn't want us to be serious. I'm leaving. He's leaving. There's no point.

But there's also the tiniest part of me that wants us to be

something...more. Something real and powerful and true. I want him to fall in love with me and want to be with me forever. What would it be like, knowing that Weston Fontaine was mine, forever?

I don't think I'm ever going to find out.

By the time we're headed out to the old building, it's dark. Almost seven o'clock. Sadie had a full bottle of vodka in her bag of goodies that she brought to my room and we pre-partied, as she called it, though I only took a few sips.

I want to keep my wits about me tonight. I've been on edge since that afternoon in my room with West, and I want to be fully functional while I'm around my classmates.

As we draw closer, we can hear the low bass of music playing. The constant murmur of multiple, excited conversations. I sneak my arm through Sadie's and clutch her close, trying to fight the nervousness bouncing in my stomach, turning what little food and vodka that's in there into a nauseating swirl.

"There are so many people here," Sadie practically squeals, resting her hand over mine as the building comes into view.

"How do we not get in trouble for doing this?" I ask weakly, my gaze scrutinizing every face I see, recognizing none of them. They either have masks on, or their faces are painted, or they're wearing a wig. Maybe even a combination of all three.

"They turn a blind eye to this party every single year. As long as things don't get too out of control, they don't mind." When I send her a questioning look Sadie explains further, "Brent told me because I asked him the same question."

I need to talk to my brother about the party he threw. I wonder if he'd be forthcoming with the details—or tell me to go to hell, which is what he usually says when I question him about anything he's done in the past.

As we draw closer to the building, the ground grows softer, my sparkly gold heels sinking into the grass. It was raining earlier this week for a few days straight, and the air is chilly. Winter is coming soon, and from what I hear, it's rather cold and dreary at Lancaster during those months.

I should feel right at home. It's the same in London during the winter.

Clusters of people are standing outside, clutching beer bottles, their happy chatter growing louder. There's lots of laughter and squealing, and I can see bodies inside the building—well, there's no roof since it burned over one hundred years ago, but there are at least still walls—moving to the music that's playing.

My feet are pinched in the heels and the dress I'm wearing is cheap and itchy, but I like the way it looks. It's white and sleeveless, sparkly thin straps holding it up, with the skirt hitting me mid-thigh. Almost the entire dress is covered in white sparkly fringe that moves when I walk, the hem of the skirt covered in white feathers. I have a thin gold headband that wraps around my head, with a white feather that sticks straight up. Ropes of actual pearls circle my neck, inherited from my great-grandmother. I'm taking a total risk wearing them, but I have never worn them before either, so I thought I might as well give them a try.

"Oh, there they are!" Sadie thrusts her hand into the air, waving excitedly at Brent and West, who are standing near the old, rickety steps that lead into the building. "Hey!"

My gaze sticks on West at the same time he sees me, his lips shifting into a smirk. I stand a little taller, my steps becoming more confident when I know he's watching me; and as I make my way toward him, he leaves Brent to meet me halfway, gathering my hands in his and spreading my arms wide so he can study me closely.

"Look at you," he says with a low whistle, his tone admiring. "Damn, girl."

"You like it?" I sound hopeful. God, I sound like Sadie, all jittery and excited when I should be trying to play it cool.

"You look fucking hot." I give a little shimmy, the sparkly white tassels swinging. "I don't know what to say."

I laugh, savoring the heady feeling of leaving West at a loss for words at my outfit.

I think that's a first.

"I love your suit," I tell him, my voice quiet. It's a standard black tux with a black bowtie and stark white, pleated front shirt, but he looks so incredibly handsome. His hair is slicked back, just like they wore it in the movie and his face is clean-shaven. I cup his cheek, unable to resist, a giggle escaping me when he kisses me in front of everyone right on the lips.

"These look real." He gently tugs at the strand of pearls around my neck. "You should be careful."

"They were my great-grandmother's," I inform him, thrilled when he drops the necklace and offers his arm for me to take. I circle mine through his and he leads me up the stairs and into the building, which is even more crowded with people.

"You better watch out," he says, dipping his head close to mine, so I can hear him over the loud music. "Don't want to break them."

"Protect me and I'm sure I'll be fine." I smile up at him, surprised when he leans in and kisses me again, leaving me dizzy.

"I'll protect you from everyone." He gives my arm a squeeze. "Promise."

He leads me to a makeshift bar and I grab a bottle of beer, taking a quick sip before I whisper in his ear, "I'm not drinking much tonight."

"I'm buzzin'," he admits, a sly smile on his face as he grabs my beer and takes a giant swig from it.

"I can tell." I glance around the room, my gaze snagging on the bodies moving to the music in the center of the floor. "We should dance."

"I have two left feet, remember?" He raises his brows.

How could I ever forget? The nightclub in Paris. Oh, I was so awful to him then, and now look at me. In a puddle just from the way this boy looks at me.

"I can dance well enough for the both of us." I take his hand, letting him keep the beer as I drag him toward the group of people dancing. "Come on."

The song ends, "Shake It Off" by Taylor Swift coming on, and while it's not a favorite, it is spectacularly easy to dance to. I move to the beat, letting the music flow through me, mouthing along to the lyrics. My dress puts on a show of its own, the sparkly tassels swinging, the feathers fluttering around my thighs. West sort of stands there, not really dancing at all though he watches me carefully, his gaze admiring. Full of emotion I don't quite recognize.

The song is over quickly, a slow song coming on, and West yanks me toward him without hesitation, his hands sliding around my waist, over my butt as we start to move. I loop my arms around his neck, my fingers toying with his soft hair.

"You're beautiful," he tells me, his gaze sincere as we dance. It's so intense, I get lost in it a little. Everyone around us fades, and it's like we're the only two in this building. Dancing to the music. Feeling each other.

"So are you," I say with a tiny smile, which makes him smile in return. "We've come a long way."

"From the mean, fake Parisian girl to the sweet little dancer that you are now? I'll say," he drawls, teasing me.

"You," I slide my hand down, giving him a light slap on the chest, "are mean."

He leans in close, inhaling as if he's trying take in my scent, his mouth drifting across my cheek before he whispers in my ear, "You like it."

He's right. I do. I'm grateful he's holding me or else I'd collapse to the floor, my knees weakened by his whispered words.

I close my eyes as we shuffle together, my forehead lightly resting against his shoulder, his arms tightening around me. This feels so right, being with him. In his arms. Forgetting everyone else and just focusing on him and the way he makes me feel.

With West, I want too much. I want everything he can give me. The more time I spend with him, the more I want to spend time with him, and I realize…

I'm becoming dependent on him. Probably too much.

It's going to hurt when it's over. I don't know if I'll be able to survive it.

But I'm a Lancaster, after all.

We can survive anything.

CHAPTER THIRTY

WEST

I'm feeling extra protective over Carolina tonight. I glare at every motherfucker who dares to look in her direction, enthralled with that damn dress she's wearing. I can't blame them. I about swallowed my tongue the moment I saw her in it. All glittery white with plenty of skin on display, that little smile on her face. Her long legs appearing even longer thanks to the sparkling gold heels on her feet.

She's gained weight over the last couple of months. She's not on that rigorous training schedule any longer and she's eating more, which I'd like to take credit for. She was monitoring every calorie that went into her mouth, and I get that she had to be strict when she was dancing, but still.

Carolina took it a little too far.

As we slow dance together, I let my gaze drift, checking out everyone in the room with us. I'm still suspicious of everyone on campus, wondering who the hell was spying on us that day in the hallway. When I had Carolina almost naked and panting on her bed, asking me to fuck her.

Only for everything to be ruined by that loud crashing sound. Had it been some random accidental fall? Or was someone actually watching us that afternoon? I don't know, and I did some investigating, but no one would talk.

Not like I could give them all the details, so I wasn't talking either. I asked a few leading questions that lead to further questions but when I didn't want to answer them, I bowed out.

And let it be.

I spot Mercedes dancing with some asshole who I don't like that's in our grade and her gaze catches mine, her lips curving into a knowing smile. I look away, not wanting her to think anything of it and I squeeze my arms around Carolina's slender waist, wishing I could take her someplace else. Anywhere else but here.

Huh. Who says I can't?

The song is almost over when I whisper, "Want to get out of here?"

She lifts her head, a little frown on her face. "Where do you want to go?"

"Back to your room?" I decide to tease her. "I'll make sure and shut and lock the door this time."

Her brows draw together in concern. "I still wonder who was there."

"I'm guessing no one." I say this to make her—and myself—feel better. "Maybe we were just hearing things. Or it was the wind."

"Sure." She sounds doubtful and I decide to change the subject.

The song ends, another fast one coming on and I grab hold of Carolina's hand, dragging her through the crowd until we're outside once more, standing at the top of the steps.

"Ready to go? Or do you want to hang out a little while longer?" I ask her.

"Oh, there's Sadie and Brent." She points to where they're standing. "Let's talk to them a few minutes and then we can leave."

"I'm going to grab another beer. I'll be right back." I kiss her cheek.

"Okay. Hurry back." She lets go of my hand and heads toward where Brent and Sadie are standing, talking with a small group of students.

I make my way back into the building, heading straight for the bar when Mercedes appears directly in front of me, stopping me in my tracks.

"What do you want?" I ask, already bored.

Her dark eyes flashing, Mercedes reaches out, poking me in the chest. "I know what you're up to. And if I were you, I'd watch out."

More empty threats from a girl who wishes she could boss all of us around. "I don't know what the hell you're talking about, but leave me alone, Mercedes. You know how I feel."

"I do know how you feel," she starts, an irritated noise escaping her when I step around her and make my way toward the bar. "I know everything, you stupid ass. And I can ruin you if I so choose."

Please. She wishes. "I'm real scared."

"You should be." She stops right next to me as I wait in line for my turn at the bar, messing around on her phone until she brings up a video, hits play and thrusts the screen in front of my face.

It's of Carolina's room, and there's no sound. It's from that afternoon, the two of us together, me on top of her, undoing the buttons on her shirt as we kiss. Fuck, I can see our tongues, I can see Carolina's bra, the way she trembles when I reach for the front of it and flick it open—

"Turn that off," I bite out, trying to steal the phone from Mercedes, but she's too quick. She thrusts it behind her back, taking a step away from me. "Where the fuck did you get that?"

"I'm resourceful," is all she says, smiling prettily. "Just—watch what you do and say, West. This can all come back to bite you in the ass someday."

I blink at her, shocked that she's not trying to purposely blackmail me.

Yet.

"Oh, and nice technique with the nipple sucking." She takes a step closer, her voice lowering so, somehow, no one else can hear. "Kind of got me hot, not going to lie."

She's gone before I can say anything, and I glance around, wondering if anyone noticed what she said. Or what she showed me.

But everyone else in this place is partying without a care in the world. No one is paying attention to me, or to Mercedes.

By the time it's my turn at the bar, the kid who's working it hands over a can of beer with a woeful expression on his face. "Watch out for her."

"Who?" And who is this asshole to warn me?

"That chick. Mercedes. She's fucking crazy. Gives a great blow job but a complete psycho."

"Give me another beer," I demand and he does what I ask with no hesitation. "And don't worry. That bitch can't touch me."

I leave him, pushing my way through the crowd, anger rushing through my veins, leaving me hot. By the time I find Carolina laughing with Brent and Sadie, I'm fucking furious, chugging the first beer before I toss the empty in a nearby garbage can and crack open the next one.

"Don't you think you should slow down?" That's the first thing Carolina says to me, and it's fucking irritating as shit.

"I'm fine." I swallow half of it, my head spinning. "Ready to go?"

"You okay, man?" This comes from Brent, who's watching me with concern.

"I'm fucking great," I snap, taking Carolina's arm. "Let's go."

She leaves with me, quiet for most of the walk back to her building, her expression completely unreadable. I nurse the rest of the beer in the can, tossing it in a bush when she enters the code and the door unlocks.

"Why isn't that implemented during the day?" I ask when we

enter the building.

"I don't know. No one's complained before," she tosses over her shoulder.

Damn it, she sounds pissed.

"Well, maybe you should. This is some bullshit, Carolina. Someone was lurking around in the hall and fucking spying on us. They need to lock the doors."

A sigh leaves her. "I'm trying not to make any waves."

"Make any waves? Someone was watching us and we were practically naked. Yet you don't want to be a troublemaker or whatever? You fucking own this school." I make a dismissive noise, my steps faltering. Shit, I practically trip over my own feet.

"You're drunk."

She's right. I am. "So?"

"So, this conversation is pointless." She stops right in front of the closed door of her suite, turning to face me. God, she's beautiful and I'm ruining the entire night by becoming a sloppy drunk and not telling this girl that I care about the truth.

That Mercedes is the one who was hanging out in the hallway. Who fucking recorded us and will most likely put us on blast somehow so everyone can see us together. It's disgusting, what she's done.

I hate her.

"You won't remember it in the morning. Maybe you should go back to your dorm room," Carolina suggests before she turns toward her door and hits the keypad, gaining entry into her room. "Go sleep it off, Weston."

Ooh, busting out the full name. I'm seriously in trouble. "You're really kicking me out?"

I follow her inside the room, pulling the door shut and twisting the lock into place.

Never going to make that mistake again.

"I think it's probably best." She turns to face me, that haughty, gorgeous expression on her face. The one that tells me she's mad. Annoyed.

I can't blame her. Mercedes ruined my fucking mood and I took it out on Carolina, which isn't fair.

"I'm sorry." I run a hand through my hair before I reach up and undo the bowtie around my neck that is suddenly strangling me. I tear it off, tossing it on the nearby desk, then start unbuttoning my shirt.

Her hungry gaze tracks my every movement, giving me hope I can rectify this situation. "For what?"

"For getting drunk and being shitty." I tug the too long shirt out of my trousers, frustrated. "You look so fucking beautiful in that dress and all I could think about was getting you back here and seeing what you were wearing underneath the white sparkles."

She goes still, blinking at me. "And that what...made you mad?"

I shrug, not wanting to explain myself. "Feeling a little frustrated, not gonna lie."

Her expression softens and she takes a couple of steps toward me, her gaze roaming over my now exposed chest. "You're probably too drunk."

"Too drunk for what?" I squint at her, my head spinning a little. I had a lot to drink, and yeah, I'm probably too drunk for whatever she's suggesting.

"For us having sex," she says, her voice small.

Okay, yeah, no. I'm not too drunk for that.

"You want to have sex?"

Carolina nods.

"With me?"

She rolls her eyes, her lips curling into the faintest smile. "Okay, you're definitely too drunk for this."

"No, no way. I wanna do it. I've been thinking about nothing else since you arrived on campus. You drove me wild, you know. With those snotty looks on your face and the way you would get so pissy with me. Fuck, it was a turn-on."

Her eyes widen in surprise. "You're lying."

"Hell no." I shake my head. "You drive me out of my mind, woman. All I can think about is how I can get you alone again. Get my mouth on you. Make you come. When you'll put your mouth on me again. You've got a great mouth, Carolina." I reach out to touch it, drifting my thumb across her lower lip.

She doesn't move but parts her lips for my thumb, and when I sink it in between her lips, she bites it, her teeth sharp enough to sting. "And you're super drunk, Weston."

"You only bring out the full name when you're mad at me. Like my mom."

The last person I want to think about. She called me earlier today to tell me the news.

My father isn't feeling well, and she thinks it's the cancer. He denies it to her, but he's thinner. Moving slower. He stops midsentence and forgets what he was talking about and his appetite has all but disappeared.

"I'm afraid it's back," she whispered to me over the phone, the fear evident in her voice. "But I'm scared to say something."

That's some shit. I don't want a relationship like that. With secrets and lies and fear. Yet here I am, keeping the biggest secret that's currently torturing me.

Wait, make that two secrets. My dad dying and that damn video Mercedes showed me.

Shit.

"Sorry. You probably don't want me to remind you of your mom," Carolina says, barely able to contain that beautiful smile that wants to spread across her equally beautiful face.

I go to her, catching her face in my hands, so I can stare at her. I let my gaze rove over her every feature, listing them in my mind. I remember when I thought she was a little funny looking. All bony and fierce. Now I look at her and see nothing but beauty.

See nothing but the girl I'm falling for.

Fuck, I'm going to ruin everything by doing this.

"Don't let me hurt you, okay?" She frowns, and I give her face a slight shake. "Just—prepare yourself for what I'm going to do."

"What are you going to do, Weston?" she asks, her voice a breathy whisper.

"I'm going to fuck everything up." I kiss her before she can respond, stealing her words, not wanting to hear what she has to say. What excuses she might make or how she thinks it's a bad idea if we do whatever she thinks we should be doing. I should've kept my mouth shut. It was a bad move, making her aware that there was some shit on the horizon and she needs to prepare.

Like we're waiting for a hurricane or whatever. She needs to batten down the hatches and make sure everything's secure before the tornado roars through and destroys everything.

I'm the tornado here. The hurricane. A natural disaster, it doesn't matter which one.

"What are you talking about?" she asks when I end the kiss to shrug out of my suit jacket.

I remember the look on her face when she first saw me in my costume. How happy she looked. How fucking beautiful she was.

Still is.

"Don't worry about it," I mutter just as I grab her and haul her into me, my hands on her face once more as I devour her mouth. The kiss is frantic. Fucking feral. I search her mouth with my tongue, letting one hand drop to her ass, so I can give it a squeeze, and she rips herself out of my grasp, backing away from me, her breathing heavy.

"You're acting strange." She wipes at her mouth with the back of her hand, her lips red from my savage kiss. Her skin blotchy and pink because she's so turned on. We stand next to each other and all I can think about is how can I get her naked.

I know she feels the same way.

"You're right." I undo the cufflinks on my wrists, letting them drop onto the floor before I practically rip my shirt off. "I might be a little drunk. But not too drunk for you."

She's backing away from me as I stalk toward her, my hands at my waist, fingers fumbling with the belt buckle. "West, please. Tell me what's wrong."

"Nothing's wrong." I undo the buckle, tackling the button and zipper of my trousers, the weight of the belt still around my hips, causing the front of my pants to hang open, my erection straining. "I want you, baby. Can't you tell."

Without warning, she grabs hold of me and practically tosses me on the bed. My confused drunk ass goes willingly, falling onto the mattress with a grunt, rolling over on my back to find her glaring down at me as she stands by the side of the bed, her hands on her hips, her face an angry mask.

"You are way too drunk to function right now, Weston Fontaine." She gestures toward me, her long, elegant fingers flicking. "You need to go to sleep."

"Come on." I hold my arms out to her. "Lay with me."

"No way." She shakes her head. "I'm taking a shower and I fully expect you to be asleep when I'm done."

"I'm not tired." My eyelids fall to half-mast.

"You look like you're falling asleep right now."

"Nope." My eyes are fully shut, but I'm still in denial. "I messed everything up, didn't I?"

The mattress shifts when she sits on the edge of the bed, her fingers drifting along my arm. "Yeah. I feel like something is bothering you, but you don't want to share it with me."

She's coming way too close to the truth. "You don't want to know."

"But I do."

We're quiet for a moment, and I swear if I concentrate enough, I can hear the party still raging on outside, the bass of the music thumping. The sounds of girls screaming, having a good time.

"I can't tell you." I sound miserable. I feel even worse. "It's family shit. You won't care anyway."

I don't mean what I say. I'm just pissed. At life. And all the curveballs that are constantly thrown at me.

"When it has to do with you, I will always care," she whispers and those words make me feel even shittier.

We don't say anything else to each other. Eventually, she rises from the bed and goes about the room, gathering her things. I shut my eyes as tight as I can, and roll over on my side, facing the wall, my back to her. She enters the bathroom and shuts the door firmly.

The last thing I remember is hearing the water turn on before I drift off to sleep.

CHAPTER THIRTY-ONE

CAROLINA

I wake up out of a dead sleep with a gasp, my eyes flashing open to find my bedroom still completely shrouded in darkness, a heavy arm draped across my waist. A wall of heat is at my back and it's currently shifting, something particularly hard poking my butt when he moves.

It's West.

He was passed out completely when I came out of the shower earlier, his shirt gone and his pants undone and shoved halfway down his hips. As if he fell asleep while trying to take them off, and as drunk as he was, I wouldn't be surprised. I tugged them off before I crawled into bed with him and fell into a deep sleep instantly.

At the party he acted so strangely. At first, he seemed happy enough, but then his mood quickly switched to anger. I blame the alcohol. He was completely shit faced, but does this mean he's an angry person deep inside? I was always told your truest self comes out when you drink.

If that's the case, West is hiding a lot of anger.

A low hum sounds close to my ear, making me shiver. I'm only in a pair of panties and his hand currently rests on my bare stomach, his fingers lightly skimming across my skin. Is he awake? I decide to test it.

"West?" My voice is more whisper than sound and I wait, holding my breath for a response.

"Hmm?" His hands wander, both of them sliding up, cupping my breasts, his thumbs playing with my nipples.

"You're awake." I hiss in a breath when he pinches a nipple.

"I am." He sounds amused, his voice a rough, raspy sound that I feel to the very core of my being.

"What are you doing?" I mean, I know what he's doing, but why now? Isn't he still drunk? Maybe not.

"What I should've done earlier but my drunk ass couldn't handle it." He chuckles. "You feel so damn good, Carolina." The sound rumbles from his chest, making my skin catch on fire and I arch my chest into his hands, sinking my teeth into my lower lip to keep from moaning.

I never want him to stop touching me.

His hands slide down my ribcage. Across my stomach. Over my hips and down further, sliding in between my thighs, pausing there. "Roll over onto your back."

West shifts away to give me room and I follow his command, lying on my back and staring up at the ceiling, my gaze falling to watch as he positions himself over me, his mouth settling on my neck. Raining hot kisses along my throat. On my shoulders. Across my collarbone and chest. The tops of my breasts. His hot breath drifts across one nipple, making me close my eyes at the sensation, a whimper leaving me when he draws the hard bit of flesh into his mouth and sucks. Hard.

I sink my fingers into his hair, holding him to me as he sucks and licks. The more he does it, the more restless I grow, until my legs are twisting and my fingers are pulling his hair. He kisses his way down my stomach, his hands back on the inside of my thighs, spreading me as wide as he can, before he attacks me with his mouth.

A teeth-rattling groan escapes me and I lift my hips, seeking more of his greedy lips. He licks me everywhere he can, his tongue teasing my entry, circling it. Thrusting inside—just before he replaces it with his fingers. I about shoot off the bed when he does that, two fingers pushing deep inside me.

"So fucking tight," he mutters as he finger-fucks me, his rhythm steady, his thumb rubbing my distended clit in tight little circles. "I wanna make you come."

His words send me over the edge, surprising me. My entire body erupts in goosebumps as the shudders wrack my body, the orgasm rolling through me. I'm grinding my pussy against his mouth, his lips sucking my clit, and it's too much. I try to roll away from him but he grabs hold of my hips, keeping me in place, his mouth softening as he kisses the sensitive skin just above my pussy.

"I want you so fucking bad, Carolina." The desperation in his voice matches the feelings currently swirling within me and I reach for him, the relief that floods me when his mouth finally finds mine almost overwhelming.

We kiss and kiss, his tongue thrusting inside of my mouth matching his fingers which are still inside of my body. I'm so wet I can hear his fingers slick through my flesh, and his cock is heavy against my stomach, insistent as it stretches the front of his boxer briefs. I reach for the waistband, trying to shove them off his body and he rolls away from me, rising to stand so he can shuck them off hurriedly.

I watch, staring at him as if I haven't seen him naked before, my gaze cataloging every single thing about him. His broad shoulders and defined arms. The flat expanse of his ridged stomach. That trail of dark hair that leads from below his navel straight to his erection. He's so big. Thick and long and I lick my lips, lifting my gaze when I hear his tortured groan.

"What's wrong?"

"You can't stare at me like that, Carolina. Like you want to devour me." His voice is pure sexual misery.

"Maybe I do."

He rejoins me on the bed, positioning himself so he hovers above me, his hands planted on the mattress, on either side of my head. He stares into my eyes, his expression soft, his lips swollen and my heart flips over itself.

I care about this boy so much. Too much. It feels dangerous right now, my emotions. Like everything could explode in my face at any given moment.

I shove the ugly thought aside, telling myself not to worry.

"You put your lips on my dick and I'll come," he says bluntly. "And I'm not wasting this on a blow job."

"But wh—"

He kisses me before I can finish the sentence and I'm lost. Lost in the press of his hot body on top of mine. The softness of his lips, the heat of his tongue. He slides his hands down my sides, his fingers curving around my hips, adjusting me and when I feel his cock resting at my entry, I know the moment is close.

We're about to have sex for the first time. My first time ever.

I press my hands against his chest, causing him to break the kiss and lift up slightly. "Are you okay?"

"You don't have to use a condom. I'm on birth control."

It took me forever to get my period—I was fourteen when it finally came and then it threw my hormones completely off balance. When I came home for the summer after I first got my period, I was a raging, hormonal bitch and my mother took me to the gynecologist and put me on birth control immediately.

It's been fairly smooth sailing ever since.

"I remember." He starts to dip his head but I push his chest again, stopping him. "What?"

"How did you know?" I'm confused.

"The night we first met. At the opera house. You told the security guard you left your birth control pills inside and you needed to get them," he reminds me.

I smile, slowly shaking my head. "At the time, I didn't think you could understand French."

"I know, and I did. I understood every single word you said." His smile is sweet and I shift my hand so it's placed directly over his heart. It thumps wildly, just like mine.

"I want to feel you," I whisper. "Every single inch of you."

He parts his lips but doesn't say anything, his gaze roaming over my face slowly. As if he too is trying to memorize my every feature so he can remember it later. "It's going to hurt."

"I don't care." I slip my arms around his neck, burying my fingers in his hair. "You'll make it better. You always do."

That's the closest I will get to saying I care about him. It's so hard for me to say the words. To express emotions that will only leave me vulnerable.

Something unrecognizable shines in his eyes just before he dips his head and kisses me again, his mouth stealing my breath, my thoughts. All I can do is feel.

He ends the kiss and wraps his fingers around his erection, brushing it against me, pressing the head to my clit. I arch beneath him, wanting more, growing tense the moment he slips just the tip inside of me.

It's so thick. I don't know if I can do this.

"Relax," he whispers. "I'll go slow. I promise."

His words ease some of my fear and I do my best to do as he says and relax, but it's difficult. He slips inside of me inch by inch, stretching me. Filling me up. I wince at the sensation, my inner walls clenching around his shaft and he goes still, breathing hard.

"Feels like you're trying to strangle me," he murmurs.

"I'm sorry."

He kisses me. "Don't apologize." Another kiss. "Just—try not to tense up."

West keeps kissing me, which helps me relax, just as he wants. His cock is hot and thick, buried deep inside of me and I swear I can feel it throbbing. Insistent. I spread my legs a little, allowing him to sink further and a moan escapes me.

That felt...good.

"I'll keep it slow," he promises as he starts to move his hips, pulling almost all of the way out of me before he pushes back inside. He keeps this pace up for a while, the slow drag and pull of his cock moving in and out of my body nearly driving me out of my mind.

It drives him out of his mind too. I can tell by the strain in his face, his muscles. The sheen of sweat coating his skin. He's holding back for my sake and I feel bad.

Drifting my hands up and down his back, I tell him, "You don't have to restrain yourself."

"I don't want to hurt you."

"It feels—better." It does. Somewhat.

Mostly.

"Go ahead," I tell him when he still hasn't said anything. When he seems to be waiting to gain my permission, which is completely unlike him. "Let go."

West begins to move again. Pumping harder. Faster. His hips are moving at an accelerated clip, his steady thrusts making that familiar feeling rise within me. And when he reaches between our bodies and starts playing with my clit?

I'm coming. Moaning his name, my inner walls squeezing around his length again and again. He groans, going still above me just before he comes, filling me with semen, his body clinging to mine, his hips shoving me up the mattress with one last push.

Until he collapses on top of me, his body damp and heavy, his mouth finding mine. He kisses me with a desperation I've never experienced before. As if he's trying to tell me something he's almost...afraid to say out loud.

I can't think about it too much. I'm too wrapped up in the moment, in him. I feel connected to West, and that is something I've never experienced before.

Almost as if this boy...

Was made for me.

CHAPTER THIRTY-TWO

CAROLINA

I wake up to the sound of notifications popping off on my phone, one after the other, from a variety of social media. I roll over, the mattress dipping, a heavy arm coming to land around me and I smile.

It's West. He spent the night with me, too tired to go back to his dorm room. And I'm glad. I've never shared the bed with anyone beyond my sister when we were really young, and this is a completely different experience.

I enjoyed it.

Don't enjoy how noisy my phone is though.

Carefully, I slide beneath West's heavy arm and roll out of bed, watching as he rolls over onto his right side, facing the wall. He must've slipped his boxers back on sometime during the night, but that's all he's wearing. Oh, and that always present, heavy watch is on his left wrist.

A flash of a memory hits me. The time I thought I caught a glimpse of ink beneath that steel band.

Ignoring my still blowing-up phone, I reach toward West's arm, turning it so I can see the inside of his wrist, my gaze on his face the entire time.

He doesn't even flinch.

With my index finger, I push the watch band up, catching sight of the ink. It's not much. A very small tattoo, really, but I can't make out what it is without taking the watch off.

My phone starts ringing, startling West awake, and he catches me with my fingers on his watch, his brows furrowed in confusion. I immediately drop his hand and go to my desk where my phone sits, answering it without seeing who's calling.

"Have you been on social media yet?" It's Sadie, and she sounds way too alert for this early in the morning.

"No."

"Um. You should check it out. Though you're not going to like what you see." Sadie's voice is actually shaking, like she might be upset on my behalf.

My stomach cramps at the implication in her unspoken words. "What are you talking about?"

"Just go look, okay? And call me if you need me." She hesitates. "Where's West?"

I decide to be truthful. "In my bed."

She doesn't even laugh or make a funny comment. "Okay. Like I said, call me. Text me. Whatever you need, I'm here."

Sadie ends the call and I immediately start checking social media, my heart leaping to my throat when I see someone shared a video.

Someone I don't even know.

Who has a video.

Of me and West.

In my bed.

"Oh my God." I cover my mouth with shaky fingers, staring in horror at the video as West unbuttons my shirt. Reaches for the front of my bra, undoing the clasp. The cups fall away, our mouths still fused and—

It's over.

"What's wrong?"

I glance over at West, who's scrubbing his face with both

hands, his hair an absolute mess, his eyes bleary when he meets my gaze. "Someone posted a video of us together and now everyone is sharing it!"

"From what, last night's party?"

"No, from my room. When we were together and thought we heard someone in the hall." I thrust my phone toward him, and he doesn't even flinch. Or react.

He just calmly takes the phone from me and watches the video on replay. Again and again, not saying a single word. Unease slips down my spine, cold and foreboding, and I take the phone out of his hand, turning it off.

"No reaction? You don't have anything to say?" I'm furious. Upset. I don't want my private business put on such public display. "We need to find out who did this and put a stop to it immediately."

He hangs his head, his fingers plucking at my comforter, his voice barely a whisper when he says, "I know who did it."

My head spins, his words on repeat.

IknowwhodiditIknowwhodiditIknowwhodidit...

"Who?" My throat aches with just that one word.

West looks up at me, pain in his gaze when he admits, "Mercedes."

"Are you fucking serious?" I open my phone back up, finding my father's phone number and immediately calling him.

"What are you doing?"

"Calling my father."

"What the hell? Are you going to tell him that a video is circulating of the two of us about to have sex?"

"I'm going to tell him a private video between the two of us is out there and I need to talk to our family lawyer immediately."

My father doesn't answer, of course, and I don't bother leaving a voicemail either. How would I describe that to him in a message?

"Don't sic the lawyers on her yet. I'll talk to her," West says as he crawls out of bed.

I glare at him, hating how good he looks standing there in just his boxers and nothing else, that tantalizing line of dark hair that leads from below his navel and disappears beneath the waistband. His hair is a disheveled, glorious mess and the stubble lining his cheeks makes him look that much more attractive, which is infuriating.

I'm so pissed, he starts to blur right in front of me. I collapse on the edge of my bed, my stomach curdling at the thought of having to face everyone.

At the realization that West admitted he knew Mercedes is responsible for this, and he did nothing to stop it.

"When did you find out?"

"Last night."

"Last night?" I repeat, rising to my feet again. I start pacing the length of my room. "You knew about this since last night and you conveniently forgot to mention it to me? I had to find out via social media that she was the one who spied on us and now, like the total bitch she is, leaked the video to people at our school so they can share it?"

"I was drunk last night, okay? And I've been going through some shit—"

"Shit you won't tell me about. Shit you keep secret because you don't want to burden me or whatever," I retort.

He runs a hand through his hair. Grips the back of his head with both hands, his elbows bent, his face turning red. Like he's embarrassed and angry and frustrated. Well good. I feel the same way.

"It's family business," he grates out through clenched teeth. "You wouldn't understand."

"If you're actually implying that I don't understand complex family relations, then you really have no clue who you're talking to, do you? My family is so fucked up, it's not even funny. And we've been talked about publicly for hundreds of years. Everyone knows the Lancasters. Everyone knows how messed up we are.

Every generation a new crop of the family comes through, and there's always a few of us who make a public spectacle."

His expression turns pained. "I'm sorry, okay? We don't actually know each other that well and—"

"Don't know each other that well?" I keep interrupting him. And I keep repeating what he said. Maybe because I'm having a difficult time comprehending what he's truly trying to explain. "We just had sex last night, West. I think we know each other pretty well."

"You know what I mean. We don't share deep dark secrets with each other, Carolina. We mess around, we talk, we hang out, but you have to admit, you can be pretty closed off sometimes."

"You are not throwing this on me." I gather up his clothes that he left on the floor and throw them at him. "Get out."

His face is one of pure shock. "What?"

"Get dressed and leave. Now."

"Carolina..."

"I don't want to hear your explanations! You knew, West. I'm guessing you probably talked to Mercedes last night at the party and she somehow dropped that little bomb on you that she was the one lingering in the hallway and that she actually recorded us together. And you didn't mention it to me. Not once. And that is so incredibly fucked up." I choke on a sob, realizing that I'm crying, but I don't even care. "You don't care about me. You only care about yourself."

He's quiet, quickly pulling on his clothes while I stand in the middle of my suite, crying. I hate him. I can't believe he didn't tell me. He had all of last night to confess and he kept it to himself.

Why, I don't know, but the why doesn't matter. He did it.

And I don't know how we will ever recover from it.

"You're really kicking me out?" He's got his hand braced on the wall as he slips on his shoes.

"You really didn't tell me what happened," I throw back at him.

At least he has the decency to appear remorseful. "I didn't know how to bring it up to you. And then I drank too much."

"Right. Drowning your worry in alcohol. Look how well that worked out for you."

He puts on the other shoe, both of them untied and I can't help but worry he might trip and fall.

Then I remind myself, it would be karma and he'd deserve it.

"I'm sorry I fucked up." He stands close to the door, looking helpless and for the shortest second, I almost feel bad for him. "I'll make this right."

"How?" I throw my arms up in the air. "I don't know how you can fix this."

"I will," he says, his voice determined. "I'll talk to Mercedes."

"Talking to her will only make it worse."

"I'll talk to Matthews."

"And get the both of us in trouble? I don't think so." I shake my head. "Just go, West."

Hanging his head, he opens the door and leaves my suite, closing it behind him with a quiet click.

My phone rings in my hands, my father's name flashing across the screen, and I answer it, the tears immediately starting.

"Darling, what's wrong? Tell me," he demands, going into full protective father mode.

I explain everything to him, leaving out a few embarrassing parts, pinning all of the blame on Mercedes.

"What's her last name again?"

"Browne. Her father is in tech."

"Curtis Browne? I know who you're talking about. I'll have my lawyer reach out to him immediately."

Satisfaction curls through my blood and I breathe out a sigh of relief. "Thank you."

"No one fucks with a Lancaster and gets away with it. I can guarantee all of these posts will be pulled down within the hour. Any mention if it will be scrubbed from the internet by the end of the day," he says, his voice so confident, I know he's speaking the truth.

"I still can't believe this happened," I admit. "I hope you don't think less of me."

"We all do stupid shit, especially when we're younger. You need to make sure you're spending your time with the right crowd, Carolina. Some people will do anything to bring us down," he reminds me.

He's right. Mercedes' intentions were never pure with me, no matter how much she tried to act like my friend when we first met. I eventually understood that and steered clear of her.

What hurts the most is West. What he did feels like a betrayal of the worst kind. And worse?

Like a fool, I trusted him.

CHAPTER THIRTY-THREE

WEST

I fucked up so bad, and I don't know how to fix it.

I show up to class because where else am I supposed to go? If I try to talk to Mercedes, I'll probably end up trying to strangle her and I don't want to end up arrested for attempted murder so I steer clear of her.

Pretty much steer clear of everyone and they do the same. There's a lot of whispering and giggling and odd looks sent my way. I can't blame them. It's scandalous, what Mercedes leaked. I've seen worse of course. Haven't we all? Thirst trap photos on someone's main account. Suggestive shots. Blatant nude photos sent to guys in confidence that are shared after they break up.

I've seen that shit a lot over the years. I've seen the majority of the girls in my class in a semi-naked pose at least once, but I've never shared any that were sent to me. And I've definitely never had a video of me involved in an intimate moment with someone else hit the internet.

Mercedes is an evil cunt. There are no other words for it. I don't know what she hoped to get out of it, but she fucked with the wrong person. And I'm not even referring to myself.

I'm talking about Carolina Lancaster.

By the time American Government rolls around, neither

Carolina nor Mercedes is in the classroom, but the rumors are already spreading.

Police were seen driving onto campus.

Carolina and Mercedes got into a physical fight.

Mercedes was hauled out of school by the police. In handcuffs.

Matthews has met with Carolina and her dad, and heads are about to roll.

I don't know how I remain unscathed up to this moment, but halfway through class, I get called to Matthews' office.

And we all know what that's about.

Everyone watches me as I get up from my desk and leave the classroom, ignoring them all. I make my way to the admin building with hurried steps, eager to get this over with, and when I walk into the office, Vivian, Matthews' secretary, gives me a look, her disappointment obvious.

"He's waiting for you in his office."

I give her a nod and head toward the open door, my steps slowing when I hear the voices coming from within.

I hear Carolina. And a woman that sounds suspiciously like her mother.

Pausing at the doorway, I wait for Matthews to acknowledge me.

"Weston. Come in." He gestures toward the open door and I settle in, ignoring the rigid woman sitting in the middle chair, her lips curled in seeming disgust.

Sylvia Lancaster. Fucking great. I don't know what's worse though. Carolina's father would probably want to murder me for what I did to his little girl.

"I'm sure you are already aware why you're here," Matthews started.

I nod, wishing I could see Carolina's face, but her mom is completely blocking her from my view.

"What happened was a complete violation of your privacy, and I need confirmation from you." He studies me, his gaze intense.

"Do you know who's responsible for creating this video of you and Miss Lancaster?"

I swallow hard, not afraid to rat out who did it, but what does this mean for me? For me and Carolina? "It was Mercedes Browne."

"And how do you know this?"

"She told me she did it. Showed me the video herself. It was on her phone."

Sylvia Lancaster's eyes are trying to burn holes through my skin.

"And when did she show you this video?"

"Last night." I clear my throat, chancing a glance in Carolina's direction, but I still can't see her face. "At the party."

Matthews' expression is one of disgust. "I hate that party. I act like it isn't happening every year."

"Then maybe you should put a stop to it. Sounds like it brings nothing but trouble," Sylvia says, her voice crisp. "Or a lawsuit waiting to happen."

"No, that would be Mercedes' little video," Carolina adds snidely.

"Okay, that's enough," Matthews says, obviously put out. "I know what Miss Browne did is both a private violation and a school one, but what the two of you did is also a violation."

Dread socks me right in the stomach. "A violation?"

"Students aren't allowed to be in dorm rooms unattended after curfew. Including the Lancaster suite."

And here I thought the Lancasters were untouchable.

"I'm sure all sorts of—things have happened in those Lancaster suites in the past," Sylvia says, her voice light. As if this entire situation isn't a big deal. "Are you trying to turn my daughter into an example of what not to do?"

"We've been able to forgive most Lancaster mistakes because there's never been any proof. Unfortunately for this one, there is proof. Video documentation of two students together, participating in an...act that they shouldn't be. And one of the worst violations of them all, quite frankly. I'm afraid I'm going to have to suspend them both."

"Suspend?" Sylvia's voice is so high pitched, I wince.

"For a week."

"I think you need to reconsider your form of punishment."

"I don't have a choice. The documentation is out there for the entire campus to see."

"Not anymore, it's not. My husband took care of that."

"Ex," Carolina adds. Sylvia goes silent, and I swear there's steam coming from her ears. "Well, it's true, Mother. You're not married anymore."

"It doesn't matter," Sylvia snaps. "I'm asking you, Mr. Matthews, to reconsider the punishment you're inflicting upon my daughter."

"What about Mr. Fontaine?"

"What about him?" Sylvia sniffs, her gaze barely coasting over me. "He's the one who put her into this predicament. He also knew who did it, yet chose not to tell anyone until it was too late. I believe the punishment is fitting for the crime."

I almost laugh. This bitch is something else.

"I'm afraid they're both at fault, which means they'll be suspended for the rest of the week. They can return to campus a week from today."

Shit. Where am I supposed to go? California to spend the rest of the week with my parents?

That is the last place I want to go.

"You'll be hearing from my lawyers," Sylvia says, rising to her feet. "Come on, Carolina."

I let them walk out first, sending a pleading look at Carolina when she briefly glances over at me, but she doesn't react. Doesn't even smile. Just lifts her head high and walks out with her mother.

"I had to do it, you know," Matthews calls out to me just as I'm leaving his office.

I turn to face him, frowning. "Do what?"

"Suspend you. And Carolina. Lancasters have been up to no good ever since I took over this school, even before that, I'm sure. Their name, their family gives them privilege nobody else has. The Lancaster antics over the years here at this school are legendary," Matthews explains.

I'm surprised he's telling me this. "What's different about this case?"

"I already told you. The video is proof. I can't not suspend you. You're lucky I didn't expel you both. Fortunately, your records are clean."

"What about Mercedes?"

His expression shutters closed. "I can't discuss that with you, but her punishment will fit accordingly."

I'm guessing she'll be expelled.

I leave the office and head for my dorm hall, my steps slowing when I catch sight of Carolina speaking to her mother at the front of the campus, near the parking lot. From the looks of it, they're having an argument. Sylvia even reaches out and tries to grab Carolina's arm, but she shrugs out of her hold and flees, heading for the building where her suite is located.

Like a complete idiot, I follow after her, calling her name, right as she starts to enter the passcode on the door lock.

Hey, at least they're locking the doors in the daytime now.

"West, go away." She doesn't even look at me, her expression determined as she re-punches in the code and reaches for the door handle.

"Let me talk to you." I lean against the door, making it shut, and she makes an irritated noise.

"There's nothing else to talk about. And we have to leave campus right now, or Matthews will be pissed." She tries to enter the passcode yet again and keeps fucking it up.

"I don't care about Matthews. Are you okay?"

A sigh leaves her and she gives up, turning to face me. "No,

I'm not okay. I'm still mad at you. I don't get why you couldn't tell me that Mercedes created that video. If you'd let me know about her last night, everything would be different."

"I can't go back and change what I did—or didn't do, okay? No matter how much I wish I could." Fuck, it pains me, how much I've hurt her. I messed everything up. "She still would've posted it and you know it."

"But at least I would've known. I would have been prepared versus having that video slap me in the face. She caught us together in one of my most vulnerable moments. And now everyone knows what we're doing."

"Is that the problem? That you don't want people knowing we've had sex?" I talk right over her when she tries to protest. "Or is it something else? Are you—*embarrassed* that we're sexually active with each other?"

"No! Of course not." She pauses. "You make it sound so clinical."

"I'm just stating facts."

She crosses her arms in front of her, on the defensive. "And now I'm being suspended. Like I care though. I wish I could leave this place forever."

I frown. "Really?"

Does she mean what she says? Or is she just mad over what happened? She has every right to be angry, but when she says stuff like that, it makes me think she doesn't give a damn about me.

Like she's just using me to get through the school year here before she returns to the life she really wants to lead.

"I don't know. My mother just tried to convince me to go to her apartment with her, but I told her I was waiting for my father. Oh, she was angry, but I don't care. I'm not spending the next week with her."

I don't like the idea of her father showing up and seeing me. He might want to take me out. "Is she that bad?"

"She's awful. And my father took care of everything already. He's on his way to pick me up now. Oh, and our lawyers have been in contact with Mercedes' parents. She won't be spying on people ever again. I can guarantee that."

I can't imagine what the lawyer threatened Mercedes' parents with.

"Where are you going this week?" Carolina asks when I still haven't said anything.

Does this mean she still cares? Or is she just curious.

"I guess I'll go to Napa and spend some time with my parents."

"Maybe you could work out your—problems."

There is nothing to work out when your dad has cancer. "What happens is going to happen. I can't change it."

She drops her arms by her sides, irritated. "I'm so tired of your ominous, mysterious statements, West. You never actually say what's going on, and it's annoying. You'd rather leave me guessing."

"I don't do it on purpose, I just—"

"—can't tell me," she finishes for me. "Yeah, I know. You've already mentioned that."

This time she taps in the correct password on the keypad and opens the door with ease. "I'll see you later."

"That's it?" I ask incredulously. "You're just going to walk away from me like nothing happened? See ya in a week, take care?"

"What else do you want me to say, West? I'll miss you? I wish this hadn't happened? I hate Mercedes for what she did to us? All of that is true, but it doesn't change anything."

"It doesn't change what? You and me? You talk like we're over."

"If you can't trust me, why are you with me?" The pointed look on her face has me immediately feeling guilty.

She's referring to my dad. Even if I do tell her now, she'll just throw it back in my face that I only did it to keep her around.

Which is the truth. I don't want to lose her. I don't want to end this.

Us.

"That's what I thought," she says when I remain silent. "And now you've proven that I can't trust you. It hurts to say that, but it's true. You kept something from me that involved me. I deserved to know what Mercedes did, and you said nothing. So yeah. Why am I with you?"

She starts to enter the building and I slap my hand against the door to prevent it from slamming shut. "I'll make this up to you, I promise. Just—wait for me, okay? I know you're mad and I broke your trust, but you mean the fucking world to me, Carolina. When I come back, I'll tell you everything, I swear."

Carolina turns to fully face me, her arms crossed again, doubt written all over her beautiful face. "Prove it, Weston."

I will, I think as I make my way to my dorm hall, my phone already ringing with a call from my father. Guess Matthews already told them what happened.

Looks like I need to prove myself to everyone.

PART 2

CHAPTER THIRTY-FOUR

CAROLINA

TWO YEARS LATER

He didn't prove shit.

As a matter of fact, Weston Fontaine never came back to the Lancaster Prep campus. He never reached out to me again. Like, who does that? He ghosted me when he swore up and down that once he returned, he would tell me everything.

I was devastated. I cried for days. Weeks, even—and I cry over no one. It felt like I didn't matter. Though we never made any promises to each other, and we were only sort of committed, so I guess if I was devastated by his seeming abandonment, that was on me.

Figures.

Of course, I now know why he didn't come back. His father died of cancer, or so it said in the otherwise vague articles I read on the internet. Just before Thanksgiving of our senior year. He should've returned to Lancaster weeks before the holiday, but he never did. Was his father already ill when he went back to California for the suspension? Did he have to stay there to help his parents out? At the very least, he could've texted and let me know. I would've understood. I'm not a total bitch.

I deserved an explanation.

After the last couple of years, I've come to the realization that West's problems had nothing to do with me. He was going through his own crap—something he mentioned to me a few times. And I have a feeling his father's cancer diagnosis had something to do with the family pressure and secrets West couldn't tell me. His father was the head of a very important company. One of the finest champagnes in the world. The House of Fontaine Champagne equals elegance. Class. Prestige. Wealth.

And while still in his teens, West somehow became the CEO of the company? With his mother's assistance, which is just…so wild to think about. Eighteen and with all that responsibility resting on his shoulders. I don't know how he did it.

How he's *still* doing it.

Once I realized West left me at Lancaster Prep to fend for myself, I got out of there as quickly as I could. That took a lot of whining to my father on my part. And begging—when I never beg. But I was desperate and couldn't stand being there any longer. I felt bad leaving Sadie, but she had Brent. She'd made friends in her class, while I had…

No one else. Not a single soul. Nothing felt the same there without West. Being at Lancaster Prep made me sad, which is the most useless, awful emotion in the world.

I called the London Dance Company and spoke to Madame Lesandre, who was overjoyed at the thought of me returning. She encouraged me to come right away, that they *needed* me there.

And that's what I did. By the beginning of the new year, I was back in London. Always shivering in the damp air, savoring those bitterly cold winter days that I didn't realize I missed so much. Hours upon hours of rigorous training were heaped upon me, Madame calling me out in class for having grown soft, which only spurred me on to work even harder. I lost all those pounds I'd gained, not that they were much, and my muscles ached in the very best way.

I had no friends upon my return—not any real ones. Not even Gideon, who left London just before my return. He was picked up by a dance company that is currently touring their way through Europe, and I'm sure he's having the time of his life.

I didn't need him, I told myself, and I was right. I soon learned that I really didn't need anyone. My time at Lancaster Prep, with West, taught me that much. Depending on someone else for your entertainment, your happiness, your emotions, got you nowhere.

It still hurt, that he abandoned me. I was forgotten like yesterday's trash, and now when I think of West, all I can imagine is me giving him a big fuck you to his face.

The satisfaction of that imagined interaction never fails to amuse me.

Now I've returned to the States to attend my brother's wedding. Whit is officially settling down, though he's been with Summer for years and they have a child, with another one on the way. Of course, I had to come home for the wedding. Though the minute I arrived at the house in Newport, I had mad regret for coming here.

The family drama was in full swing. Mother was lamenting that Summer didn't allow her to participate in the wedding or reception arrangements, meaning she was afraid Summer would put together something that would end up looking like a tacky mess. I was annoyed that Father still let our mother stay at the house while we were all there for the wedding, but it's large enough that her room could be on one end of a wing and his could be on the opposite side, so they'd never really run into each other unless they had to.

Mother also came crying to me over Sylvie. How my sister chooses to ignore her, when all she wants to do is love her – direct quote.

I just smile and nod, counting down the days until I can leave.

The wedding day itself dawns bright and sunny, everything

coming together beautifully while I stay out of the way. Summer gets ready at the house and invites me to have my makeup and hair done with her, so I join her in the salon, surprised at how friendly she is toward me, when we haven't spent much time with each other. She's so warm and thoughtful, and I appreciate that.

The complete opposite of my brother, though I suppose we owe Summer for being the reason Whit has mellowed out so much.

The wedding is beautiful and the reception is perfect. Spring is my favorite season and I dress accordingly in a simple, pale pink satin sheath dress. I "borrowed" it from my mother's closet and plan on never returning it, because it's beautiful in its simplicity and it fits me perfectly. Plus, it's from Calvin Klein's collection in the mid-nineties—it's vintage. When I told the makeup artist what I was wearing, she got excited and claimed she wanted to give me the "Hailey Bieber at Met Gala 2019 face" and I wasn't disappointed.

A subtle cat eye with thin black liner and pink eyeshadow, and the most beautiful pink, shimmering highlighter on my cheeks. I've been on the stage countless times, worn a variety of cosmetics over the years, and I swear, this is the prettiest I've ever felt.

I'm moving about the crowd at the reception, stopping to chat with various relatives and people I know here and there, when I run into my younger cousin Arch Lancaster, who is currently hiding behind a large flower arrangement, drinking straight from a champagne bottle.

A Fontaine bottle, I might add, because of course he is.

"What are you doing?" I put on my best shocked mother voice, which causes Arch to spill some of the champagne he's drinking down the front of his suit.

"What the hell, Carolina?" He's coughing and sputtering and I can't help but smile. As the youngest in my family, I could never pick on anyone.

They all picked on me.

"You shouldn't be drinking."

"If I was in Europe I could. Archaic, puritanical laws in this country, I swear to God," Arch mutters, looking disgusted.

"You're not even old enough to drink in Europe," I point out.

"I will be eventually." He wipes at the front of his tie, which is stained with droplets of champagne. "Why the hell did you just scare me like that anyway?"

Arch Lancaster is the oldest son of George, my father's younger brother. Arch is sixteen and awful. Much like my brother. There is something about those oldest Lancaster boys that make them behave so terribly.

"Because I could," I say simply, smiling at him. "How's school?"

"Miserable. Only two more years in that hellhole and then I'm out for good."

"Please. You aren't enjoying your time at Lancaster Prep?" Every Lancaster boy seems to because they get away with almost anything, which is completely misogynistic and totally unfair.

"Fine, it's not terrible." That's all he says, a sly smile appearing on his classically handsome face. "I've heard some stories about you, though."

I have learned to dodge these questions about my tenure at the family prep school. "I was barely there."

"Long enough to have a sex tape go viral." He holds up his hand for a high five. "Pretty scandalous, Carolina. Didn't know you had it in you."

I stare at his proffered hand before I silently shake my head and walk away, annoyed he would bring up such a thing.

Men. They're the worst. Even when they're sixteen.

Especially when they're sixteen.

I wander around the ballroom where the reception is being held—yes, the house is big enough to have its own ballroom. It was built during a different time and is grandiose and completely over the top, but I love it. I spot Spencer Donato, Sylvie's first love, and I turn to go in the opposite direction.

I've already talked to him enough today. The poor man is still completely besotted with my sister and seems even a little angry over it. I don't feel like analyzing their relationship yet again.

"Darling! Oh my goodness, I've been looking for you! I want you to meet someone."

I turn to find my mother standing before me, an overly bright smile on her narrow face. She's been on some sort of diet that's left her thinner than usual and she doesn't look well. And I think she's been indulging in too many cosmetic procedures too. "Who?"

This is the same woman who wanted to speak to Sylvie alone earlier, so she banished me from the conversation with a few pointed words. Now she acts like she wants to be my best friend.

"Her name is Madison Collins. Oh, she's a sweet girl. Tall and blonde. Actually, she reminds me of you. She's now seeing someone you're terribly familiar with and I think you might like her. Oh, Madison!" Mother's voice rises and she waves her hand, gaining the attention of an attractive blonde woman who was engaged in conversation with a few other wedding attendees.

She disengages herself from the group and makes her way over to us, her expression curious. "Sylvia, it's so good to see you again."

"Lovely to see you too, Mads."

Mads? What, like they're best friends?

"I wanted to introduce you to my youngest daughter." Mother smiles at me, her eyes sparkling. "This is Carolina."

Madison's expression falters for the briefest moment, but then corrects itself, her smile smooth as she offers her hand to me. "Carolina, it's lovely to finally meet you in person. I've followed your career for a while."

I'm shaking her hand, trying not to frown. A little thrown by her comment. "You have?"

"Oh yes. When I was little, I wanted to be a ballet dancer so badly, but I always skipped class. I've always admired your dancing. I've even seen you perform." She releases my hand and steps back, that smile still stretching her mouth. It almost looks painful. "We also...share an acquaintance or two. Well, mainly only one."

"We do?" I'm full-blown frowning now, curious as to who she's referring to. I don't know this woman. I don't recognize her either, and I wish I did. She does remind me of someone, but I can't place who.

Madison nods. "I came with him tonight."

Him? Now I'm even more confused. I figured our mutual someone was a female, though no clue why. "Who are you here with?"

Mother laughs, the sound reminding me of a tinkling bell. Though it's more like a warning clang of impending doom. "Oh, darling, you remember Weston Fontaine, don't you?"

I blink at my mother, her question on repeat in my brain. It may have been over two years since the last time I saw that asshole, but I haven't forgotten him.

How could I?

"You know West?" I ask Madison.

"Yes. I'm his date tonight." Madison's smile fades, and I realize in that moment she knows exactly who I am—and who I was to West.

My gaze shifts to Mother, who's watching this all unfold with glee dancing in her gaze.

God, she made sure this little encounter happened, didn't she?

Of course she did.

CHAPTER THIRTY-FIVE

CAROLINA

"West is here?" I practically gasp, panic clawing at my throat. I don't mean to have such a strong reaction, but that was the last thing I expected to hear. My heart is hammering in my chest and my skin grows hot, and I do my best not to swivel my head around in search of him.

How did he get invited to my brother's wedding and I didn't know? Who did this?

"He was invited," Mother says, and realization hits.

She did this. I don't know how exactly, but she made sure West would be here and she is the biggest bitch in the world to spring it on me by using his girlfriend or whatever she is as some sort of torture tool.

"Who invited him?" I ask through barely clenched teeth. My head feels like it might explode, I'm so angry at her.

"Why, I did. We've always moved in the same social circles with his parents, and it was such a shame when his father died. I spoke to his mother upon her return to New York, and next thing I know, we're meeting for lunch dates on a regular basis. His mother is here tonight too," Mother explains with an excited lilt in her voice.

I stare at her in disbelief, trying to process everything she just said, but I'm stuck on one thing.

West.

He's here. Right now.

I need to keep it together before my mother tries to make it worse.

"How nice." My gaze goes to Madison, who's watching me with laser focus. "You'll have to tell West I say hello."

"I will. There are so many people here, I'm sure you won't bump into him." Her laughter is overly false and I know she absolutely does not want me to run into West.

"I should go. I'm so thirsty. I need another glass of champagne. I did notice it was Fontaine." I reach out and rest my hand lightly on Madison's arm, offering her a faint smile. "Only the best at a Lancaster event, don't you know."

"Yes, of course," Madison murmurs. "Lovely to meet you."

"You too." I send a scathing glare in my mother's direction before I turn and push my way through the crowd, headed for a bar, so I can actually grab another glass of champagne. I need to drench my fury in alcohol. I'm so mad I'm practically fuming.

I scan every face I pass by, annoyance flitting through my veins when people try to stop me and make conversation. I act as if I have no time, keeping my pace hurried, the bar finally in sight and when I approach it, resting my arms on the ledge as I make my request for a glass of champagne, I hear a familiar voice come from behind me.

"I was hoping I'd see you."

Closing my eyes for the briefest moment, I mentally ask for strength before I pop them open and turn to face Weston.

In the flesh.

Oh, and what beautiful flesh he is, clad in a light gray suit and white shirt that's open at the collar, no tie in sight. His neck and that tantalizing glimpse of chest are smooth and tanned, and he looks so much older, yet just the same.

"Really? I figured you would be hiding from me. You're really good at that."

He grins, the bastard. "You hate me."

I incline my head toward him. "Yes."

"Miss, your champagne."

I turn to the bartender and take the proffered glass, flashing him my best, sweetest smile. "Thank you."

He smiles in return, dazzled. "You're welcome, Miss Lancaster."

"Slaying everyone in your path still I see," West drawls when I return my focus to him.

I take a sip of the champagne. Cool and crisp, the bubbles pleasant on my tongue. "Why are you here, West?"

He rests his hand against his chest as if I offended him, my gaze settling on those long fingers, remembering what they could do to me. I shake my head once and take another fortifying swallow from my glass, needing the alcohol for courage.

"I was invited," he says.

"By my mother."

His smile fades, his expression turning sincere. "I know you two have your issues, but she's been very kind to my mother since we returned to New York."

I want to ask him when he returned and why didn't he call. I want to tell him my mother is using his mother for whatever sick and twisted game she's concocted, and I want to know when he looks at Madison, is he reminded of me.

Because it hits me right then that's who she reminds me of. Not someone I know, but of my own self.

And that's seriously fucked up.

"That's wonderful. I'm so glad our mothers can become friends and that my mother approves so heartily of your girlfriend." I offer him a demure smile and sip from my glass before I say something that I might regret.

His expression doesn't even falter. "Did you meet Madison?"

I raise the glass toward him in a toast. "She's lovely."

He leans back on his heels, shoving his open jacket aside so he can rest his hands on his lean hips and damn him, he's never looked finer. "This is fucking awkward."

"It's fine. You ghosted me when we were teenagers and now here we are, having to be polite adults interacting at my brother's wedding as if we're old, dear friends while you bring the woman you fuck as your date. It's wonderful. The perfect reunion." I down the rest of the glass, hating that I lost my cool and referred to Madison as the woman he fucks.

"Carolina..."

"I don't want to hear your excuses," I say, interrupting him. "It's fine. We were young and stupid and you did enough damage while we were together at school. How much worse could you make it if you simply didn't contact me anymore? I understand. I left Lancaster Prep not too soon after you did."

"I saw that," he says quietly, his deep voice making every hair on my body stand on end.

"Keeping tabs? I see your girlfriend likes to do that too." I glance into my empty glass, whirling in frustration and offering it to the bartender, who takes it despite helping someone else. "Another one please?"

"Coming right up," he says with a nod.

"Can we go somewhere more private and talk about this?" West asks.

I turn toward the boy who broke my heart yet again, trying to study him with objective eyes, but it's no use. I'm angry at him. Hurt by him. What he did...

Is hard to recover from. Still.

"There's nowhere private I can take you." Lies. This house is full of unoccupied rooms. "And I don't want to hear what you have to say."

Another lie. I'm dying to know what he has to say. How he can explain what he did and make it all right—which he can't. But I will never know.

Because I'm not about to subject myself to that story.

He rears back a little, surprised? Please. "Really."

I slowly shake my head, taking the fresh champagne glass from the bartender before I step away from the bar itself, West following me, damn it. "Go back to your girlfriend and enjoy having your continued conversations about me."

"Conversations about you?" He frowns, which is a good look for him. And now I want to smack his handsome face. "What are you talking about?"

"She mentioned she's followed my career. She's seen me perform." My expression turns snotty, I can feel it. "That's fan behavior if you ask me."

The asshole actually starts to laugh. "Oh, Carolina. Never change."

I'm so infuriated by his reaction, I give him the finger.

Just before I turn and walk away.

I'm headed for the stairwell that leads to our bedrooms when I hear my mother's voice call out my name. I come to a stop, waiting for her, ready to unleash.

"Where are you going?"

"Away from here," I snap, shaking off her hold when she tries to touch my arm. "How dare you invite him."

"Invite who?" The innocent expression on her face is so aggravating because it's so goddamn phony.

"Stop playing games. I'm not your puppet like Sylvie. You can't manipulate me," I practically hiss.

She already did though. I don't understand why she gets off on putting her children through horribly uncomfortable situations, but here we are. She's done this to every single one of us time and again, but especially Sylvie.

"I wasn't trying to manipulate anyone. It's smart to have West Fontaine on our side. He's rather powerful, and being so young, it's even more tantalizing than usual." Her smile is sly, and I hate that she used the word tantalizing when describing West.

She's old enough to be his mother. She better keep away from him or I'll—

Inhaling deeply, I mentally tell myself to calm down. This is what she wants. What she gets off on.

A reaction.

"What West and I shared is over," I tell her with a finality I don't quite mean. "We were kids."

"Who were together."

"You never approved."

"I never said that. I wasn't thrilled that the two of you were suspended for your...antics, but I didn't disapprove of Weston Fontaine. On the contrary, I believe he'd be perfect for you." She pauses, letting her words sink in. "You saw Madison, did you not? She resembles you."

"It's weird."

"Men have a type, and you're his type. Sometimes that old, young love feeling never fades. You'd be smart to chase after him."

"I'm returning to London in two days. I'm busy."

"You should never be too busy to set up your future, Carolina. And that man could be your future if you play your cards right."

"Why do you care?" I ask, baffled as ever by her motives. "What does it matter who I end up with?"

"We have an image to maintain, darling. You and Weston are a proper match. You both move in the same social circles and his family's wealth is vast. Word on the street is he's preparing to sell Fontaine." She makes a tsking noise. "That will be a very... interesting move for him to make. It'll draw a lot of attention."

It will also make him an absolute load of money.

"And once he does that, the possibilities are endless. You would be smart to set your sights on him. Why do you think I befriended dear old Mads?" She lifts her brows.

Oh, she looks so pleased with herself. My mother is devious. So is my sister and brother.

So am I.

"I'm not going to sabotage his relationship." I refuse to play by my mother's tactics. Her children may be devious like she is, but she takes it to a whole other level.

"It would take nothing to sabotage it. Their relationship is so brand new, and Madison is extremely insecure. She knows about your history with West. It would take nothing to decimate them—and her." Mother smiles and grabs hold of my shoulders, giving me a gentle shove toward the stairs. It happens so quickly I don't have time to react to her touching me, which she very rarely does. "Think about it."

Thanks to what she told me, it's all I can think about for the rest of the evening.

CHAPTER THIRTY-SIX

CAROLINA

I return to London two days later, relieved to be back in my routine. My safe place. My little London flat with the creaky pipes and the dim lighting, since I never seem to get any direct sunlight through the windows. I have more than enough money to live in some fancy townhouse in the more affluent part of the city, but I chose to live in the neighborhood where the theatre is. It's older and quaint and some things are run down but almost lovingly. Like your grandmother's cherished treasures in her home, it's older yet well-kept.

Much like the theatre. Being part of the London Dance Company, going from the school to the performing troupe, is not as much of an honor as I once thought it was. While LDC is one of the most well-known and respected companies in the UK, it's definitely not the best. That would be the Royal Ballet, who Gideon dances for now.

Yes, my Gideon. We're still friendly and talk often. We even get together for a meal on occasion, though it mostly consists of us picking at our salads while we share a cigarette or five while eating outside.

I picked the terrible habit back up but only on occasion. It gives me that buzz I need. And it makes me forget to eat, which is also what I need. I can quit any time.

I swear I can.

Luckily my brother's wedding was scheduled during a break in our performance schedule, but now we're back to performing five nights a week and two on Saturday. It's a lot. I'm exhausted, but I'm also completely preoccupied and unable to think about the things that bother me that keep me up at night.

Or people that bother me.

Specifically men.

Specifically Weston.

Mother's words didn't help. She put ideas in my head I couldn't shake. Ideas that made me toss and turn in my old bed in the Newport house, the sound of the ocean pounding the surf keeping me from falling asleep.

Well, the ocean and my thoughts. All of them having to do with West. Looking too good to exist in that damn gray suit. His hair in casual disarray, his eyes just as dark and all-seeing as they always were. The amusement on his stupidly handsome face when I said something that made him laugh.

I was trying to be mean and he laughed at me. God, I hate him.

I do.

Getting out of the States was the right thing to do. I wish I would've left sooner. The moment I returned to London, I threw myself back into practice. Back into the rigorous training and the constant time in the studio. At the barre. On the stage. Going through the same moves over and over. Running through the same routine again and again. The music on repeat in my head, in my body, in my sleep.

Muscle memory is a wondrous thing. I hear the song start to play and my body shifts into position.

The first night we're scheduled to perform, I arrive at the theatre and head to the dressing room, stopping short when I see the giant bouquet of flowers sitting on my vanity table.

One of the women in the dance troupe, who also happens to sit at the vanity next to mine, is grinning at me in the reflection of her mirror.

"Looks like you have a secret admirer," Cressida says in her posh English accent.

I grimace, trying to ignore the nerves pinging in my stomach as I approach my table, my gaze never straying from the pale pink long-stemmed roses. I stare at them for a moment, realizing no one has ever sent me flowers before a performance before. Not since the recital days, when my father would bring me a bouquet and I would pose for photos under the hot lights afterward, my face drenched with sweat and my makeup smeared.

There have to be at least two dozen in this bouquet. Maybe even three. And they are absolutely perfect.

Tearing open the little envelope included in the arrangement, I read the card.

Pink roses will forever remind me of you. Good luck tonight.
Xo,
West

"Who are they from?" Cressida asks, her eyes gleaming with curiosity.

"An old friend." I stuff the card back into the envelope and shove it into my bag, mentally cursing myself that I didn't throw it away already. There is no reason for me to keep the card.

Absolutely none.

I get ready with a fierce determination that I haven't felt in ages. Push myself to the limit on stage, dancing until I'm out of breath, throwing my whole body and soul into the performance. I'm not the lead, but I'm a secondary, and when the curtain drops, men and women leap to their feet, many of them shouting, "Brava!"

And when the curtains draw back and we bow to our beloved

audience, flowers are gently thrown onto the stage, the majority of them landing at my feet. At the encouragement of the rest of the cast, I gather them up in my arms, bowing and smiling, my gaze running over the audience. Their nondescript faces, their mouths stretched into wide smiles. Only one isn't smiling. A man.

He's familiar.

All the joy from the performance leaves me in a gust and my shoulders fall when I see him.

Weston fucking Fontaine.

I look away, smiling at the other dancers, grateful when the curtain once again drops. My entire act deflates, a scowl forming on my face as I stomp my way backstage. I change out of my costume quickly, throwing on an old pair of sweatpants and a tank top that lie wrinkled in my bag, slipping on a pair of Birkenstock clogs that are lined with fur and keep my always cold, always battered feet warm.

Staring at my reflection in the mirror, I rub the makeup off my face with exaggerated jerks, ignoring the way Cressida stares at me, the concern in her eyes infuriating though I don't know why.

I am a contradiction. I want to perform on stage, yet I don't want anyone paying attention to me. I want to shine in the spotlight, yet I wish no one knew my name.

I make no sense, even to myself.

"Are you okay?" Cressida asks after watching me for long, most likely torturous minutes. I'm acting like a savage and I'm sure she notices.

"I'm fine." I throw away the cotton rounds I used to remove my makeup, staring at my blank, boring face. It's still always a shock to see myself after the makeup is gone. We wear so much when we perform, we're downright plain when it's gone.

Well, some of us aren't plain. There's the lovely English rose Cressida, who has naturally bright pink lips and the prettiest cheekbones. I sort of hate her.

No, I don't. She's sweet and caring, nothing at all like me and I'm just mad because the one boy—man—who I let toy with my heart is, once again, trying to toy with my heart, and I'd much rather take his heart and stomp all over it until it is nothing but a bloody lump that's barely beating.

There is clearly something wrong with me, that I'm not happy that West sent me flowers. That he sought me out by flying clear across the Atlantic to watch me perform. He most likely is waiting for me and will suggest we talk, and I sort of want to tell him fuck you to his face in reply. How will he react? Will I make him mad? Will he leave me alone for good?

Do I want him to leave me alone?

No, a little voice whispers deep in my mind and I hate that voice so much.

"I'm fine," I finally say, offering her a brittle smile.

She looks away, pretending to be preoccupied by her phone, and I say nothing. Just gather up my things—but leave the roses there—and flee the backstage area, pushing through a door that leads outside.

I normally walk home if the weather is nice and it's not too dark, or I take the tube. Tonight is a tube night for sure, and I'm about to head toward the station when I hear a steady, slow clapping coming from somewhere behind me.

Coming to a stop, I turn my face up to the sky and close my eyes, quietly asking for strength. I should've known he'd find me immediately.

He always seems to—but only when he wants to find me.

Slowly, I turn to face him, standing up straighter, putting on my invisible armor. "Weston."

"Carolina." He stops clapping and I stare at him, hating how attractive he looks leaning against the side of a very expensive sports car, clad in dark gray trousers and a blue button down that's open at the collar yet again. Why do I get so aroused by the sight of his neck and that tiny glimpse of his chest? Every time I see it, I want to put my mouth right there and kiss him.

Or bite him.

"What are you doing in London?"

"Business. Thought it was the perfect excuse to come see you."

"We just saw each other."

"It wasn't long enough."

"Funny how you want to see me now, after disappearing from my life for the last two years." I start walking, my steps determined, my head held high. I can hear him follow me, his steps just as determined, irritation obvious in his deep voice when he speaks.

"Where are you going?"

"I'm taking the tube home," I toss over my shoulder.

"I have a car. I can drive you home."

"I am not getting into a car with you." I start walking faster but he keeps up, the bastard. His stride is longer. I can feel him practically upon me, and I squeal when he snags hold of my wrist, wrenching myself out of his grip. I whirl on him, breathing so hard my chest is heaving. He backs away, holding his hands up in pure defensive mode.

"Carolina, come on." He pauses, his gaze holding mine. "I need to talk to you."

"There's nothing left to say. You leaving two years ago without a word was enough. I get it. Go home, Weston." I turn away and start walking, and this time, I can tell he's not following. My footsteps are heavy against the sidewalk, the sound echoing, the sound of traffic in the near distance, and I blink hard, trying to staunch the tears from flowing.

"I want to explain what happened," he calls to me.

I glance at him from over my shoulder, my steps slowing. "It doesn't matter anymore."

"I suppose you're right. Still want to explain though." Another hesitation. "You get my flowers?"

"Yes. I threw them in the trash." I turn to face him yet again, crossing my arms. I look a mess. Barefaced in clothes that probably need a wash. Still sweaty from the performance and desperate for a shower.

Yet he's looking at me as if I'm the prettiest thing he's ever seen, his gaze coasting over me, touching on each part of me. My hair, my face. My neck and chest. Drifting down the length of my body before he meets my gaze once more. "Please tell me you didn't. Those roses cost me five hundred pounds."

I may be wealthy, but at least I'm not foolish and wasting a ton of cash on flowers to a woman who may or may not hate your guts.

"I'm fairly certain you can afford them with all of your champagne money," I retort.

The man grins. I swear he enjoys it when I'm rude. "I've missed you, Carolina."

I hate what he just said. I hate worse how my heart leaped when he said it. "Not enough to call."

The smile barely fades. "I was a fucking idiot."

I snort. "Definitely."

"I want to make it up to you."

Impossible. "What about your girlfriend?"

"What about her?"

He doesn't deny he has one still, and that's even more infuriating.

An angry noise leaves me and I give him the bird just like I did at Whit's wedding reception, before I turn on my heel and practically run down the sidewalk.

With his laughter chasing me all the way to the tube station.

CHAPTER THIRTY-SEVEN

CAROLINA

Weston Fontaine comes to the next five performances at our little theatre, including the double one on Saturday, both in the afternoon and the evening. His seat gets better every single time, and by the Saturday evening performance, he's sitting front and center in the very first row, his gaze trailing me the entire time I'm on stage. His applause is louder than anyone else's when it's over, with him shouting my name and even whistling like the tacky American he is.

It's annoying. It's wonderful. I can't stand him. Deep down, I still adore him and I hate myself for it.

I have no idea what he wants from me.

He's alone at every performance, too. No insecure Madison in sight, and I wonder where she is. I'm tempted to call my mother and ask, but then she'll ask her own questions and know I'm scheming, and I don't want to involve her in any of my digging.

Instead, late at night when I'm lying in my bed and scrolling social media, I look up Madison. There are no photos of West on her grid, which fills me with relief. Why, I don't know. It doesn't matter who he's with. Or maybe they've broken up and he's already with someone else now. It sounds impossible, but West always moved fast. Whoever he could've found would be prettier and not as harsh as me. Someone who enjoys physical touch and isn't afraid to talk about her feelings.

God, I hate people like that.

I let my imagination get the worst of me all the time.

West also continues to send me flowers. A fresh bouquet every evening, always pink roses, and Cressida is beside herself with curiosity, ready to burst when I don't outwardly react to the daily arrangements that appear at my vanity. Though deep down, I'm dying inside, thrilled he would do such a thing, and his persistence in his pursuit of me.

I still haven't told poor Cressida who they're from and she acts like I'm torturing her, whining that she deserves to know.

Maybe I am, I don't know. I don't mean to. I refuse to say his name out loud. To acknowledge him with others means something is happening between us and I don't know what that is, so it's better to keep him a secret. Like he doesn't exist.

It's easier that way.

After the Saturday night performance, I find him waiting for me in the same spot as the first night I ran across him. Leaning against the same fancy sports car, his entire face lighting up when he sees me, like I'm the best thing to happen to him. He's wearing another one of those light gray suits, his shirt the palest pink, matching the roses he keeps sending me, and the car matches him, because it's silver. An Aston Martin.

Fast and sleek and very British.

"Is that your car?" is how I greet him.

He glances back at it, his smile pleased when his gaze meets mine. "I'm leasing it. You like it?"

"It looks like a death trap."

"The way I drive, it probably is."

My heart lurches in fear of him wrecking this stupid car and mangling himself. I swear, my knees actually wobble.

"Your performance tonight was amazing," he continues. "Best one so far."

Him being in the audience, knowing he's watching, is making me even harder on myself than usual, and it shows in my performances. Even the director has noticed, and acknowledged my—quote—breathtaking work. I begrudgingly admit to only myself that it has everything to do with West.

"Thank you," I tell him, keeping my response simple. I'm in fight or flight mode. Should I argue with him or run away? Both options are tempting.

"Are you getting my roses?"

I nod my acknowledgement. "They're too much."

"Still tossing them in the trash?"

"Of course." I'm lying. They've completely overtaken my table and some have migrated their way to Cressida's vanity too.

His smile is sweet enough to make me ache. "Come to dinner with me, Carolina."

"It's late." I sniff. "And I'm not hungry."

"Then come with me and watch me eat. I'm starved. Watching you night after night leaves me ravenous."

There is something so sexual about his comment that I actually shiver.

"I have something else for you."

A groan leaves me. "No more gifts. Please."

"This one you'll like. I promise."

I take a tentative step forward, stopping myself just in time.

"What about your girlfriend?"

I hate that I have to ask about her. That we have to acknowledge that she exists, but we must.

"What about her?"

"Does she know you're here? That you're with me?"

His expression smooth as glass, he pushes himself off the car and slowly starts to approach me. "Madison is not my girlfriend."

I frown, confused, and he stops. "I was told she was."

"By who?"

"My mother." Did she actually use the word girlfriend in

reference to Madison? I can't remember.

"You two talk about me?" West appears far too pleased with that idea.

"Never." I roll my eyes. "She introduced me to Madison. You were there. You know what happened."

He shoves his hands in his pockets, chuckling. "I'm sure my mother might have mentioned something to your mother about Madison, but it's not true. We're not together. We never really were."

"What does that mean?" It's the *really* that throws me.

"It means we went out a couple of times. Nothing serious. I brought her to your brother's wedding as my defensive date."

"Defensive? Defense against what?" I am sure I already know the answer.

"You. I was worried if you saw me there unaccompanied, you might take me out." He smiles, immediately wiping it from his face with a sweep of his hand.

"I wanted to take you out the moment I knew you brought a date." Oh, I hate that I just admitted such a thing. I want to pretend he doesn't matter, that he doesn't affect me, but I just gave myself away.

"A big mistake on my part then," he drawls, his gaze intensifying. "I never want to make you mad, Carolina. Even though that seems to be all I can do when it comes to you."

"If you don't want to make me mad, then what do you want to do to me?" The words scrape against my throat, my voice raw.

"I'm afraid if I tell you, you might run away for good."

"It doesn't matter what you say. I feel like I always want to run away from you." And that's the truth.

"I'm trying to keep you around here." His smile is direct, aimed at me like a weapon, and my heart flips over itself as if in surrender.

The relief that floats through me is heady, my knees wobbling yet again. "I'm still mad at you."

"You should be. I'm hoping you'll let me explain and set things right with you." He pauses. "With us."

His words fill me with pain, and I can't explain why.

There is no us, is what I want to scream while I stomp my foot like a toddler having a tantrum. But I do none of that.

Instead, I smile as I glide toward him, stopping close enough that our toes almost touch. "Then take me to dinner and I'll watch you eat. But you have to promise me one thing."

"Anything," he says without hesitation.

"Don't drive too recklessly." I point at the car. "That thing looks fast."

"It is." He pulls the key fob from his pocket, dangling it from his fingers. "Ready?"

No. I'm not even close to being ready to get into a car with him.

"Yes," I say with far more assurance than I feel, approaching the car with the utmost confidence. I'm wearing a black dress that's clean and no underwear beneath because what's the point. I figured I was going straight home after a quick squabble on the street with West, but I still wanted to look decent.

At least more decent than he's seen me prior. The impression I've left on him can't be much, yet he still sends me flowers, still waits for me outside when it's time to leave.

He rushes ahead of me and opens the passenger side door, waving his hand and indicating I should step inside. I do so, sitting delicately in the passenger seat, startling when he slams the door.

The interior of the car is beautiful, black leather everything with enough silver knobs to confuse me—and it smells like him, which is some sort of torture that I can't help but wonder if he planned it all.

He slides into the driver's seat seconds later, filling up the space, his shoulder nearly nudging mine and I recoil from his closeness, pressing myself against the door.

"Do you have any preference where we go?" He turns that

intense gaze upon me and I feel rooted in place. Unable to move. I didn't bank on being so close to him and how it would make me feel. I'm close enough to touch him. Smell him. To lean in and press my face into his neck, inhaling his familiar, woodsy scent.

I banish the last thought from my mind.

"I'm not hungry, remember?"

"You will be once I take you to this place." He starts the car, revs the engine because of course he does, he's a man and he's ridiculous, and then pulls away from the curb with the tires squealing on the pavement. I can even feel the car's back end sway and I send him a stern look when he comes to a stop at the next light, the engine rumbling, the grin on his face telling me he's extremely pleased with himself.

"You're dangerous."

"I thought that's why you liked me."

"I never said I *liked* you, Weston." I stare out the passenger window, fighting the smile that wants to grow.

"At some point you must've. Why else did we do what we did?"

"What exactly are you referring to?" I keep my gaze firmly fixed on the window.

"You remember." His voice is low and full of unspoken meaning. "Or do you?"

He's the only person I've ever done that sort of thing with so, of course, I remember.

And this makes me wonder how many women has he been with the past two years? He's very successful, and very young. And also, extremely good looking. I'm sure women have thrown themselves at him and he's had his pick.

So, what is he doing here with me?

He takes me to a restaurant that's not too far from the theatre and that must be very popular. It's crowded with well-dressed couples, a large cluster of people waiting in the lobby, yet the moment West tells the hostess his name, she's leading us deeper into the restaurant, seating us at a small table not too far from the bar, which is absolutely packed. The low murmur of conversation fills the space, the scent in the air absolutely divine and my stomach grumbles despite my constant protests that I'm not hungry.

"Have you been here before?" he asks once the hostess leaves us with our menus.

"No, never." I flip open the menu, my mouth almost watering at the descriptions of the food. "I don't get out much."

"No one trying to take you out?"

I send him a look. "Don't dig, West."

"Why not?"

"It's none of your business."

He shrugs. "I had to try."

There's a votive in the center of the table, the candlelight flickering upon his face and I don't know if I've ever seen him look more handsome. He's downright breathtaking and as I stare at him, I realize something.

My feelings for him have never really dimmed. I still think about him constantly, but instead of wanting him, I want to yell at him. Ask him why. Why did he leave? More than anything, I want to beg him to give me every single detail of what he's experienced over the last two plus years.

Not that I do that. I won't beg this man for any information. Instead, I play it cool, reading over all the restaurant has to offer, not planning to choose a single thing.

"I'm having the lobster." He glances up at me. "Want to share an appetizer?"

My stomach growls loudly on cue and I almost want to die with embarrassment.

"Whatever you want to get," I say weakly.

"We're getting the scallops. You like seafood?" When I nod, he slaps the menu shut. "Then it's settled. I'm starving. And I want something from the bar. Do you? They have a great martini."

"You've been here before?"

"After you've rejected me so soundly the last couple of nights? Yes." He ducks his head, seemingly bashful, though we both know that's a crock of shit. Besides, he's chuckling, like my rejection is amusing, and maybe it is. "After the first night, I came here and sat at the bar and drank myself into oblivion."

"Really?" He took my rejection that badly? I was pretty awful.

"You were really mean. And when you're mean," he rubs at his chest, right in the vicinity of his heart, "it can hurt, you know?"

I roll my eyes. "Come on, West."

He drops his hand, leaning across the table as if he's trying to get closer to me. "Come on, Carolina. You've been mean to me since the first time we met."

I was terrible to him in Paris. When I first started at Lancaster Prep. And now here in London. I can't help it. He brings out the worst in me. "There's something about you that I find so…"

"Irritating?" he offers.

"You frustrate me. With your pretty face and charming words," I finish.

"You think I'm pretty?" He leans back in his chair, his legs splayed wide, looking every ounce the confident man that he surely is. "I don't know how I feel about that. I'd much prefer handsome. Attractive. Good-looking. Even hot. But *pretty?*"

I nod. "Your face is very pretty."

He scowls. "I hate that."

My smile is small, and I'm lying. My brother has a pretty face. I think that's what makes his nasty attitude so shocking. And while West is definitely handsome, and could even be considered pretty, especially when he was younger, I wouldn't say that's an accurate word to describe him.

But the word annoys him so it's fun to say.

"Maybe you hate me too," I finally say.

"No, that's how you feel about me." His expression turns somber. "Which I suppose I've earned, since I fucked everything up."

I part my lips, ready to ask why exactly he did what he did, when the server shows up, asking if we want to start with drinks or an appetizer. West orders for me—an espresso martini, I can't wait—plus the scallop appetizer, and once the server is gone, I prop my elbows on the table, curling my hands together and resting my chin on top of them.

"You need to start explaining."

"Where should I start?" He frowns.

"From the beginning."

CHAPTER THIRTY-EIGHT

WEST

Just having Carolina sitting across from me and being able to stare at her gorgeous face makes my heart ache—my entire body aches with wanting her. She's so close yet still so distant, and I know without a doubt...

I can't fuck this up. I just wasted the last two years of my life without her in it, and now I need to work on winning her back.

Did I ever really have her though? At one point in time, I believe I did. She was all in. And then I had to go and ruin it all. I could've handled my father's death better. I could've handled the Mercedes' situation better too. That's where I really fucked up. Keeping that from Carolina was my downfall.

But I'm persistent. I knew I could break down her walls and get her to at least leave with me, and now here she is, sitting in public with me, about to down an espresso martini and I can't wait to get a little liquor in her. Maybe she'll loosen up. She's always so damn tense, especially around me.

Not when she's on stage though. Being able to watch her in her element, see her perform night after night, was awe-inspiring. I never got tired of seeing the same performance. She's a beautiful dancer, her body fluid when she moves. I swear to God she got better and better with each performance. To the point that I leapt to my feet when it was over earlier, clapping and shouting her name like I was at a football game.

I wasn't the least bit embarrassed, though I think she might've been.

"Do you mean the day we were suspended?" I ask when I realize she's waiting for me to speak. Not a moment I want to relive.

Talk about an asshole move. I regret what I said. What I did to her. How abandoned she must've felt by me.

Will I ever be able to make it up to her?

"How about why you never came back to Lancaster Prep after our week suspension?" She lifts her brows, the challenge on her face obvious.

I stare at her for a bit because I can, and I cherish each second as I track her every feature. In the darkest of days, right after my dad's death, I never thought I'd see her face again. My dad told me I couldn't return to Lancaster Prep the moment I arrived at their sprawling home in Napa, saying he needed me. I took one look at his face, the pallor of his skin, the haunted look in his eyes, and I knew.

He was dying—near death. And he knew it too.

I opted out of school early. I had enough credits to graduate. I was going because who wants to grow up yet? Not me. Yet I was saddled with all of the responsibilities of running a fucking champagne business that makes hundreds of millions of dollars a year—assisted by men who were much older than me. Some of them are even old enough to be my grandfather.

Clearing my throat, I tell her exactly that. About my father and how ill he was when I arrived in Napa. How he made me stay with them so he could train me. Show me everything he did in what little time he had left. Less than a month later, he was dead. My mother was beside herself. Crying hysterically and asking me what we were going to do, wailing and falling to her knees. I had to be strong. Bear the brunt of the tragedy, the business. I had to be the adult and I was only eighteen years old.

The sympathy in Carolina's gaze is surprising—and relieving. "I'm sorry for your loss. That sounds like it was…rough."

"It was terrible." I don't bother delving into all the details.

"I'm sure you were consumed with learning the business."

"Yeah, I tried. I'm still trying." Thank God for having a board and competent staff who run everything for you. There may be many of them who resent me, but there are also plenty of men and women who worked for my father and only wanted to help me. They were already rewarded with the proper pay and bonus structure, and I still bonused some of them even more after that first year of me being at the so-called helm.

Her voice is soft. "That's a lot of responsibility."

"Too much," I agree.

"Did it take up all of your time?"

"Between working constantly, trying to manage the estate with my mother, who was paralyzed with grief and unable to make a decision for at least a year, yeah. I was fucking swamped." I scrub a hand over my mouth, hating that I sound like I'm complaining, but if I can't be real with this woman, then what's the point of pursuing her?

"I can't even imagine."

"Yeah, it wasn't much fun." My gaze locks with hers. "Just know that I thought about you, Carolina. You were on my mind always. I missed you."

She never saw it, though she came close to discovering it. Maybe I should show her—

Or maybe she'll think I'm a complete stalker who had a low-key obsession with her. Now might not be the time to show her anything.

Carolina digests what I said silently, her gaze dropping from mine, like she can't look at me for a moment, and my mind spins at what she might say next. When she finally speaks, I brace myself.

"What I don't understand is why you couldn't at least send me a text. Let me know you were okay. Or that you weren't okay and you never wanted to talk to me again. Whatever. I just—I deserved to hear from you. At least once in the last two years." She presses her lips together, sadness glimmering in her eyes, and I feel like a world-class asshole.

"I have no explanation for it," I say without hesitation, and it's the goddamn truth. "I was so caught up in my grief, and then I couldn't grieve anymore. I didn't have time for it. I had to work. I had to learn how to manage the House of Fontaine, and deal with the crotchety assholes who resented me for taking over the business. Thank God there weren't too many of them, but they caused enough problems that shit got stressful real quick. Every day was a fucking challenge. I worked from sun up to sun down. I'd go home, collapse into bed and then wake up the next morning to start all over again."

"Sounds like a grind."

"It was. And I'm sorry for...all of it. Everything. I just—I didn't handle things well. I still won't. I'm a work-in-progress." I offer her a small smile.

She returns it and damn if that isn't a relief. "Aren't we all?"

I need her to understand that I didn't forget about her. I just didn't know how to deal with my life at that time. Everything hit me at once.

"After everything that happened, it's not that I wasn't thinking of you, Carolina. I just...was incapable of dealing with everything at that point. I was completely overwhelmed. I had nothing left to give. Not for myself or anyone else."

"I'm sorry about your father." She reaches out and rests her hand on top of my arm for the briefest moment. Voluntarily touching me, which isn't like Carolina. "I'm sorry you lost him."

"Thank you." Her fingers on my arm burn, even through my suit jacket and shirt. She might electrocute me if she touched my bare skin.

She removes her hand when the server appears with our drinks and she sips from her espresso martini eagerly once he's gone, making a low humming noise that is like a shot to my dick.

"This is delicious," she murmurs, licking her lips.

Jesus.

To distract myself, I raise my glass and she hurriedly raises hers, some of the liquid spilling over, little brown drops on the pristine white linen tablecloth. "To old friends."

"To old friends." She smiles as we clink our glasses together, our gazes never breaking as we each take a sip of our drinks. "I'm still mad at you, West."

"I know, Carolina. I fucked up." I don't even bother trying to deny it.

Her expression turns stern. "You did. I'm still not over it."

"I wouldn't be either if I were you." I take a long swallow from my martini, noticing that she watches me the entire time, and when I set the glass on the table, I ask, "Everything okay?"

She nods a little too frantically, her cheeks pink. "Everything is fine. It's great. You know what?"

"What?"

Her smile is slow. Lethal as fuck. "I find that I'm suddenly ravenous."

CHAPTER THIRTY-NINE

CAROLINA

I should be absolutely furious at Weston Fontaine.
I should've shoved him in a puddle on the street and told him to go to hell.

But I didn't do any of those things. Instead, I let him drive me in his fancy British car and take me to an equally fancy British restaurant, and he kept ordering me these fancy little espresso martinis and now I'm drunk. I'm seeing two Weston Fontaines in front of me, and that blows my mind so profusely I can't help but start laughing because what are the odds of having two Westons in front of me? Obviously, I'm not thinking straight.

And then I immediately sober up when I realize who I owe this to.

My treacherous, only out for herself, scary as hell mother.

The earlier effects of two and a half martinis consumed are gone in a flash thanks to that horrible realization.

"What's wrong?"

Glancing up, I find West watching me, his brows wrinkled in concern. This meal with him has been so pleasant. It truly has felt like old friends catching up. We gossiped, we talked about people we knew in high school and where they are now. He knew much more than I did about the various people we went to school with but that's only because I wasn't at Lancaster Prep for long. I do love hearing the stories though.

I could listen to him talk all day. That dreamy deep voice. The low chuckles and the flash of a naughty smile. My panties would light on fire if he kept that up, but oops, I'm not wearing any, so I guess there's no chance of that happening.

I press my thighs together at the thought.

"Carolina." His sharp voice pulls me from my thoughts. "Are you all right?"

"Oh, yes. I'm sorry. I just—how close are our mothers?"

His frown deepens. "I believe it's the ladies who lunch type of friendship. Once my mom returned to Manhattan, she picked up with her old friend group and your mother was a part of that group. They gravitated to each other. I guess they have a lot in common?"

I really hope West's mother is nothing like mine. "Not many women have things in common with my mother. She's rather… unique."

My mother had to broaden her horizons and find new friends to spend time with since she drove away all of the old ones. She'd always gripe that my father got their friends in the divorce, but that's not quite true. Not really. Yes, he may have kept a few of his old friends and their wives as part of his social circle, but my mother also turned into a raging bitch who did nothing but complain about Father nonstop. Her friends got so tired of hearing about it they eventually shut her out.

I can't half blame them. I shut her out as much as possible, but I can only do so much since she is, after all, my mother.

"My mom seems to like her a lot."

"Yes, my mother made it sound like they've been spending a lot of time together." I frown, staring into the half empty martini glass. "I can't lie, I'm a little wary over them being close."

"What's the harm in it? My mom needs as many friends as she can get right now. She still mourns over my father. I even suggested she try dating again, but she said it was much too soon." He shrugs. "I don't like the idea of her with another man yet anyway so maybe she's right. But eventually I think it might be good for her. I can't imagine her being alone for the rest of her life. She's still got a lot of years left."

I need to backpedal. He might ask what's wrong with my mother and there's not enough time in the world to list all the ways that Sylvia Lancaster is completely fucked up. "Look I think it's nice that our mothers are friends, but you have to know that mine is…not a nice person."

His frown deepens, and I continue on, "She's manipulative. Scheming. I'd even go so far as to say sometimes even—dangerous." I sit up straight, grab my glass and drain it of every last drop in one swallow.

"A little dramatic much? You're being very ominous. I feel like I'm in a movie right now, Carolina." He shakes his head, obviously amused, and I bang my fist on the table, making the silverware clatter against our mostly empty plates. "What the hell?"

"I'm serious. My mother is *not* to be trusted." It pains me to say that. I don't like admitting to people that something is wrong with my mother. She's not normal. She's devious and conniving and I'm worried there's some ulterior motive as to why she's become so friendly with Weston's mother. "Maybe you should warn your mother about her. Don't tell her I said anything though."

"I can't do that. What am I going to say? 'Hey, Mom, word on the street is you can't trust Sylvia Lancaster. She's kind of a psycho.' She'll want to know who said that and she'll want facts. Reasons."

"I don't think you'll need to say much more than that. I'm sure there are plenty of people back home who would confirm that assessment." I nod.

His expression is incredulous. "I was kidding."

"I'm not. Please, just—say something to her. You don't have to get all ominous and warn your mom her life is in danger, because I don't believe that's the case. You can tell her that you've heard some things about Sylvia Lancaster and that she should be on guard around her. And your mom should definitely not tell her any secrets. My mother could use them against yours."

He studies me for a moment, like he needs to take the time to think over what I just said. "Are you afraid of her?"

I blink at him, unsure how to answer.

"Like, are you scared for your own safety?"

This is a tricky question. "Not really. Not for myself. If anyone should be scared, it's my sister." I wince. "Sylvie refuses to spend time alone with her."

"What the fuck? Why?"

"It's a long story." I can't get any more into it without making my entire family sound like a bunch of lunatics, so I wave a hand, dismissing the conversation. "You never told me about one person in particular."

He raises his brows but says nothing about my subject change. "Who are you wondering about?"

"Mercedes."

"Ah." West leans back in his chair, his shirt molded to his lean torso, my gaze lingering there, wondering what he looks like under those clothes. Just as good as he did when we were younger? I'd guess even better. He's bigger. Broader. "She's in California."

"Wait, seriously?" Jealousy rises, making me see green, and I mentally tamp it down. "Why?"

"Her dad was in tech, remember? She got kicked out of Lancaster Prep but ended up graduating high school when she went back to California, then went on a European vacation over the summer, started at Berkeley her freshman year and then flunked out during the first semester. She hooked up with a musician soon after that, and got into heavy drugs. Then I guess she got clean and now she's living with that guy in Oakland and pregnant with his baby."

"*What?*" I'm shocked. Positively floored.

"Right?" He's nodding, his eyes half-lidded, giving him a sleepy/sexy look. He hasn't drunk as much as me, one and half martinis to my three, and he's consumed nothing but water for the last thirty minutes at least. Bet he's trying to sober up since he drove that fancy Aston Martin here. "I never thought she'd end up like that."

"I hope she's miserable," I say with as much sincerity as I can muster. "I hope she's a huge disappointment to her parents and that she regrets all of her life choices."

My words, my tone are both vicious, and I see the worry flicker in West's gaze. "You're still pissed at her. So am I."

"Of course, I am. She got us suspended from school, West. She shared that video of us together with everyone she knows and she encouraged them to share it. She's a horrible human. She's getting exactly what she deserves." I won't back down from my feelings. Mercedes is a nasty person and I hope I never see her again.

"She was pretty shitty for what she did," West agrees. "It just feels like so long ago now."

He's not wrong. It was a long time ago. A lot of things have happened, most of them good, at least for me, and I guess it's easier to forget about that one horrible thing that happened to us in high school.

But being in front of West, remembering how devastated I was over the incident and how he handled it. How angry I was at him.

God, that hurt the most of all.

"Why didn't you tell me you knew she recorded us?" I ask, my voice small.

"Ah, Carolina." He runs his hand over his jaw. His cheek. Like my question made him uncomfortable. Sometimes I wonder if I'm the only one who calls West out for his bad behavior. "I was dealing with a lot of shit because of my dad. Remember when I disappeared for a couple of days and I saw him? He told me then he was dying but made me promise I wouldn't say anything to anyone. He even lied to my mom and said he was in remission. He lied to the entire board at Fontaine. The staff, everyone he worked with, even those closest to him. They all believed everything was status quo, and then I went to Napa on November first and was put right to work on the second. And it wasn't a normal 'bring your son to work day' either. The writing was on the wall. I think they all realized it then, just like I did. And not even three weeks later, he was dead."

I didn't realize his father burdened him with that secret. How unfair. Our parents act like we owe them for raising us, but a lot of the time, they take advantage of us and do their damage just because they can. They think they have the right to control our lives and make us miserable because they "made" us.

If I ever have children, I will never do that.

"This is a heavy conversation and I didn't mean for it to get so serious." He smiles, his gaze appreciative as it drifts over my face. "I like having you sit across from me."

I say nothing. Just press my thighs together again because I can't handle it when he looks at me like that.

"I'm probably asking for too much, but I want you back in my life, Carolina. I know you have your career here in London, but things are happening in my own life that will allow me to do pretty much anything I want here soon. I can live anywhere, go anywhere. My freedom is just on the horizon," he explains.

I'm filled with both joy and dread at what he suggests. I love my life here in London. I really do. But I don't know what it would be like to have him in it. I don't know if I trust him. After everything he did, how he just up and left me...

What's to say he won't do it again?

"Why is your freedom just on the horizon?" I ask, using the

exact words he just said.

He sits up straight, looking pleased with himself. "We're currently brokering a deal to sell the House of Fontaine. A large luxury conglomerate has made an offer we can't refuse, and it's going to be announced soon."

"That's wonderful."

He nods. "It's not what my father would've wanted, but I've discussed it with my mom and she approves. I was never interested in running that company. And the money is hard to resist."

"When you sell it, what's next for you?"

"I don't know." His gaze locks with mine. "It depends on what you want."

CHAPTER FORTY

CAROLINA

My heart stops at his words.

It depends on what you want.

No one has ever really cared about what I want. Not my parents. Not the few friends I've had. Not my siblings. They're too wrapped up in their own shit and I don't blame them. My parents claim they only want what they think is best for me, but who knows. Only by sheer determination and will am I here now, living my life in London and dancing on the stage.

Is it because of who I am? The family connections and the wealth my last name brings isn't a deterrent in this situation and I take advantage of it. Why wouldn't I? At least I'm not sitting on my ass and doing nothing, which is what I could be doing with my trust fund.

But this man sitting in front of me is wanting to frame his life around mine. Around my wants and desires and needs. That is...

Shocking.

Overwhelming.

In the very best way.

"You said something to me earlier."

He tilts his head. "What did I say?"

"That you had a gift for me." I smile at him, resting my hands in my lap. "Was that a lie?"

"I would never lie to you." He reaches around for his jacket, digging into it and withdrawing a small, black velvet box. Jewelry. A ring box.

My stomach starts churning with nerves. What in the world? That better not be—

"Don't look into it too deeply. It's not what you think." He sets the box in the center of the table. "For you."

I stare at it like it might be a snake ready to strike, lifting my gaze to find West watching me with amusement.

"It won't bite." He waves a hand at the tiny box. "Open it."

Reaching for the box, I slowly crack it open to find a gorgeous ring nestled inside. The round stone is large and a vivid blue, surrounded by tiny diamonds, and the band is paved with diamonds as well.

"It's tanzanite, set in platinum," West explains. "When I saw it, it reminded me of you. Your eyes."

I'm speechless. It's truly the most beautiful piece of jewelry I've ever seen, and I did absolutely nothing to deserve it. "It's too much."

"No, it's not. Try it on."

I pull the ring from the box and hold it up to the light, the diamonds sparkling. It's beautiful. And I stand by my statement— it's definitely too much.

I'm about to put it on my ring finger on my right hand when West's voice stops me.

"Try it on your middle finger."

I do as he says, and it's a perfect fit. I never wear rings, so it feels heavy. Holding up my hand, I splay out my fingers, staring at the ring for a quiet moment.

"I bought it specifically for your middle finger so when you feel the need to flip me off again—which I'm sure you will—I can see the ring that I bought you and know that you belong to me."

My startled gaze meets his.

"I'm getting ahead of myself but come on, Carolina. You know the truth."

The air grows heavier the longer we both stay silent until finally I can't stand it any longer.

I aim my new ring in his direction, lowering all of my fingers until only the middle one is up, the ring glinting from the flickering candle in the votive.

West smiles. "I like it."

"You would." I jab my middle finger in the air before I drop my hand to the table, my gaze still stuck on the ring.

It's exquisite. Too much. I don't even want to know what he spent on it, or what this all really means.

"If you're uncomfortable wearing it, I understand," he says quietly.

"I'm not uncomfortable, West. It's just—this is so wild. I haven't seen you in two years. Then you just show up out of the blue in London like we're old friends and have no weird shared past. Like, shit went down between us. Your leaving Lancaster Prep and never coming back…"

Broke my heart. Ruined me for anyone else. Tore me to pieces and made me realize I'd be a fool to let anyone into my life. Not to mention his utter lack of concern for my feelings when it came to the whole Mercedes thing.

That still hurts too. Way too much.

"It was wrong, and I'm sorry," he finishes for me.

Unable to resist, I flip him off, making sure he gets a good, long look at the ring he gave me before I drop my hand into my lap. "Thank you for the apology."

"I do feel like shit for what happened. I have no excuses. I was young and stupid and overwhelmed."

I nod.

"And I didn't understand how to navigate the relationship thing, you know? I wasn't very good at it."

"I'll say," I retort. Though really, I was exceptionally terrible at it too.

"But I want to make up for it. I'm here for however long it takes, Carolina. I don't need to be in the States. All the paperwork has been done and I'm just a phone call away for anyone who needs me. The only person I want to be with right now is you. Even if you're flipping me off and telling me to go to hell, I'm going to do my damnedest to make you see that we're perfect for each other."

I actually snort, immediately covering my lips with my fingers, the ring heavy. A symbol of how I'm feeling.

Heavy with emotion. With doubt. With joy.

Can you be both happy and sad about something? I think so.

"I know. Kind of a crazy concept, am I right?" West shifts in his chair, his expression dead serious. "I want to try again."

"You're going to have to try really hard," I warn him.

"I'm prepared for that." His look is almost like a warning. "Are you?"

A fter West pays for dinner, he escorts me out of the building, guiding me with his hand low on my back, his fingers burning through the thin cotton of my dress. I'm ultra-aware of his nearness, his scent, the fact that I'm not wearing anything under my dress and I'm tempted to tell him exactly that.

But then I think better of it and decide to keep my mouth shut.

We exit the restaurant, the cool breeze hitting us, making me shiver.

"Cold?" His voice is low and terribly close to my ear and I nod, rubbing my upper arms briskly with my hands.

He comes to a stop on the sidewalk and so do I, watching as he shrugs out of his jacket and slips it carefully over my shoulders.

It's huge, engulfing me almost completely and most likely making me look like I'm not wearing anything under the jacket. He's standing directly in front of me, tugging on the lapels to cover me completely, his knuckles brushing against the front of my dress, that light touch making my nipples harden almost painfully.

"That good?" he asks, his hands still gripping the lapels, his gaze lifting to mine in question.

I nod, my breath lodged in my throat, swallowing the whimper that wants to escape when he slides his hands down, those knuckles brushing me the entire way until he finally lets go.

"I'll drive you back to your flat." He starts walking once more and I keep up with him, noting how tall he is next to me. How protected I feel when I'm with him.

I glance down at my hands that are clutching the front of his jacket, the ring shining up at me as a reminder that I'm wearing it. That I agreed—to a certain extent—that I'm his.

The anxiety rises and I try to tamp it down, but by the time we're approaching the gorgeous Aston Martin, I swear I'm in a full-blown panic attack.

"Carolina? Are you all right?"

I realize I'm breathing loudly. And I'm shivering. West grabs hold of me, wrapping his arms around my waist, pulling me into him and he's so solid and warm. It's like being enveloped by an oven, and I rest my head against his chest, listening to his rapid heartbeat. He allows me to stand there silently for long, agonizing minutes, running his hand over my hair, his tone gentle as he reassures me.

"You're going to be all right. Just breathe."

I cling to his words as much as I cling to him and I've got my face fully shoved into chest. His shirt is unbuttoned a few extra buttons and I sort of want to press my nose to his skin and breathe deep his scent but...

I don't want to seem like I've completely lost it so I restrain myself.

"You seem better," he says a few minutes later, his fingers still tangled in my hair. "Are you ready to go?"

I nod, keeping my head bent, almost afraid to face him. He slips his fingers beneath my chin and tilts my head up, my gaze meeting his and all I see is warmth and acceptance there. I don't remember West ever looking at me like this when we were younger.

"I'm rushing you."

"Completely."

"I don't mean to. I'm just—eager." He releases my chin, his thumb touching the corner of my mouth. "I've missed you."

His finger on my lips burns right through me and I close my eyes, leaning into him. He cups the side of my face, his voice a raw whisper when he says, "I'm asking too much from you. It's just that you're so damn beautiful. You're all I've thought about for I don't want to admit how long. And after seeing you at your brother's wedding, I knew I had to come to you. I had to convince you that what we could have is real."

"You scare me." I open my eyes, wishing he knew just how badly he does. "I don't know if you deserve me."

"I don't." He dips his head, his mouth brushing against mine when he speaks. "But I'm going to work hard to prove to you that I do."

He kisses me then, his lips warm and soft. He doesn't push, doesn't ask for anything else from me, and when he eventually pulls away, I try to ignore my disappointment.

"Come on." He steers me toward the car, heading for the passenger side. "Let's get you home."

He deposits me into the passenger seat and shuts the door for me, rounding the car and sliding into the driver's seat seconds later. There's no showy revving of the engine this time, though it rumbles when he starts it, all of that restrained power reminding me of him.

I watch him blatantly as he drives, too far gone to care. He maneuvers through the streets of London with ease, as if he was born driving in England his entire life, and I'm impressed. I'm not much of a driver in the first place and I don't dare try and drive here. I'd much rather take public transit and leave it to the professionals or those from here.

"You're staring," he says at one point when he's stopped at a light, glancing over at me with a knowing look.

"I can't help it. I'm impressed with your driving abilities." I decide to be truthful. "I'm also shocked that you're here. That I'm in your car and wearing the ring."

"The ring means nothing."

"It means a lot," I correct, my voice thick with emotion. "You don't just buy me a ring so you can see it when I flip you off."

"I can guarantee you're going to flip me off again, and it's going to be sooner rather than later." He sounds amused.

The light turns green and he guns the engine, the car roaring down the street. It's late and traffic is light and I realize I didn't give him my address, yet he knows exactly where to go.

"How do you know where I live?"

His expression turns sheepish. "You told me."

"Did not."

"Pretty sure you did."

"Weston." My voice is firm.

"Carolina."

"How do you know?"

A sigh leaves him as he makes a sharp right onto my street. "I followed you."

"You *stalked* me?"

"*Followed* you," he says again.

I sit up straighter, faintly alarmed. "Why would you do that?"

"I wanted to make sure you got home safe." He shrugs one shoulder. "I trailed you home on the tube one night."

"What?" My mouth drops open in shock. Is he serious?

"Yeah. You didn't notice me, which is also concerning because clearly you aren't paying attention to your surroundings. I got off on the same stop you did and lurked in the shadows as you made your way home."

"That's terrifying."

"I know. I was terrified for your safety. You had AirPods in your ears, Carolina. Anyone could've snuck up on you and you would've never heard them."

How did this turn around into me being reckless with my safety versus my questioning his borderline criminal behavior by admitting he followed me home while, and I quote, "lurking in the shadows?"

Though there is a part of me buried deep that is thrilled at his wanting to make sure I'm safe. It's almost sweet of him.

He pulls next to the curb in front of my building, putting the car in park and shutting off the engine. "You're mad."

"More like I'm disturbed. Though maybe you're the disturbed one here."

His smile is rueful. "Like I said, I was worried about you. You're rather oblivious."

"I guess I don't expect my ex to follow me around like a stalker."

"Jesus, I'm not a stalker." He leans back in his seat, exhaling roughly. "It's going to be difficult winning you back, huh."

"You deserve a challenge."

He turns his head, the grin on his face stealing my breath. "I'm ready for it."

CHAPTER FORTY-ONE

CAROLINA

The man is persistent, I'll give him that.

He still shows up at the theatre night after night, if not sitting out in the audience, then he's at least waiting for me after it's over. I don't take the tube home any longer. I allow him to drive me home, never inviting him up to my flat, though I know he's dying for me to do so. I can see it in his eyes, read it in his body language, and while I would love to invite him up, I know I'm not ready.

It's best to make the man wait.

But it's been a week since the night he took me to dinner and gave me a too expensive ring, and my resolve is starting to waver. I blame it on the way he looks at me, as if he's thinking of all the ways he can get me naked, and I wish I could confess that my imagination is running away from me too.

He's stopped sending a daily flower arrangement. Instead, they appear every two days, and Cressida finally got me to admit who they're from, and who West is to me. She's a bone-deep romantic and thinks this is the most adorable thing she's ever witnessed while I keep blowing the situation off by saying he's not that serious.

I'm starting not to believe myself though. Weston Fontaine

is dead serious in his pursuit of me and I'm loving every minute of it. And while I can't wear the ring he gave me while I practice and perform, I make sure and bring it with me to the theatre every single day, slipping it on before I leave at night, greeting him with a subtle wave of my middle finger upon first sight of him.

He laughs at my greeting every single time, that rich, deep chuckle making my insides quiver. I want him badly. I want his hands and his mouth on me. I want to hear him whisper dirty words in my ear and tell me what to do. I want to give in to his demands willingly and allow him to use me in any way he wants, because I know he'll take care of me.

Once upon a time, for a very brief moment, he did exactly that, and I know he would do it again.

When he doesn't attend the nightly performance, he dresses much more casually when he picks me up, but he always looks devastatingly handsome. Last night he greeted me while wearing a pair of black joggers and a white hoodie sweatshirt, then took me to a pub where he watched me eat way too much food, protesting the entire time. Just like he told me watching me perform makes him ravenous, spending so much time with him leaves me feeling ravenous as well.

Hungry for him.

Tonight he came to watch, wearing that damn gray suit again, the one that I find so sexy, his white shirt unbuttoned halfway down his chest like he's trying to purposely distract me. Once everything's over, I hurry to wipe off my makeup until my face is scrubbed shiny and clean, Cressida watching me with a careful eye from her perch right next to me.

"I want to meet him," she declares.

I send her a look in her mirror's reflection. "Absolutely not."

"I have witnessed this entire thing unfold. The very least I deserve is to meet this man who sends you every pink rose that must exist in all of Covent Garden. I want to hear his voice. I want to see what's so dreamy about him," Cressida explains.

"He's not dreamy," I protest. The look she sends me calls me on my bullshit. "He's not, I swear."

"I have eyes, Carolina. I see him sitting out there night after night, watching you as if you're the most beautiful thing he's ever seen. Of course, he's dreamy. And he's completely in love with you."

"There is no love involved."

Another stern look from Cressida. "Who are you trying to convince of that? Me? Or yourself?"

Her words linger as I change into yet another dress. This one pale pink with a flowy skirt and thin straps that tie on my shoulders. My shoulders are mostly bare as is my collarbone and I can't help but wonder if I could tempt him into kissing me there. I can imagine him tugging the top of my dress down and my breasts coming free. He would touch them. Kiss them. Hopefully suck...

"I'm walking out with you when it's time to leave. You're going to introduce me to your new boyfriend," Cressida says, her firm voice interrupting my lurid thoughts.

Once I'm dressed and ready to go, I find that Cressida is as well, her bag slung over her shoulder, her expression bright and friendly. Her gaze drops to the ring on my finger—she never sees the ring on my finger. I don't normally slip it on until she's completely out of sight—and her eyes widen the slightest bit.

"He gave that to you."

I nod.

She laughs. "He's so in love with you. That ring is gargantuan."

"It's not a diamond so it doesn't count."

When I draw closer, she grabs at my hand, bringing it up to her face so she can examine the ring closely. "I see diamonds. That's close enough."

Seconds later we're exiting through the back door of the theatre, West in his normal spot leaning against the back of the Aston Martin, his arms crossed and a smile on his face. It goes up a notch when he spots Cressida, and I see two bright spots of color on her cheeks, as if she too is entranced with his handsome looks and undeniable charm.

"You're bringing a friend?" His gaze shifts to Cressida. "I recognize you. You're a dancer."

Her blush deepens. "Cressida. I've been dying to meet you."

His grin widens. "Lovely to meet you. I'm West."

He takes her hand and she giggles. She can barely look at him, as if she's afraid he might try to wield some sort of power over her, and I stand there awkwardly, listening to their small talk as she rambles on about the beautiful flowers that he sends me. How he attends so many of our performances and isn't he sick of it yet?

"I could never be sick of watching Carolina perform." His gaze finds mine, his smile different when it's aimed in my direction. Much more intimate. "I love watching her."

Cressida literally clutches her hands in front of her chest as if she might swoon. "That is the sweetest thing I've ever heard."

"You are far too much of a romantic for me," I tell her, shifting her out of my way so I can approach West and stake my claim on him. Not that I'm afraid of Cressida trying to take my man—heck, is he even my man to take? "Should we go?"

"Of course." West slips his hand behind me so it's resting on my lower back, standing by my side as if we're an established couple. I can't deny that it feels good, being with him like this. Like I belong with him. To him. "Cressida, it was wonderful to meet you."

"Lovely to meet you too, West!" She's also far too cheery for me tonight. Well, pretty much all the time. I appreciate her enthusiasm but it's just…not me.

"I hope our paths cross again soon," West continues, so very polite.

That's one thing I've noticed about him since we've reunited. He seems so much more grown up and handles almost every situation with such quiet control. He's polite and respectful and acts like he knows what he's doing, while I'm awkward, sometimes unintentionally rude and really, I have no idea what I'm doing.

"Oh, I'm sure our paths will cross again very soon." The cheeky grin she flashes our way is almost infuriating. "See you tomorrow, Carolina."

"Bye." I wave at her, wishing I could give her the finger and let her get a good, long look at my ring, but I don't mean it. Cressida is harmless. I like her.

More than anything, I appreciate her.

"She's nice," West says once she's gone.

"Mmm, hmm." His hand still rests on my back and I wish it would drop even lower.

"She knew a lot about the flowers." He glances down at me. "Are you talking about them? Talking about me?"

Always fishing for more information. Always hoping I'm telling everyone I know about him.

"Her table is next to mine. We get ready together before every performance. She sees the flower deliveries and always asks about them," I explain.

"I like her. She doesn't seem like someone you would want to hang out with, but I like that you spend time with her. She seems sweet."

"Don't get any crazy ideas," I warn him. "I doubt her sweetness wore off on me."

"I don't think I'd want you too sweet." He leans down and drops the briefest kiss on my forehead. "I like you just the way you are."

His words go straight to my head, leaving me dizzy. Has anyone ever said that to me before? I don't think so. Not even my parents. They always wanted me striving for more. Do more, be better. You're a Lancaster, you can do it.

That was always my father's angle. Encouraging me by saying my name alone could get me what I wanted in life, and I suppose he's right in some cases, but not everything.

Living up to the family name is intimidating. This is why I'm grateful for dance. It gives me something to focus on outside of the family and the money, rather than be worried over what I might accomplish as a Lancaster.

It's a blessing and a curse.

"What do you want to do tonight?" he asks. Normally we go out for dinner and talk while we eat. That first night we drank a little too much, but we haven't done it since, which is better. I prefer to keep my wits about me and it's difficult enough, trying to be logical when in West's presence.

"I'm tired."

"You are?"

I nod, lying as per usual to get what I want. But is it wrong when I'm thinking this might be what West wants too?

"I want to do something different," I suggest.

"Like what?"

"Like maybe…grab something to eat to-go and hang out at my place?"

That is the first time I've made the offer, and I can see the impact my suggestion has on West. His brows shoot up and hope flickers in his brown gaze.

"Are you sure?"

I nod.

"You're finally going to let me into your palace?" Those beautiful eyes are now dancing with mischief. He does enjoy giving me a hard time. Much more lighthearted than before, when he was a morose, broody teenager who hated everyone.

I roll my eyes. "It's not a palace. It's quite small, and I don't have a lot of furniture."

"I'm sure it's nice."

"It's okay. There's a couch and a bed. The important things, right?" My question is suggestive.

I'm tired of waiting. We keep dancing around the subject,

without coming right out and saying it—or even better, doing it.

Having sex. He's barely even kissed me. It's almost like he's afraid of me, afraid of what might happen if we take it to the next level.

Well, I want to make something happen between us. I've spent so much time with West this last week getting to know him all over again, and I want more.

I want to be *with* him.

"The important things," West repeats, his smile slow. "I agree. What should we order for dinner?"

We end up grabbing sushi at a restaurant not too far from my building. West carries the bag of to-go containers up the stairs, following behind me as I race up them, not even bothered by running up three stories. By the time we're at my front door, I'm not even out of breath and impressed that he isn't either.

I like that he's in shape. I wonder if he still runs. I'd guess, yes.

As he looms behind me while I unlock my door, I swear he's taller than he was when we were in high school. And he's most definitely broader. I guarantee his chest is more defined and I'm curious to know what he looks like naked.

Because of course I am.

"Here we are," I announce as I hit the wall switch and the single lamp that sits on the rickety end table next to the couch flickers on. "Like I said, it's not much."

He enters my little sanctuary and I close and lock the door, leaning against it while I watch him survey my flat. It's tiny and a little drab but it's in a safe, quiet building and it's close to the theatre and the dance studio. The location is what sold me, but I've come to like it here. I don't need a lot of fancy trappings like what I've grown up with.

None of that is really me. I just want to dance. And retreat somewhere quiet and calm so I can just…be.

"I like it," West announces, moving into my tiny kitchen and turning on the light before he sets the to-go bag on the counter.

"Where are your plates?"

I walk into the kitchen, stopping right beside him. "I don't really have any."

"You don't?"

"I'm not much of a cook."

"Me neither." He tears open the bag and pulls out the containers. "We'll just eat out of these then."

I check the fridge to see what I have to drink and find a couple bottles of beer that someone from the dance company left behind a long time ago, when I had them over after the final night of the previous production we worked on. "I have beer."

"That will work."

We sip beer and eat sushi at the old dining table that was left behind by the previous tenants. The landlord said it would be gone once I moved in, and I immediately told him I'd keep it. I could've bought anything I wanted and had it delivered but I didn't even want to think about it.

Much easier to use what was left behind.

"This is good," West says before he shoves another red dragon roll into his mouth. He uses the chopsticks with ease, uses far too much wasabi for my tastes, and he's already finished off more than half of his beer. Is he nervous?

"It's delicious. My favorite sushi place in all of London, and I just happen to live close to it." I set my chopsticks on the edge of the container and wipe at my mouth with my napkin, realizing West is watching my every move. "Do I have rice on my nose or something?"

"No." He shakes his head. "I'm just—glad to be here with you. In your flat. Eating sushi."

"Just another typical night then." I'm trying to make light of this. He is far too serious right now.

"Not even close. My nights the last two years were spent pouring over the Fontaine books. Going over the assets and liabilities. Looking for ways to cut costs and increase revenue.

It was fucking awful, but I had to learn it. I had to figure it out to ensure my and my mother's future," he explains, letting his chopsticks drop into his mostly empty container. "The best thing about tonight is I'm not looking at a spreadsheet."

I burst out laughing. "I'm better to look at than a spreadsheet?"

"You don't even know how much." He's not smiling. Just staring at me intently, his arms propped on the edge of the table, his upper body leaning toward mine. Like he wants to be close.

Actually, he appears ready to pounce.

"What are we doing, West?" I ask softly, my heart starting to race. I want the answer, yet I don't. The mystery of this, the anticipation, is excruciating.

"What do you want to do, Carolina?"

I decide to be truthful. "Everything."

CHAPTER FORTY-TWO

WEST

Everything.

My head, my heart, my fucking soul and even my dick are pounding at that one simple word falling from Carolina's lush mouth.

Finally.

I've been patient. Respectful. I didn't want to push. Didn't want to come at her too hard because I know she's skittish like a wild animal and one wrong move, she'd be gone. She doesn't like to be touched, so I don't do much touching, even though it fucking kills me. All I want to do is touch her. Kiss her. Fuck her into oblivion if she'd let me.

"Well?" she asks after I'm silent too long for her liking. "You have nothing to say to that?"

I clear my throat. "I'm trying to keep myself under control."

"What would you do if you lost all control?" Her cheeks turn the faintest pink.

"I'd lunge across this table and kiss you."

"That doesn't sound very comfortable." Her voice is light. Teasing.

"This isn't about being comfortable. It's about getting what I want."

"And are you saying you want me?"

"Maybe." Now I'm the one teasing.

She flashes me the finger, the ring I gave her prominent, filling me with pride that she wears it as much as she can.

"I'm going to clean up our mess." She rises to her feet and closes her sushi container. "Do you want something else to drink?"

"I'm good." I've already finished my beer, but I don't need another one. The last thing I want is to be drunk or even buzzed tonight. Things are shifting between us and I need to be sober.

"A mint?" She grabs a tin from the kitchen counter and offers it to me. "All of that wasabi you just consumed."

"And sriracha." I shrug, taking the tin from her and popping it open. "What can I say, I like spicy things."

"Is that why you like me?" She laughs, the sexy sound going straight to my dick. "I'm sorry. That was really cheesy."

"But accurate." I pop the mint in my mouth, wincing at the overpowering flavor. "You're pretty fucking spicy. And sexy."

She rushes into the narrow kitchen, shoving her sushi container into the fridge before she returns to the table. She's got that familiar flush coating her skin. The way she used to look when we were hooking up. Or when she was embarrassed prior to our hooking up.

"You really think I'm sexy?"

"Come on, Carolina. Are you fishing for compliments? You know I think you're sexy." I pause, deciding to be truthful. "You're all I think about."

She blinks at me and I continue.

"When I wake up in the morning, you're on my mind. When I'm in bed, I drift off to thoughts of you. In the shower, I jerk off while thinking about you."

Her cheeks are bright red, her voice a squeak when she says, "You do?"

I nod. "We didn't do near enough together when we were younger."

Carolina takes a step forward, gripping the back of her chair. "I've done nothing else since you."

My entire body freezes when her words sink in.

She's done nothing else. Been with no one else. It's especially shocking because...

"Me neither."

Her mouth drops open. "I don't believe you."

"It's true."

"Come on, West." She waves a hand at me. "Look at you."

I glance down at myself, then lift my head, returning my gaze to hers. "What about me?"

"You're gorgeous."

"So are you."

"Successful."

"Not on my own merits. You're far more successful than I am."

"I don't dance for the most prestigious company in the world, but I love it." She makes a face. "If I was really good, I'd be with the Royal Ballet."

"Don't underestimate yourself. You're still young. It could happen."

She curls her fingers around the top of the chair, her knuckles white. "No one else believes in me like you do."

Her voice is raw, and the look on her face makes my heart ache. I stand without thinking and go to her, turning her so she's facing me and circling my arms around her waist. "You deserve the world."

Carolina rests her hands on my chest, her gaze imploring. "I never thought I did. No one makes me feel as if I'm worthy of anything like you do, West."

"I want to give you the world. Whatever you want, whatever you need, I want to take care of you. Be with you." I duck down, my mouth hovering just above hers. "Will you let me?"

Her voice is the barest whisper. "Yes."

I crush her mouth with mine, kissing her fiercely, absolutely no finesse involved. I thrust my tongue into her mouth, sliding it against hers, groaning at the first delicious taste of her. Her scent wraps around me, reminding me of a cool ocean breeze, and I remove my hands from her waist to cup her face, cradling her cheeks. As if she's the most precious thing.

Which she is. To me.

We kiss as we stumble around her apartment, looking for a soft place to land. I eventually collapse on the couch, bringing her with me, her landing on top. She doesn't look like she weighs much, but she's solid muscle, and I can feel the subtle strength of her as I run my hands over her body. Her arms and sides and legs.

Hard as rock. This woman could probably squeeze me to death with her thighs, but I'd go willingly.

Fuck, I'm an idiot over her.

She breaks away from my still seeking lips at one point and I lean back against the couch, staring at her as she sits up straight, her eyes never straying from mine as she slides down the straps of her dress from her shoulders. She tugs at the bodice, her small breasts popping out and I reach for them, cupping them both, my thumbs flicking her nipples.

They're hard and bright pink, reminding me of the roses I can't stop sending her.

Groaning, I lean in and draw one of those pretty nipples into my mouth, sucking hard. She wraps her hand around the back of my head, holding me to her before I shift to the other nipple and give it the same attention.

My cock throbs. It's been far too long since I've been with her. I'm sure she won't believe me, but after my father's death, I had no time for a relationship. Not even a hook-up. Nothing happened between Madison and me beyond a few brief kissing sessions that did nothing for me.

All I have to do is look at Carolina and I'm rock hard. The power she wields over me is startling.

I return my mouth to hers, the kiss turning languid.

Downright filthy. Our tongues are busy as are my hands, which are currently sliding up the outside of her thighs, burrowing beneath the skirt of her dress, all the way up to her hips.

"You're not wearing panties," I murmur against her lips.

She licks at the corner of my mouth. "I haven't worn panties or a bra since the moment you showed up on the street waiting for me."

"Are you serious?"

Carolina rears back a little, nodding. Looking extremely pleased with herself.

"Fuck." My hands are now curved around her perfect ass and I give it a squeeze, my fingers teasing the crack. "We've wasted a lot of time."

"We needed to do this." She kisses me deep and I let her take over for a moment as her tongue searches my mouth, her hands in my hair, fingers tugging as she essentially devours me. "We needed to wait."

She's probably right, I think as I knead her ass, my fingers digging into her skin, making her whimper against my mouth. My sweet, fiery Carolina Lancaster is not a fast mover. She needs to be lured in slowly.

I shift one hand to rest on top of her thigh briefly before I let it slide down, until I'm cupping her pussy. The heat of her scorches my skin and I gently press, noting the way she stiffens, how she holds her breath. When I press my fingers against her fully, she angles her hips, my fingers sinking in, finding her wet.

So fucking wet.

"Oh God," she chokes out when I press against her clit.

I rub her clit with my thumb, drawing tight circles around it, the wet sounds filling the room. I never take my eyes off of her and she throws back her head, essentially riding my hand as I stroke her into oblivion.

"Don't stop." She gasps at one point when I hit a particular spot that I continue to keep touching. "Oh my God, just like that."

Like I'd stop. Watching her is making me harder than I've ever been in my life. Her tits are out, shaking as she bounces, the scent of her hitting my nostrils and making my mouth water. I want to taste her. Making her come with my tongue and then again on my cock.

"West." Her head pops up, her eyes open when they meet mine as she chokes out my name. I don't look away. It's like I can't, and I increase my pace, desperate to get her off. She thrusts her hips against my hand, her breath stuttering in her lungs, her lips falling open but no sound coming out when she goes completely still.

And then falls completely apart.

It's a beautiful thing, witnessing a woman come because of what you're doing to her. I keep stroking her pussy, my fingers slicking through her juices, feeling the way she trembles as the orgasm sweeps over her. I thrust a finger inside her tight sheath, her inner walls clenching around it so tight, I wonder how I'll ever be able to fuck her.

"Oh my God," she repeats when it's over, her entire body starting to relax. She basically melts into me, slumping her body all around me, and I remove my hand from her pussy at the last second, wrapping my arms around her so I can hold her close. "That was…"

Her voice drifts, her mouth moving against my neck, making me shiver, and I run my fingers up and down her bare back, quietly marveling at her smooth skin.

"Amazing," she finally finishes, slowly pulling away so our gazes can meet. "Let's do that again."

When I say nothing but only lift my brows, she tacks on a soft, "Please?"

As if I could resist her. I'll give this girl anything she wants.

All she has to do is ask.

CHAPTER FORTY-THREE

CAROLINA

It's the way he watches me, his expression completely unguarded. None of the defenses or walls are up, it's just West studying me with pure emotion shining in his eyes. All of that emotion is for me.

And no one else.

My body still shaking with the remnants of my orgasm, I carefully climb off his lap, my dress falling to my feet in a soft heap. I kick it aside, completely naked, as I head for my bedroom, but West remains in place on the couch like he can't move.

I stop, glancing over my shoulder to find him watching me with a burning intensity that could probably scorch me where I stand. "Are you coming?"

"I'm about to," he says as he leaps to his feet, heading straight for me.

Before I can move, he's got a hold of me, tossing me over his shoulder so my head is hanging upside down, my hair covering my face. I squeal and pound on his back with my fists, nervous as he carries me into my bedroom, carefully dropping me onto the bed.

"Are you a caveman?" I ask once I've got my hair out of my face.

He's standing at the foot of the bed, already undoing the buttons on his sleeves before he reaches for the front of his shirt. "Apparently."

I don't complain. How could I? He picked me up with such ease, which is a complete turn-on.

Everything he does turns me on.

I scooch backwards on the bed, propping my back against the pile of pillows, slowly spreading my legs so he can see every part of me. I'm too far gone to care anymore. The embarrassment is gone. The worry over what he might think of me, or that he might touch me, gone.

I want all of it. I want him to see me, to want me, to touch me. My body feels like it's vibrating, I'm so aroused. And I came only minutes ago.

"Look at you," he murmurs, his gaze dropping to the spot between my legs. I swear I get wetter just from him staring at me.

"Hurry up," I urge, resting my hand on my stomach before I start to slide it lower.

He stops unbuttoning his shirt. "Keep doing what you're doing."

"You like to watch?" Who am I right now? I remember when he asked me that same question two years ago. In my dance studio that one night. I hold my fingers just above my pussy, my clit tingling in anticipation.

"I like to watch you," he clarifies. "Touch yourself, Carolina."

My fingers go lower, not quite there yet. I'm completely waxed—it's just so much easier while dancing—and I wonder if he likes it too. "Tell me what to do and I will."

I've masturbated before. Lately, to thoughts of him late at night while still in my bed, unable to sleep. My mind too full of him, going over our conversations, the way he looks at me. The things he says.

"Use your middle finger," he suggests, his voice hoarse. "I want to see my ring on your cunt."

My pussy floods with moisture at his choice of words and I do as he says, my finger sinking between my lower lips, the large ring protruding between them as I test the wetness there. I spread my thighs wider, showing him everything I've got, my finger poised and ready to do his bidding. "What next?"

"Touch your clit." I do as he asks, sucking in a harsh breath. "Rub it."

I rub the distended bit of flesh, my legs already shaking, on the verge of orgasm just from the heat of his gaze, the lightest touch of my finger. The ring is heavy, a reminder of what it represents and I lazily stroke my flesh, everything inside of me throbbing.

"Slip a finger inside. Your middle finger." His voice is low. Extra deep. He sheds the shirt, letting it drop, and I stare, my mouth dry as I take him in.

He's just as glorious as I'd hoped. All smooth skin over ridged muscle. His pecs are firm and his stomach is almost a washboard. I'm around beautiful bodies day in and day out, including male ones, but no one makes me feel like West does.

I push my finger inside me, until the ring stops my progress and hold it there, letting my pussy get used to it. I don't really fuck myself with my fingers. More like I test. I play. I pay attention to my clit more than anything else because that's what gets me off.

"Fuck yourself." I do as he says, my finger thrusting, my body squeezing around it, needing more. Needing something thicker. "Yeah, just like that."

Tilting my hips up, I fuck myself harder, my thumb brushing against my clit, the ring rubbing against my sensitive skin too, making me light up. It's all too much. Not enough. I need something more. Something harder. Something bigger.

"Stick another finger inside you." I do it automatically, stretching myself full.

A moan falls from my lips and I rest my head back on the pillows, my eyes closed as I fuck myself harder. I'm so wet, the juicy sounds are obvious, and any other moment I would be embarrassed.

But not now. Not here. It's so much better, knowing he's watching me. Telling me what to do.

Next thing I know he's on the bed, lying between my spread legs, his face right at my pussy. He pulls my fingers out, wrapping his lips around them and licking them with his tongue, and I lift my head, whimpering as I watch him lick them clean.

Just before he dips his head and licks me from ass to clit.

I swear to God I scream, my hands immediately going to his hair, tugging on the soft strands as he laps at my clit, circling it over and over. I hold him to me, my grip strong like he's going to stop, but he doesn't. He keeps licking and sucking as if he's enjoying his favorite meal, his hands sliding under my butt so he can hold me to him. His fingers tickle at my crack before they slide lower, brushing against my asshole and I stiffen.

"You don't like that?" My hands fall away from his hair when he lifts his head, his mouth wet from me, his brows furrowed in question.

"I just—I don't hate it." I bite my lower lip, feeling shy. How do I explain to him that I'm willing to do whatever he wants, wherever he wants to? I'm only hesitant because I've never had someone touch me there before, but I liked it.

I did.

"I want to taste you everywhere." He sticks his tongue out, licking me in an exaggerated manner that has my heart racing and thighs quaking. "I want to fuck you with my mouth and my fingers and my cock."

I can't speak.

"I want to fuck your cunt and your ass and your mouth. I want to come on your face. I want to come inside you." He frowns. "Are you still on birth control?"

"Yes."

"Thank Christ," West mutters just before he draws my clit

between his lips.

That's all it takes. A couple of tugs from his lips, his tongue laving against the sensitive bit of flesh, and then I completely fall apart with a keening cry, my fingers plunging into his hair yet again as I pull it tight. He never lets up, his mouth moving against me, drawing the orgasm out until finally I'm pushing him away, unable to take it anymore, rolling over on my side when he lifts up from me.

I'm still shaking, trying to control my breathing, watching him out of the corner of my eye as he wipes at his face with the back of his hand, still licking at his lips.

Filthy man.

Taking slow, deep breaths, I eventually calm my racing heart, my gaze locked on West as he takes off his pants, kicking them aside. His cock strains against the front of his cotton boxers and my entire body lights up.

He's about to take those boxers off when I stop him with a question.

"Why don't you ever take off your watch?"

It's the same one he's worn since high school. Heavy and expensive with that wide, steel band. He glances at it, his gaze lifting to mine, and I swear his cheeks color with...

Embarrassment?

It comes back to me then. The edge of a tattoo.

I sit up fully. "Let me see it."

"See what?" He's playing stupid on purpose.

"The tattoo."

"What tattoo?"

"The one beneath the watch." I roll my eyes when he hesitates. "I know it exists, West. I saw it once."

His eyes nearly bug out of his head. "You did? When?"

"Halloween night our senior year." The first and last night we spent together, just before our entire world shifted.

"So you know what it is." His voice is flat. Tinged with worry.

"Not quite."

"What do you mean, 'not quite'?"

"West." I shift so I'm on my hands and knees, crawling across the bed until I'm right in front of him. I rise up on my knees and wag my hand at him. "Let me see."

With extreme reluctance, he holds out his hand palm up and I reach for the clasp of his watch, carefully undoing it. The band goes loose and I slide it off, the watch landing on the mattress with a soft thud, neither of us caring because I'm staring at the tiny tattoo and he's staring at me.

My lips part and my mind races. Wait a second. I...

I recognize that.

"That's my drawing." My gaze lifts to his, his face like a mask. I absolutely cannot read him. "From the night in Paris."

He exhales, worry etched in his features. "Yeah."

"You had it tattooed on your skin?"

Swallowing hard, he nods.

"This is permanent." I rub at the tattoo like I expect it to smear.

"No shit, Carolina." He doesn't sound amused, but he doesn't sound angry either. I can't figure out what his mood is.

I curl my finger around his wrist and trace it along the delicate edges of the costume I drew on his skin. The straps, the bodice. The little dots I added that were supposed to represent sparkles. The layers of tulle that make up the skirt. I'm no artist and I made the drawing so quickly. The memory is still vivid in my mind. The sensation of his warm skin beneath my fingertips, how he held himself there so carefully while I drew on him, his gaze never straying.

"I can't believe you did this," I finally say, meeting his gaze. "Why did you get this tattoo?"

He shrugs, seemingly uncomfortable, and when he tries to pull out of my hold, I don't let go.

"Why, West?"

"It was stupid. I wanted to remember the night. Remember you. You left an impression." His gaze drops, like he can't look at me when he admits, "I wanted you to always be with me, even in such a small way."

My heart aches at his words. At the meaning behind them. "So you had someone tattoo it on your skin."

"Right after I left you on the street. I went straight to a dingy tattoo parlor and asked the artist to draw over it. He thought I was crazy."

I stare at it yet again, touching it. "I love it."

"You do?" He sounds surprised.

Nodding, I lift his hand to my mouth, brushing a soft kiss to the tattoo on the inside of his wrist. "It's the sweetest thing anyone has ever done for me."

"Sweeter than the flowers?"

I nod.

"Sweeter than the ring?" He lifts his brows when I let go of his hand.

"The ring is pretty sweet." I smile.

He cups the side of my face, his finger drifting down my cheek. "It was an impulsive decision that I was sure I would regret once it was over and I paid for it."

Of course, it was. He barely knew me. We should've never seen each other again.

"But I don't regret it, Carolina. You've always been with me. Both on my skin and in my heart." His smile is rueful. "That was cheesy as hell, but you know what I mean."

I throw myself at him, wrapping my arms around his neck, our upper bodies pressed close. Skin on skin. He feels so good. My breasts crushed against his wall of muscle, his heat seeping into me.

He realizes it too. I can tell by the way his hold on me changes. Becomes firmer, pulling me closer. I can feel his erection brush against my stomach, even through the soft cotton of his boxers, and I reach for him, my finger sliding over him, making him groan.

Oh God.

I think I'm falling in love with West Fontaine.

CHAPTER FORTY-FOUR

CAROLINA

West rids himself of his boxers and guides me so we're both lying on our sides on the bed, face to face. He strokes my face with his fingertips, letting them trail down my neck, across my shoulder, along my arm. I'm shivering, overwhelmed with emotion and need, and I'm aching to be filled.

But I'm also scared. Is it going to hurt again? It might. I've only ever had sex once, on Halloween night, two years ago, right before our world imploded.

I remember how big he was, and how thick he felt back then. It even hurt earlier when he pushed two fingers inside me and I was wet. Well, it wasn't too much pain. It just took a little time to adjust. And after a few seconds, it felt good.

"You look scared," he says as if he can read my thoughts.

"I've only ever had sex that one time," I admit. "Remember?"

His gaze softens. "Yeah."

I nod. "I don't want to worry about pain. I just want to feel good."

"I'll make sure it feels good. I promise." I love those promises he makes me. "It's been a long time for me too. The same amount of time. And tonight, this moment, you—it matters to me."

It doesn't even bother me that there was someone else before me. It was a long time ago. And I love that he said I matter.

"You know that, right?" he asks when I haven't said anything. "*You* matter to me, Carolina."

"I know," I whisper, nodding, my hair rustling against the pillow. This feels like a moment. Like something important is happening between us and I don't want to forget a single detail of this night.

Not a one.

"I care about you." He touches my face. Presses his thumb against my lips. "I'm falling in love with you."

I'm breathing heavier and I swallow hard, trying to calm my suddenly riotous emotions. I don't know how to answer him. I care about him, I do, but I don't know how to say it. Or what I'm feeling for West might actually be love.

I think it is, but I'm not sure.

"You don't have to say it back." He kisses me so gently I think I might cry. "I just wanted you to know."

He tries to pull away, but I don't let him, keeping him with me, my mouth finding his. We kiss for so long, my mouth aches. He's got my back pressed against the mattress and he's lying on top of me, my legs spread, his lower body snug against mine and his insistent erection nudging against my belly.

"We don't have to do this if you don't want to," he says at one point, after he spends approximately five minutes on each of my nipples. He's panting, his body covered in a sheen of sweat and I realize that I do this to him.

He wants me just as badly as I want him—maybe even more so.

"I want to," I tell him, reaching between us so I can brush my hand against his dick. I feel it leap beneath my fingertips, as if it has a mind of its own, and I slip my hand beneath his boxers, curling my fingers around his length.

His agonized groan lights me up inside, encouraging me. I start to stroke him, finding a rhythm, going with him when he rolls away from me until he lands on his back. I tug on his boxers, trying to get rid of them and he helps me, until he's lying there as naked as I am.

Leaning back on my haunches, I study him blatantly, my gaze roving over every inch of exposed skin. He's smooth and lean, his stomach flat, his cock thick and long and fully erect. He's got the lightest smattering of hair between his pecs, around his navel and narrowing into a line below it. This delicious little trail that leads to his cock, and oh my God, I really am nervous about that thing fitting inside me.

"You're staring," he eventually says, his voice strained.

"You're big," I return, my gaze never wavering from his erection. "Did it fit last time?"

He's grinning at my silly question. "It fit."

"I don't know…"

"Trust me." He's on me in an instant, and I'm flat on my back again, staring up at him. "It's going to fit. And it might hurt, but I doubt it."

"You doubt it?"

"We've already been through this once. You'll be fine."

"You're a man." I swat at his chest, but before I can make contact, he's got his fingers around my wrist, stopping me. "You don't have to worry."

He grabs my other wrist and holds my arms above my head, pinning them to the mattress. "I'm going to make sure you're ready."

"How are you going to do that?" My voice turns breathless when he runs his mouth down my neck. Across my collarbone. He lets go of my wrists.

"Watch," he whispers, and I do.

I watch him as he rains kisses all over my skin. His mouth is everywhere, kissing me in places I never thought could feel so good. On the inside of my wrist, behind my elbow. My rib cage. My hipbone.

He completely ignores where I want him the most, slipping down to kiss along my calves, the inside of my knees. The tops of my thighs, his grin wicked when he flashes it my way after catching me staring.

I'm trembling, my muscles taut with anticipation, the pulse between my thighs throbbing. I can't think. All I want is for his mouth to be on my pussy, bringing me pleasure just like he did only a few minutes ago.

But the man doesn't deliver. He teases and taunts. He flips me over and kisses my lower back. My ass. Drawing closer and closer...

"Get on your knees," he demands, and I automatically do what he says. "Spread them wider."

I do that too. I'm so wet, I can feel it drip down the inside of my thighs.

"Fuck, look at you," he whispers just as he kisses the very bottom of my right ass cheek. "You're glistening."

"West." His name is a moan on my lips, a shuddery breath leaving me when I feel his finger teasing. Testing my wetness.

"You're so open to me." He slips his finger inside me with ease. "You're almost ready."

I gasp when he adds a second finger and starts to pump them in and out of my body, his movements slow but smooth. I rear back, trying to create friction, dying for him to move faster. Harder.

He removes his fingers from my body and I cry out, disappointment flooding me. He strokes me, his fingers toying with my clit, strumming it and I angle my hips, rubbing against his fingers shamelessly, desperate to come.

"You're a fucking mess," he murmurs, making it sound like an endearment.

"Please," I beg, unsure of what I'm asking for. Just knowing that he's the only one who can give it to me. "Please, West."

He readjusts himself, his head sliding between my legs, my

pussy hovering above his face. He grabs hold of my ass and pulls me down, his mouth open, sucking as much of my sensitive flesh between his lips as he can, his tongue lashing at my clit over and over.

I grind against his face, gripping the headboard, my hips working as I rub against his mouth and chin. The orgasm hovers, my entire body tightening, my belly tingling and when he hits a certain spot, I'm done for.

The orgasm slams into me, so strong I swear I almost black out. I'm shaking. Moaning. My pussy pulsates, my body quaking as the tremors race through me. He clamps his hands around me, holding me to his face as I come and come, until I finally roll over, worried I might've smothered him.

"Are you okay?" I'm on my side above him, resting on my arm, despite the fact that my limbs are weak and I'm afraid I might collapse at any moment.

He smiles at me, his entire face smelling like my pussy. "I think you're ready."

Within seconds, we're positioned once more with West above me, his cock probing at my entrance. I close my eyes and exhale deeply, trying to calm my racing heart.

"Relax," he murmurs, his lips brushing against my forehead. "You're so tense, Carolina."

I do my best to imagine my muscles slowly melting and it helps. He eases his way inside me, just the head slipping inside and I immediately tense up once more, my inner walls trying to strangle him, just like the first time.

"Fuck," he bites out, pressing his forehead to mine as he inhales sharply. "Spread your legs wider."

I do as he says and he works his way inside me. Deep. Deeper. Inch by inch filling me up until I'm wincing, a soft moan escaping me.

"Does it hurt?"

"Not really." It feels amazing.

He kisses me. A sweet, tongue-filled kiss that doesn't stop for what feels like forever. It has the right effect on me because the next thing I know, I've got my arms around his neck, my fingers in his hair, stroking him. He starts to move, pulling all the way out before he plunges back in, that delicious friction making me forget all of my worries when I moan.

"Better?" he asks.

"Don't stop," I encourage.

He starts to go faster, his hips working as he thrusts his cock inside of me again and again, filling me up. I glance down, trying to see it, and I catch a glimpse of his cock sliding out before it disappears inside of me yet again and my inner walls grip him tight.

"Fuck," he groans, pausing. Like he needs to before he loses control. "I'm gonna come."

"Go ahead," I encourage.

"Are you close?"

"I don't know. Not really." I was just enjoying the ride. I've already come twice tonight. I didn't expect for it to happen again.

"I want to make you come." He reaches between us, his fingers brushing against my clit and my pussy pulses around his cock, making him groan yet again. "You like that?"

"I like all of this," I say on a gasp, throwing my head back when he fucks me into the mattress.

His pace is fast, our sweaty skin slapping against each other, our moans mingling in the air. He grunts with every thrust, his fingers pinching my clit, setting me on fire, until I'm a gasping, shaking mess and he's shouting. I feel it then. That first burst of semen spurting into me, filling me, and he grunts yet again, one last final thrust before he goes completely still, hovering above me with his hands braced on the mattress on either side of my head.

"Fuck me," he mutters, his chest heaving, his breaths harsh. I watch him in complete and utter fascination, marveling that our bodies are still connected. That he's still inside me, a part of me.

I think he always will be. It doesn't matter what happens.

He's mine.

And I'm his.

I wake up in his arms a few hours later, the predawn light already starting to creep in through the cracks of the blinds on the windows. I lift my head to watch him sleep, mesmerized by how soft his face looks. How boyish.

He's still so young and he's dealt with so much responsibility. He could have anyone in the world. Be anywhere he wants, and here he lies with me.

With me.

I touch his cheek, his stubble prickling my palm. I give his face a gentle shake and his eyes flutter open, his mouth curling into a slow smile.

"What?"

An idea has come to me and I start to laugh.

"Carolina, what the fuck? You're freaking me out."

"I want you to do something," I say between laughs.

He frowns. "Okay."

"Draw on me." I scoot across the mattress, stretching across him so I can reach for the drawer on my nightstand. I pull it open and scramble around until I find what I'm looking for. "With this."

I hand him a pen.

"What do you want me to draw?"

"Whatever you want." I roll over so I'm lying on my stomach. "Maybe something on my back. My ribcage? Maybe right here." I point at my side, just below my ribs. "Something meaningful. Or cute."

"Why?" He sounds wary. And sleepy. The poor man.

"I want to get it tattooed on my skin. So I will never forget this night."

He smiles faintly, scrubbing at his chin. "I don't think I'll ever forget it. And I don't need a tattoo to remember it."

"I don't either." I roll my eyes, feeling playful. Carefree. Cared for. "But I want one. I'm jealous of yours."

He glances at the tiny drawing on the inside of his wrist before he meets my gaze. "I love mine."

"I want one to love too." I point at the pen in his fingers. "Start drawing."

"I can't draw."

I blow an exasperated breath. "Then write something sweet. Like, 'Carolina is the most beautiful woman in the world.'"

"You are. You don't need me to tell you that."

"I do," I whisper, like the insecure being that I am, and he leans in, delivering a sweet kiss.

"You're the most beautiful woman in the world."

"Thank you." I tap his chest with my finger, then shove him gently. "Now write something."

He thinks about it for a while, tapping the pen against his lips as he surveys my body. Looking for the perfect spot to write my future tattoo. Finally, he decides on the spot, right along the curve of my hip. He writes and writes, at least five words and I frown, trying to see what it is.

"Don't look," he warns, his voice fierce. "Wait until it's done."

"What if I hate it?" I'm teasing.

I won't hate it.

"You won't," he says confidently, and when he's finished, he leans back, admiring his work. "I like it."

"Can I look at it?"

"Absolutely not." He climbs out of bed. "Let's get dressed. And you better put some panties on."

We don't even bother taking a shower. I'm sure our skin smells of sweat and sex, but we don't care. I throw on a tank and a skirt, pull on a pair of full coverage panties at West's insistence while he slips on his suit pants and his shoes, walking out to his car with no shirt on like it's no big deal.

He looks delicious. Rumpled and sexy and exposed. I should probably drag him back into my bed and have my way with him but I also really want to get this tattoo.

"You can't go like that," I insist, and he pops open the trunk of his sleek Aston Martin, digging into a travel bag that's nestled inside, whipping out a black T-shirt, and yanking it on within seconds.

"Am I presentable now?"

His disappearing abs make me pout but then he's slapping my ass and encouraging me to get into the car, so I do.

We're at the twenty-four-hour tattoo shop minutes later after a harrowing journey on the mostly empty city streets, and I'm able to get right into the chair. West explains the tattoo he wants to the artist, a beautiful woman with long, jet black hair and very little clothing on, her skin covered in ink.

"Your tattoos are amazing," I tell her when she approaches me, fear making my heart beat faster.

"Thank you." She smiles gently. "He told me you don't like being touched by strangers."

I'm touched he would even mention it.

"Or anyone really," I amend. "Except for him."

"Will it bother you if I touch you?"

I shake my head. "I want this."

"Okay." She pats my arm, her gloved hand not bothering me in the least. "You're going to like this tattoo, I promise."

I lie on my side and let her work on me, the steady hum of the tattoo gun nearly lulling me to sleep. It hurts, but after a while, I completely zone out, almost enjoying the pain, and when she's finished, I'm almost disappointed.

"Want to see it?" she asks, sounding excited, and I nod my response.

She leads me over to the full-length mirror leaning against the wall, my dress covering it, the fabric brushing against the sensitive skin and making me hiss. West appears at my side, pulling the skirt up until the tattoo is exposed, my skin glowing red, the black ink traced over the words that he wrote. They're in French.

Je serais toujours avec toi.

I frown, concentrating on each word, translating them to English in my head.

I'll always be with you.

My gaze lifts to find West watching me, the worry on his face making my heart melt. "Do you like it?"

"I love it," I whisper, tears welling in my eyes. I blink hard, trying to make them stop but one slips down my cheek and he reaches around, wiping it away with his thumb.

"I love you," he whispers back, his hands settling on my shoulders and giving them a squeeze.

I lean my head to the right, resting my cheek against his fingers. I wish I could say the words in return, but I'm too overwhelmed.

Someday, I tell myself.

Someday.

CHAPTER FORTY-FIVE

WEST

We spend the next few days together as much as possible. When she's not at the studio or at the theatre, she's with me. And when she's not with me, I'm at my hotel suite, working. On the phone, texting, Zoom meetings, responding to emails.

The deal is almost done. We're going to announce in the next couple of weeks that the House of Fontaine is being sold and it'll merge with one of the biggest luxury brand conglomerates in the world. It's a large deal. We're going to make a lot of money. I won't have to worry about finances for the rest of my life, and my children and my children's children will probably be taken care of as well.

But is that all I want out of life? To live off of the billions I'll make from selling my father's legacy? What would I do?

I need to figure that out. I'm only twenty. I still have time.

All I know is I want Carolina with me. By my side always. She's the happiest I've ever seen her and I'm the happiest I've ever been. We were made for each other.

I've had to be careful with her after she got the tattoo, making sure I didn't touch her there. Seeing her tear up when she realized what I wrote damn near had me in tears, and I don't cry. Not really. I shed a few at my father's funeral but then I was right back to work. I didn't have the proper time to grieve, my mother said like a warning.

She's right. I still haven't had the time to grieve. For all I know, once everything settles down, I might fall completely apart.

We shall see.

By Saturday evening, I'm at Carolina's performance, sitting in the second row, enraptured as usual with her dancing. She glides across the stage effortlessly, her feet barely touching the ground and she leaps into the air, landing with a wobble.

And a wince.

I sit up straighter, watching her carefully, noting how she moves. Her expression is impassive, her eyes flashing with what I think is pain and the moment the performance is over and the curtain drops, I'm already out of my chair, muttering "excuse me" as I make my way past the irritated people in my row.

The curtain lifts, the performers in a line on the stage and Carolina is not with them.

My heart feels like it might burst from my chest.

I'm running down the aisle and toward the side of the stage, running up the short set of stairs that leads to the backstage. A tall, thin man acting as a bodyguard tries to stop me but I make eye contact with Carolina who's sitting in a chair, a man kneeling at her feet.

"Please let him in," she shouts and the bodyguard steps aside so I can go to her.

I'm kneeling beside her on the other side of the chair, my gaze fixed on her face as she watches the man touch her ankle. "What happened?"

"Oh my God, right there." She grimaces in pain, nearly jumping out of the chair when he touches her in a certain spot. "Do you think I broke it?"

My head pounds and I take her hand, interlacing our fingers. Her fearful gaze meets mine and I give her hand a squeeze, letting her know that I'm here for her.

I've got her.

"I don't think so," the man says. "But you should probably go get examined."

"I'll take you," I say without hesitation. "Are you ready?"

"But…" Her eyes meet mine once more, her chin trembling. "I probably just sprained it, right?"

"You need to double-check and make sure you know exactly what your injury is," the man recommends. "You don't want to take any chances."

The man gets up, leaving us alone as the rest of the cast rushes in off the stage. I glance down at Carolina's leg, noting the swelling of her ankle, and I know I can't just stand by and wait for her decision. "I'm taking you to the hospital."

"But…"

"No buts." I rise to my feet, bending down so I can scoop her into my arms. She makes a protesting noise at first but goes willingly, letting me walk her out of the theatre and straight to my car.

"You're really carrying me the whole way?"

"I'll carry you into the hospital too," I say firmly. "Don't argue with me, Carolina. You don't need to be on that ankle. What if you make it worse?"

She clamps her lips shut, remaining silent.

I drive at a decent speed so I don't scare her, barely able to contain my worry. Dance is everything to her. It's what helped her cope when shit got rough. It's her identity. What if her injury means she can no longer dance? What will she do then?

It didn't even happen to me and I can barely handle the thought. I need to make sure that she's going to be all right.

We end up in the emergency room at a hospital not too far from the theatre. The place is busy, but we only end up sitting in the waiting area for about an hour before they call her back into one of the private examination rooms. There we wait another hour until finally the doctor enters the room, his stride brisk and his expression serious.

"A dancer, hmm?" He's glancing over her file.

"Yes. I twisted my ankle while performing tonight."

"Who do you perform with?"

"The London Dance Company."

His expression turns less stern in an instant. "We were at your theatre last week. The performance was lovely."

"I'm glad you enjoyed it." She looks pleased, and I'm grateful that he praised her. Not enough people do that, and she deserves the accolades.

The doctor pushes and probes at her ankle, then asks for an X-ray to be done. The ankle is swollen and turning purple already, and she can barely put any pressure on it.

"Sprained," he announces after he checks the X-ray. "Severely. Looks like you'll be off your feet for at least a month."

"A month?" She sounds incredulous.

"Maybe longer." The doctor shrugs. "I'm recommending at least four weeks off. No dancing. No performing. After a couple of weeks and as long as the swelling's gone down, you can do some light exercises but nothing strenuous. You could make the injury worse if you push yourself."

Her shoulders fall, her defeat obvious. "All I've done my entire life is push myself."

"It stops today," the doctor says cryptically, his gaze sliding to mine. "Are you two together?"

I don't bother looking at her. Just nod my confirmation. "Yes."

"You need to watch over her."

"I will."

By the time we're leaving the hospital, it's late. Almost two in the morning and Carolina is tired. And grumpy. "I don't know what I'm going to do."

"You're going to rest."

"I can't rest. I don't know how." She bangs her head against the car seat, closing her eyes. The doctor bandaged her ankle up nicely, prescribed some pain meds that she's already insisted she won't take and even suggested she use crutches. "My understudy will have to replace me. There's so much I need to teach her."

"You're not teaching her shit." Her eyes flying open, she glares at me. "I mean it. You heard the doctor. Do you want to make your ankle worse?"

"I can't just sit around in my tiny little flat and wait for it to heal. I need to be at the studio."

"Why don't you return to New York with me," I suggest.

She goes quiet for so long, I finally glance over at her to make sure she hasn't passed out.

"Well?" I ask. Does she think my suggestion is ridiculous? Is she going to tell me no?

She better not tell me no. I'm bringing her with me whether she wants to go or not.

"My family. Well, my parents." Carolina is quiet for a moment, as if she needs the time to find the proper answer. "They like to play games against each other. It's a power struggle between them. My father, of course, is the most powerful one with the name, the money and the influence. My mother wanted that. She wanted to be on his same level, and she could never get there. It frustrated her. He frustrated her. He also ignored her and found other women to have affairs with. A lot of them. My mother needed someone to control, and who better than her children? Well, Whit wouldn't tolerate it, and I avoided her at all costs, so my sister is the one she controls."

I turn onto the apartment building's street, noting how she said that last sentence. "Does she still control your sister?"

"As much as she possibly can, yes, she does. Though I do believe Sylvie has learned how to get away from her. Somewhat. It takes drastic measures, like marrying a man who was old enough to be her father, but it worked. Funny, considering my mother was the one who arranged that marriage."

"This sounds a little…"

"Fucked up? Yes, those two words describe my family perfectly." She smiles, and despite the weariness and the pain and the disappointment etched on her face, she's still the most beautiful woman I've ever seen.

"Is she abusive?" I can only come to that conclusion because of everything I've heard. "Your mother."

"Not toward me." She turns those big eyes on me. "Toward my sister? I suspect so."

Anger fills me. "You need to stay away from that woman."

"That's why I'm here."

"But I want you to go with me to New York."

"I don't know..."

"You don't have to tell her you're there. It's none of her business where you are. Let her think you're still here."

"She'll figure it out. She'll hear from a friend and the next thing you know, she'll be calling me. Texting me. Complaining about how much I hurt her and asking why I don't ever want to see her anymore. She said all of that to me at the wedding."

"I fuckin' hate this." I punch the steering wheel, annoyed. "You're coming with me to New York and there's no way I'll let her see you, I swear."

"Do I have a choice in the matter?"

I glance over at her, exhaling loudly. "I sound like an asshole."

"No, you sound worried about me."

"I am." I stare straight ahead, parking the car directly in front of Carolina's building. "I have to go to New York. I can't put them off any longer. They need me there to sign paperwork and go over a few things before the announcement is made. And while I hate that you're hurt, you have to agree that the timing is good. You can come with me and we can spend some time in the city together."

"Are you telling me I have to go or are you asking?"

Reaching out, I settle my hand on her thigh, giving it a squeeze. "Asking. With a hint of telling."

I look at her, our gazes locking, and I try and convey to her through my eyes that I care about her. That I'm watching out for her. That I love her and want to protect her and no one—I mean no one—is going to touch a hair on this woman's head. Not even her mother.

Does she understand that? Does she see?

"Okay," she finally whispers. "I'll go to New York with you. But I don't know how much time I'll be able to spend in the city. My ankle is killing me and I have to stay off of it, remember?"

The pointed look she gives sends her message to me loud and clear.

"I won't make you tour around the city." Leaning in, I press my mouth to hers. "I just want you with me always."

"And I want to be with you always." She cups the side of my face. "But I can fight my own demons, West. I don't need you to be my savior."

"Even if I want to be?"

"Even then."

CHAPTER FORTY-SIX

CAROLINA

New York City in the summertime is hot and boring. No one is around during the weekends because they all get the hell out of this place, going to the Hamptons to escape the oppressive heat. The city is dirty and gritty, and the hot air makes everyone so grumpy.

This is why I remain holed up in the penthouse apartment West leased for us. It's on the Upper West Side, in a beautifully quiet neighborhood full of elegant brownstones filled with equally elegant families. We're not too far from Central Park and the New York City Ballet is nearby as well. I haven't had a chance to go and watch a performance yet.

I'm not in the mood to make myself sad.

The ankle is getting better, though it's still not perfect. Most of the swelling has gone down and I can put light pressure on my foot. West hovers like a nagging mother every time I'm on my feet, watching my every move like a hawk, and it's annoying yet somehow also sweet, because it shows that he cares.

At least someone does.

I have lunch with my father and he asks endless questions about West while I give him only minimal answers. He doesn't need to know about my relationship, and I know that drives him out of his mind because I'm leaving him in the dark and he hates that. He wants to know everything.

Let him wonder. He doesn't need to know every single detail.

I see my sister often. She's back together with her first love, Spencer. They seem really happy together and she looks good. The best I've ever seen her. She's pushed our mother out of her life almost completely and I think that helps. Doesn't hurt that Spencer is so attentive, wanting to make sure she's safe. He's so in love with her and I can't help but think of my relationship with West.

I don't tell my sister much about us either. I spend time with Whit and Summer, and I don't even bring up his name. It's not that I'm trying to hide him or keep him a secret from everyone, I just don't want to have to explain to them what's going on. Especially when I don't even know what's really going on.

I'm in the dark, just like everyone else.

We've already been here for two weeks and West spends most of his days away at the New York offices of Fontaine, or at the lawyer's office. Going over the paperwork, making sure everything is in order for the transition. This deal is so huge, he knows that people are watching. Every single moving part has to fall into place perfectly or it could be a potential disaster.

Today he's been at his attorney's office all afternoon, while I've been stuck in this apartment bored out of my mind. When he finally texts me that he's almost finished, I send him a text in return, demanding he take me out to dinner.

West: *Be ready in thirty minutes. Meet me downstairs. I'll let you know when I'm there.*

Within thirty minutes, I'm out on the street after carefully making my way down the steps, clad in a cream-colored sundress with tiny pale pink flowers scattered all over the fabric and a flat, brown leather sandal on one foot, a walking boot on the other. It's awkward and it makes getting around difficult most of the time, but it definitely helps.

My hair is scraped up into a tight bun on top of my head and I have no makeup on, deciding to go natural. I might not look my best, but I feel good. Better than I have in weeks and I practically skip toward his car—a boring old BMW, I miss the Aston Martin—when he finally pulls up to the curb.

The window slides down, revealing West sitting in the driver's seat wearing a crisp white shirt with black trousers. No tie of course. It's too hot for one and he's got his shirt unbuttoned halfway down his torso like he's some sort of sex-crazed dancer in a 1970's disco. All that he's missing is a gold chain.

"What is up with the shirt?" I hobble over to the car so I can lean in through the passenger side window.

He grins, not even offended. "You don't like it?"

"The longer I get to know you, the more buttons you leave undone on your shirts. I don't think I like it."

West jumps out of the car and rounds the front, opening the door for me like a gentleman. "Get in," he instructs with a wave of his hand.

I settle into the seat, amused at him slamming the door and jogging around the car before he slips back into the driver's seat. "Are you telling me you don't want me wearing my shirts like this?"

"I don't want women seeing what I've already got."

"You trying to keep me under wraps?" Oh, he appears even more pleased with himself. I should not indulge this man's ego.

But it's like I can't help myself.

"Maybe," I tease.

He touches my leg, his fingers curving around toward the inside of my thigh. "I like the dress."

"Thank you."

"You look pretty." He removes his hand, and I miss it.

"Even with the boot?" I point toward the unwieldly contraption on my foot.

"Especially with the boot." He frowns. "Is your ankle

bothering you? Should we do this another time?"

"Oh my God, no. I need to get out. Please. I really haven't gone anywhere since we got here." Oh, I did go to my sister's "tea party," which turned into an epic disaster. We were having so much fun hanging out with family and friends. Even my father was enjoyable, regaling us with stories of his youth.

Then our mother showed up to cause a scene and ruined everything.

Typical.

"I have a suggestion for dinner." West pulls out onto the street, merging seamlessly with the heavy traffic.

"Where do you want to go?"

"There's a French restaurant that opened up not even a year ago in Soho and everyone raves about it." He glances over at me quickly before returning his attention to the road. "I want to take you there. In honor of where we first met."

"You mean Paris?"

He grins, his gaze sliding to mine. Oh, he looks handsome. I really don't mind the open shirt front. It's quite sexy. "I mean Paris."

"Where you met the stupid girl who pretended to be French and you forgot to mention that you're fluent?"

"Ha, yeah." He settles his hand on my leg once more, his touch possessive. "And the woman wasn't stupid. She was just—young. And beautiful. I was completely gone for her."

I smile, ducking my head. I love it when he says things like that. "You were so cocky."

"Was I?"

"Definitely."

"I thought I was more...persistent than arrogant."

"You were that too." I shake my head, remembering the night vividly. "I was a terror."

"A sexy terror."

"Rude and abrasive. I said the worst things."

"I loved every moment of that night." His fingers slide up, terribly close to my panties. "I wouldn't change a single thing."

"You still would've got the tattoo?"

"I definitely would've got the tattoo. I don't regret that decision at all."

"I don't regret mine either." It means so much, his words on my skin. I stare at it sometimes in the mirror, after I've gotten out of the shower. When he wrote the words and how it tickled. The meaning behind the words, and how much he matters to me.

He's the most thoughtful man. I'm so lucky he's mine.

"Is this place good?" I ask, changing the subject. "The restaurant we're going to?"

"That's what I keep hearing. Plus, it looks fun."

"Fun?"

"The food is good. The drinks, excellent, and the atmosphere is...sexy." He smirks.

"Sexy?" I keep saying everything like it's a question. How annoying.

Yet West doesn't seem bothered at all.

"There's an evening burlesque show. Red lights. Bottle service. It's like a big party every single night."

"How sexy will I feel with this stupid boot on my foot?" I glare at it, suddenly hating that I still have to wear it.

"You're sexy no matter what."

"And I'm not twenty-one yet."

"No one will care." His hand slides up, the side of it brushing the front of my panties. "They'll let me in. It won't matter."

"Oh, and I can't get in on my name?" I arch a brow, feeling challenged.

He laughs. "Fontaine is currently in everyone's mouths."

"Better not be." He sends me a questioning look. "I'm the only one who should have a Fontaine in my mouth."

More laughter, and it sounds so good. "Trust me, baby. You are."

· · ·

The restaurant is just as West described. Moody elegance with an impressive bar that nearly takes up an entire wall. We walk into a crowded lobby, my gaze scanning the room, noting that every table appears occupied.

No need to worry, though. West drops his last name to the host and without hesitation the man leads us to a quiet table with deep blue velvet booth seats. I scoot in somewhat awkwardly thanks to the boot, West directly behind me, settling in so close I worry how we'll eat without elbowing each other in the face.

"What do you think?" he asks once the host leaves us alone. He glances around the room as he slides his arm along the back of the booth, his fingers dangling close to my bare shoulder.

"It's beautiful." I check the drink menu, concentrating on the many choices listed. Our server appears, asking if we'd like any drinks to start and West lets him know what we want without hesitation, ordering the cocktail that sounds closest to an espresso martini on the menu.

"How did you know that's what I wanted?" I ask him once the server leaves.

"I know what you like." West smiles at me, his fingers tickling my bare shoulder. "What do you want to eat?"

"I need to look at the menu first." I scan my options, deciding on the fish while West declares he's going to order the filet mignon. He gives me an update on what's going on with the House of Fontaine and I let my gaze wander around the room, noting how happy everyone looks here. People are smiling and laughing. Conversations are loud and every server rushes around the place with big grins on their faces.

"Why are you smiling?" West's arm drops to my shoulders, pulling me in close, and I lean my head against his side, sighing when he kisses my forehead.

"*Everyone* in this restaurant is smiling. It's so…refreshing."

"You haven't been happy?" The concern in his voice is obvious.

I pull away slightly so I can look into his eyes, noting the faint worry there. "My entire life, I don't think I've been happy. Not really. Until…"

"Until what?" he asks quietly.

All the noise surrounding us blurs and all I can concentrate on is West. His handsome face and beautiful eyes. The way he's watching me, his arm a solid weight on my shoulders, his fingers drifting over my skin. It's as if he can't stop touching me, and I rest my hand on his thigh, needing the contact.

"Until I met you," I admit.

He yanks me in for a crushing hug, and I'm thankful for the booth seating and how it allows us to touch each other easily. "I almost fucked everything up."

"What do you mean?"

He lets go of me, though he remains close, his arm still slung around my shoulders. "I was an idiot for not contacting you sooner. For letting you go for two years. I could've lost you. I *did* lose you."

My heart pangs. "You earned your way back in."

"And I was in pure panic mode the entire time," he admits.

"You were?" I'm surprised.

He nods, his gaze never straying from mine. It's like he can't stop looking at me. "I thought for sure you'd reject me. I deserved to be rejected. What I did…I hurt you, Carolina. So fucking bad. I feel terrible for how I treated you. It wasn't fair, how I left and never contacted you for two entire years. Like…what the hell was wrong with me?"

West sounds tormented. He looks even worse. His eyes are glassy and his cheeks are ruddy. He's so upset at the thought of what he did to me, and that makes my heart swell with emotion.

"It's okay." I touch his cheek, cupping the side of his face and he leans into my palm, his eyes falling closed for the briefest moment. "Don't let it bother you. Not anymore. We're together now. You were young and you were overwhelmed. Grieving."

"I was drowning," he adds, turning his face so he can kiss my palm, his warm lips sending a shiver up my arm. "And then I realized one day I had to work my hardest to get you back into my life."

"When you saw me at Whit's wedding?"

"Before that."

My mouth drops open. "Before that? What, when you were dating Madison and realized she looks like me?"

He starts to laugh, my hand falling away from his face, and I try to be mad, but it's no use.

I can't be mad at him. Not anymore.

"No, before Madison. When I came back to New York with my mother. I knew you were in London. The invitation to your brother's wedding sort of fell into my lap and I felt like it was fate."

Fate with a lot of help from my scheming mother, but I don't mention that.

"I knew I would always be with you," he continues, his gaze glowing as he takes me in. "And now here we are."

My smile is small, pleasure suffusing my body at the idea that we were always meant to be. "Here we are."

The server appears with our drinks and takes our dinner order, rushing away the minute West finishes speaking. I lift my glass in a toast and West does the same, waiting for me.

"To us," I murmur.

He clinks his glass with mine. "To us."

We drink, never taking our eyes off of each other, and the alcohol slips through my veins, warming my skin. My belly. I keep sipping, eventually finishing the entire glass in a short amount of time. I can't help but laugh when a bunch of servers come out of the back dressed in costume, looking like they're about to fight in a revolution, wearing white wigs and carrying fake guns that shoot out glittery confetti. The lights dim and music starts to play. People start dancing, taking their white cloth napkins and twirling them above their heads. Some of them are even dancing on the bar top. Bottle sparklers shine in the darkness and all I can do is stare.

It's not even nine o'clock and we're in full party mode.

"Fun, right?" West murmurs close to my ear.

Nodding, I turn to him, letting him kiss me. No one is paying attention to us, and even if they were, I have enough alcohol coursing through my veins already that it doesn't really matter.

I'm enjoying myself too much to care.

CHAPTER FORTY-SEVEN

WEST

I can't stop staring at Carolina.

When I suggested going to this restaurant, I didn't realize just how much she would enjoy herself. She's approximately two and a half drinks in, swaying to the music, laughing when one of the servers appears in front of our table and fills a shot glass for her while holding it in his mouth. I give the guy a dirty look because even I can see he's attractive and making eyes at the woman I love, and unfortunately, she notices.

"Don't be jealous," she chastises once the guy leaves. "I'm with you tonight, hmm?"

She rests her hand on my thigh yet again. She keeps doing that, and I'm now sitting in the middle of a very crowded restaurant, trying to finish my filet mignon while sporting an erection.

The things I do for this woman.

No complaining though. Not when I see the joy on her face and the way her gaze dances when it meets mine. When she lifts her glass and shouts along with the other diners in the restaurant the moment someone jumps up on the bar and starts playing a trumpet. It's loud and obnoxious and completely over the top, and I love that Carolina is totally into it.

This is a version of my girl that I've never seen before, and I'm so grateful I'm witnessing this moment. I want to see more of *this* woman. Full of joy and laughter and finding constant delight in everything that surrounds her. She hums with satisfaction every time she sips from her drink. Groans in delicious agony each time she takes a bite. She is enjoying herself so thoroughly, when normally this sort of atmosphere would send her into complete stimulation overload.

"I'm stuffed," she says with a little moan as she leans back against the soft blue velvet booth that we're sitting in. It's intimate and cozy and I love how her thigh constantly presses against mine. "I don't think I can eat another bite."

"But I wanted to get dessert."

"You can eat it. I'll just watch."

"Oh, you'll join me eating our dessert." I lean in and drop a kiss to her perfect lips, and she smiles, her face tilted up toward mine, her gaze thoughtful.

"Really? You think you can convince me?" She's challenging me, a teasing lilt to her voice and I press my forehead to hers, dropping my hand to the outside of her thigh, gathering up some of her skirt with my fingers.

"I can persuade you to do just about anything," I murmur.

She actually squeals with laughter, pulling away from me and reaching for her drink, which she drains in one long swallow. I stare at the elegant column of her throat, the way it gently moves when she drinks, and I'm filled with the sudden need to touch her.

Inappropriately. While in public.

"You want another one?" I ask.

"I shouldn't," she murmurs, staring at the empty glass with longing.

Our server magically appears, as if summoned by Carolina's wishes, and asks if we want another one.

"Please," I say for her. "For the both of us."

"Will do." The man nods and heads for the bar.

I lean back in the seat, my gaze never straying from Carolina.

She shifts and sways in the booth, a constant smile on her face and she glances over at me to catch me staring. "What are you looking at?"

"You. You're enjoying yourself."

"I am." She claps her hands and that's when I realize she might be a little drunk. "Such a wonderful night."

"Want to enjoy yourself more?" I arch a brow.

"What more could happen to make this night better?"

I lean in close to her, my mouth right at her ear, lips brushing the sensitive skin when I whisper, "I want to make you come."

She goes completely still, as if she needs to absorb what I said, before slowly, she angles her head toward mine. "What exactly are you plotting, hmm?"

"Wait and see." I lean back against the booth, spreading both of my arms out along the top of it.

She contemplates me, curiosity in her bright blue gaze. "Are you meaning here?"

I nod.

"Right here?" Another nod. "In public?"

"No one will notice."

"I couldn't." She shakes her head, but I see the excitement in her eyes. She's thinking about it. "Someone would notice."

"I don't know."

The lights dim as if on cue, going completely dark for the briefest second before red lights come on, a single red beam shining on the short runway in the center of the restaurant, a scantily clad woman standing there.

Music starts, slow and sensual and the woman swings her hips, turning her back to us, her entire ass on display. I reach out and tug on a strand of Carolina's hair, sending her a knowing look when she glances over at me, and she turns away quickly, giggling.

The server stops by our table with new drinks and Carolina accepts her eagerly, taking a sip. I sip from mine as well, tugging her toward me when she sets her glass on the table, nuzzling the side of her face.

"Let me under your skirt," I whisper.

She shakes her head. "You're naughty."

"You like it." I pause, my voice firm when I tell her, "Lift your skirt, Carolina."

Her gaze meets mine, her face painted in red light, achingly gorgeous. "I don't have any panties on."

I smile. "You came prepared."

"You are so bad." She's shaking her head once more as she reaches beneath the table, her hands busy gathering her skirt and lifting it upward. "What if someone catches us?"

"No one will notice." It's so dark in here, and the music is loud. The booth is high all around us, cutting off anyone's view. They'd have to know what they were looking for to find her on display.

Glancing down, I see that her skirt is bundled up to her waist, her lower half completely bare. My cock surges in my pants and I silently curse my choices right now. This is going to be torture. "Show me what you've got, baby. Spread your legs."

"Weston." She reaches for a drink and takes a big sip before setting it back down and slowly but surely, spreading her legs.

I dip my head, studying her. Pink and glistening wet. All for me. "Touch yourself."

Her gaze holding mine, she reaches down and strokes her pussy with her index finger, holding it out toward me. It's wet, coated with her and I grab hold of her wrist, licking at her fingertip with my tongue.

"Delicious," I croon, noting her dilated pupils. "My turn."

Scooting closer, I rest my hand on her bare thigh, skimming my fingers across her smooth skin, drawing closer and closer to her cunt. I can smell her. Musky sweet and so aroused, I wouldn't doubt she'll leave a wet stain on the velvet when I'm done with her.

Oh well.

My hand hovers just above her like a ghost and she whimpers, her hips lifting, causing my fingers to brush against her pussy. She hisses out a breath and I rest my hand directly over that needy spot between her legs, holding it there.

She's breathing hard, her chest rising and falling rapidly, her skin flushed. I can tell, even in the red light. She's aroused. Dying for it.

Dying for me.

"Think anyone knows what we're doing?" I ask casually as I begin to stroke her, my fingers sliding through her folds.

Carolina frantically shakes her head, her breaths turning into little pants. "N-no."

"You get off on doing something like this in public?" I strum her clit, rubbing it in those tight little circles she enjoys so much.

"Yes."

I smile, pleased with her honesty. Leaning in, I kiss her, my tongue thrusting against hers, just as I slide a finger into her tight pussy. She rises up, accommodating my hand, and I add another one to the first, filling her.

Fucking her with my fingers.

The music continues, the burlesque dancer moving provocatively about the stage. The room is quiet save for the loud music, everyone seemingly entranced by the woman performing with the exception of me.

I'm too caught up in the sounds Carolina makes. The way she feels. Her scent, her eyes, her lips. She tastes amazing, she feels even better and when she clamps her thighs tight around my hand and wrist, I break the kiss, frowning.

"I'm close," she whispers, sounding frantic. Breathless.

"Tell me what you need." I remove my hand from her completely like a sadistic bastard, despite the hold her strong thighs had on me, and I sink my fingers into her mouth, heat coursing through my blood when she sucks and licks them almost desperately.

"I need your fingers," she whispers when I pull them from her mouth. "And I need you to keep kissing me."

I give her what she wants, kissing her slowly, my tongue doing a thorough search of her mouth. My fingers slip in between her thighs once more, teasing her clit. Teasing every part of her I can reach. Cracking my eyes open, I glance around, making sure that no one is paying any attention to us. Closing them once more when I'm reassured that they're not.

Increasing my speed, I thrust my fingers inside of her, my thumb toying with her clit. She gasps against my lips, her hips straining and I can tell when the orgasm hits her. Her body stills and I swallow her moans, kissing her deeply, keeping my fingers buried inside of her, my thumb on her clit as she rides out her orgasm on my hand.

The moment she's done the song ends and there's a round of applause. I slowly pull my hand from her body, bringing her fingers to my mouth. The scent of her hits me and I lick my fingers, making her laugh.

"Your timing is impeccable," she compliments me.

"No, baby, that was all you."

Her expression turns serious and she leans in, kissing me softly. "I never want this night to end."

"Don't worry." I cup the back of her head, keeping her close. "We have the rest of our lives together. I promise."

CHAPTER FORTY-EIGHT

CAROLINA

I'm a nervous wreck all morning in anticipation of calling my mother, which is dumb. I should just do it and get it over with.

But I need to work up to this moment, this...conversation. She's not an easy woman to talk to, especially when what I have to say to her will make her upset. Plus, she sleeps in every morning. Now that she has no children to take care of—or terrorize—she stays up till all hours of the night and sleeps in until ten, almost every morning, according to Sylvie. She is not a lady who does brunch. She is all about the lunch.

Maybe that's what I should do. Meet her for lunch somewhere in public and extremely busy, and tell her to butt out of my life. Telling her via phone or text won't have the same effect. Saying it to her face in a restaurant, where she can't cause a scene, is the right move.

The smart move.

When I discovered that Mother was talking about me with West's mom—she's always dropping little tidbits to him about me and she basically said exactly that when all three of us met for dinner last week. Laura Fontaine is a lovely woman. I like her.

What I don't like is my mother feeding her information about me that I should tell her myself. Mother is stepping over as per usual and I'm tired of it.

Tired of her.

Instead of running away from my problems, for once I'm confronting them head-on.

So, I send her a text asking her to meet me for lunch at a restaurant not too far from where she lives and she readily agrees, most likely thrilled that I would do such a thing. None of us actually seek her out so this must feel important to her.

I'm only going to crush her with my requests, but I don't care. She's toxic. We all know it. Pretty sure she knows it too. I can't have that in my life. I've avoided her for so long. All these years in London, dancing, dancing. Always dancing so I wouldn't think about anything else. Trying to push her out of my thoughts, my life.

I wear a thin black dress with a very expensive black bra and panty set I picked up recently while I was out shopping—something I'm not always a fan of but have been doing more because I'm bored without dance and West is so busy during the day. Black flat sandals on my feet—the boot is finally gone, thank goodness—my hair scraped back into a tight bun. Very light makeup on my face and the giant Lancaster diamond studs in my ears, a gift from my father when I turned eighteen.

The entire outfit is armor against my mother and I stride into that restaurant with as much confidence as I can muster, keeping the sunglasses firmly on my face, so she can't see the fear flashing in my eyes.

She sees even a glimmer of terror and she'll grasp on to that visible emotion, feeding on it until she has you wanting to run screaming from the room.

"Carolina, my goodness you look so chic." This is how my mother greets me when she sweeps into the restaurant minutes later. I'm already seated at our table, which is situated close to the front, where almost everyone can see us. "Sorry I'm late."

Another tactic she uses to keep people on edge, making them wait for her. "It's fine. I was late as well."

I rise to my feet and let her hug me, remaining stiff in her embrace, only patting her back for a brief moment before I take a step back. Her arms fall away from me, the disappointment clear on her face, and I think, point to me.

This is terrible, but our relationship has always worked this way. As sick and twisted as it is, I don't know anything else.

"Taking after your mother after all, aren't you." She sits down across from me, a pleased smile on her face.

I stare at her, my gaze assessing her carefully. She's been refreshed, meaning she's had some work done, and she looks abnormally young. Startlingly reminding me of Sylvie.

It's eerie.

Mother catches me studying her and leans over the table as if she's going to share a big secret with me. "I've had a little touch-up done recently. It looks fabulous, doesn't it?"

A *little* touch-up? More like a lot.

"You look very…young." She looks like so many of the other women in this city who are desperate not to lose their youthful appearance. I'm not against plastic surgery, but there is something about a woman in her late fifties who is trying to appear like she's in her twenties. It doesn't look natural.

"Isn't it great?" She sighs happily, flashing her smile at the server, who's young and handsome and overly solicitous as he lists the drink specials. I ask for water. Mother orders a skinny spicy margarita on the rocks without a salted rim. The moment he's gone, I send her a look.

"A margarita?"

"I need something to spice up my day." She shrugs, not looking bothered by my question. "Get to my age, darling, and then you can judge me."

This is going to be a long lunch.

We order our food and I listen to Mother complain about

everything. Whit and Summer and how she can't see her own grandson.

"They barely let me visit and heaven forbid they drop the darling boy off at my place so I can spend a few hours with him. I would assume they'd love a break here and here. Raising a toddler isn't easy and she's about to have another one." Mother shakes her head, sipping from her margarita. "I don't understand it."

I do. I wouldn't leave my child alone with my mother either.

"And then there's your sister." She brings up Sylvie after our meals are brought to us, and that must be some sort of record. "I still cannot believe she had that party and invited every single one of you but me."

"Mother." I rest my fork on the edge of the large bowl of salad I ordered. "You know she doesn't want anything to do with you."

She visibly flinches. "I don't deserve this kind of treatment from my daughter."

"She is literally terrified of you. That's why she doesn't want you around her."

"What in the world did I do to make her react that way?" Mother actually rests her hand against her chest, aghast at the possibilities.

I'm not about to go into a list of all the reasons why Sylvie doesn't want anything to do with her, but I take this moment as my segue into why I asked her to lunch in the first place.

"Actually, I wanted to talk to you about something."

Her face is an innocent mask. "What is it?"

"Laura Fontaine."

"Oh Laura. A lovely woman. A little…rustic for my taste sometimes, but I blame that on her wandering through the Napa Valley vineyards for so long." Mother laughs.

"You talk about me to her," I say. "A lot."

"Of course, I do. You're dating her son. We could end up being relatives." Her smile is serene, her gaze dancing with unknown thoughts. Emotions. Whatever.

Sometimes I'd like to know what makes my mother do the things she does, and other times, I am too scared to think about it.

"I don't want you doing that. In fact, I don't think you should spend as much time with Laura as you do."

The smile is gone, just like that. "You cannot tell me what to do."

"I'm asking you politely." My appetite disappears at the way Mother's face transforms. It goes from friendly and light to dark and foreboding in the blink of an eye. "You don't need to talk about me with Laura."

"She asks questions."

"Let her ask West or even me. We just had dinner together."

"I know." Mother's smile is triumphant. "She told me. Said that you're a lovely girl and that we're very much alike."

My finger curls around my fork and I have the sudden image of me lunging for her. Stabbing her in her ugly black heart with it. I shake it away, disturbed. "I don't like this."

"There's nothing you can do to change it. We're friends. I'm not going to stop talking to her. How do you want me to do that? 'Oh sorry, Carolina asked me to keep away from you.' How will that look, darling? Laura will be scandalized. She'll think less of you and you need that woman on your side. She has so much influence over West."

I stare at her, hating how logical her explanation is. "I want you to stay out of my personal business."

Her eyes flash, her expression turning fierce. "I know how you are, and I'm sure this is making your little controlling heart nearly collapse with palpitations, but you don't control this situation, Carolina. Laura Fontaine is my friend and there's nothing you can do to change that. And you can't expect me to not talk about you. I'm your mother. You're involved with her son. We're going to talk about our children."

I'm so angry I can barely see straight. Whit never lets her get the better of him. Sylvie either agrees with whatever she says or runs away. I usually just stayed out of the way, but every time I talk to her lately, I find myself unable to convince her of anything. Most of the time, I'm actually agreeing with her.

It's frustrating. Infuriating.

"I hear you're going back to London in a couple of weeks?" She smoothly changes the subject and I automatically answer, grateful to talk about something else.

"Yes. I need to be there to start practicing for the next production."

"I think it's a mistake." She takes a sip of her drink.

"Me going back to London?"

She nods. "Leaving West behind? Have you discussed this with him?"

No. Not at all. We don't talk about the future beyond the House of Fontaine merging with the luxury conglomerate, which is happening soon. It's too scary to think about anything after that happens, let alone say out loud.

"Sort of," I hedge.

Her disapproval is obvious. "Carolina. Really?"

"What do you expect me to do? Stay here forever, marry the man and have his babies?" I make it sound like torture when I secretly adore the idea.

Which means maybe I care about him—dare I say love him— more than I thought.

"Absolutely," she says without hesitation. "If you were smart, that's what you would be doing. Darling, Weston Fontaine is an absolute catch. And once the sale of the House of Fontaine is announced, the man will have women swarming him. He's young, he's attractive and he will be filthy rich. The sole heir to all of that champagne money."

"It was never about the money with West," I protest, and she laughs.

"It must be so nice to be you. Perfectly insulated in your rich little world. Never having to worry about a thing. You have more money than anyone you know. Even West Fontaine." Her smile turns shrewd. "Merging those fortunes together is a smart move, darling. And he knows you won't be using him for his money. He'll never be able to trust another woman after you. He'll always wonder if they're with him because of his name, or his bank account."

I can't stand the thought of West with another woman after me. Not after everything we've shared. He's had my drawing tattooed on his skin since he was seventeen. I have his words tattooed on me. That means something.

"I don't want to push." This is about as real as I will ever get with her, I realize. Because there is one thing my mother understands. How to lure a man in.

She also knows how to push one away, though I'm sure she'd never admit it.

"I'm sure he's smitten with you. If you behave like you usually do, I'm sure he's completely gone over you." She drains the last of her margarita, then lifts her glass into the air. The waiter notices, of course, and acknowledges he'll bring her a fresh one with a quick nod of his head.

Unreal.

"What are you talking about?"

"Your utter indifference about everything, darling. The more you act like you don't care, the more they want to be with you, so they can make you care." Her smile is knowing. "I'm sure he's madly in love with you by now."

I say nothing, thinking of that night after the tattoo, when he told me he loved me. He's never said it again. I'm sure he thinks I'll freak out if he utters those three words, and back when he first told me, he would've been right.

But now, I'm tempted to hear him say those words again. I'm even tempted to try and say them on my own. I don't know if I'll be able to get past the lump in my throat that will undoubtedly form, or the anxiety that will have its evil clutches wrapped around my heart, but I want to try.

I want to tell him how I feel.

I arrive home from my too long lunch with my mother to find West already there, pacing around the living room, pausing in front of the floor-to-ceiling windows, staring out at the cityscape with his phone pressed to his ear. He's not doing a lot of talking, only interjecting here and there, and I wonder who's on the other end.

He's in shorts and a T-shirt—a look I don't see him wear much at all, and I let my gaze drift over the length of him, lingering on his broad shoulders. The curve of his ass beneath those shorts. His long legs covered in hair. Not too much though. It's just enough. Perfect even.

West glances over his shoulder and catches me staring, his lips curving into the faintest frown, a question in those beautiful brown eyes. I smile at him, clutching on to the positive feelings my mother stirred inside me. The ones that remind me I have a good man by my side, who's only going to grow into a better man. He's smart and caring and attentive to my every need. He's more than proven he cares about me.

I'd be a fool to let him go. To leave him behind so I can dance.

It's still important to me. Ballet. Performing. But it can't be everything. I'm good enough to dance for a smaller company, but I will never be a part of the most renowned dance troupes in the world, and…

I'm at peace with that.

Everything is going to be okay.

"All right," he says into the phone. "That all sounds perfect. I'll talk to you later." He ends the call, turning to face me, that question still glowing in his eyes. "I take it your lunch with your mother went well."

I texted him to let him know what I was doing and where I was going. Just in case. That's how paranoid the woman makes me feel.

"It was good." That's all I offer, all I'm willing to say, and I think he can tell.

"I'm glad. I don't want you two hating each other. Family is important. My mother is all I have." His smile is slow. "Well, and then there's you."

"Do you consider me a part of your family?"

His expression becomes serious—enough to make my heart catch and my breath stall. "You're in my heart. On my skin. Forever, Carolina."

"West." My throat aches with the words I want to say and I close my eyes for a moment, taking a deep breath before I say, "I'm not going back to London."

He blinks in confusion. "Why not?"

"I don't want to dance anymore. I mean, I don't want to stop dancing, but I don't feel the need to perform anymore."

"What do you want to do?"

"I want to stay here." I swallow hard. "With you."

CHAPTER FORTY-NINE

WEST

Did Carolina say what I think she just said?

"You won't return to London then?"

She slowly shakes her head, her lips parting at the last second. "Wait. I'll need to go back and get all of my stuff. Move out of my flat. But no, I'm done with the London Dance Company."

"Are you sure?" I'm surprised. Dance was—is—her life. It's all she's ever talked about. All she's ever wanted to do. She's made it the entire focus of her life and now she's willing to just… quit? "Why?"

"I don't need it anymore." She shrugs.

"And why is that?"

"Because I have you." She takes a step forward. Then another one. Slowly approaching me. "I've been running away from my life since I was a child. Trying to get away from everything that made me, me. I wasn't proud of being a Lancaster. I didn't like my family and I didn't like myself. So I became someone else."

"Carolina," I start, cutting her off. "Much of who you are is because of dance. You aren't just your family. You became your own self too."

"I know." She takes another step closer. I can smell her. That same ocean scent, the one I can't figure out where it comes from.

A mix of her body wash and lotion? Her shampoo? Or is it just her? "And for once in my life, I like myself. I'm comfortable with who I am. That's all because of you."

She comes another step closer and reaches out, resting her hands on my chest, her fingers curling slightly in the soft cotton of my T-shirt. "Why would I leave that? This? You?"

"You want to stay here with me." It's a statement, not a question.

"Yes." She nods, her eyes gleaming.

I snag her waist and yank her to me, holding her close, the relief flooding me making me weak. Only this woman could do that to me. I've been strong for everyone and everything else for so damn long. "Thank God. I was going to demand you stay, even if I had to wait until you started making plans and buying plane tickets or what the fuck ever. Or I would've just followed you back to London and stayed with you until you were ready to come back to the States with me."

"You would've done that for me?" She sounds surprised.

Nodding, I reach out to brush a stray strand of her hair away from her face. "My little dancer. I would follow you to the ends of the earth to keep you in my life."

She presses her lips together for the briefest moment, as if she needs to contain all of her emotions to keep them from spilling out. "I love you."

Finally. I've been waiting. Not wanting to push. After she got my words inked on her skin, I had to tell her how I felt. Too overwhelmed with the moment, unable to hold back. Her eyes had flickered then, and I knew, deep down, she felt the same way, it's just hard for her to say it.

To finally hear her make that declaration feels pretty fucking amazing.

Cupping the side of her face, I stare into her eyes, noting how clear and shiny they are. "I love you too."

"I didn't disintegrate and turn to dust." Her smile is tremulous.

"I don't know why it's so scary to say those words. To feel that emotion for someone else."

"Love is powerful. That's why it's so damn scary." I brush my thumb across her lips, my skin tightening when they part and cling. "My feelings for you drive just about every fucking thing I do right now."

"I don't believe you."

"It's true." I start to chuckle because I can't help it. Everything is coming together perfectly after two long, hard years, and I'm ready to fucking celebrate. "The deal is done. They're announcing it tomorrow."

"Oh." Her smile is beautiful. Full of so much joy that I crush her to me once more. "Oh, West. I'm so happy for you. I know you've been stressed."

"Not anymore. Everything is finished. We were putting the final touches on the press release that's going out tomorrow when you came home." I like the sound of those two words.

Came home.

This woman is my home. There is nowhere else I would rather be than with her.

"We should celebrate," she says as she pulls away slightly to look up at me. "What do you want to do?"

"Stay home with you, order in and drink Fontaine Champagne one last time before it belongs to someone else," I answer truthfully.

Carolina lifts her brows. "Doesn't it already belong to someone else?"

"Semantics, woman." I lean down and kiss the tip of her nose. "Just indulge me."

"Okay. That I can do." She squeezes her arms around me, her hands slipping down until they're sliding over my ass. "What's up with the shorts and T-shirt look?"

"I was going to go for a run when I got the call," I answer.

Her smile turns sly. Even a little naughty. "I can give you a workout."

"What about your ankle?" We've had sex since the night of her injury—I can't keep my hands off of her. But I don't push too hard. She's in pain and it's awkward, and I'm content with just holding her most nights.

Well, I'm not necessarily content. I usually end up with a raging hard-on and the urge to conquer her like a fucking beast, but then I remember that she's hurt so I leave her alone.

And jack off in the shower instead.

"It's a lot better. I can put pressure on it now."

I noticed she walks easier on it. No more limping around, and she never did try and use the crutches. I can't blame her. "You're not overdoing it, are you?"

"Not at all." She shakes her head and pulls out of my hold completely, heading down the hall toward our bedroom. "You should follow me."

I don't even protest. I just do as she suggests, trailing after her down the hall, until we're both in the bedroom and she's directing me to sit on the edge of the mattress.

Again, I do as she says, letting her take control for once. Two of the four walls in the bedroom are nothing but windows and they're both completely open, offering us a view of the entire city surrounding us.

But I'm not paying attention to the view outside. I'm watching the girl I love fall to her knees in front of me, her hands running up the tops of my thighs. "I've missed you. Missed this."

"Missed what?" I play dumb on purpose, wincing when she tunnels her hand beneath my shorts and pinches my leg.

"Being with you. You've been very respectful of my injury, but I'm not completely fragile, West."

"I didn't want to hurt you. And you seemed tired some nights." When we first got here, she slept for hours for at least three days straight.

"I needed to catch up. All I've been doing is dancing and performing and stretching and just...I never had time for myself.

Ever." Her eyes glow with sincerity. "You taught me how to slow down and take care of myself."

That's funny, considering I feel like all I've been doing for the last two years is taking care of the House of Fontaine and all the responsibilities that came with it. "I'm here for you, baby."

"I do love it when you call me baby." She rears up, her hand curling around the back of my neck, pulling me down for a kiss.

I drown in her taste. The stroke of her tongue against mine. I tug on her lithe body, pulling her up, taking her with me when I fall back on the bed with her sprawled all over me. Our mouths are still fused, our tongues busy, my hands wandering all over her. Sliding beneath the skirt of her black dress, running my fingers up the back of her firm thighs. Teasing along the edge of her panties, the heat of her already radiating. I'm sure she's wet.

Soaked for me.

Quickly I flip her over, so she's on her back, tugging at the front of her dress, catching a glimpse of the sleek black bra she has on. The fabric is smooth and shiny, trimmed with delicate lace. "Nice."

"It's new." She shrugs out of her sleeves, the dress falling down, exposing the bra completely. "My panties match."

"Need to see this." I shift away and help her rid herself of the dress, whistling low as I take in what she's wearing. "Fucking sexy."

Her entire body flushes pink, but she doesn't shy away or try to hide herself. "Thank you."

"So polite." I lean over her, pressing my mouth to the soft flesh just beneath her navel. She quivers beneath my lips, her fingers threading through my hair.

"This was supposed to be about you," she protests as she starts to gently squirm, as if she's trying to get away from my mouth. I wrap my hands around her hips, keeping her in place.

"But this is what I want." I lift my gaze to hers. "You."

CHAPTER FIFTY

CAROLINA

West is positioned between my thighs, his mouth hovering above my panties, a filthy smile curling his lips after he just said he wanted me.

I will never grow tired of hearing him say that.

"But I wanted to give you—pleasure," I finish somewhat lamely, feeling a little silly that I'm even complaining. If this is what he wants, who am I to tell him no?

"This gives me pleasure, Carolina." He bends down, resting his face against the front of my panties. His breath is hot, and when he exhales, it's like he touched every single part of me, lighting me up inside. "Just—let me do this."

I give in without a word, a sigh leaving me when he nudges my panties with his nose, inhaling my scent. He hooks his fingers into them, slipping beneath the thin fabric, brushing my skin. It's a barely-there touch, not insistent or hard or purposeful at all. More light teasing and, oh God, it sends a streak of lightning straight to my clit, tumbling down my legs and curling my toes.

He gently skims his fingers across the top of my pussy and I suck in a breath. It's been far, far too long since we've done something like this. I tilt my head down, watching as he studies me with utter fascination, his gaze fixed on his fingers moving and shifting beneath my panties.

Just before he shoves them aside and leans in, he braces his hand on my belly, spreading me open and teasing my clit with the tip of his tongue. A moan leaves me and I try to lift my hips, seeking more of his mouth and tongue, but his fingers clamp tighter around my hips and I'm unable to move.

"West," I cry, but he shushes me, his mouth moving over my skin, his tongue licking every crevice, every fold, every bit of my flesh as he spreads me wide, his lips in constant motion. My entire body trembles as he continues his torment, and when he shifts his hands to rest beneath my thighs, pushing me up, I go willingly.

Until my ass is in the air, still covered by my now stretched-out panties.

"We need to get rid of these," he says, removing them from my body with efficiency. I'm in a daze, the pleasure swarming me, making me dizzy, and when he leans back in to lick at my pussy yet again, he moves farther down, his tongue teasing my ass, the ridged skin there.

A gasp leaves me and I freeze, my body stiff. He goes still as well, waiting. Ready to stop if I tell him to, I'm sure.

But I don't tell him to stop. My body slowly relaxes, a sigh leaving me when he licks me there again and I close my eyes, losing myself to the pleasure of the forbidden. It feels downright naughty, what he's doing. Where he's licking me, and when he slips his fingers inside my pussy, pumping them in and out of my body slowly, I know I'm close.

Already. It takes nothing for the man to make me come and I can't even be ashamed of it.

I'm in love him. This boy who quickly turned into a man. A man who's already sold his family's company and made sure his mother would never have to worry about anything again. A man who chased after me and waited patiently until I eventually came around. A man who gave me a ring to wear on my middle finger so he could see it every time I flipped him off.

A man who tattooed my drawing on his wrist the first night we met. Who wrote words of love and devotion on my skin for me to etch them permanently, so I could look at them forever.

I adore this man so much. I love him. I didn't know it could be like this. Could feel like this. He adores me. He loves me.

And when he increases his pace, his fingers sliding in and out of my body, his tongue working my flesh, the orgasm sweeps over me out of nowhere. I'm trembling, whimpering, an absolute mess. He pulls away from me and I can hear the rustle of clothing, impatient murmurs while I lie on the bed still shuddering.

West reaches for me and I go willingly, letting him position me until I'm on my hands and knees, my ass in the air. He looms over me from behind, his hands returning to my hips, his cock entering me. I move with him, the sound of our sweaty skin connecting filling the room, his grunts growing louder with his every thrust. He fucks me hard, his fingers digging into my hips, his cock driving deep inside me, hitting a spot that has me seeing stars every. Single. Time.

The orgasm grows, this one bigger. Stronger. His rhythm becomes sloppy, more frantic, his groans louder until finally he slams inside me, holding himself there. I can feel his cock throbbing within my body, just before he spills, flooding me with his semen.

He begins to fuck me again, in short, sharp jabs, moaning with each one, hitting that spot again. And again. The orgasm builds, my stomach clenching, my clit pulsing, until finally it hits, a keening cry leaving me.

West grabs hold of me, lifting me up, his cock still embedded deep inside, my body shuddering as he holds me to him, my back to his front, his fingers curling around the front of my throat, holding me there. He presses his cheek against mine, his mouth moving against my skin as he whispers, "I love you."

We're both breathing heavily, in tandem with each other, my pussy clenching around his cock. I feel so connected to him in this moment. Literally and figuratively. We're melded together, in this together.

Always together.

Forever.

The next day, we stay home, witnessing the merger announcement via social media. Flower arrangements are sent by the dozens congratulating him. A cake, two dozen cupcakes, a charcuterie board and fruit formed into colorful flowers are also included in the gifts various people and businesses sent.

"We can snack on everything they've sent you for a week," I say as he opens the charcuterie board, letting me thumb through the cheeses and meats.

"So far things have been positive," he says, smiling at me from across the kitchen counter.

"You didn't think it would be viewed that way?"

"I didn't know." He shrugs. "I still have some guilt. This was my father's legacy, and I know he passed it on to me in the hopes that I would preserve it and carry on. But I never viewed it as a legacy. More like a burden."

"You were too young," I remind him.

"I could've let someone else take over while I ran amok and did whatever the fuck I wanted. But that didn't feel right either." He grips the edge of the counter, his gaze locking with mine. "This felt right. Taking care of my mother, and me. I don't know shit about running a champagne company. And I could've learned—I tried to learn, but being involved in this business never felt like it was me. More like it was something placed upon me."

"Then you did the right thing."

"That's what I'm thinking. My mother said the same thing. I talked to her earlier, when you were in the shower. She said she's getting a lot of flower arrangements too. Like it's a funeral." His expression turns sheepish. "If she'd said that to me a year ago, we both probably would've cried. Especially her. But now she can laugh about it. I consider that progress."

"I'm glad you're both healing." I round the kitchen counter, just about to pull him in for a hug when I receive a phone call.

From Sylvie. Who rarely calls. We usually just text.

"Who is it?" West asks. He must notice my confusion.

"My sister." I answer it, barely able to get out my hello before Sylvie starts babbling incoherently. She's crying and carrying on, breathing heavy and not making a lick of sense. "Sylvie, calm down. What's wrong?"

My heart races as she tries to compose herself before she says, "Oh, Carolina. I don't know how to tell you this but…Mother. She's gone. She's dead."

I lean heavily against the kitchen counter, my knees nearly giving out on me, and West rushes toward me, wrapping his arms around my waist to support me. "What?"

"I'm at the Newport house and she just…she showed up unannounced and she was so scary, Carolina. I've never seen her act like that. She was coming for me. Cornering me. Saying the craziest things."

The last time I saw my mother, we actually got along. Things felt somewhat…normal. Not that our relationship would ever be normal, but I left that lunch not hating her or resenting her.

And now she's dead.

"Did she hurt you?" I ask. "Are you alone?"

I'll drop everything and go to her right now if she needs me.

"N-no. She tried to, though. And Spencer is here. He's with me." Sylvie is sobbing, her words thick with tears. "She's always hated me, Lina. She's wanted to destroy me for years."

I never understood their relationship, and I'm not sure I ever will, but in this moment, I know that Sylvie is grieving. She's falling apart and she'll struggle over my mother's death.

We all will.

But ultimately, for Sylvie, it's for the best.

Now she'll be free of our mother's torment, once and for all.

"Do you want me to come out there?" I ask, leaning my head against West's chest. "I could leave right now and be there with you."

"It's…" her voice lowers and she whispers, "the house is a crime scene. I don't think you want to come out here."

"A crime scene?" West stiffens when I say that.

"She fell, Carolina. She fell down the stairs and cracked the back of her skull open. The police are talking to the both of us and making sure everything's okay. That it was an accident like we said."

Something like doubt prickles my skin. "Was it an accident?"

"Of course, it was! I can't believe you would even ask."

"I'm just making sure, okay?" A sigh leaves me. "Call me when you know more. And when I can see you. Have you called Daddy?"

"Yes. And Whit. They both said they'll take care of everything."

"I'm sure they will. It's going to be okay, Sylvie." I gentle my tone, feeling sorry for her. She's crying so hard still. And she's been through so much. Mostly at the hands of our mother. "You're going to be okay."

"You're right. I know. It's just so hard. I saw it all happen and…" Another sob, this one ending with a wail, and tears spring to my eyes, hearing how much pain my sister is in.

I can hear a male voice saying her name, talking to her in low tones and then a muffled sound, Spencer's voice suddenly in my ear.

"Can she call you back later, Carolina? I'm so sorry about your mom. Things are hectic here right now and the police want to speak with us."

"Are you two going to be okay?" I ask, my fingers curling tightly around my phone.

"We're going to be all right. Eventually. Whit is on his way out now. Your father is on the phone, trying to take care of things."

I don't even know what my father could be taking care of, but I'm glad they're handling it and not me.

"Okay. Please call me when you can. Or have Sylvie call me. Whit. Whoever." I feel helpless. Like I should rush out there and be with them, with Sylvie. But I know Spencer will take care of her far better than I ever could.

We end the call and I glance up to find West watching me intently, his hand smoothing up and down my back in a soothing gesture. "Your mom?"

I nod once. "She's dead."

"Oh, Carolina." He pulls me into him, holding me close. I begin to tremble, my entire body shaking, tears spilling from my eyes, down my face. I don't know how to feel. How to react. I'm numb. Cold. My teeth are chattering and I cling to him, my fingers curling around his shoulders, my tears getting his shirt wet in seconds. "I'm so sorry."

Sadness leaves me raw and aching, and I quietly marvel that I'm completely overwhelmed with emotion. Something I rarely experience. I handle any difficulty or tragedy with the usual stoic reaction, desperate to keep it bottled in.

This time, at the loss of my mother, a woman I both feared and disgusted, I can't help but sob the hardest I've ever cried.

"It's okay," West murmurs against my hair, his deep voice reassuring. "It's going to be okay."

If anyone can understand what I'm going through, it's West. He lost his father. Now I've lost my mother.

But at least we have each other.

Chapter Fifty-One

CAROLINA

The day of my mother's funeral, there's a heat wave in New York City.

Of course, there is. It makes perfect sense. Whit tries to make a joke about hell welcoming our mother home, but Summer jabs him in the ribs to shut him up.

I almost giggled but corrected myself at the last second.

Sylvie acts like a zombie—an impeccably dressed zombie but still. She moves slow. Doesn't respond to our questions like she doesn't even hear them. She flat out doesn't say much at all while Spencer guides her through the motions, as if she can't even walk or talk on her own. I'm sure she's still in a state of shock. While their relationship wasn't normal, they were close, no matter how much Sylvie tried to get away from her.

I stay and sit with my family at the church while West sits with his mother, who is beside herself with grief. She was close to my mother for such a brief time, and another death in her life only two years after her husband's pushed her over the edge, West explained to me before the funeral started.

"If you want me by your side, I will be there," he said, his voice firm, his gaze serious. "But I also don't want to intrude on your family either. I know this is a difficult time for all of you. I remember how it is."

It's better this way, I think as I sit with my father, who holds my hand throughout the entire service. West can console his mother while my father consoles me. Augustus Lancaster loved my mother at one point, yet he also hated her. Their divorce was nasty. All sorts of fighting over money and the children, though we were all shipped off by then. Mother just wanted the status and the name by the end of it all. That's all she cared about.

My parents may have been divorced, but deep down, he still cared about her. She still mattered. She was the mother of his children.

A sea of Lancasters attend the funeral as well, most of them showing up to pay their respects to Sylvia. I'm surrounded by them, all of us sitting together at the front of the church none of us attend unless for weddings and funerals. The occasional baptism. A Christmas service or for Easter. Some of us could benefit from spending a little more time in church, but that's a discussion for another day.

Once the service is over, we all walk out of the church together as a family, so many people murmuring their respects. I teared up a little during the service, but I feel all cried out today. I'm not much of a crier in the first place and shedding so many tears the last few days has completely wiped me out.

"Come straight over to the apartment," Father announces. "I've already told everyone. There's food and drink, and an entire staff to serve it. I hired a piano player and everything."

"Mother would love this type of party," Sylvie says.

"She would," Whit agrees.

"At least someone is playing the piano in Daddy's apartment," I say with a little shrug.

"Carolina," Sylvie says out of nowhere.

I turn to look at her. "Yes?"

"I love you." She shifts closer, pulling me into a hug.

I cling to her, closing my eyes for a brief moment before I

turn my head and press my lips to her cheek, saying the words back to her. "I love you, too."

When was the last time we said that to each other? I have no idea. Most of the time I believed Sylvie resented me. That she hated me for being able to escape the house while she was stuck behind.

But maybe not. Maybe she envied me. Perhaps she even missed me. I know sometimes—a lot of the time—I missed her and Whit. They might've been shitty to me as only older siblings can be, but I did miss them.

With our mother gone, maybe we can be closer now.

We're about to load up in the limo to head for my father's apartment when West calls my name. I turn to find him, standing off to the side, his mother standing next to him with red-rimmed eyes.

"How are you?" he asks when I draw closer.

I offer them both a weak smile. "I'm dealing."

"That's all you can do." He brings me in with one arm slung around my shoulders, kissing my forehead.

"I'm so sorry for your loss," Laura says, and West releases me so I can hug his mother. "You're so strong. I would be a sobbing mess."

"You were a sobbing mess," West says, his voice lightly teasing, trying to ease the heaviness that lingers.

There's no use though. That heaviness is going to be with me—with us—for a while.

"I'm just so sick over what happened. I know how hard it is to lose someone." Laura releases her hold on me and I realize it's so much easier to let people touch me now. I don't even flinch.

How...strange.

I think I owe it all to West.

"It's been difficult," I agree, because I know that's what I should say.

We might've been on better terms lately, but my mother

wasn't a good person. She was manipulative and abusive toward Sylvie. I also think she suffered from mental issues, yet she never sought help.

I wish she would've. Things might've ended up differently.

"Your father asked everyone to come to his apartment," West says.

"Please do. I'll be there. I'm going to ride over with them." I hug him once more, needing to absorb his calmness, his strength for a little bit longer. "See you there?"

"We'll be there." He kisses me, quick and soft, and I'm not embarrassed that his mother saw it. I might've been a few months ago.

But not anymore.

I ride over to my father's house with him, shocked to receive a group text to all of us from Whit that they had to make a detour to the hospital because his wife has gone into labor.

"Summer is going to have the baby," I announce to him.

He jerks his head in my direction, his brows drawn together in confusion. "Right now?"

I'm reading the texts from Sylvie, who's explaining that they're stopping by the hospital to drop Whit and Summer off before they come to the gathering. "Yes, right now. Can you believe it?"

"You lost your mother and you're gaining a niece, and me a granddaughter, all in the same day." Father shakes his head, a faint smile on his face. "It won't be just a day to mourn any longer."

I smile at him in return, the tears returning to my eyes. I try to fight them, but it's no use, and I let them flow, wiping them off with my index finger. "Is it odd to feel happy right now? About the baby coming?"

"Not at all." Father reaches out and pats my knee. "It's a good thing, this baby being born today. Your mother would've loved that."

Would she? The baby is stealing her thunder. This day is supposed to be about Sylvia Lancaster, not the next generation.

But then again, she's not here anymore, and there's no thunder to steal. This feels like divine intervention. Both of my parents would call it a gift from God.

"Do you think she knows?" My question is a whisper, and I'm referring to my mother. I feel silly asking it, but I can't help but wonder. "About the baby?"

"Carolina, I'm positive that your mother not only knows, she's the one who made this happen." He offers me a reassuring smile. "One last gift from Sylvia."

I'm shocked by my father speaking so kindly of her, but I suppose he still had a bit of affection for the woman. She was the mother of his children, even if she was not necessarily a good one.

I too would rather think of her in a positive light than a negative one today, so I'm going to have to agree with his statement.

When we arrive at my father's apartment, he turns it on for the crowd that has gathered. The eternal host. Ready to entertain and tell his stories while surrounded by an audience. He launches into multiple ones about our mother, sharing old details about things I've never heard about her before. I listen for a while, relieved when I spot West and his mother entering the apartment, and I go to them immediately.

"Summer is at the hospital. She's in labor," I announce.

"No shit?" West grins, his mother slapping him on the arm.

"Watch your language. We were just at a funeral," she chastises.

"Yes. She was having contractions all through the funeral, I guess. Whit demanded the limo driver take them to the hospital right away. The baby is going to be born today. Whit is giving us updates," I explain.

"Aw, I love that. There's something about this moment that feels very full circle, don't you think?" Laura asks.

I nod, hooking my arm through West's, so I can lean my

head against his chest. "Very full circle. We lose someone in the family and gain someone, all in the same day."

"That's sweet," Laura says, getting misty-eyed.

I smile at her. I like that she has a soft heart. That she isn't hard like my mother was. Sylvia Lancaster was jaded. Cynical. Always trying to find a way to get something out of someone. From what I see with West's mother, she's not like that at all.

And I love that. It means that West has some of her soft heart too.

After a few minutes of conversation with West and his mom, I wander around the apartment and chat with various people, including my relatives. I spend a little time with my cousin Crew and his brothers, Finn and Grant. I catch up with Charlotte and her handsome husband, Perry. I give my younger cousin Arch some shit because he's a devil just like my brother and Grant, and he deserves it. I spot the terror twins, the youngest sons of my father's youngest brother, Fitz. Not sure where his daughter is though. We're closer in age and when we were little, we played together a lot.

There is so much family here, and while I've avoided them for the last eight years of my life for the most part, every one of them is warm and welcoming toward me, asking me plenty of questions, seemingly interested in my life. Well, most of them. Some are grumpy.

Most though, are fairly decent.

After I chat with yet another friendly relative, I realize that I regret treating my family like an afterthought. Family is important. I should connect with them more. Spend quality time with them. All of them. My brother and sister and father. My cousins and my aunts and uncles. When I was a little girl, we would get together all the time for various family events. As we got older and my parents went through their difficult divorce, everyone scattered in different directions, and it was never the same.

I'd like to change that and soon. We can't just let funerals and weddings bring us together. We should actually want to spend more time with each other.

And I want to include West in these celebrations too. And his mother. They only have each other while I have this big, welcoming family that will surely take them in.

Well, I might be stretching it a bit when I use the word welcoming. The Lancasters can be a snobbish bunch when they want to be.

"Hey." I turn at the sound of West's voice to see him lingering near the entry to the kitchen, and I go to him, letting him wrap me up in his embrace. "We're probably going to leave soon."

"Okay." I close my eyes when he kisses me on the forehead. I love it when he delivers those. Why did I ever want to flip him off again? I feel like a completely different version of myself. "I'm going to stay here a little while longer."

"You want me to come back and pick you up?" The concern in his gaze, the offer he just made, makes me feel safe.

No one has ever done that for me. Not really. Not ever.

Until West.

"That would be nice." I smile at him just before he kisses me.

"Give me like an hour. I'll be back. Text me if you need anything."

I hug Laura, thanking her for her sympathetic words, appreciating her too. Appreciating both of them. What was supposed to be a time of celebration for them with the sale of the House of Fontaine has turned into something sad. But they don't blame me for it.

I don't blame myself either. This is just life.

And sometimes things don't go as planned.

CHAPTER FIFTY-TWO

CAROLINA

"Oh my God, she's so precious," I croon, completely enraptured with my new niece's little face.

Her mother is holding baby Iris, who is wrapped in a soft blanket of the palest pink, her eyes wide open and staring into mine. I touch her cheek with my finger, amazed at how soft it is, yanking my hand away when she squirms and makes a fussing noise.

"Did I upset her?" My gaze flies to Summer's, who offers me a kind smile.

"No, she's just cranky like her daddy."

"Hey, watch it," Whit says mildly. He's planted right by Summer's side, his arm around her shoulders, his gaze fixed on his daughter. He looks amazed. Like he can't believe he made that and I have to admit…

I can't believe he made sweet baby Iris either. And her big brother August. They are the most adorable children on the planet.

I am, of course, biased because they're my niece and nephew, but I think everyone can admit that Whit and Summer produce beautiful children.

West and I came to visit them a week after Iris was born.

Whit called me and invited us to see her and, of course, I said yes. While they've been sending lots of photos in the group text chat we have, seeing Iris in the flesh is such a better experience.

"Do you want to hold her?" Summer asks me.

"Oh, I couldn't—"

"Just do it," Whit interrupts, glaring at me. "Don't be scared."

I swallow the lump of fear in my throat and nod once. "Okay."

I settle more comfortably on the couch next to Summer, holding out my arms like she instructs before she carefully settles the bundle into them. I hold Iris awkwardly, staring down at her with awe. She doesn't move. Her face is smooth, her eyes now closed, her little rosebud lips pursed.

She is absolutely beautiful.

"Aw, I love her." My body slowly relaxes as I continue holding her, and I bring her closer, leaning down to press my lips to her soft black hair. I breathe in her sweet baby scent, pulling away slightly when her eyes flash open, locking with mine.

I know a baby's vision isn't the best when they're born. But I feel like this child is looking deep into my soul, and she understands it. Understands me.

Then she screws up her face and begins to cry.

"Oh no, I'm so sorry. Shh." I start to bounce her like some sort of natural instinct and she stops crying immediately, little whimpers still leaving her, her butt wiggling beneath my palm. A loud noise sounds from her diaper and I jerk my head up, panicked.

Whit and Summer start to laugh.

"She's very gassy," Summer says.

"The girl puts up a nasty stink," Whit adds.

"Here." Summer holds out her arms and I give her back her daughter. "I'll go change her."

She leaves the living room so it's just me, Whit and West. My brother leans back against the couch, spreading his arms out, contemplating me before his gaze shifts to West.

"You two are serious, huh?"

My stomach clenches. "Define serious."

At the same time West offers a simple, "Yes."

Whit sends me a look. "You're basically living together. I call that serious."

"Do you disapprove?"

"Not at all. Whatever makes you happy. Just watching out for you." He sends a skeptical look West's way. "Congratulations on the sale of Fontaine, by the way."

"Thank you." West nods.

"What are your plans now?" Whit's gaze shifts to mine.

"I'm going back to London soon."

"To dance?" Whit's eyebrows shoot up.

"To retire," I amend. "I'm done dancing."

"Wait a minute. Are you serious? You love dance. That's all you've done the majority of your life. Why give it up now?"

"That's what I told her," West says.

"Was the injury more serious than you let on? Is that why you're quitting?" Whit asks me.

"No, not at all. I just…I love dance, but I will never be a prima ballerina. Not like I want to. And while I don't regret all the years I dedicated to dance and ballet, I think it's time for me to hang up my toe shoes, so to speak." I shrug, not knowing how else to explain it.

I will miss dancing. It's been a part of my life for so long, it's going to be difficult giving it up completely. Though maybe after a couple of months, I will want to go somewhere and dance again; for now, I need to take some time for myself and figure out what I want to do next. I'm only twenty. I have my entire life ahead of me.

Perhaps West and I can travel the world. I truly believed that would happen with the internationally acclaimed dance troupe I joined someday, but that's not going to happen for me. So, I'm going to make my own plans.

Do my own thing.

"You're going to have a lot of free time then," Whit observes.

"Well, I think West and I are going to travel for a bit." West smiles at me, nodding his confirmation that, that is definitely our plan.

"And after you get tired of traveling?"

"We'll see what happens next." I shrug, actually enjoying that there's nothing on the horizon for me. I used to be so rigid. I needed a plan for everything. I had to know what was going to happen at least five to seven steps ahead.

Now? I'm throwing caution to the wind and seeing where I land. And it's the most liberating feeling.

"How about you come work for me?" Whit's expression doesn't change a bit. He sounds and looks like he could be talking about the weather.

"Work for you? Doing what?" I laugh.

Whit's face is dead serious. He doesn't say a word. In fact, I think I offended him by laughing.

I clamp my lips shut, resting my hands in my lap. "Come on, Whit. What are you talking about?"

"I'm starting a nonprofit. For kids who were…abused."

His words sink in slowly, leaving me silent for a moment as I absorb exactly what he's saying. "What do you mean?"

"It's still in the works. Sylvie wants to help. It's going to take a while to build, but I've been talking to people and we want to do something to help out children." Whit glances down at the baby blanket that was left behind and he smooths his fingers over it. "I have my own now. I can't imagine anyone—and I mean anyone—wanting to hurt their own children to benefit themselves."

His words sink in, letting me know who he's referring to.

Our own mother.

Sylvie and I have been talking a lot. She's told me some things that made me uncomfortable, but that I needed to hear. Mother was definitely abusive toward her. Both mentally and physically, and I don't think Sylvie is over it. She's in therapy. She has Spencer. She will be okay.

"I want to help too," I tell Whit, and he smiles at me, the relief on his face obvious.

"I was hoping you'd say that. You two have about a year. Maybe eighteen months. And then I'll need you." Whit glares at West. "So don't go and move out of the country or anything like that."

"I'm not the one who wants to live outside the US. That's on her." West points at me and I start laughing again, unable to hold back. They both join me and I realize that we're all going to be okay.

Despite everything.

I say exactly that to West when we drive back to our place.

"We're going to be okay, you know," I tell him, resting my hand on his thigh. The very hand with the ring that he gave me on my middle finger.

"I know." His hand drops from the steering wheel to cover mine briefly. "I'm glad you feel that way. I know it's been a tough few weeks on you."

"A tough month," I say in agreement. "I need to go back to London."

"When?"

"Soon. I already called my landlord. He's looking into leasing out my flat, but I need to get my stuff out of there. Plus, I have things at the studio. At the theatre."

"Let's plan to go over there soon and pick up your things," he suggests.

"I'm sure my father would let me use the plane." We have a private jet because, of course, we do. "I'll need it to load up all of my things."

"What are you saying? That you're going to bring furniture back?"

"No, not at all." I grip his thigh, giving it a squeeze. "I just have a lot of clothes and things. You know, stuff."

"Stuff." He shakes his head. "You could probably leave it all and not miss it."

"That's not true." I think of my pointe shoes. My favorite leotards and sports bras and I can't just leave that stuff behind. It all belongs to me. "I want it."

He grabs my hand and brings it to his mouth, kissing the back of it before he places it back in my lap. "Then we'll go get it."

I love how he just assumes I want him to go with me—which I do.

"After that, what should we do?"

He stops at a light, glancing over at me. "What do *you* want to do?"

"I've always wanted to go to Australia." A dreamy sigh escapes me as I stare off into the distance.

"You've never been?"

I shake my head. "Nope."

"We should go."

"You're right." I smile over at him. "We should."

"Let's plan the trip when we get home."

Excitement floods my veins. "Are you serious?"

"Definitely. We've got the time and the money." He grins, hitting the gas as soon as the light turns green, the wheels squealing. "We can do whatever you want. As long as I'm always with you."

"I don't want to do this without you," I admit.

"Do what?"

"Life. I need you by my side. In my heart." I stare at his handsome profile, exhaling softly. "On my skin."

His grin is adorable. "You're stuck with the tattoo."

"Not that I regret it."

"I don't regret mine either."

I wish I could grab his arm and kiss the very tattoo I drew on him, but I can't since he's driving, so I restrain myself. "I love you."

"I love you too."

"Are we really going to do this?" I laugh, turning to stare out the window as we speed past the tall buildings. The city is nothing but a blur of light, and the night air is still warm. The sky as clear as my heart.

I've never felt lighter.

"Fuck yeah, we are." He jerks the BMW to the right, pulling up to the empty curb and putting the car in park, the engine rumbling. Leaning over the console, he reaches for me, cupping my face, forcing me to look into his eyes, his thumbs streaking across my cheeks. "We're in this together, Carolina. You're stuck with me."

"There's no one else I'd rather be stuck with," I admit, just before he kisses me.

No one else.

Just him.

EPILOGUE

WEST

TWO YEARS LATER

I stand on the peripheral of the ballroom dance floor, watching my fiancée talking with a group of people, her lips curved into the biggest smile I think I've ever seen. She laughs at something her cousin Crew says to her, covering her mouth for the briefest moment. The four-carat pink diamond that sits on her left ring finger flashes in the light that shines down upon us from the glittering chandeliers above.

I gave her that ring only a month ago, on New Year's Day in Paris. Down on one knee like the sap I am for her in our hotel suite at the George V, my nerves shot to shit when I asked her to marry me. Like I was worried she'd say no.

She didn't.

Carolina hugs her cousin, her head swiveling slowly, as if she's looking for someone. The moment her gaze settles on me, her smile grows and she starts toward me, crossing the room. She's extra beautiful tonight, wearing a strapless pale pink dress that matches the ring. It's covered in multiple layers of ostrich feathers and hits just above her knees, a silver crystal band wrapped around her waist. She glides across the wide expanse of the ballroom, the feathers fluttering in the breeze, and when she's finally standing in front of me, I hook my arm around her waist and bring her in close, pressing my lips to hers in a soft kiss.

"You are beautiful," I murmur against her lips, which are slicked in a pale pink the same shade as her dress.

She pulls away slightly, laughing. "That is the tenth time you've told me that."

"I can't get over you in that dress." I pull away slightly, my gaze eating her up. Her shoulders gleam, there's a hint of cleavage on display, and all I can suddenly think about is when can we leave so I can get her naked.

"It's so fabulous." She pulls out of my hold completely and does a spin, the feathers moving with her. "My most favorite costume yet."

I smile at her. "Costume?"

"So much of my life has felt like a performance. As if it were all fake," she admits, her blue eyes going wide. "But the best thing about what we share is that it's real. All of these things are really happening to me. To us."

Carolina lifts her glass full of pink champagne in a toast. I do the same.

"To us." I touch my glass to hers before I take a drink and she does the same.

I will never get over how those words sound.

"Aw, you two."

We both turn to find my mother smiling at us, the happiness on her face undeniable. She's come a long way from the sad woman who lost so much. She has a solid group of friends. She's traveling a lot and she's even met someone. Maurice is her boyfriend. He's wealthy—he owns a chain of dry cleaners in New York and New Jersey, and he makes my mother laugh. Something my father really didn't do, especially during those last few years.

I just want her happy and I think she is. Which in turn makes me happy.

"You look stunning, Carolina," Mom gushes, wrapping her up in a big hug before she pulls away holding on to Carolina's hands so she can examine her closely. "And that dress! So gorgeous."

"Isn't it beautiful? It's Dolce and Gabbana," Carolina says, and Mom nods her approval.

With Sylvia Lancaster's death, my mom has sort of stepped in and become a mother figure to my fiancée. I love that they get along so well. Everything has come together so beautifully the last few years.

Carolina and I embarked on traveling the world since she left her dance company. We've been all over the place. Europe and Asia. South America. Before we left France, she confessed to me that she was tired of traveling.

"I want to put down some roots," she confessed, her gaze on her hand and that pink diamond. "Plus, now there's a wedding to plan…"

I agreed because I feel the same way. It's been an adventure, traveling with Carolina, but I'm tired of it too. We need a break, so we've moved back to the city, in an apartment that belongs to the Lancaster family. They own so many all over the city, we only had to pick and choose, and Carolina fell in love with the brownstone that's not too far from where her cousin Crew lives with his wife, Wren. We've been spending more time together lately, the four of us meeting up for dinner at least once a week since our return to the States.

And Whit's nonprofit is finally about to launch—and we're helping with it. We're both on the board, as well as Sylvie and Summer. It's an important endeavor for all of us and I'm proud to be a part of it.

Carolina is too.

"I adore the dress," Mom says, bringing me back to our— their—conversation. "So, I wanted to ask you, Carolina…"

Her voice drifts and Carolina frowns. "Ask me what?"

"Is it true, that you're wanting to open a dance studio and

start teaching classes?"

Carolina glances over her shoulder at me before she turns to face my mother once more. "Actually...yes. I thought it might be fun, to offer a few classes. Nothing too strenuous. Beginning ballet and some barre exercise sessions a couple of times a week. I'll be busy with my brother's nonprofit, so I can only do this part-time."

"I think offering dance classes is a great idea. I would love to sign up as soon as you have some available," Mom says.

"You're just saying that." Carolina rolls her eyes.

Always trying to tear down her worth, still. She doesn't see the sincerity shining in my mother's eyes.

"No, I'm not. And I have plenty of friends who would enjoy a class like that too. West mentioned you've already leased a studio."

Cat is out of the bag, I want to tell Carolina, but I remain quiet.

"Well, isn't he revealing all my secrets."

They chat for a few minutes longer before Mom is whisked away by her boyfriend. The moment she's gone, Carolina is on me, giving me an earful.

"I can't believe you already told your mother about the studio."

I shrug. "I knew she'd want to be a part of it. And not just because of who you are to me. She loves you. And she's always talking about how she wants to find her core."

Carolina smiles. "The best way to find it is doing ballet."

"That's what she said." I slip my arm around her waist, leaning in to kiss her cheek. "My mom is proud of you. I'm proud of you. And you're going to end up with a bunch of high society ladies in your dance class, hoping to relive their youthful days from ballet class. Just watch."

She smiles up at me, her eyes shiny. Like she might cry at any moment, which is the last thing I want. "Thank you for always believing in me."

How could I not? She always believes in me too. No matter what I say or do. "I love you," I murmur, drifting my fingers across her cheek.

"I love you, too." She turns her head, delivering a quick kiss to my palm before she tilts her head back, smiling at me, circling her arms around my waist. I think of the girl I first met, who pretended to speak French and didn't want me to touch her. She's a completely different woman now.

I'd like to think I had something to do with that, but I know the truth.

Carolina came into herself on her own.

I'm just the lucky man she also happens to be in love with.

ACKNOWLEDGMENTS

Carolina Lancaster, whew. I love her. But Weston Fontaine? I might love West even more. He's dreamy! Writing their story put me through all of the emotions. Spoiler alert (you should be reading this after reading the book but I still warned you): originally, you as the reader would've known West got that tattoo. The scene was written in the first part of the book. I deleted that scene because Nina said, keep it a secret from everyone, including the reader. So I did. But maybe I'll share that scene someday. It has a great line in it, so that's what made it so tough to delete…

Another spoiler: I have to admit, it was a lot of fun to bring Sylvia back. That woman is the worst! But when they're the worst, that means (at least for me) they're my favorite to write. There is nothing better than a villain. Well, it's even better when the villain is actually the hero, but that's not the case in this book (that's Whit's story ha ha).

As always, a big, giant thank you to everyone who reads my books. I cannot do this without you, and you mean so much to me. I need to shout out a special thank you to Rebecca Hilsdon and the rest of the team at Michael Joseph/Penguin Random House UK for bringing the Lancasters to the UK Commonwealth. Your enthusiasm and love for my books mean so much to me, and there is nothing better than seeing an email from you in my inbox.

I also want to thank everyone at Valentine PR for taking care of me - Nina, Kim, Valentine, Daisy, Sarah, Kelley, AMY (my kid, lol) - you ladies are the best! Nina, thank you as always for your insight. I took all of your suggestions and added I think four or five more chapters to this book so everyone thank Nina for making it longer.

Always must thank my editor Rebecca for all that you do and especially this go around to my proofreader Sarah for keeping the timeline straight! All those chapter additions kind of messed it up so thank you for catching them all! I must always thank Emily Wittig for yet another gorgeous cover - I'm in love. Your support for the romance reading community is so appreciated.

p.s. - If you enjoyed I'LL ALWAYS BE WITH YOU, it would mean the world to me if you left a review on the retailer site you bought it from, or on Goodreads. Thank you so much!

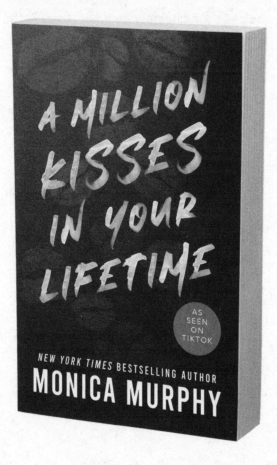

AMARA
an imprint of Entangled Publishing LLC